THE
BABY-SITTERS CLUB

CLAUDIA AND THE NEW GIRL

DON'T MISS THE OTHER
BABY-SITTERS CLUB GRAPHIC NOVELS!

KRISTY'S GREAT IDEA

THE TRUTH ABOUT STACEY

MARY ANNE SAVES THE DAY

CLAUDIA AND MEAN JANINE

DAWN AND THE IMPOSSIBLE THREE

KRISTY'S BIG DAY

BOY-CRAZY STACEY

LOGAN LIKES MARY ANNE!

ANN M. MARTIN

THE BABY-SITTERS CLUB®

CLAUDIA AND THE NEW GIRL

A GRAPHIC NOVEL BY

GABRIELA EPSTEIN

WITH COLOR BY BRADEN LAMB

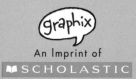

An Imprint of
SCHOLASTIC

Library of Congress Control Number: 2019957379

ISBN 978-1-338-30458-9 (hardcover)
ISBN 978-1-338-30457-2 (paperback)

10 9 8 7 6 5 4 3 2 1   21 22 23 24 25

Printed in China   62
First edition, February 2021

Edited by Cassandra Pelham Fulton and David Levithan
Book design by Phil Falco
Publisher: David Saylor

This is for the loyal readers of the Baby-sitters Club books

A. M. M.

For my mom, who breathed life into our house
with her pottery and paintings, and my dad, who
showed me the political power of comics.

Thank you to DK and Shep, whose classes and advice
made me fall in love with learning again and changed my
life for the better. And to both my grandmas, Barbie
and Sonia, for being my biggest cheerleaders.

G. E.

KRISTY THOMAS
PRESIDENT

CLAUDIA KISHI
VICE PRESIDENT

MARY ANNE SPIER
SECRETARY

STACEY MCGILL
TREASURER

DAWN SCHAFER
ALTERNATE OFFICER

MALLORY PIKE
JUNIOR OFFICER

JESSI RAMSEY
JUNIOR OFFICER

CHAPTER 1

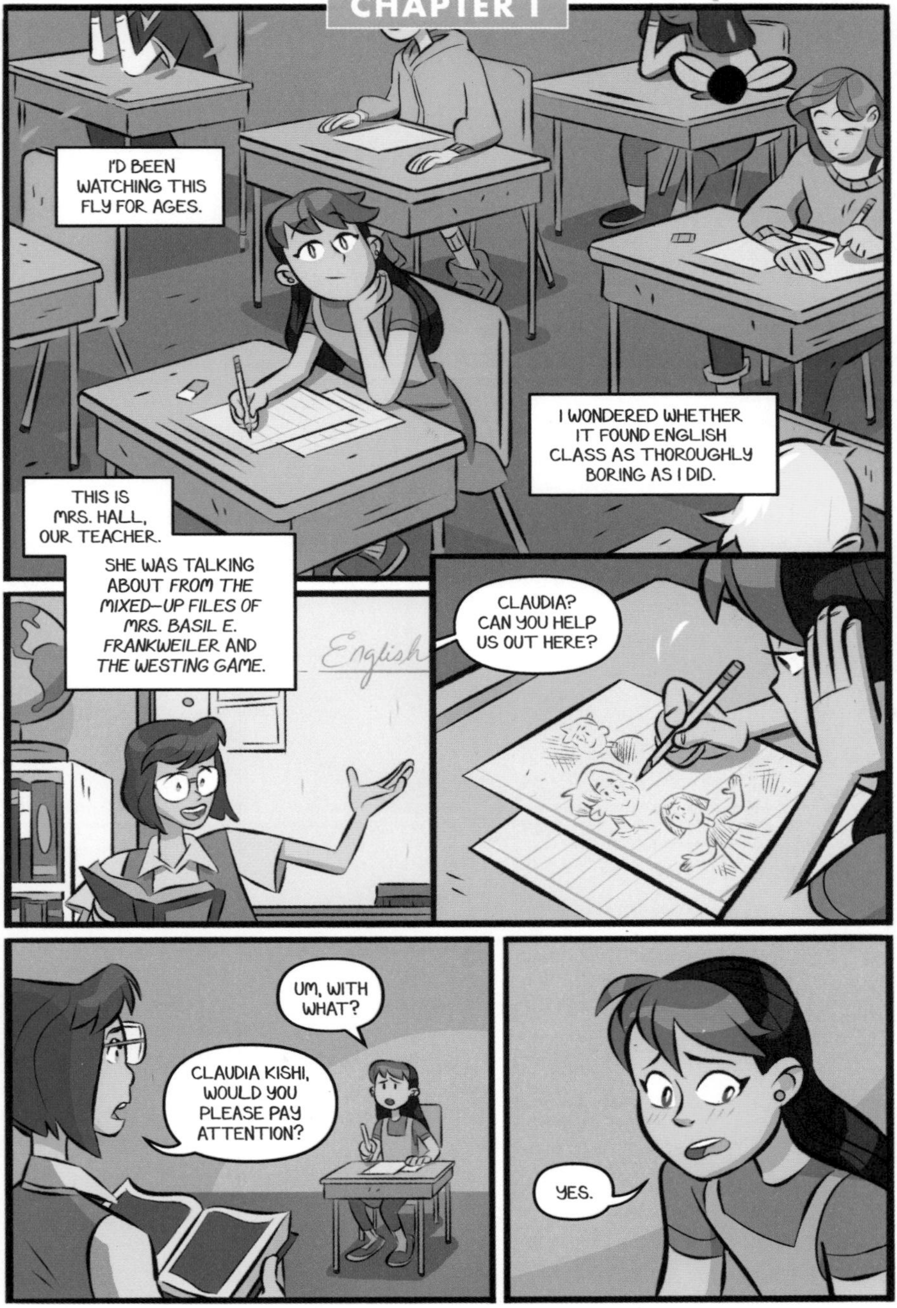

I'D BEEN WATCHING THIS FLY FOR AGES.
I WONDERED WHETHER IT FOUND ENGLISH CLASS AS THOROUGHLY BORING AS I DID.
THIS IS MRS. HALL, OUR TEACHER.
SHE WAS TALKING ABOUT *FROM THE MIXED-UP FILES OF MRS. BASIL E. FRANKWEILER* AND *THE WESTING GAME*.
English
CLAUDIA? CAN YOU HELP US OUT HERE?
UM, WITH WHAT?
CLAUDIA KISHI, WOULD YOU PLEASE PAY ATTENTION?
YES.

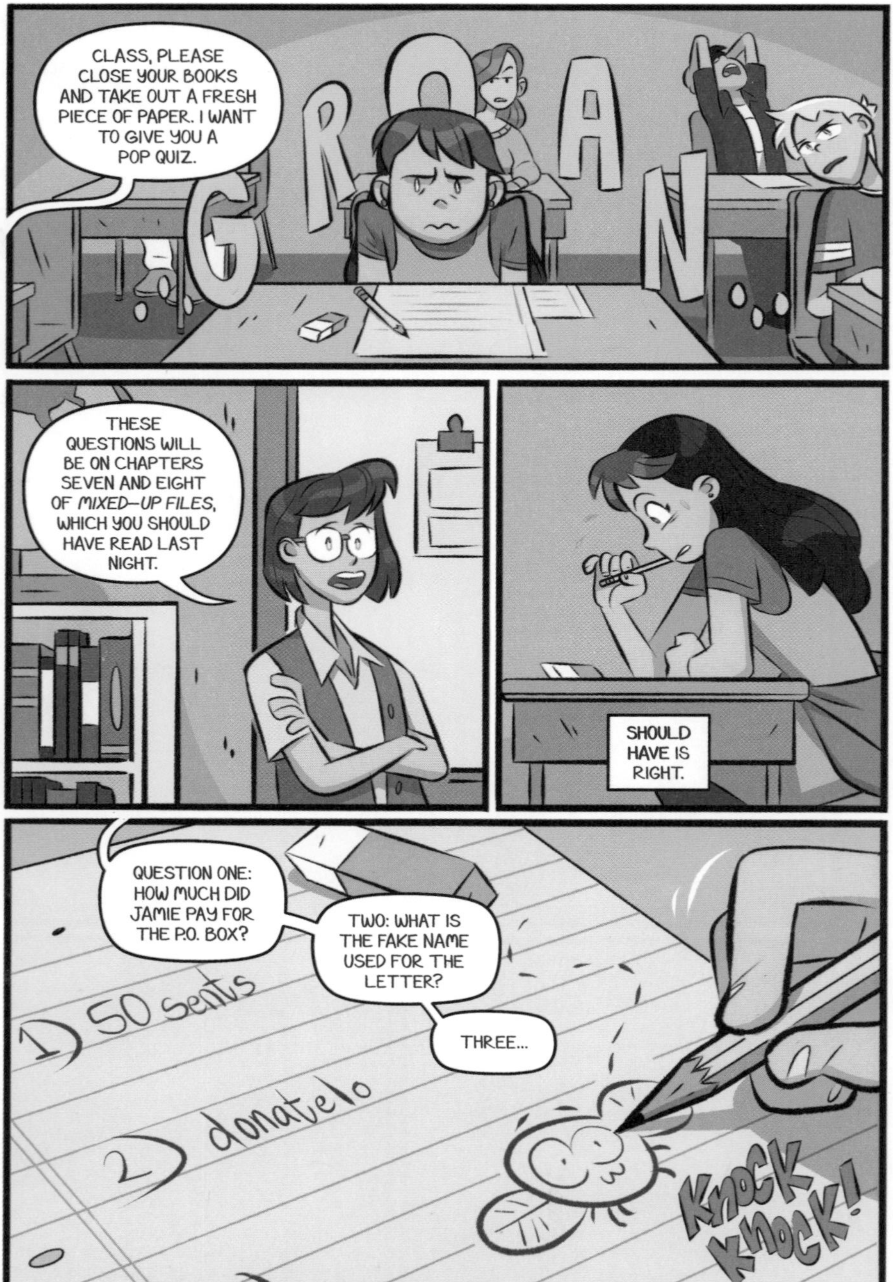
CLASS, PLEASE CLOSE YOUR BOOKS AND TAKE OUT A FRESH PIECE OF PAPER. I WANT TO GIVE YOU A POP QUIZ.
GROAN
THESE QUESTIONS WILL BE ON CHAPTERS SEVEN AND EIGHT OF *MIXED-UP FILES*, WHICH YOU SHOULD HAVE READ LAST NIGHT.
SHOULD HAVE IS RIGHT.
QUESTION ONE: HOW MUCH DID JAMIE PAY FOR THE P.O. BOX?
TWO: WHAT IS THE FAKE NAME USED FOR THE LETTER?
THREE...
1) 50 sents
2) donatelo
KNOCK KNOCK!

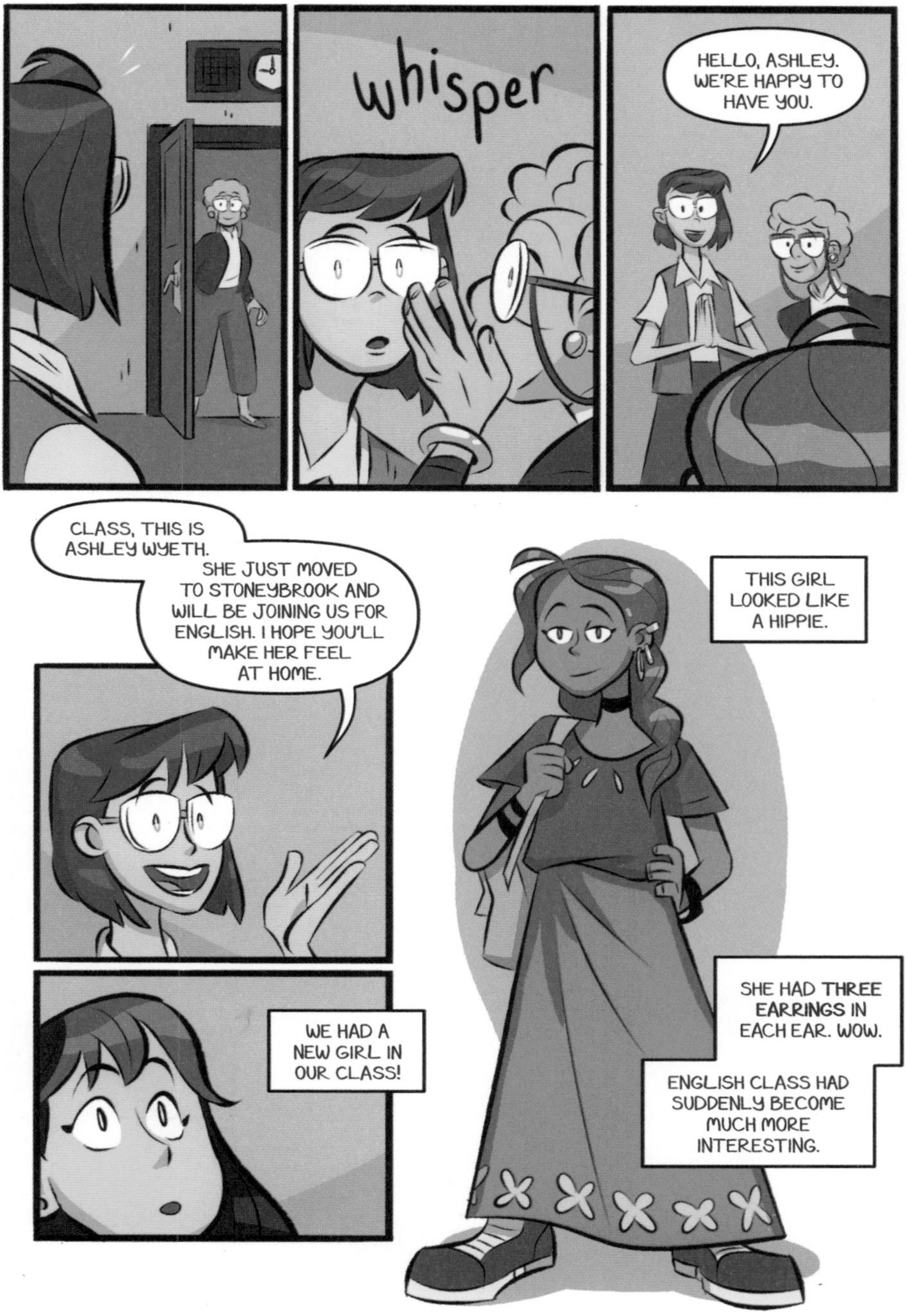
whisper
HELLO, ASHLEY. WE'RE HAPPY TO HAVE YOU.
CLASS, THIS IS ASHLEY WYETH.
SHE JUST MOVED TO STONEYBROOK AND WILL BE JOINING US FOR ENGLISH. I HOPE YOU'LL MAKE HER FEEL AT HOME.
WE HAD A NEW GIRL IN OUR CLASS!
THIS GIRL LOOKED LIKE A HIPPIE.
SHE HAD THREE EARRINGS IN EACH EAR. WOW.
ENGLISH CLASS HAD SUDDENLY BECOME MUCH MORE INTERESTING.

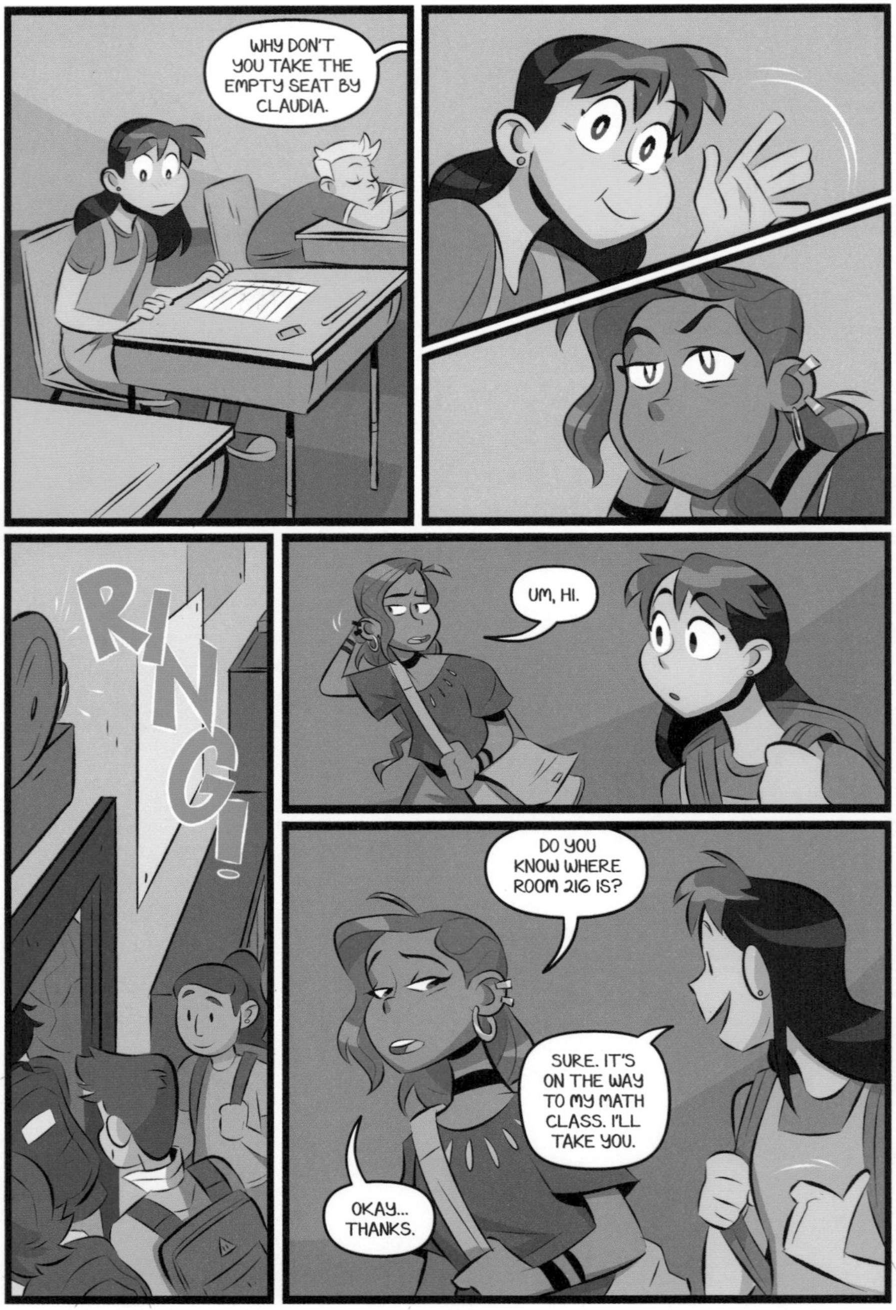
WHY DON'T YOU TAKE THE EMPTY SEAT BY CLAUDIA.
RING!
UM, HI.
DO YOU KNOW WHERE ROOM 216 IS?
SURE. IT'S ON THE WAY TO MY MATH CLASS. I'LL TAKE YOU.
OKAY... THANKS.

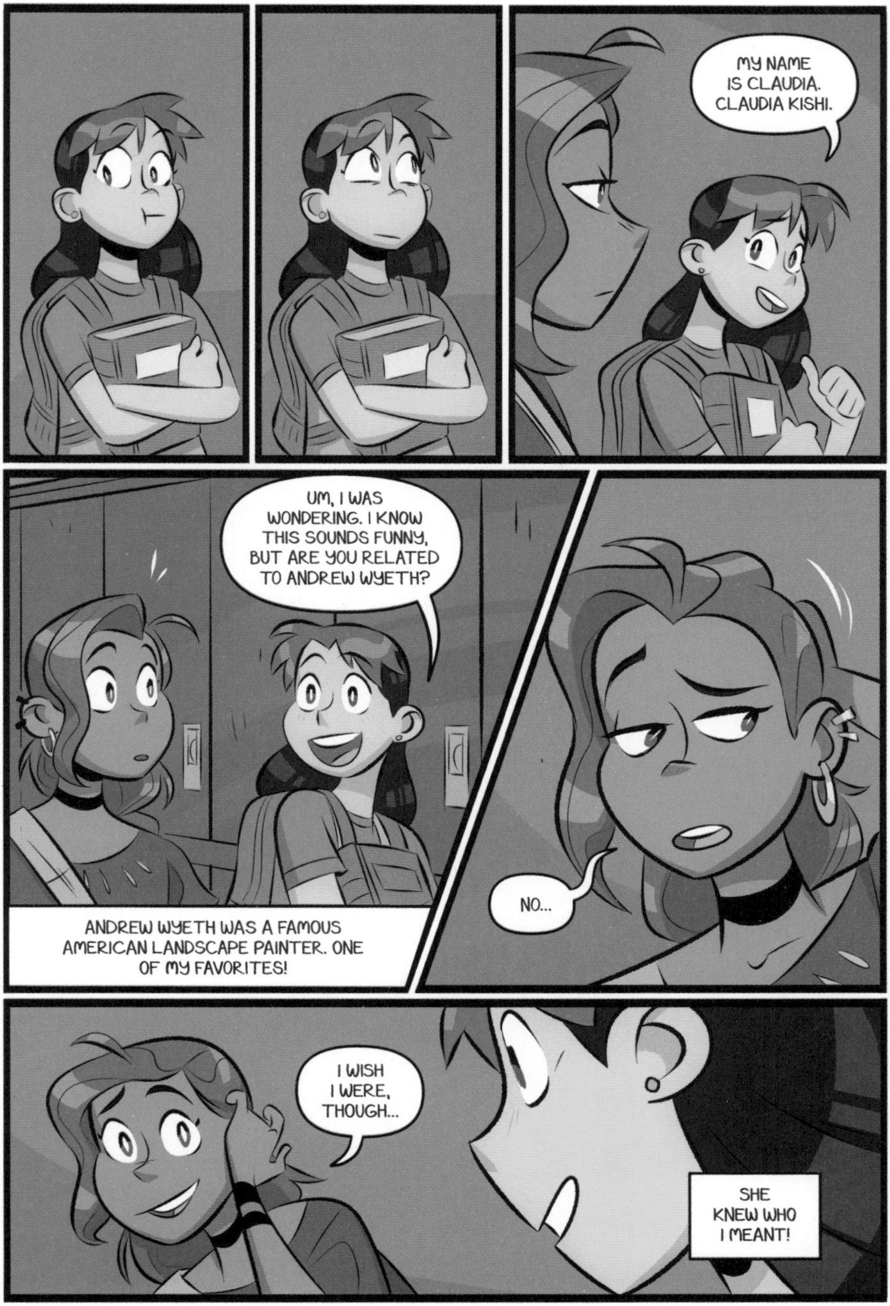
MY NAME IS CLAUDIA. CLAUDIA KISHI.
UM, I WAS WONDERING. I KNOW THIS SOUNDS FUNNY, BUT ARE YOU RELATED TO ANDREW WYETH?
ANDREW WYETH WAS A FAMOUS AMERICAN LANDSCAPE PAINTER. ONE OF MY FAVORITES!
NO...
I WISH I WERE, THOUGH...
SHE KNEW WHO I MEANT!

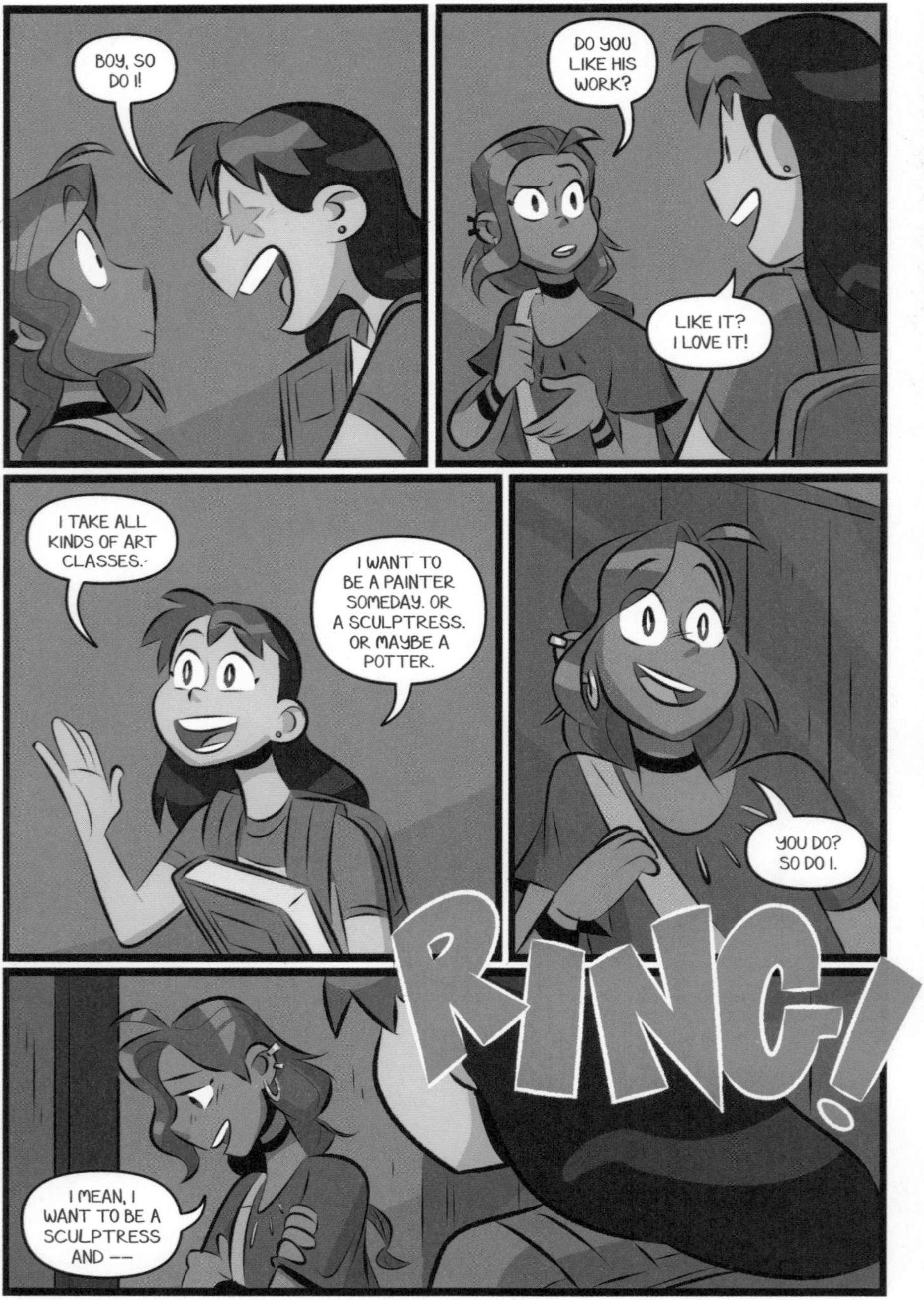
BOY, SO DO I!
DO YOU LIKE HIS WORK?
LIKE IT? I LOVE IT!
I TAKE ALL KINDS OF ART CLASSES.
I WANT TO BE A PAINTER SOMEDAY. OR A SCULPTRESS. OR MAYBE A POTTER.
YOU DO? SO DO I.
RING!
I MEAN, I WANT TO BE A SCULPTRESS AND --

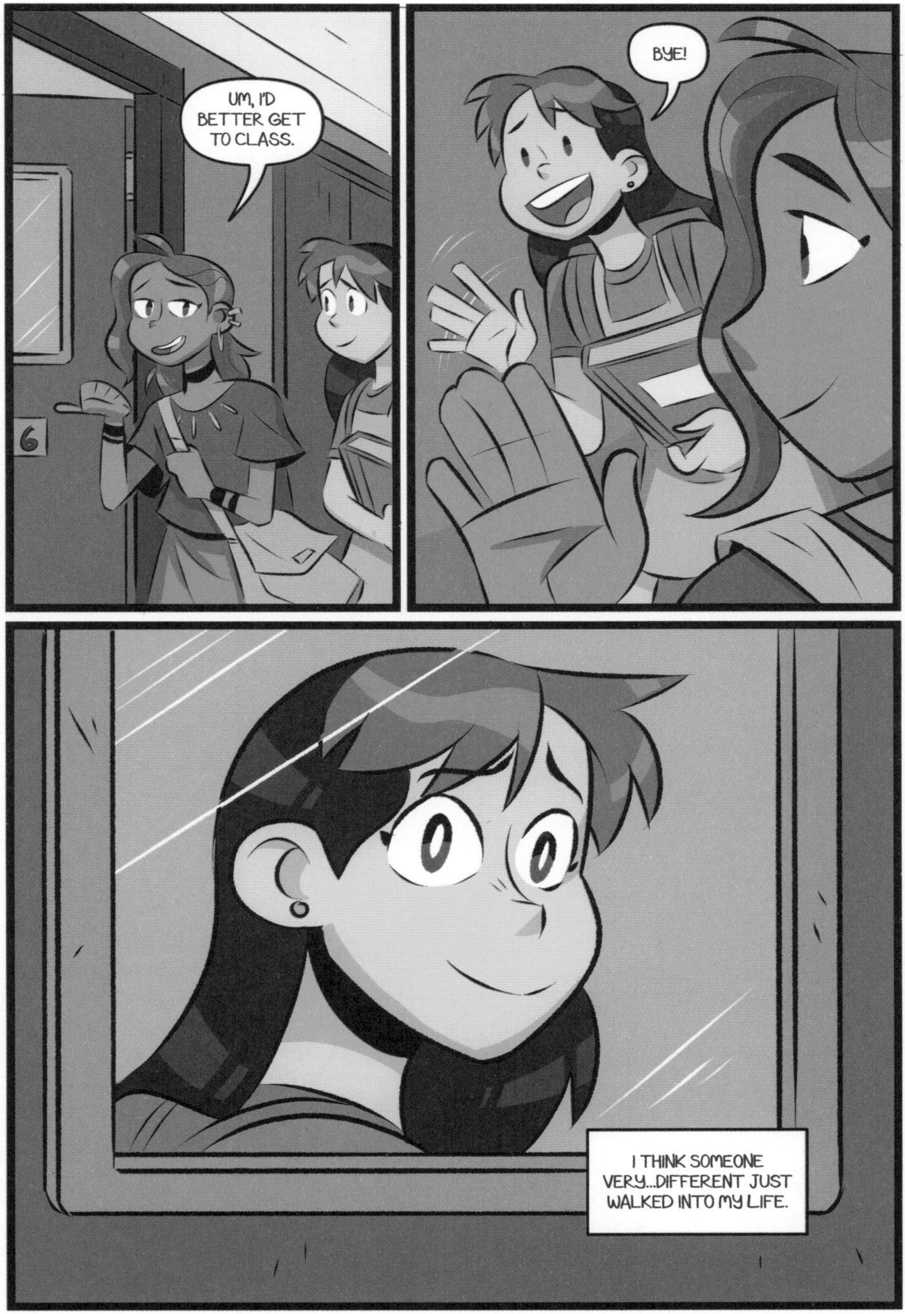
UM, I'D BETTER GET TO CLASS.
BYE!
I THINK SOMEONE VERY...DIFFERENT JUST WALKED INTO MY LIFE.

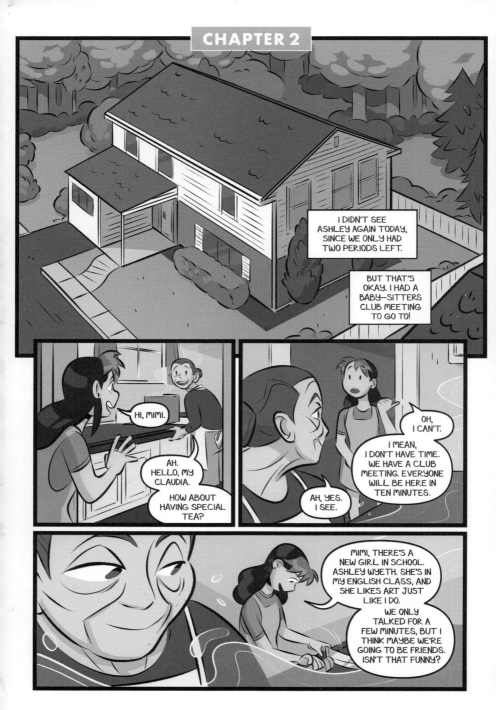

CHAPTER 2

I DIDN'T SEE ASHLEY AGAIN TODAY, SINCE WE ONLY HAD TWO PERIODS LEFT.

BUT THAT'S OKAY. I HAD A BABY-SITTERS CLUB MEETING TO GO TO!

HI, MIMI.

AH. HELLO, MY CLAUDIA.

HOW ABOUT HAVING SPECIAL TEA?

OH, I CAN'T.

I MEAN, I DON'T HAVE TIME. WE HAVE A CLUB MEETING. EVERYONE WILL BE HERE IN TEN MINUTES.

AH, YES. I SEE.

MIMI, THERE'S A NEW GIRL IN SCHOOL. ASHLEY WYETH. SHE'S IN MY ENGLISH CLASS, AND SHE LIKES ART JUST LIKE I DO.

WE ONLY TALKED FOR A FEW MINUTES, BUT I THINK MAYBE WE'RE GOING TO BE FRIENDS. ISN'T THAT FUNNY?

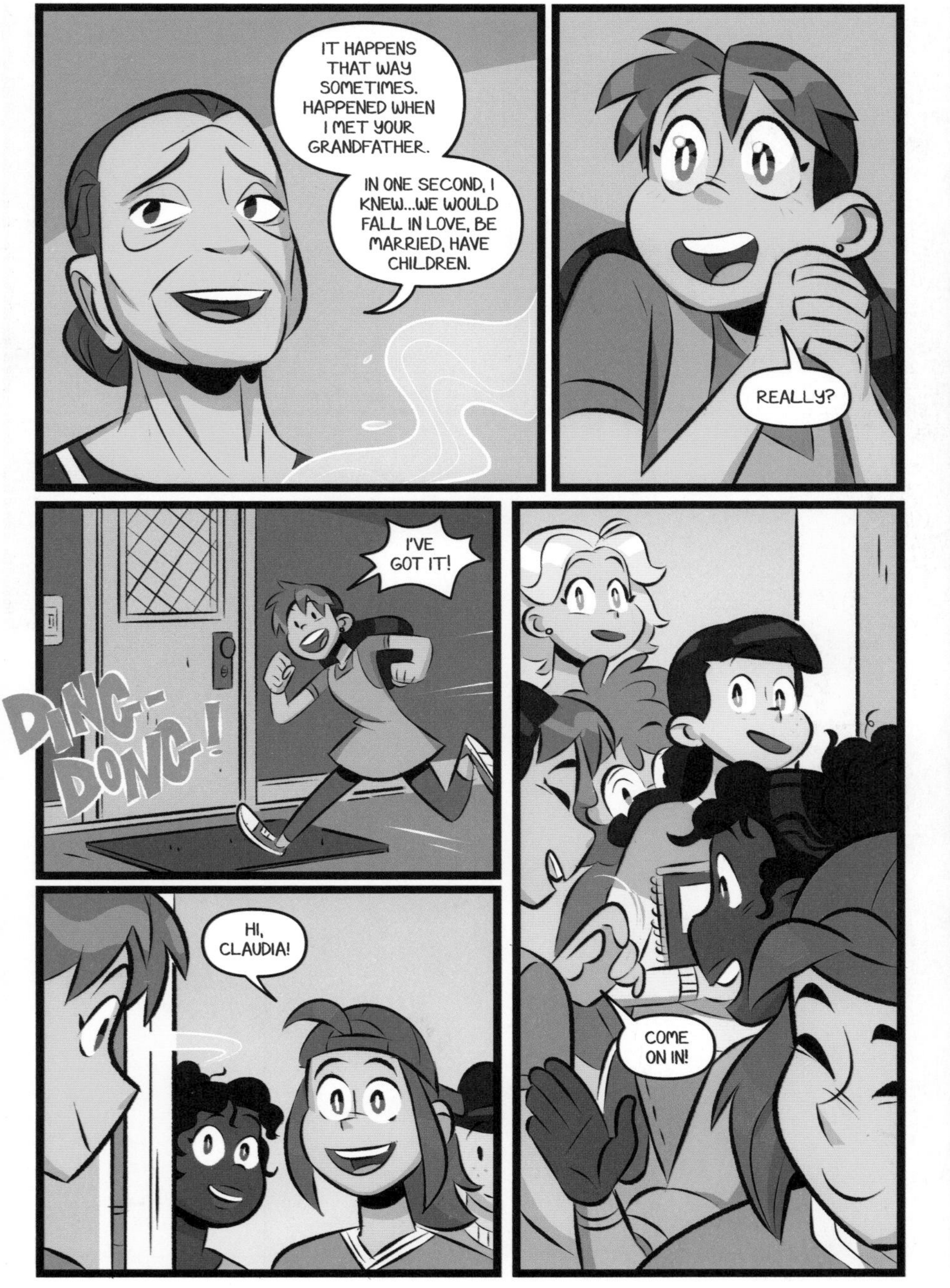
IT HAPPENS THAT WAY SOMETIMES. HAPPENED WHEN I MET YOUR GRANDFATHER.
IN ONE SECOND, I KNEW...WE WOULD FALL IN LOVE, BE MARRIED, HAVE CHILDREN.
REALLY?
DING-DONG!
I'VE GOT IT!
HI, CLAUDIA!
COME ON IN!

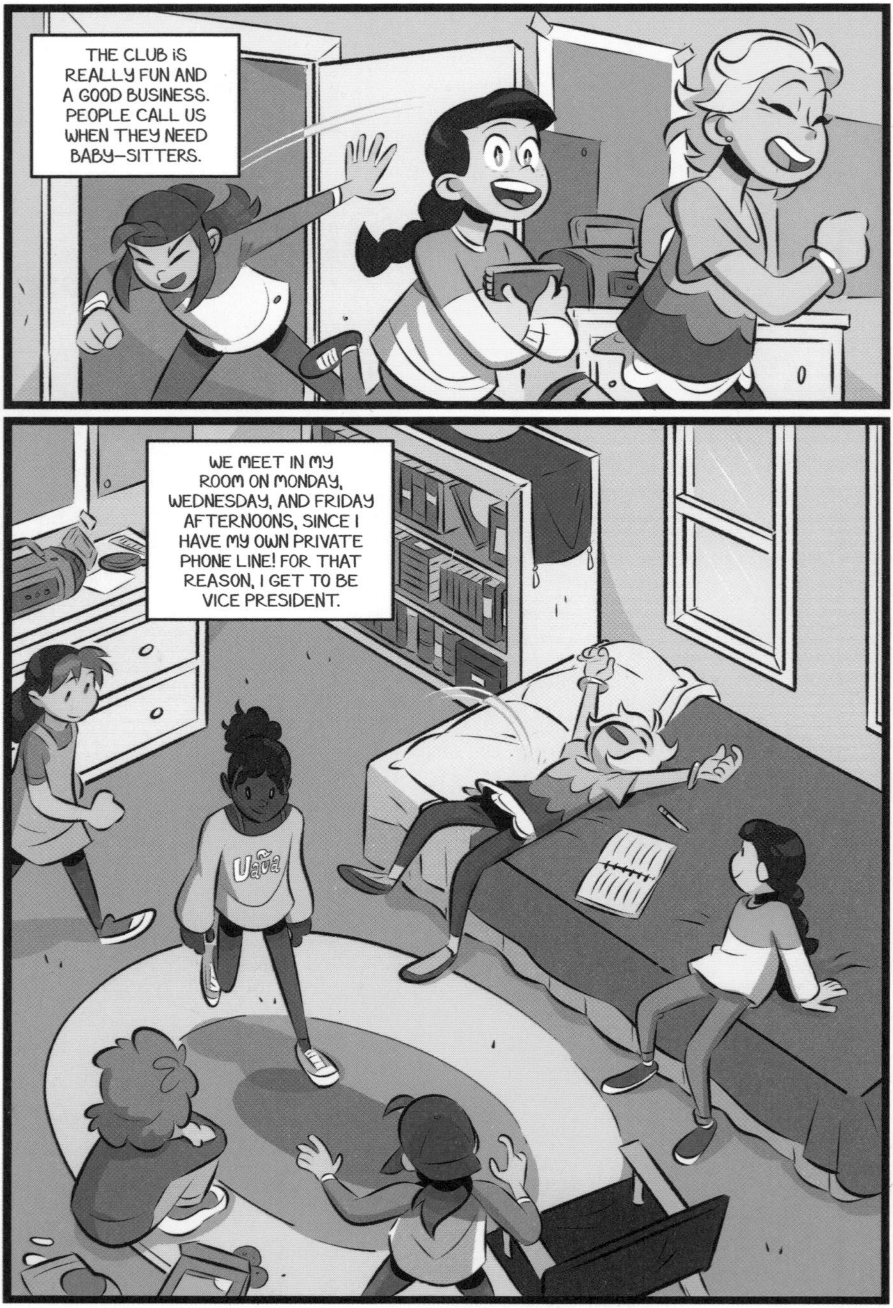
THE CLUB iS REALLY FUN AND A GOOD BUSINESS. PEOPLE CALL US WHEN THEY NEED BABY-SITTERS.
WE MEET IN MY ROOM ON MONDAY, WEDNESDAY, AND FRIDAY AFTERNOONS, SINCE I HAVE MY OWN PRIVATE PHONE LINE! FOR THAT REASON, I GET TO BE VICE PRESIDENT.

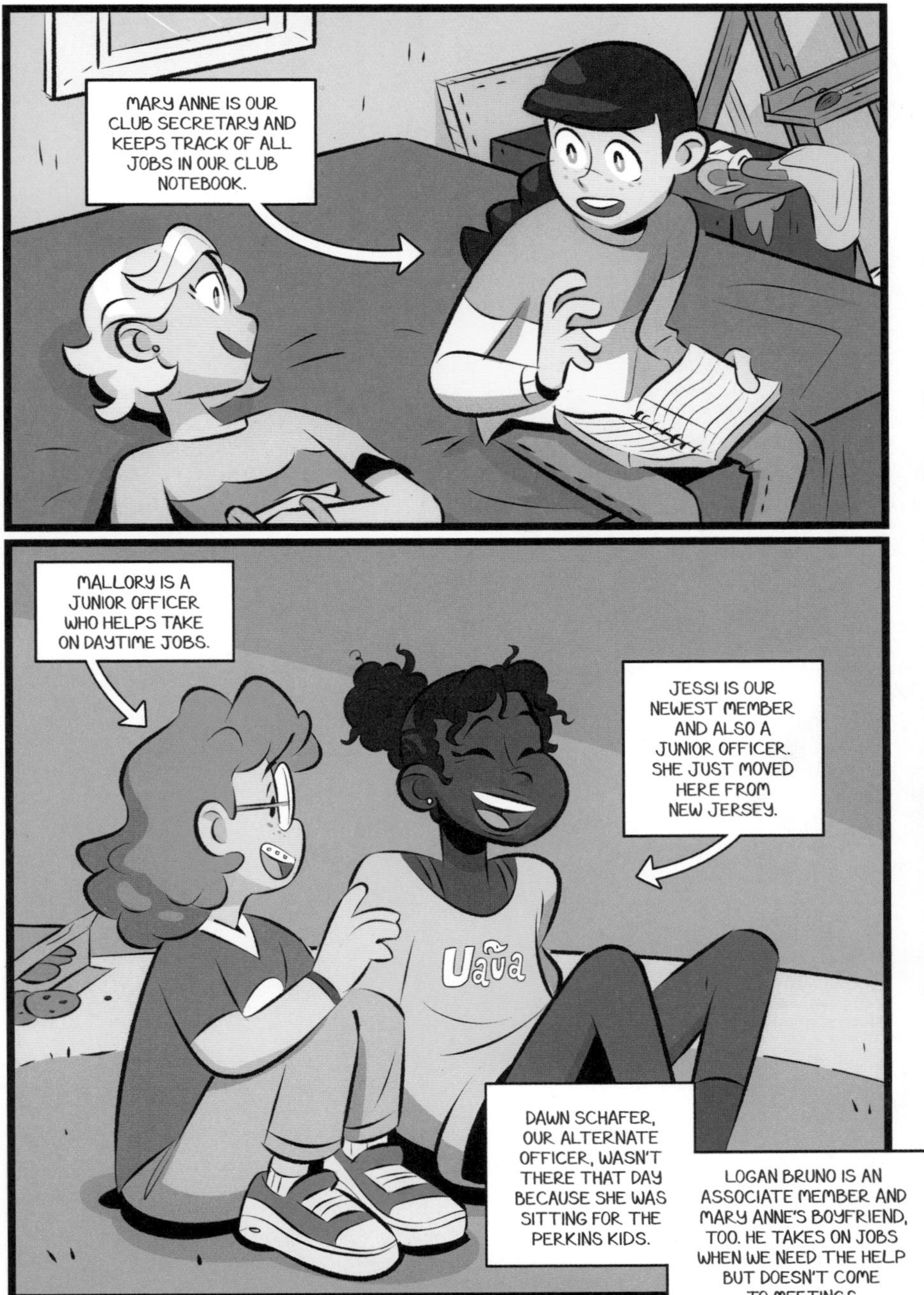
MARY ANNE IS OUR CLUB SECRETARY AND KEEPS TRACK OF ALL JOBS IN OUR CLUB NOTEBOOK.
MALLORY IS A JUNIOR OFFICER WHO HELPS TAKE ON DAYTIME JOBS.
JESSI IS OUR NEWEST MEMBER AND ALSO A JUNIOR OFFICER. SHE JUST MOVED HERE FROM NEW JERSEY.
DAWN SCHAFER, OUR ALTERNATE OFFICER, WASN'T THERE THAT DAY BECAUSE SHE WAS SITTING FOR THE PERKINS KIDS.
LOGAN BRUNO IS AN ASSOCIATE MEMBER AND MARY ANNE'S BOYFRIEND, TOO. HE TAKES ON JOBS WHEN WE NEED THE HELP BUT DOESN'T COME TO MEETINGS.

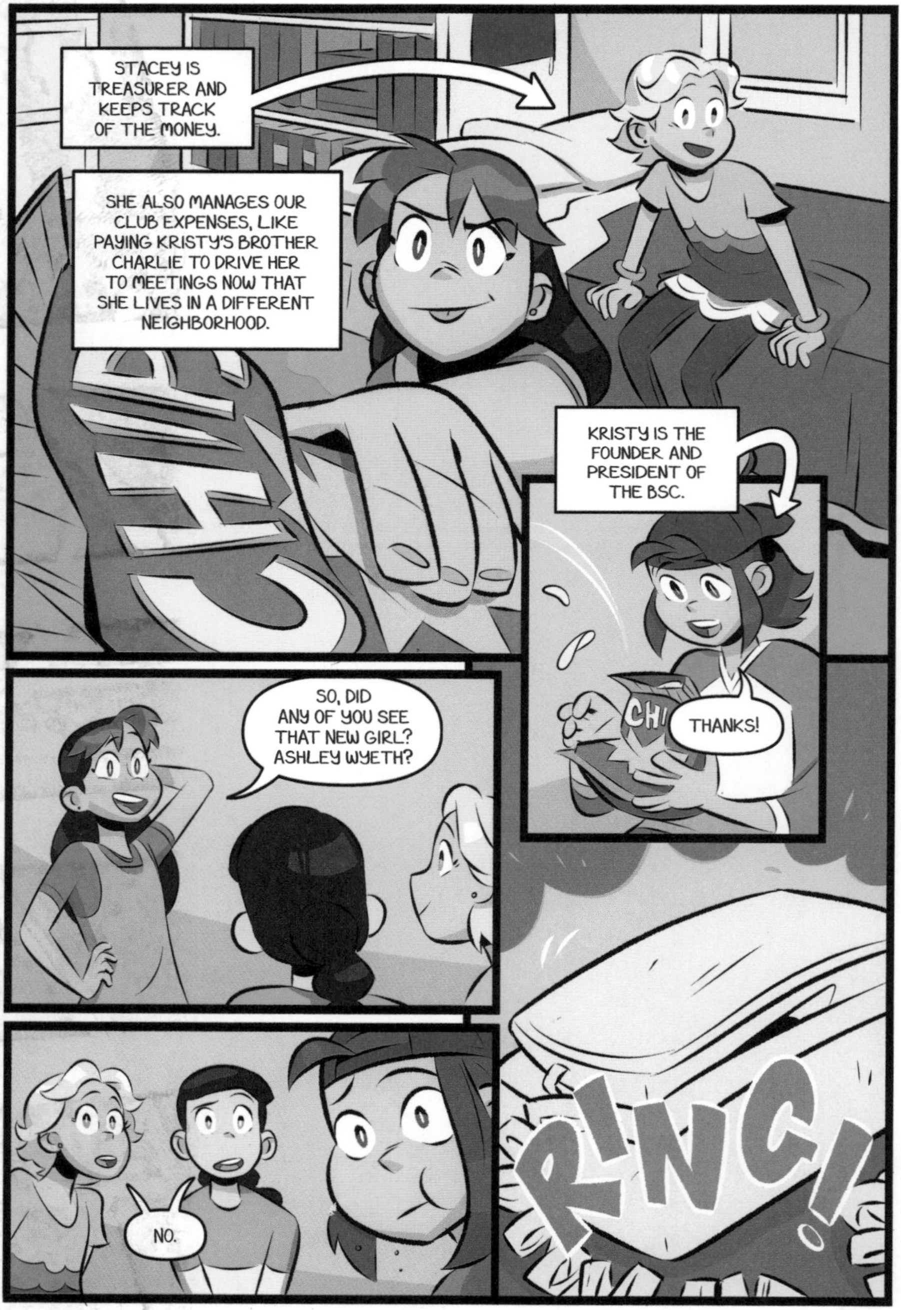
STACEY IS TREASURER AND KEEPS TRACK OF THE MONEY.
SHE ALSO MANAGES OUR CLUB EXPENSES, LIKE PAYING KRISTY'S BROTHER CHARLIE TO DRIVE HER TO MEETINGS NOW THAT SHE LIVES IN A DIFFERENT NEIGHBORHOOD.
KRISTY IS THE FOUNDER AND PRESIDENT OF THE BSC.
THANKS!
SO, DID ANY OF YOU SEE THAT NEW GIRL? ASHLEY WYETH?
NO.
RING!

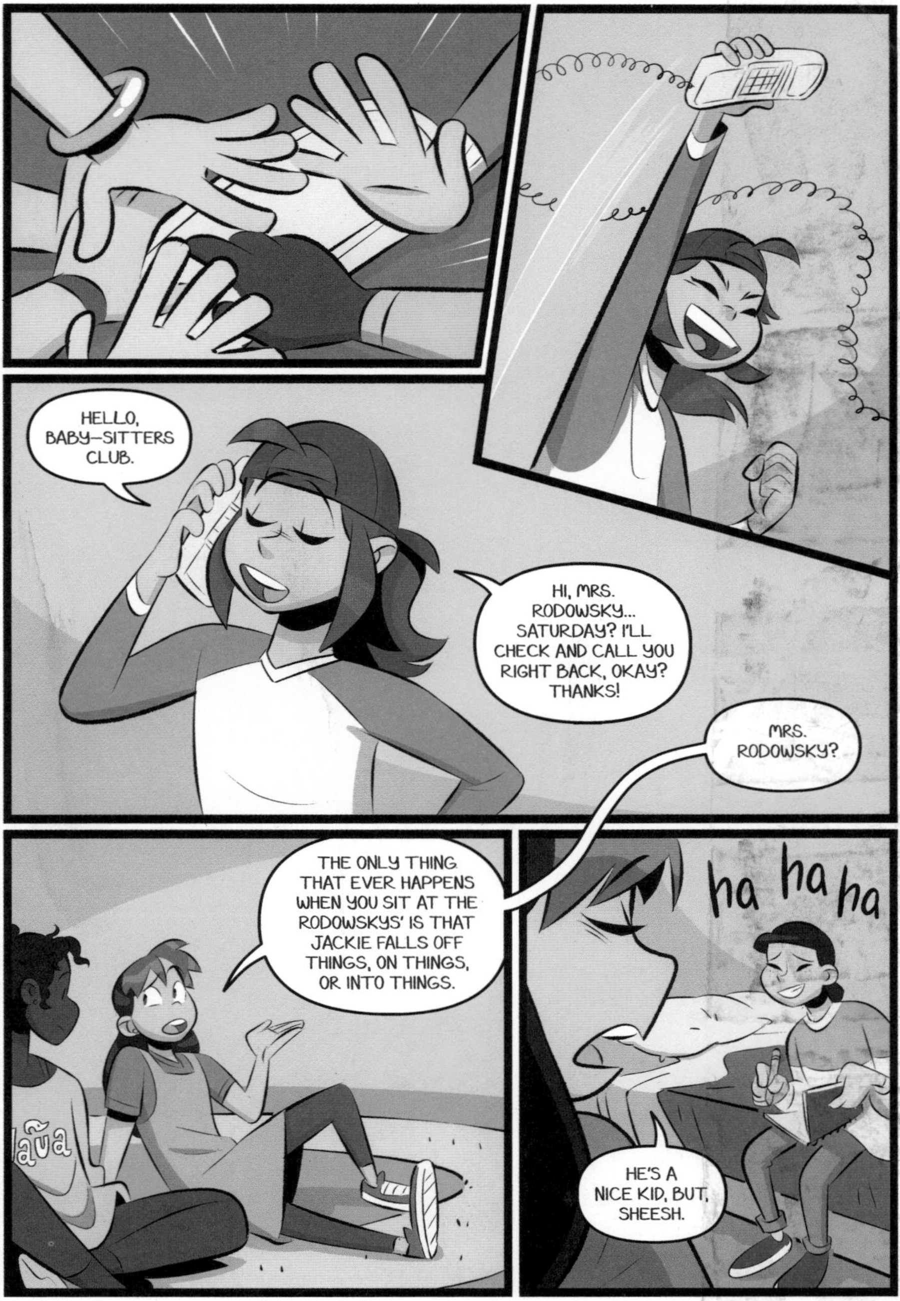
HELLO, BABY-SITTERS CLUB.
HI, MRS. RODOWSKY... SATURDAY? I'LL CHECK AND CALL YOU RIGHT BACK, OKAY? THANKS!
MRS. RODOWSKY?
THE ONLY THING THAT EVER HAPPENS WHEN YOU SIT AT THE RODOWSKYS' IS THAT JACKIE FALLS OFF THINGS, ON THINGS, OR INTO THINGS.
ha ha ha
HE'S A NICE KID, BUT, SHEESH.

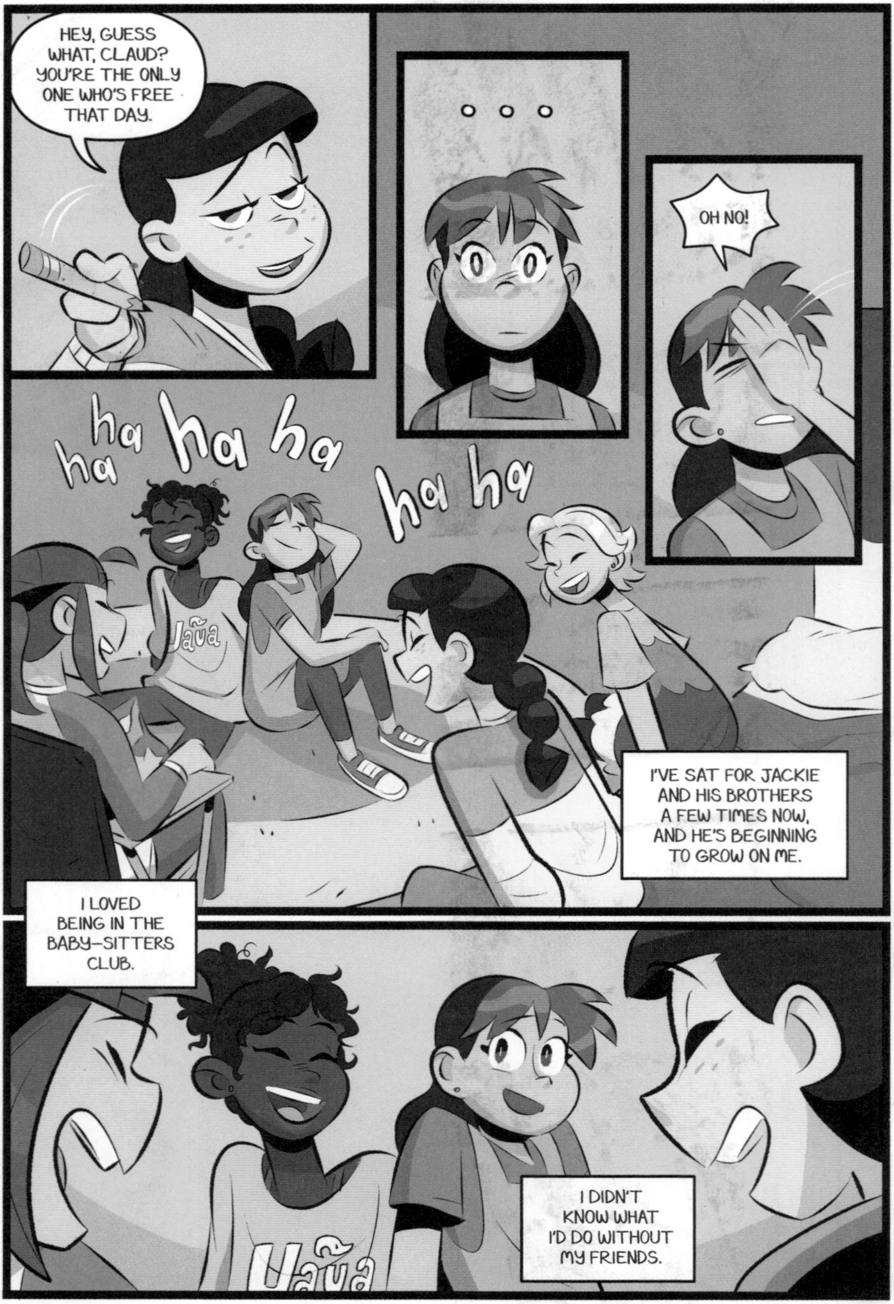
HEY, GUESS WHAT, CLAUD? YOU'RE THE ONLY ONE WHO'S FREE THAT DAY.
...
OH NO!
ha ha ha ha
ha ha
I'VE SAT FOR JACKIE AND HIS BROTHERS A FEW TIMES NOW, AND HE'S BEGINNING TO GROW ON ME.
I LOVED BEING IN THE BABY-SITTERS CLUB.
I DIDN'T KNOW WHAT I'D DO WITHOUT MY FRIENDS.

CHAPTER 3

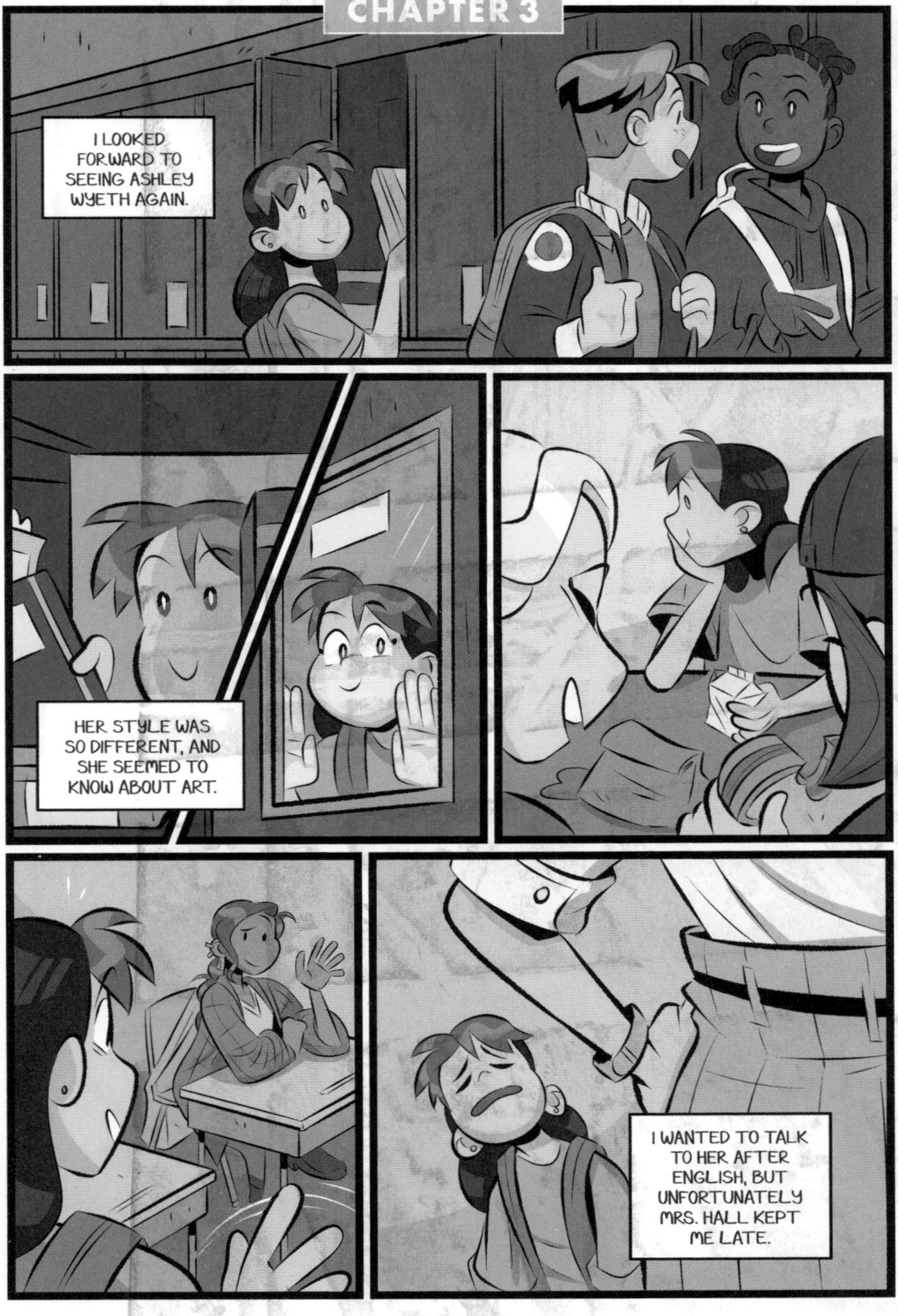
I LOOKED FORWARD TO SEEING ASHLEY WYETH AGAIN.
HER STYLE WAS SO DIFFERENT, AND SHE SEEMED TO KNOW ABOUT ART.
I WANTED TO TALK TO HER AFTER ENGLISH, BUT UNFORTUNATELY MRS. HALL KEPT ME LATE.

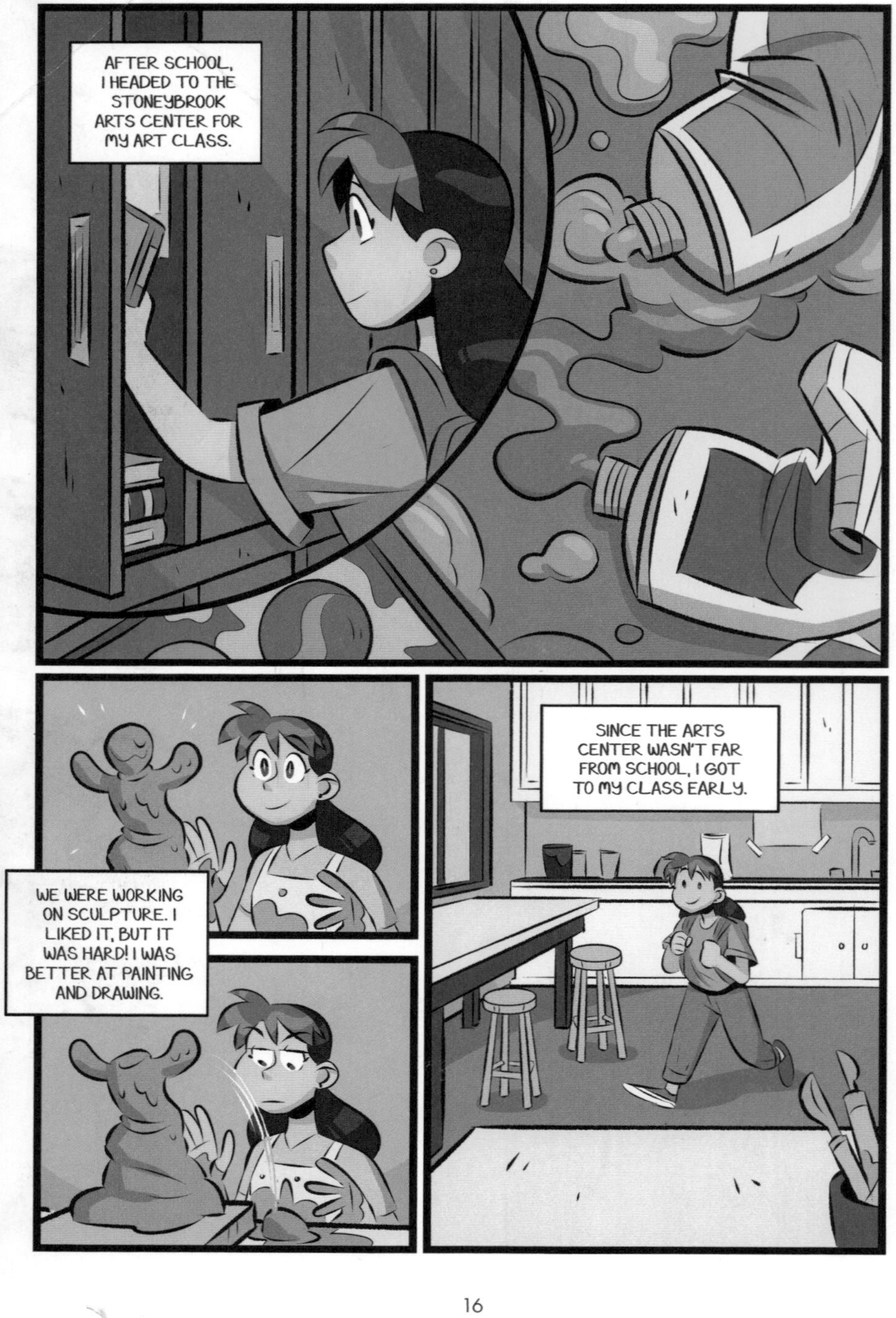
AFTER SCHOOL, I HEADED TO THE STONEYBROOK ARTS CENTER FOR MY ART CLASS.
WE WERE WORKING ON SCULPTURE. I LIKED IT, BUT IT WAS HARD! I WAS BETTER AT PAINTING AND DRAWING.
SINCE THE ARTS CENTER WASN'T FAR FROM SCHOOL, I GOT TO MY CLASS EARLY.

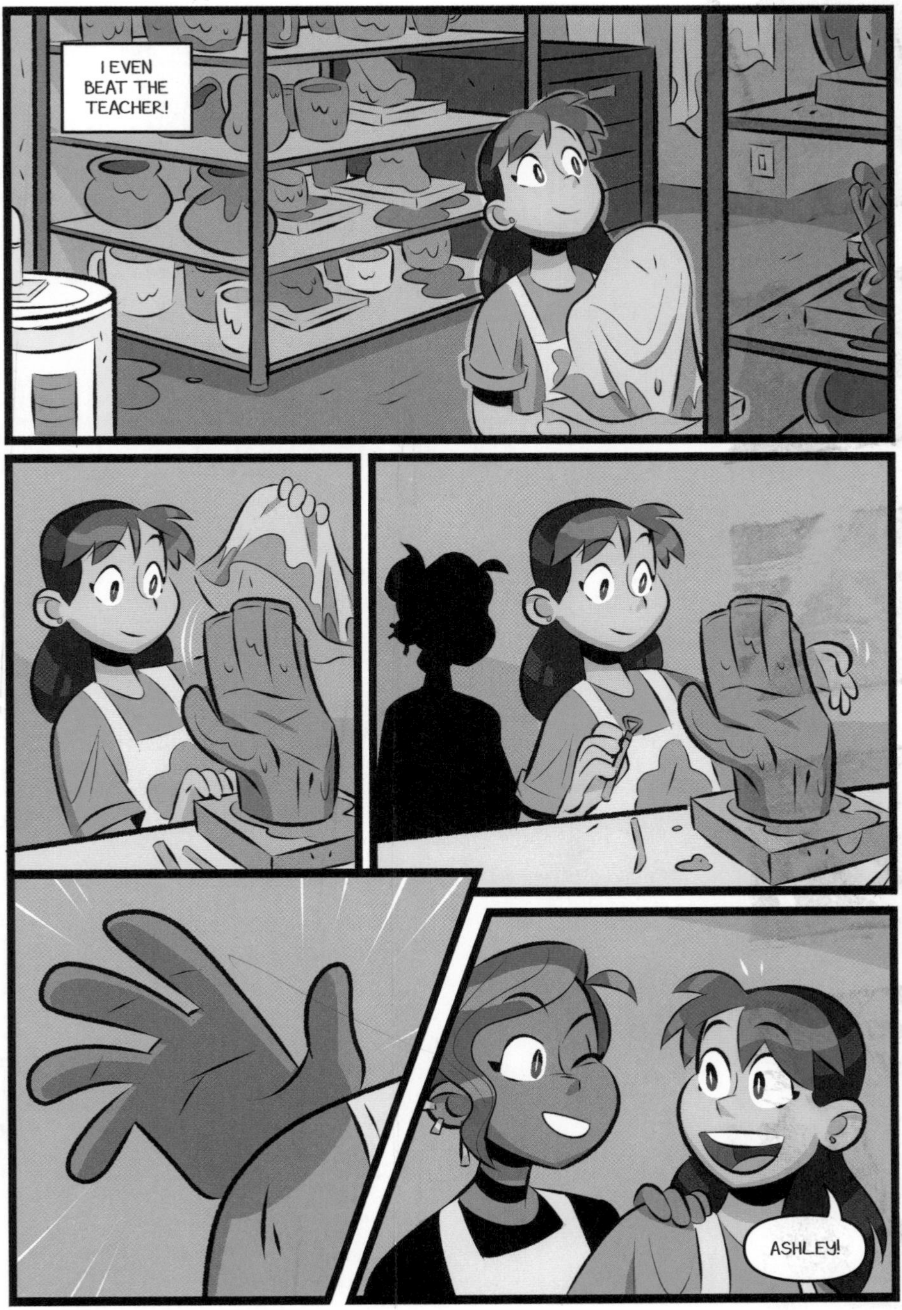
I EVEN BEAT THE TEACHER!
ASHLEY!

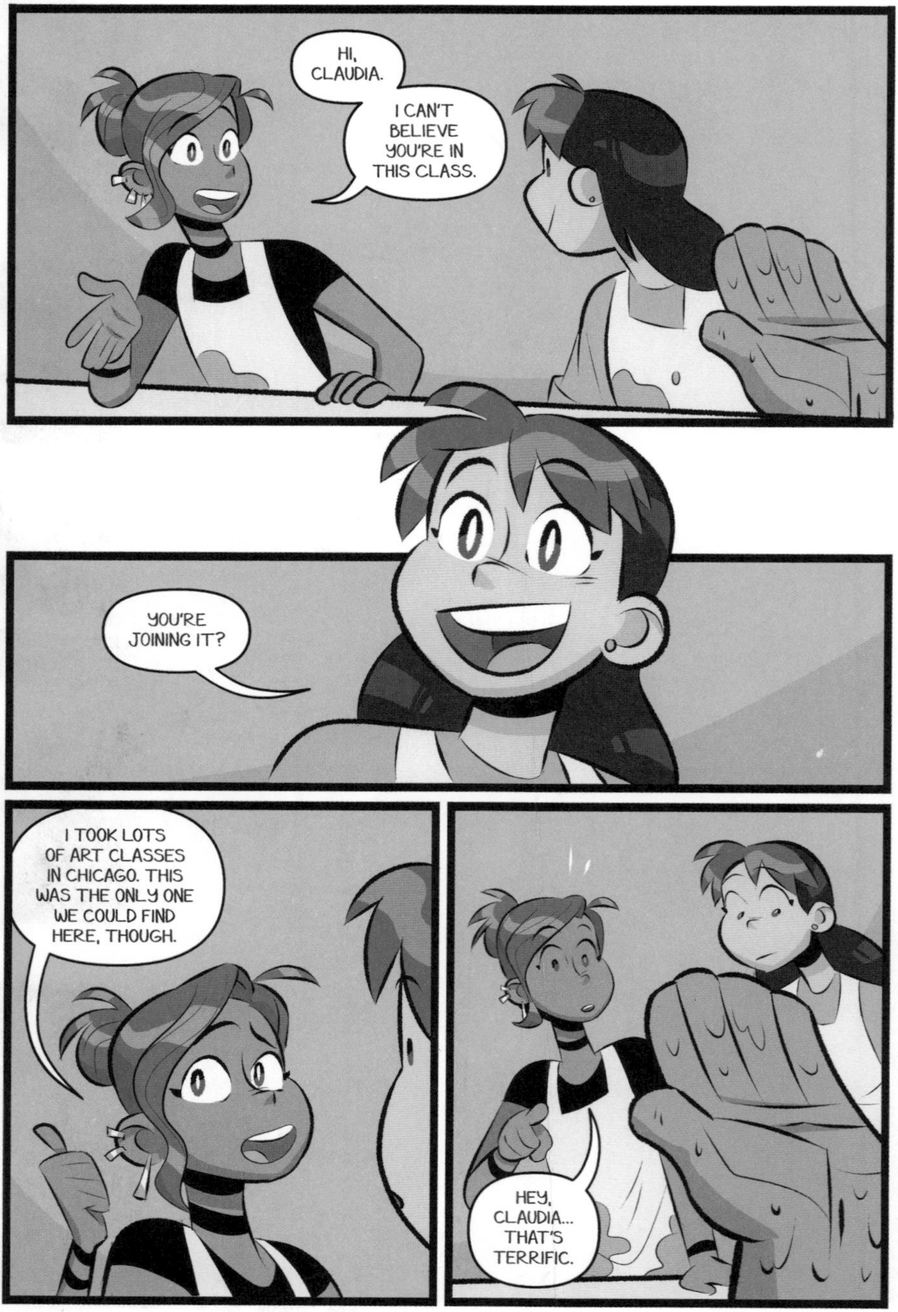
HI, CLAUDIA.
I CAN'T BELIEVE YOU'RE IN THIS CLASS.
YOU'RE JOINING IT?
I TOOK LOTS OF ART CLASSES IN CHICAGO. THIS WAS THE ONLY ONE WE COULD FIND HERE, THOUGH.
HEY, CLAUDIA... THAT'S TERRIFIC.

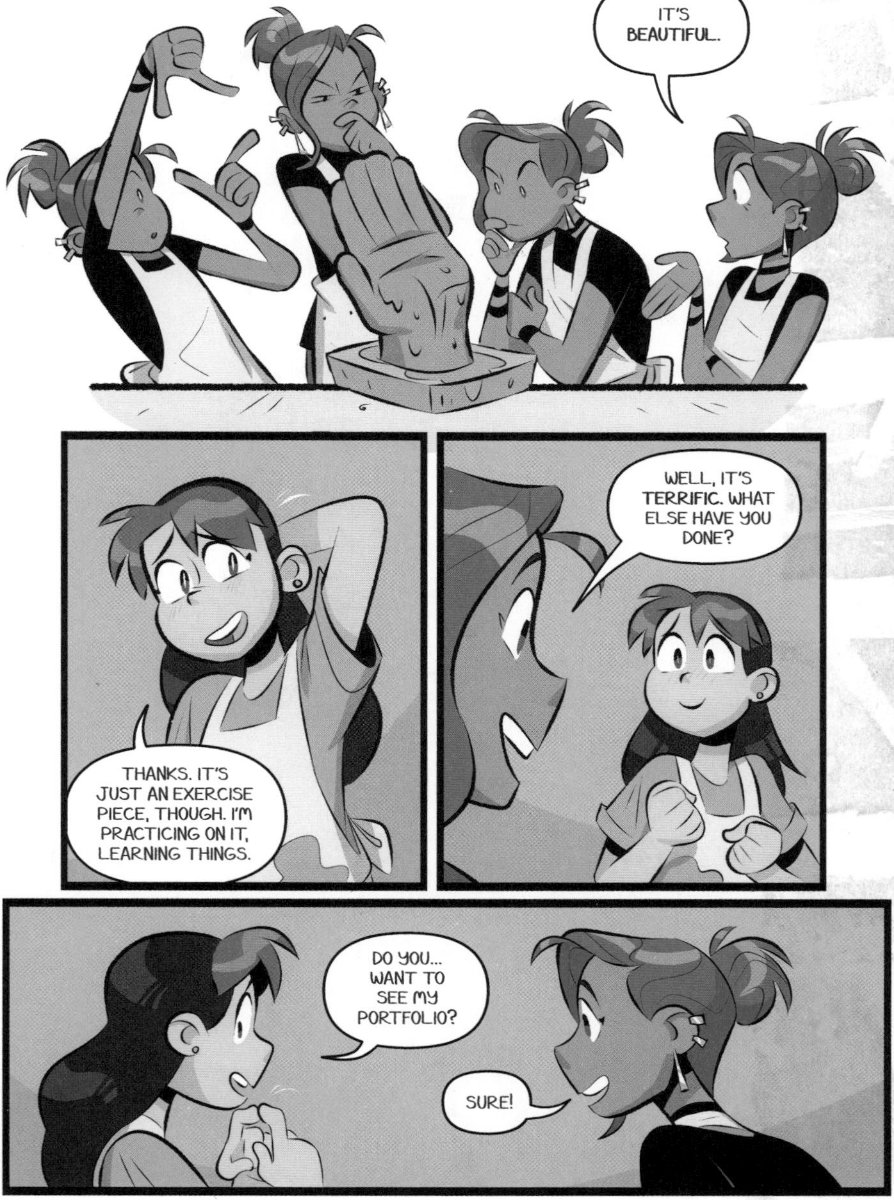

IT'S BEAUTIFUL.
THANKS. IT'S JUST AN EXERCISE PIECE, THOUGH. I'M PRACTICING ON IT, LEARNING THINGS.
WELL, IT'S TERRIFIC. WHAT ELSE HAVE YOU DONE?
DO YOU... WANT TO SEE MY PORTFOLIO?
SURE!

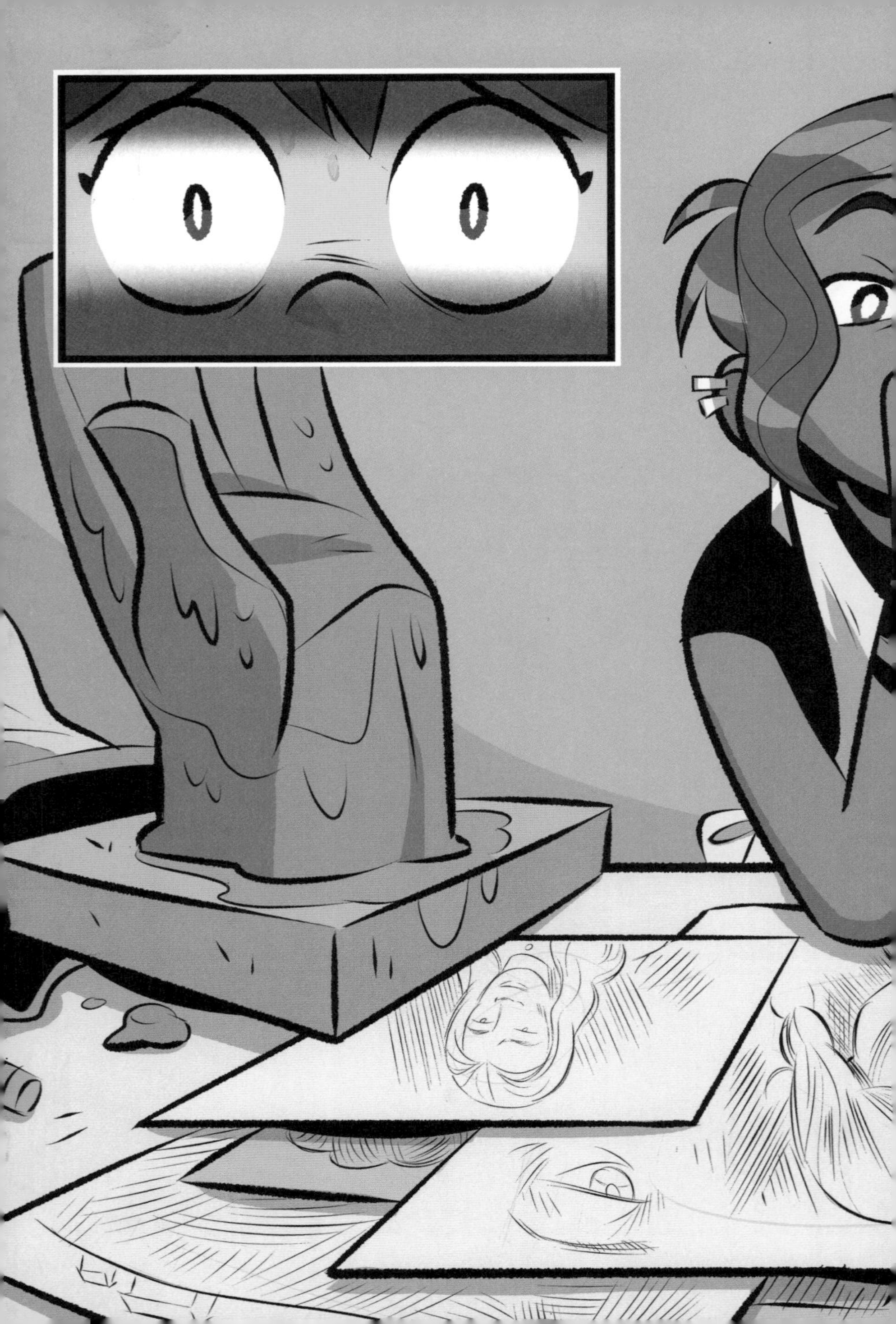

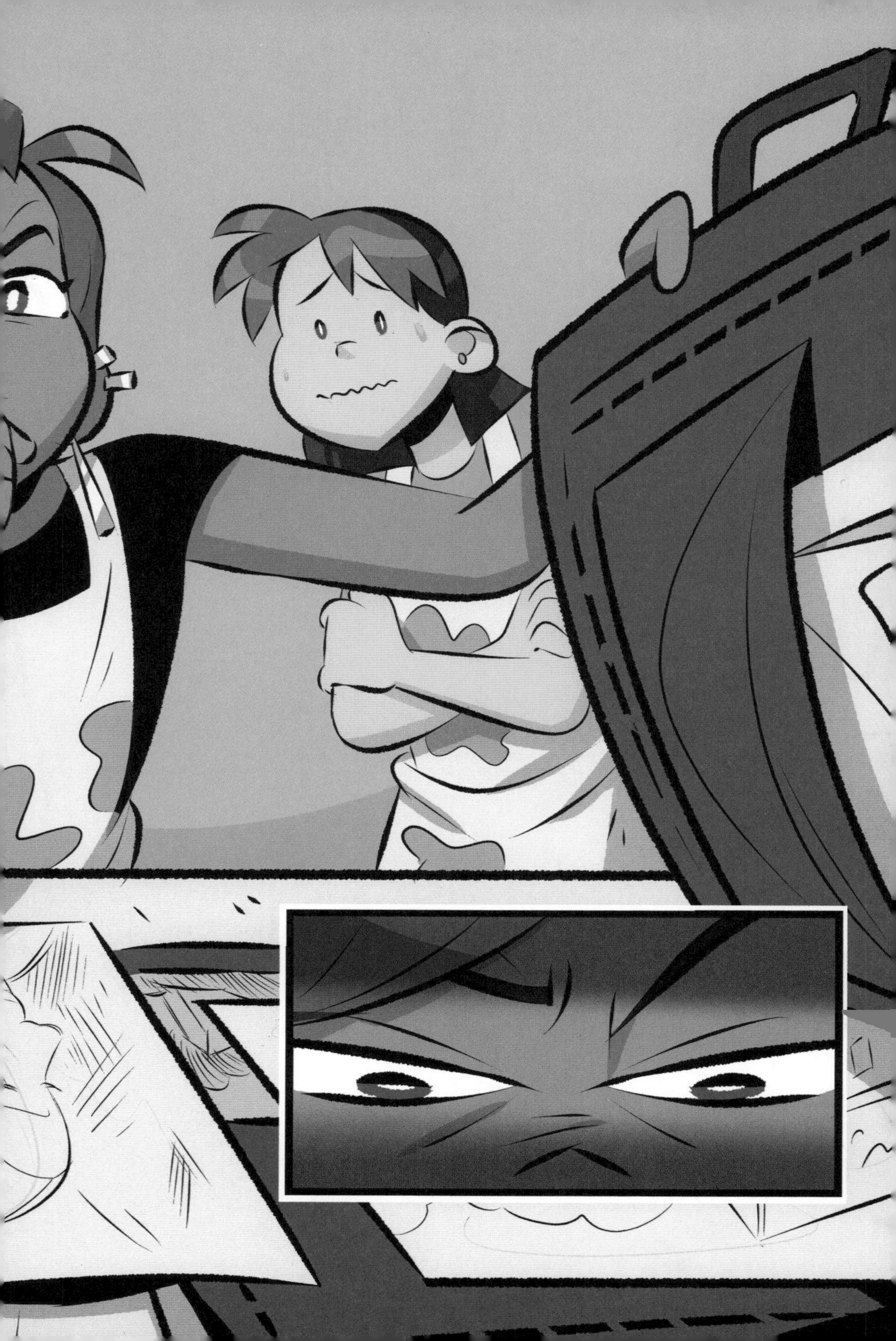

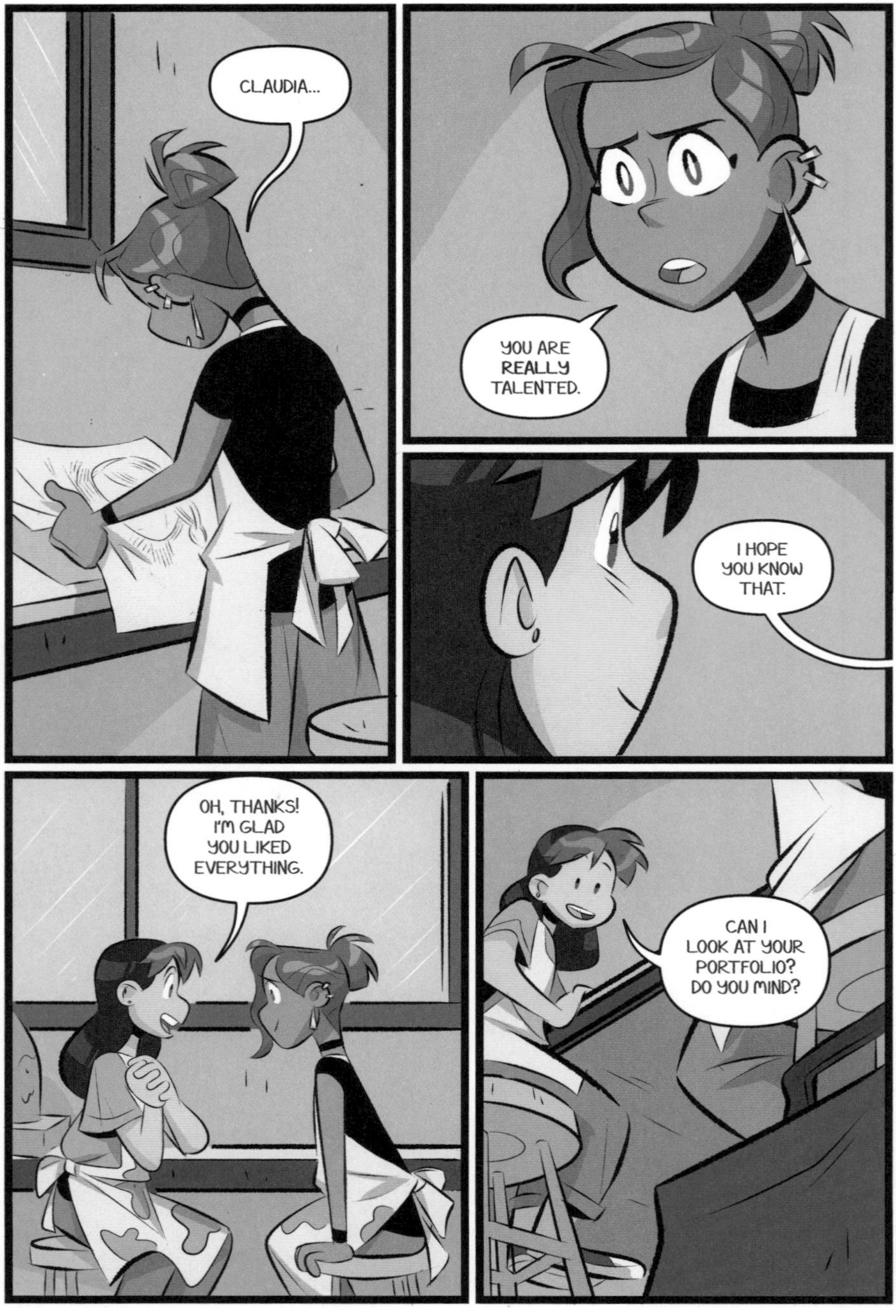
CLAUDIA...
YOU ARE REALLY TALENTED.
I HOPE YOU KNOW THAT.
OH, THANKS! I'M GLAD YOU LIKED EVERYTHING.
CAN I LOOK AT YOUR PORTFOLIO? DO YOU MIND?

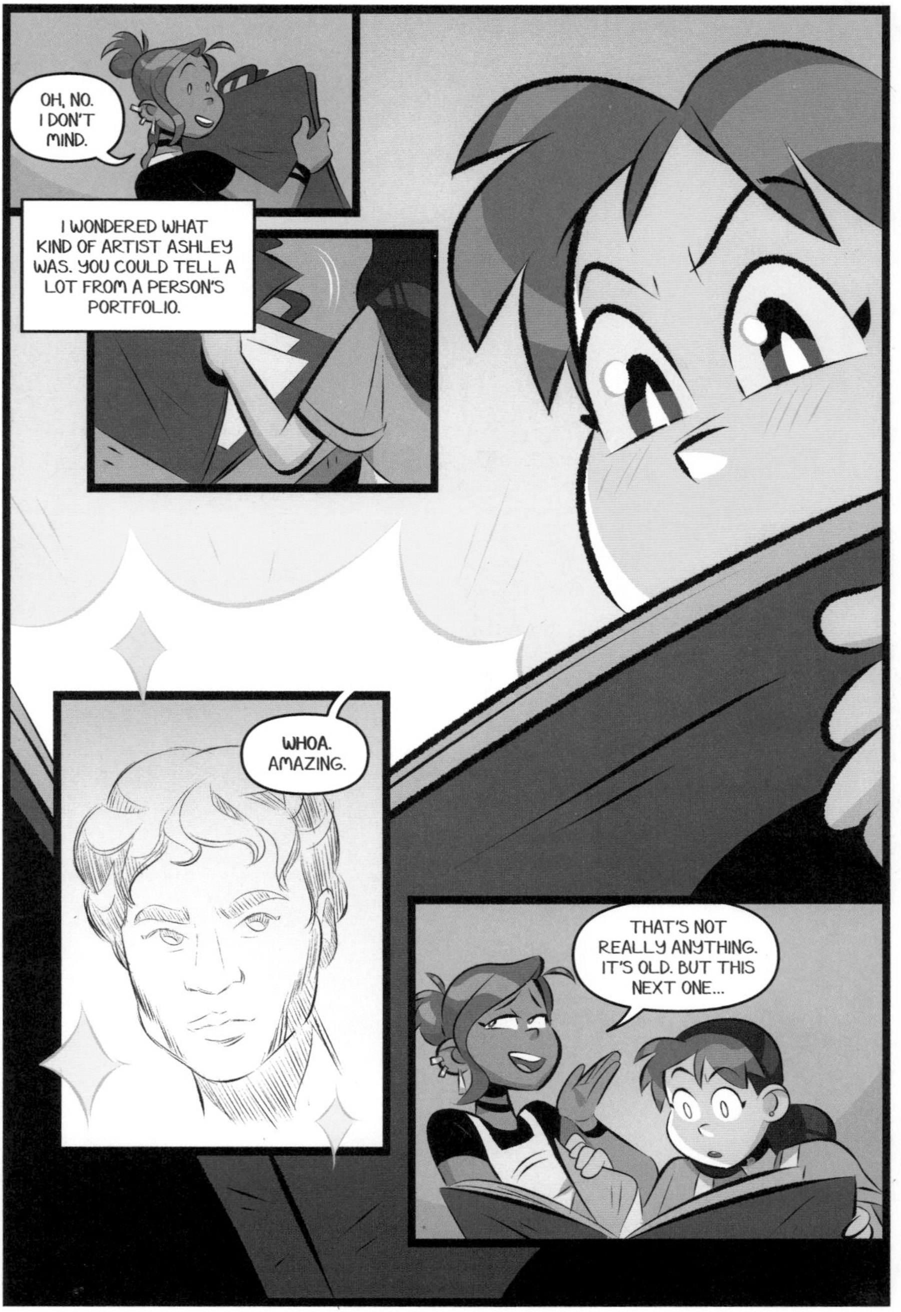
OH, NO. I DON'T MIND.
I WONDERED WHAT KIND OF ARTIST ASHLEY WAS. YOU COULD TELL A LOT FROM A PERSON'S PORTFOLIO.
WHOA. AMAZING.
THAT'S NOT REALLY ANYTHING. IT'S OLD. BUT THIS NEXT ONE...

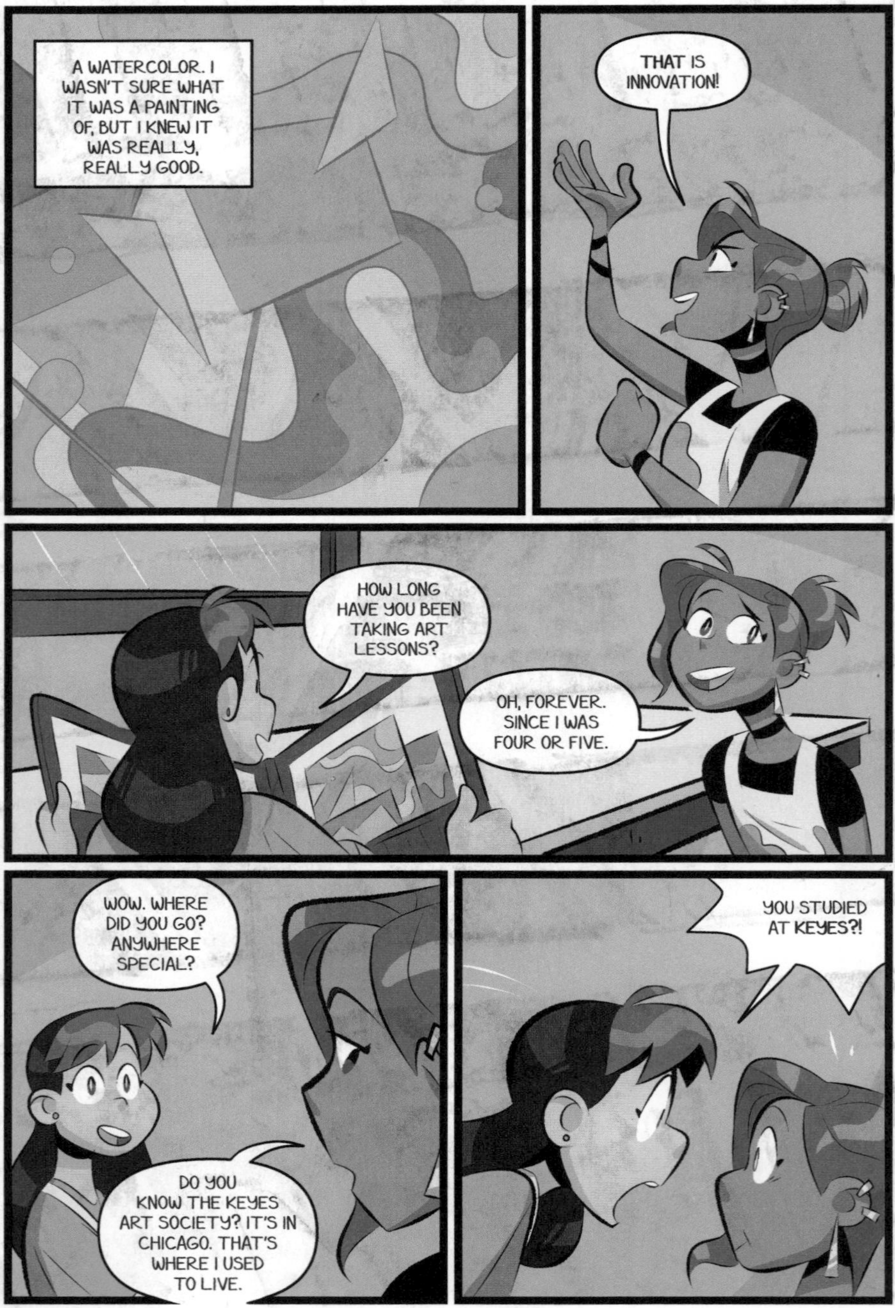
A WATERCOLOR. I WASN'T SURE WHAT IT WAS A PAINTING OF, BUT I KNEW IT WAS REALLY, REALLY GOOD.
THAT IS INNOVATION!
HOW LONG HAVE YOU BEEN TAKING ART LESSONS?
OH, FOREVER. SINCE I WAS FOUR OR FIVE.
WOW. WHERE DID YOU GO? ANYWHERE SPECIAL?
DO YOU KNOW THE KEYES ART SOCIETY? IT'S IN CHICAGO. THAT'S WHERE I USED TO LIVE.
YOU STUDIED AT KEYES?!

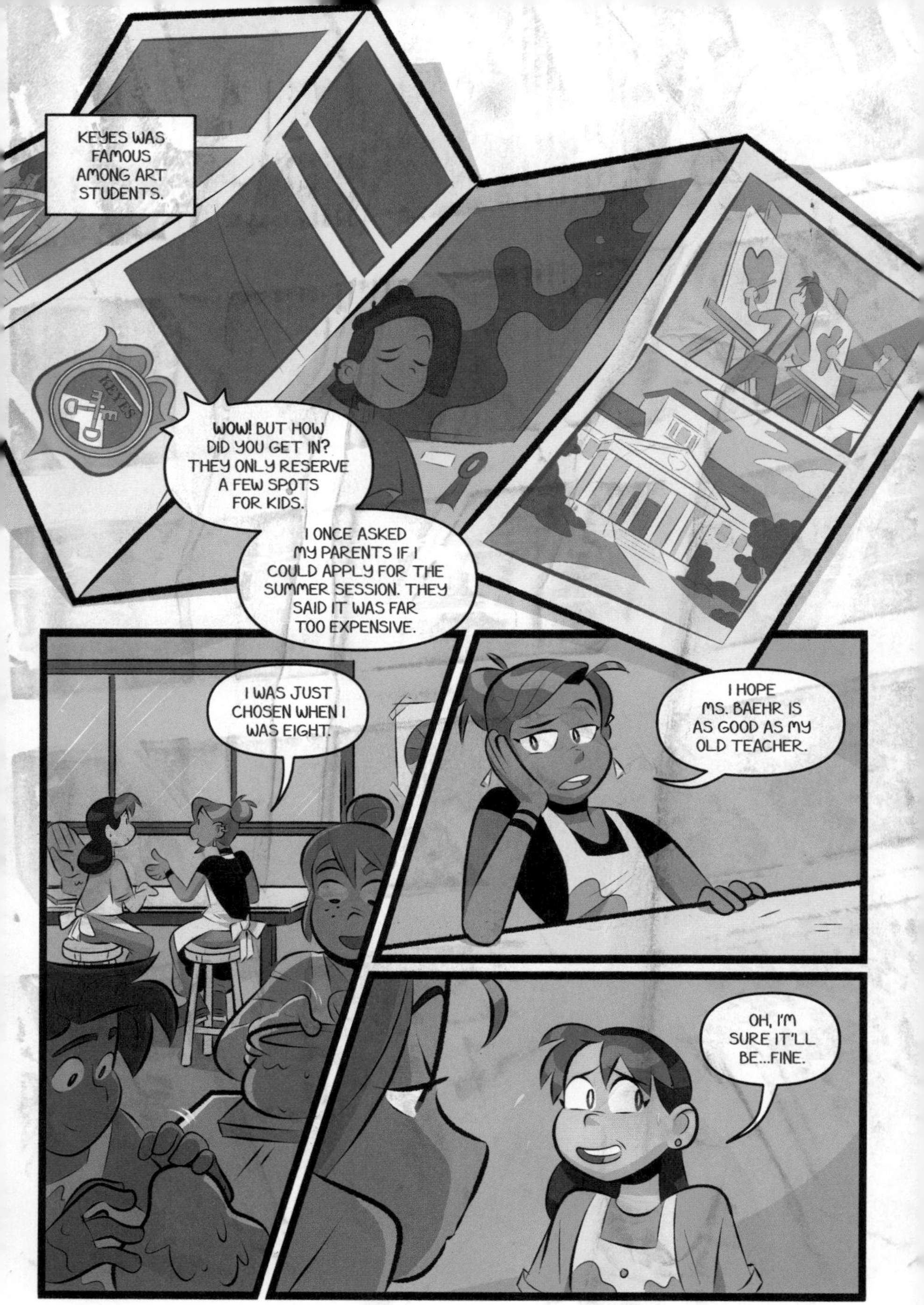
KEYES WAS FAMOUS AMONG ART STUDENTS.
KEYES
WOW! BUT HOW DID YOU GET IN? THEY ONLY RESERVE A FEW SPOTS FOR KIDS.
I ONCE ASKED MY PARENTS IF I COULD APPLY FOR THE SUMMER SESSION. THEY SAID IT WAS FAR TOO EXPENSIVE.
I WAS JUST CHOSEN WHEN I WAS EIGHT.
I HOPE MS. BAEHR IS AS GOOD AS MY OLD TEACHER.
OH, I'M SURE IT'LL BE...FINE.

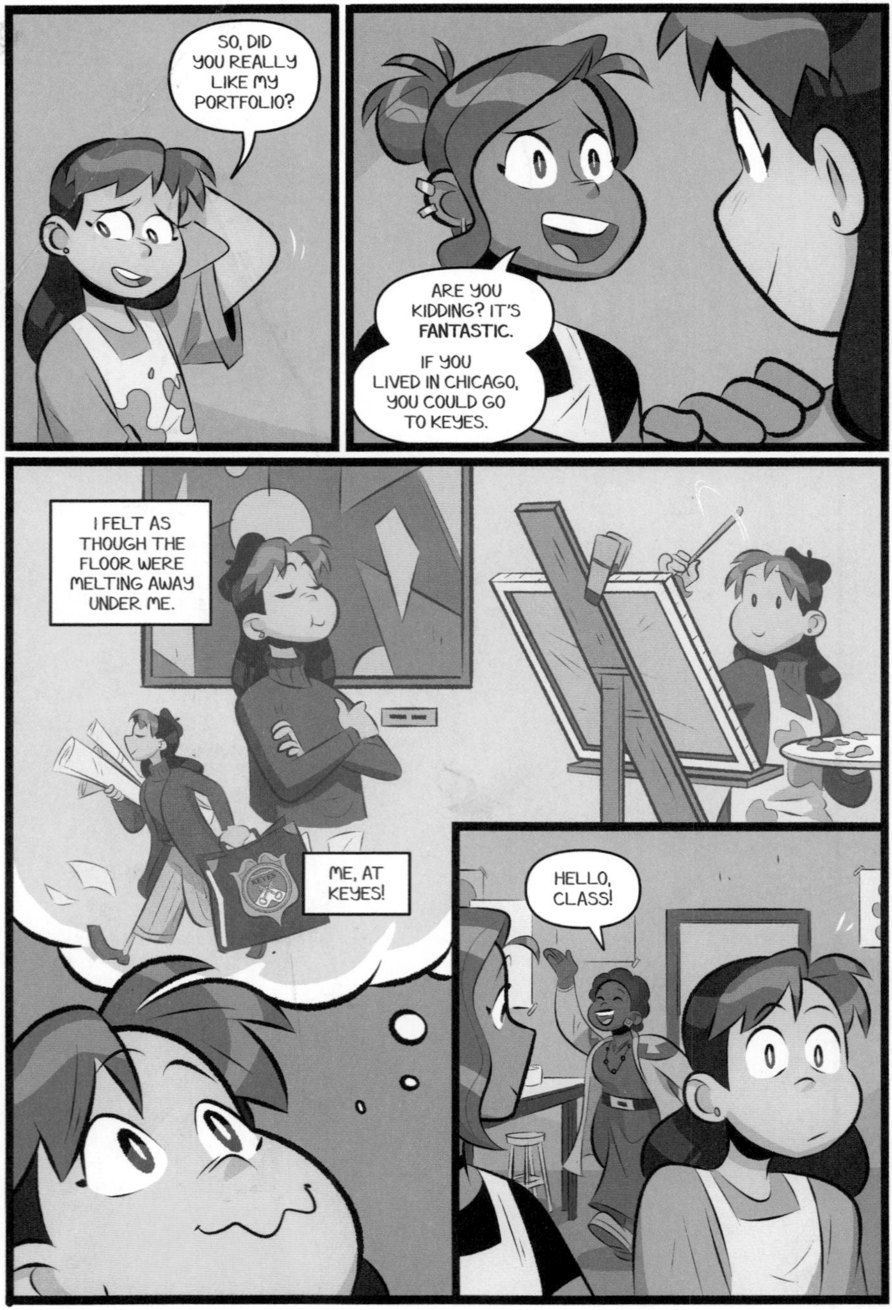
SO, DID YOU REALLY LIKE MY PORTFOLIO?
ARE YOU KIDDING? IT'S **FANTASTIC.**
IF YOU LIVED IN CHICAGO, YOU COULD GO TO KEYES.
I FELT AS THOUGH THE FLOOR WERE MELTING AWAY UNDER ME.
ME, AT KEYES!
HELLO, CLASS!

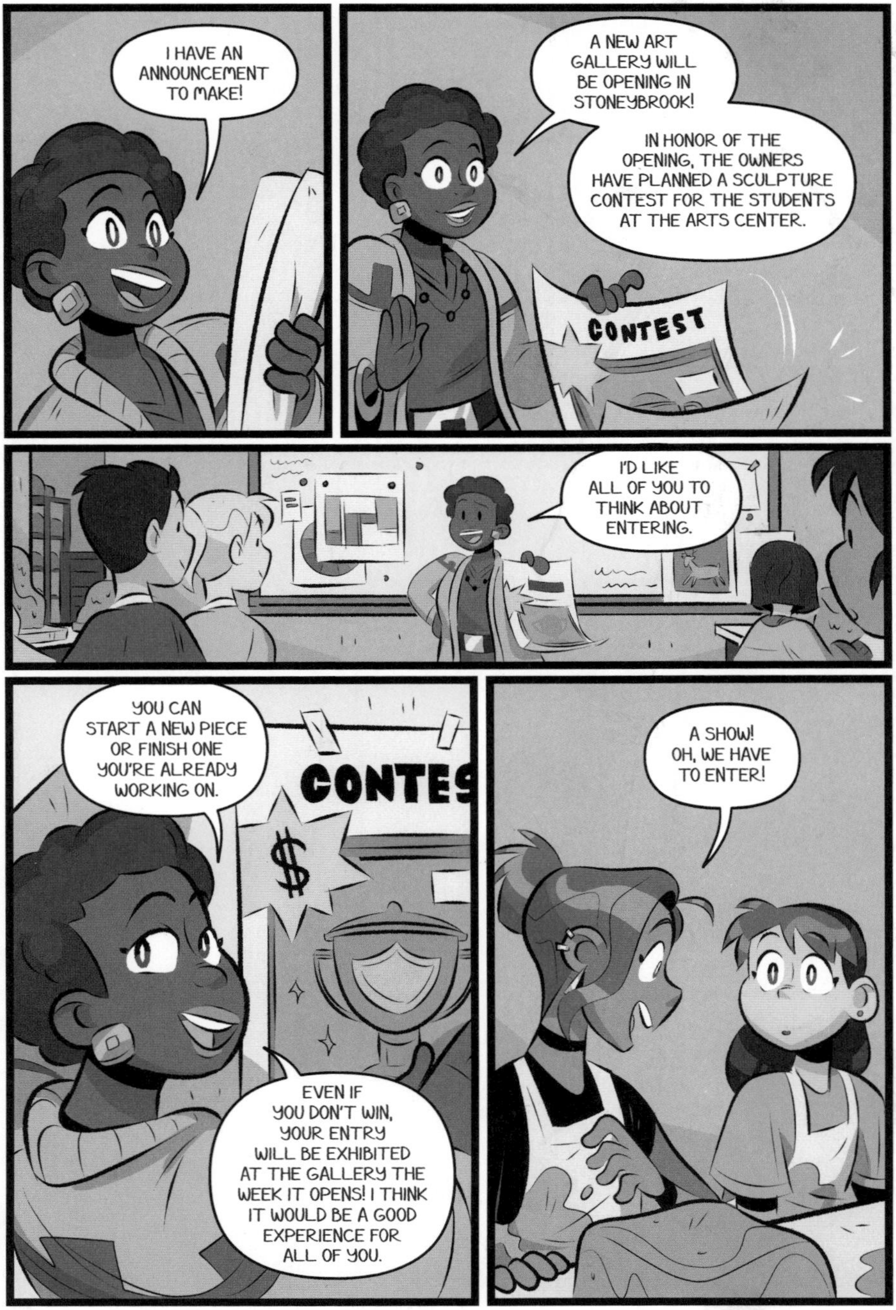
I HAVE AN ANNOUNCEMENT TO MAKE!
A NEW ART GALLERY WILL BE OPENING IN STONEYBROOK!
IN HONOR OF THE OPENING, THE OWNERS HAVE PLANNED A SCULPTURE CONTEST FOR THE STUDENTS AT THE ARTS CENTER.
CONTEST
I'D LIKE ALL OF YOU TO THINK ABOUT ENTERING.
YOU CAN START A NEW PIECE OR FINISH ONE YOU'RE ALREADY WORKING ON.
CONTES
$
EVEN IF YOU DON'T WIN, YOUR ENTRY WILL BE EXHIBITED AT THE GALLERY THE WEEK IT OPENS! I THINK IT WOULD BE A GOOD EXPERIENCE FOR ALL OF YOU.
A SHOW! OH, WE HAVE TO ENTER!

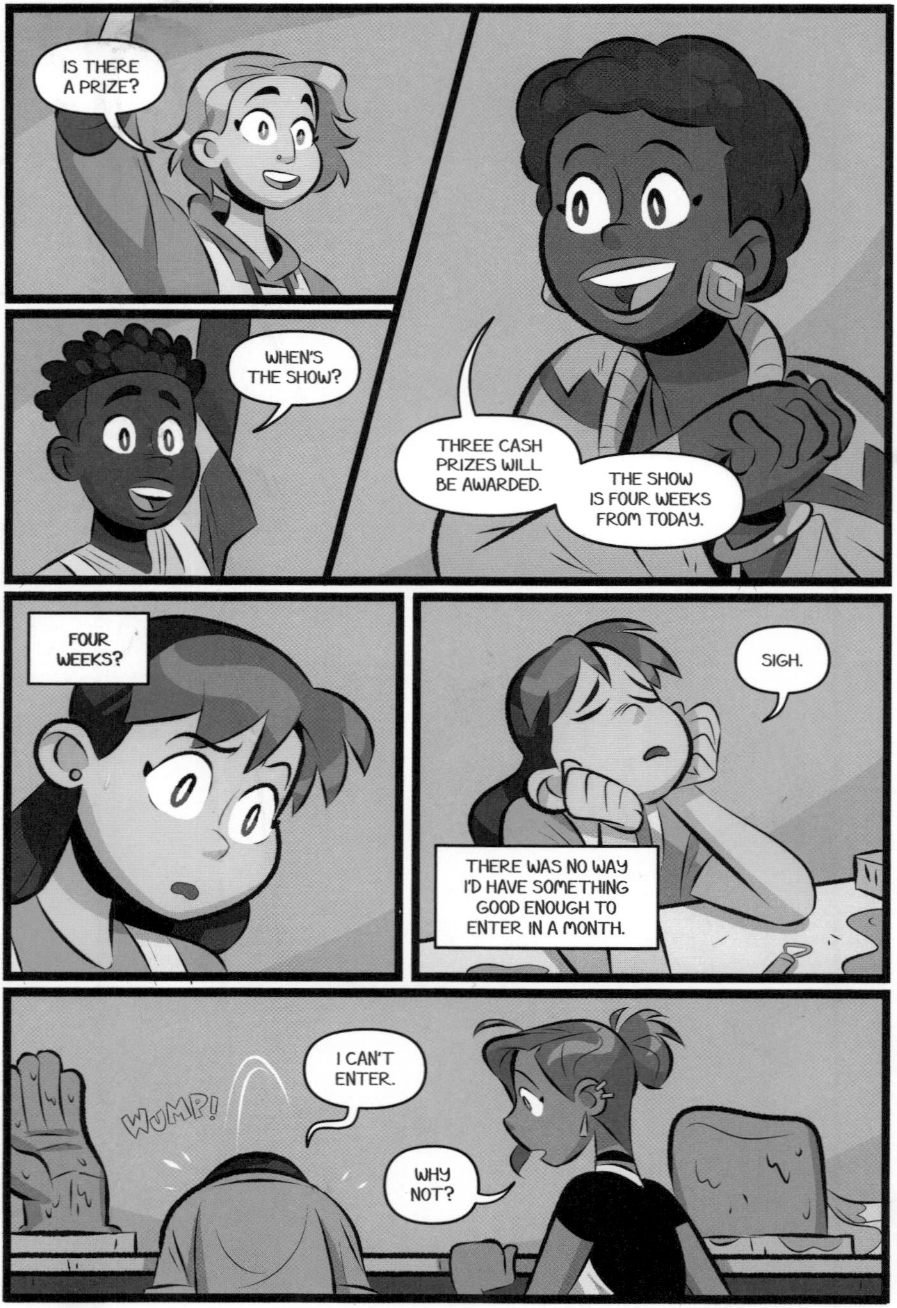

IS THERE A PRIZE?
WHEN'S THE SHOW?
THREE CASH PRIZES WILL BE AWARDED.
THE SHOW IS FOUR WEEKS FROM TODAY.
FOUR WEEKS?
SIGH.
THERE WAS NO WAY I'D HAVE SOMETHING GOOD ENOUGH TO ENTER IN A MONTH.
WUMP!
I CAN'T ENTER.
WHY NOT?

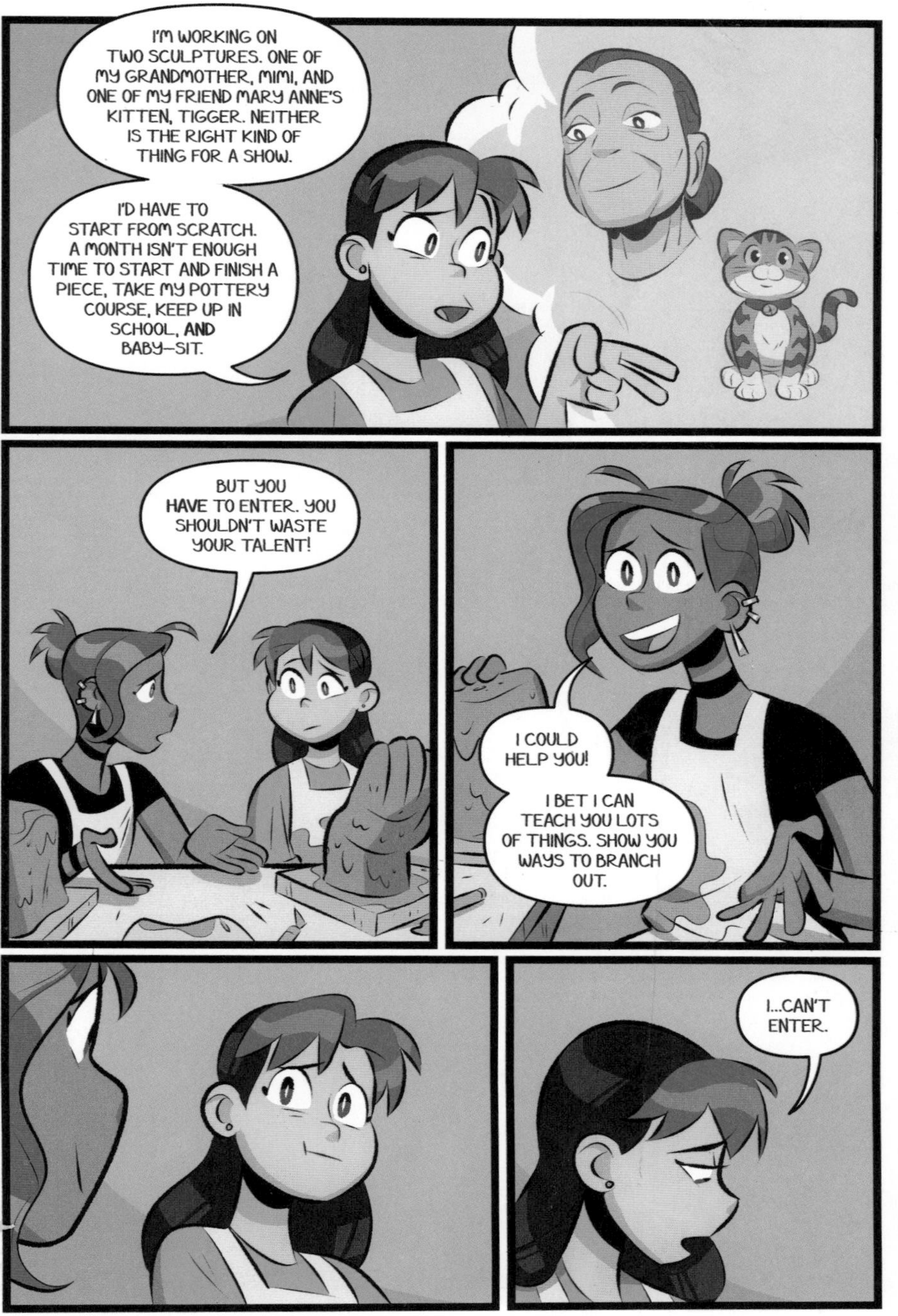
I'M WORKING ON TWO SCULPTURES. ONE OF MY GRANDMOTHER, MIMI, AND ONE OF MY FRIEND MARY ANNE'S KITTEN, TIGGER. NEITHER IS THE RIGHT KIND OF THING FOR A SHOW.
I'D HAVE TO START FROM SCRATCH. A MONTH ISN'T ENOUGH TIME TO START AND FINISH A PIECE, TAKE MY POTTERY COURSE, KEEP UP IN SCHOOL, AND BABY-SIT.
BUT YOU HAVE TO ENTER. YOU SHOULDN'T WASTE YOUR TALENT!
I COULD HELP YOU!
I BET I CAN TEACH YOU LOTS OF THINGS. SHOW YOU WAYS TO BRANCH OUT.
I...CAN'T ENTER.

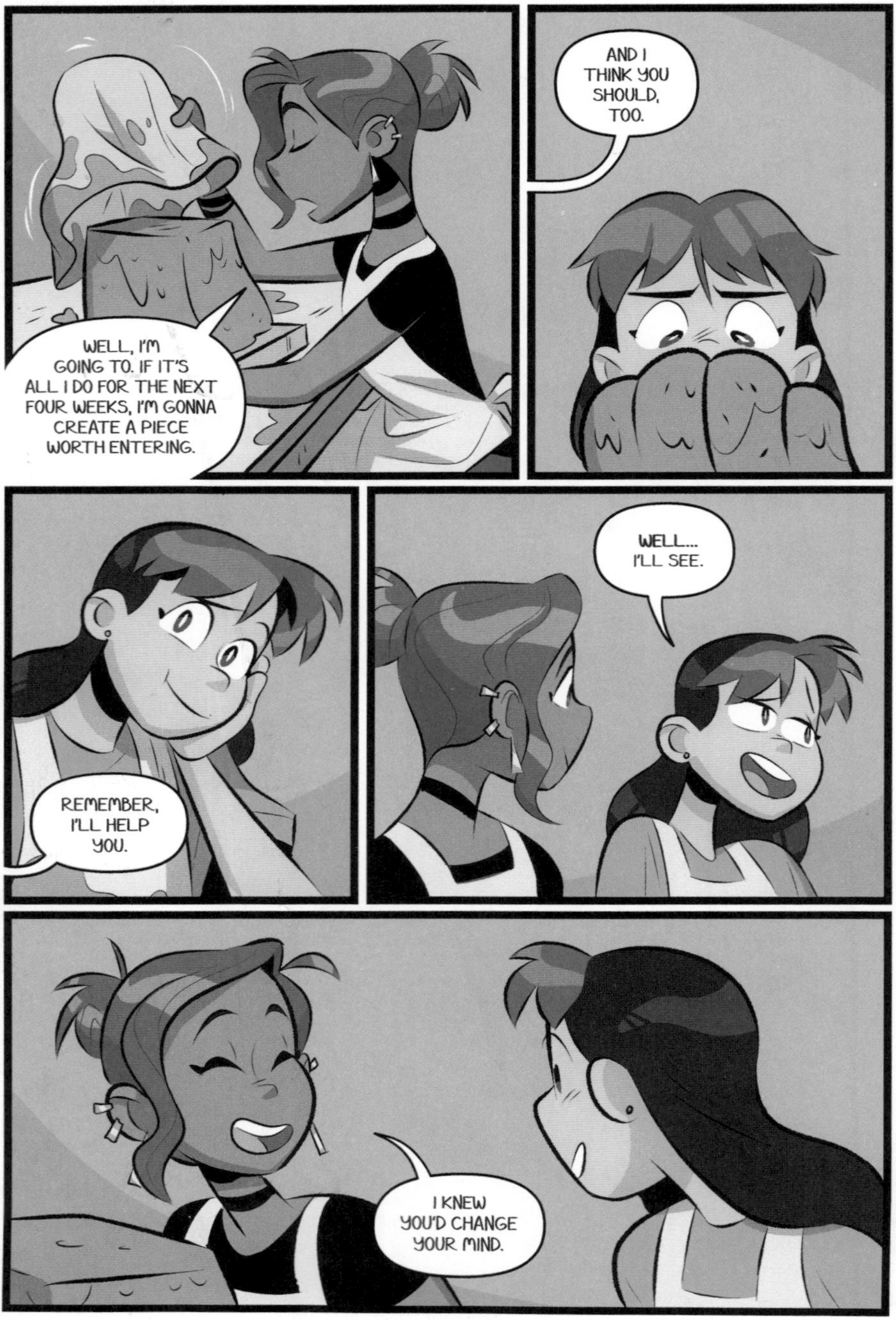
WELL, I'M GOING TO. IF IT'S ALL I DO FOR THE NEXT FOUR WEEKS, I'M GONNA CREATE A PIECE WORTH ENTERING.
AND I THINK YOU SHOULD, TOO.
REMEMBER, I'LL HELP YOU.
WELL... I'LL SEE.
I KNEW YOU'D CHANGE YOUR MIND.

CHAPTER 4

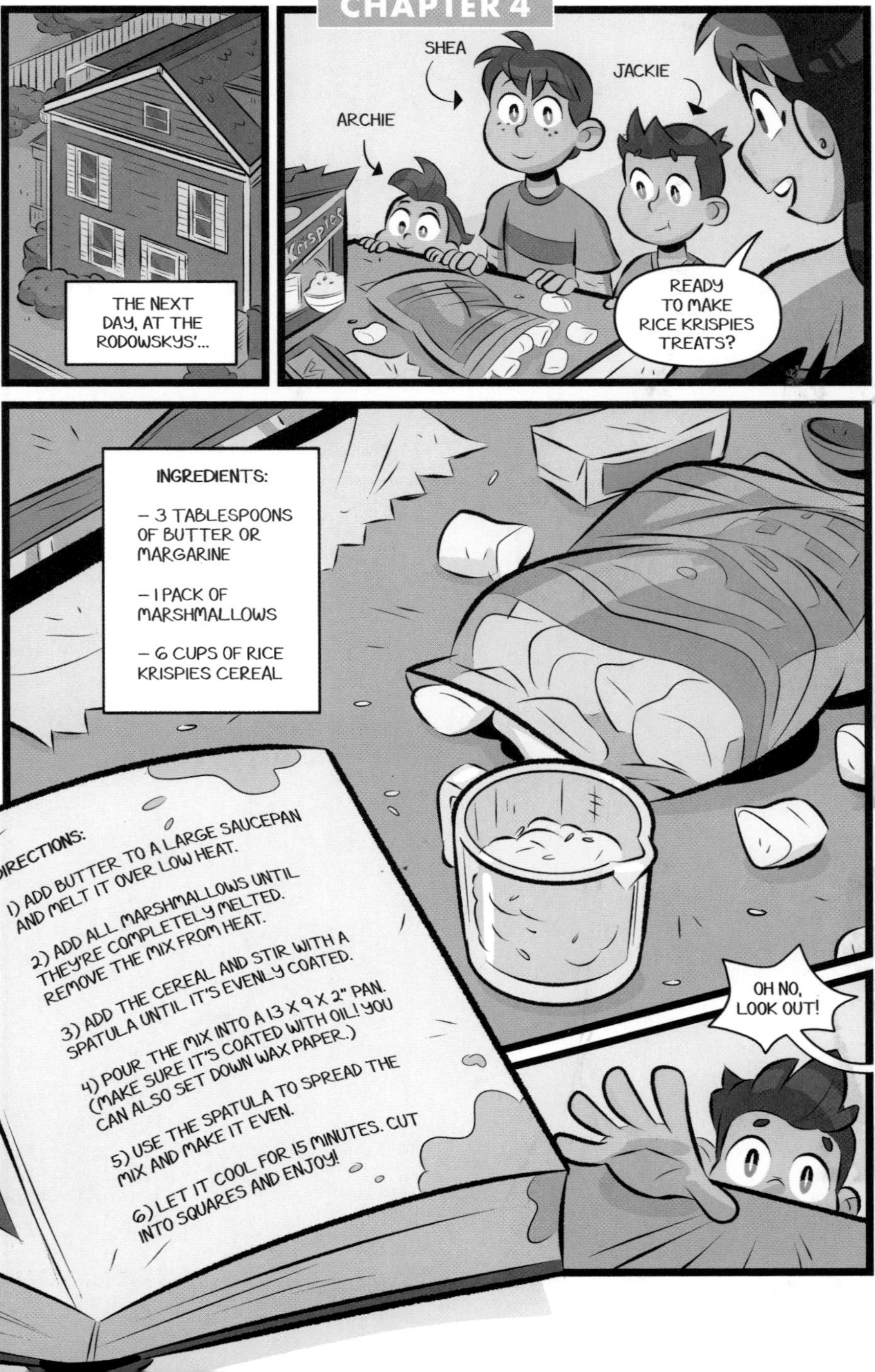
THE NEXT DAY, AT THE RODOWSKYS'...
SHEA
JACKIE
ARCHIE
READY TO MAKE RICE KRISPIES TREATS?
Krispies
INGREDIENTS:
– 3 TABLESPOONS OF BUTTER OR MARGARINE
– 1 PACK OF MARSHMALLOWS
– 6 CUPS OF RICE KRISPIES CEREAL
DIRECTIONS:
1) ADD BUTTER TO A LARGE SAUCEPAN AND MELT IT OVER LOW HEAT.
2) ADD ALL MARSHMALLOWS UNTIL THEY'RE COMPLETELY MELTED. REMOVE THE MIX FROM HEAT.
3) ADD THE CEREAL AND STIR WITH A SPATULA UNTIL IT'S EVENLY COATED.
4) POUR THE MIX INTO A 13 X 9 X 2" PAN. (MAKE SURE IT'S COATED WITH OIL! YOU CAN ALSO SET DOWN WAX PAPER.)
5) USE THE SPATULA TO SPREAD THE MIX AND MAKE IT EVEN.
6) LET IT COOL FOR 15 MINUTES. CUT INTO SQUARES AND ENJOY!
OH NO, LOOK OUT!

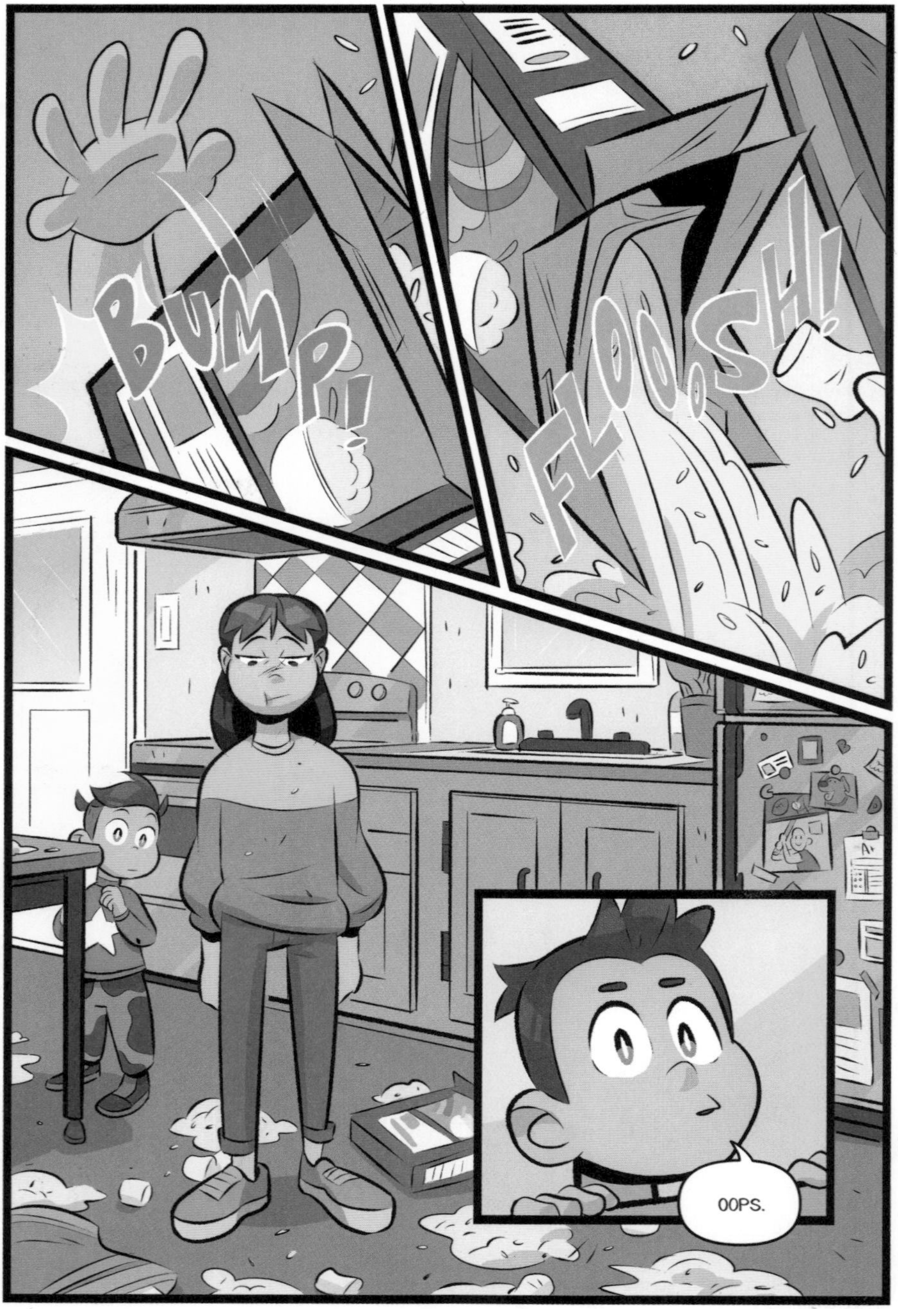
BUMP!
FLOOOSH!
OOPS.

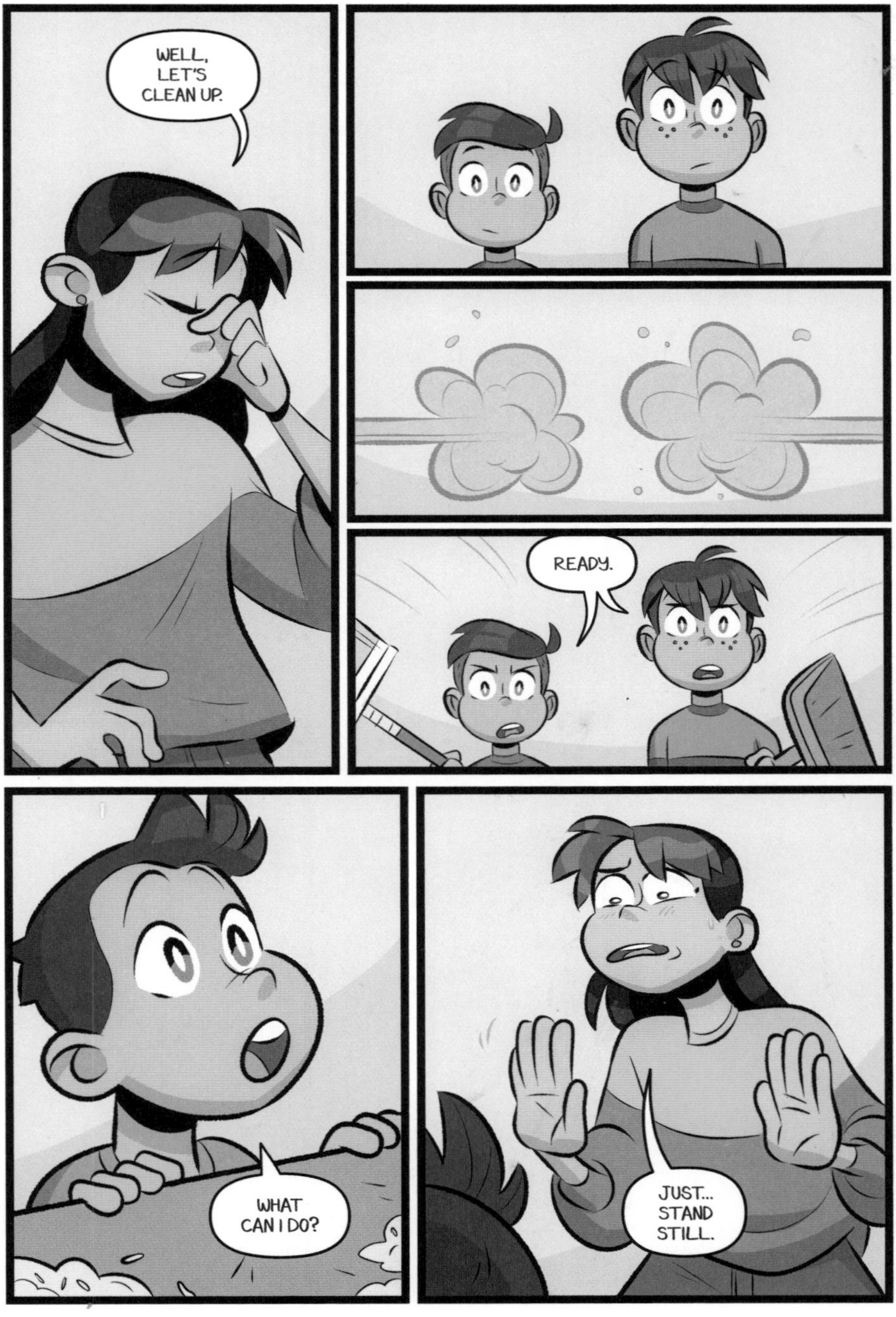
WELL, LET'S CLEAN UP.
READY.
WHAT CAN I DO?
JUST... STAND STILL.

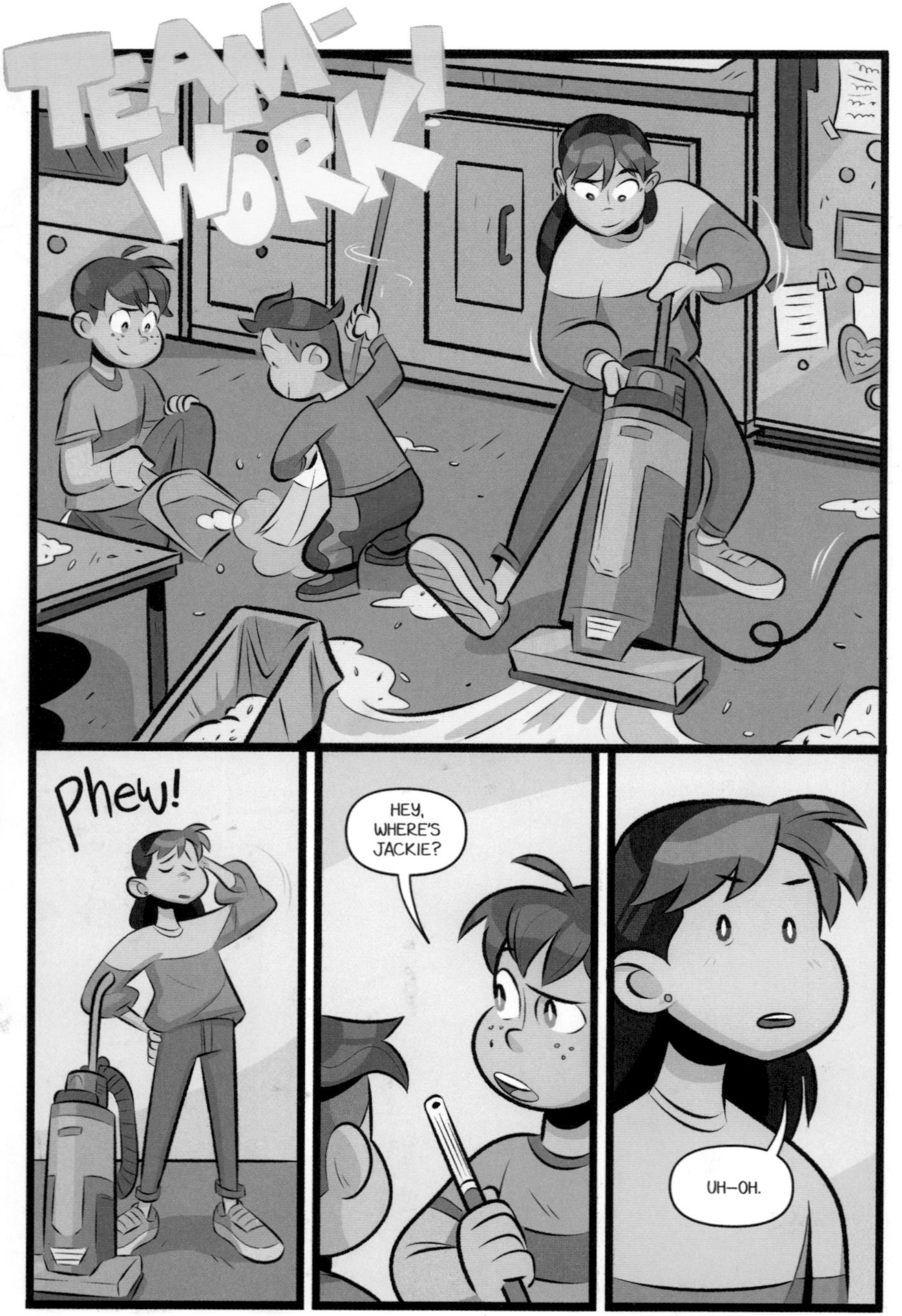
TEAM-WORK!
Phew!
HEY, WHERE'S JACKIE?
UH-OH.

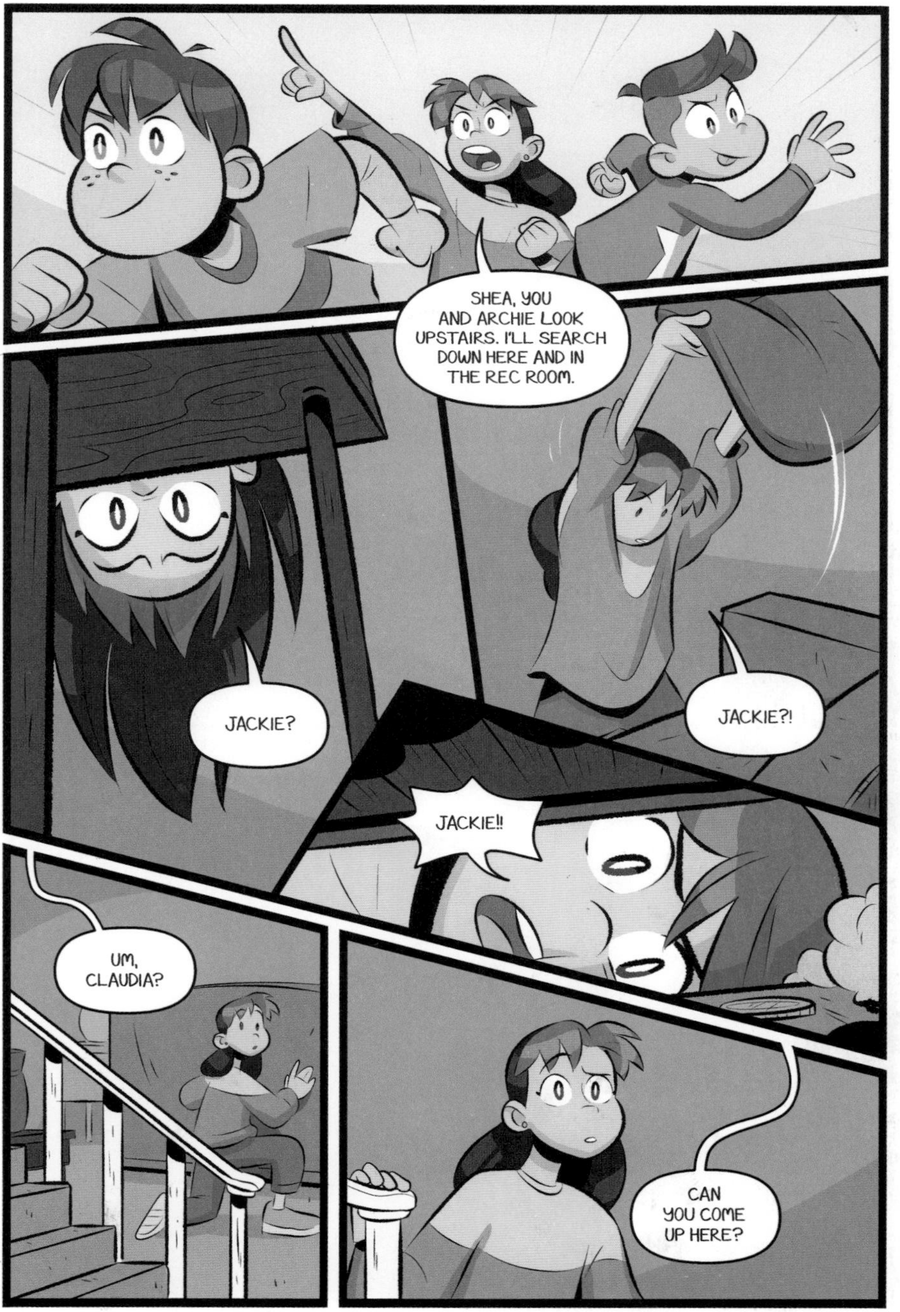
SHEA, YOU AND ARCHIE LOOK UPSTAIRS. I'LL SEARCH DOWN HERE AND IN THE REC ROOM.
JACKIE?
JACKIE?!
JACKIE!!
UM, CLAUDIA?
CAN YOU COME UP HERE?

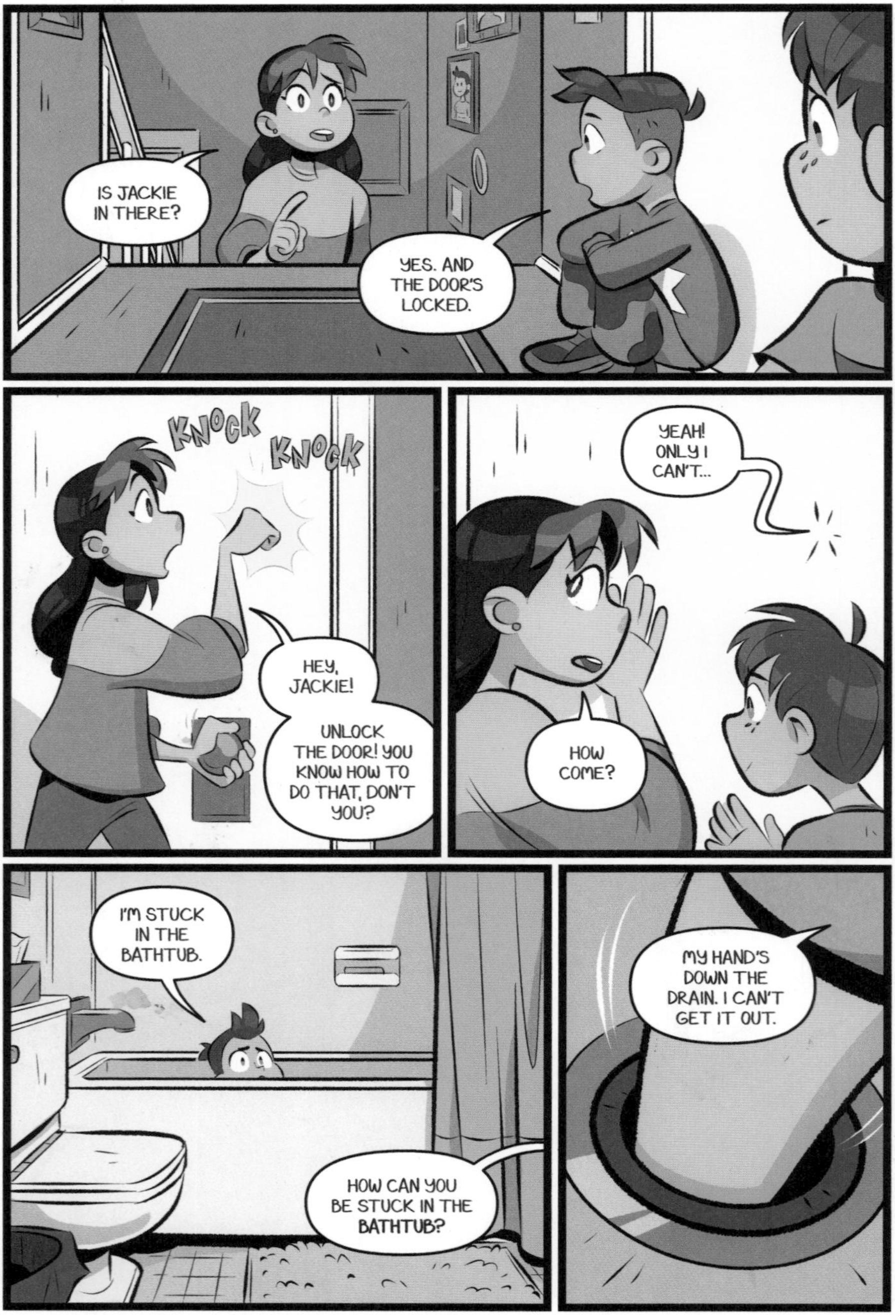
IS JACKIE IN THERE?
YES. AND THE DOOR'S LOCKED.
KNOCK KNOCK
HEY, JACKIE!
UNLOCK THE DOOR! YOU KNOW HOW TO DO THAT, DON'T YOU?
YEAH! ONLY I CAN'T...
HOW COME?
I'M STUCK IN THE BATHTUB.
HOW CAN YOU BE STUCK IN THE **BATHTUB**?
MY HAND'S DOWN THE DRAIN. I CAN'T GET IT OUT.

HE'S TRYING TO GET HIS BLASTO-PLANE. IT GURGLED DOWN THE DRAIN LAST NIGHT.

OH, FOR HEAVEN'S SAKE.

ALL RIGHT. SHEA, WHERE'S THE KEY TO THE BATHROOM?

GENERALLY, WE BABY-SITTERS ASKED PARENTS A LOT OF QUESTIONS, SUCH AS WHERE THE FIRST-AID KIT WAS, OR IF THE CHILDREN HAD ALLERGIES.

I'D NEVER BOTHERED TO ASK ABOUT THE KEY TO THE BATHROOM.

YOU DON'T KNOW?!

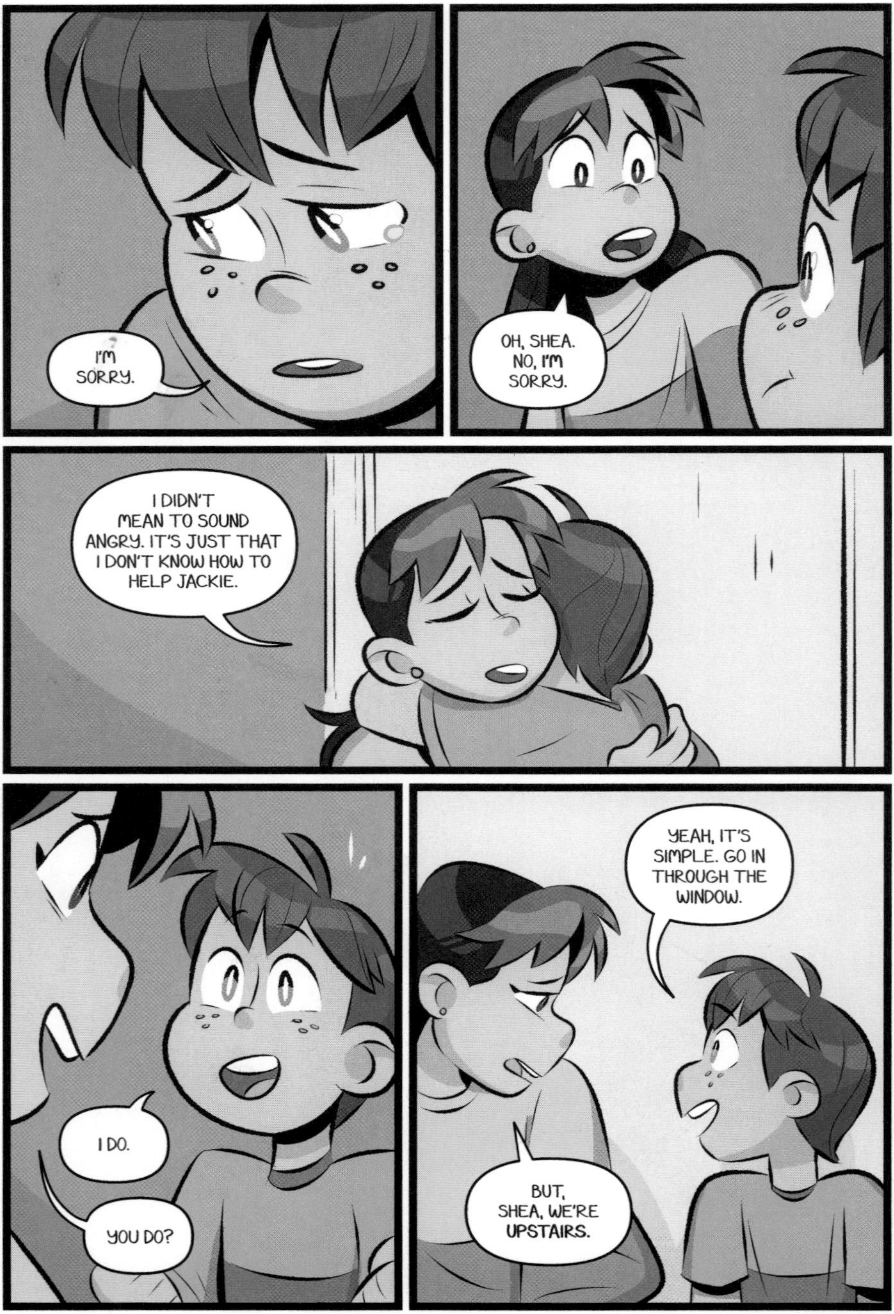
I'M SORRY.
OH, SHEA. NO, I'M SORRY.
I DIDN'T MEAN TO SOUND ANGRY. IT'S JUST THAT I DON'T KNOW HOW TO HELP JACKIE.
I DO.
YOU DO?
YEAH, IT'S SIMPLE. GO IN THROUGH THE WINDOW.
BUT, SHEA, WE'RE **UPSTAIRS.**

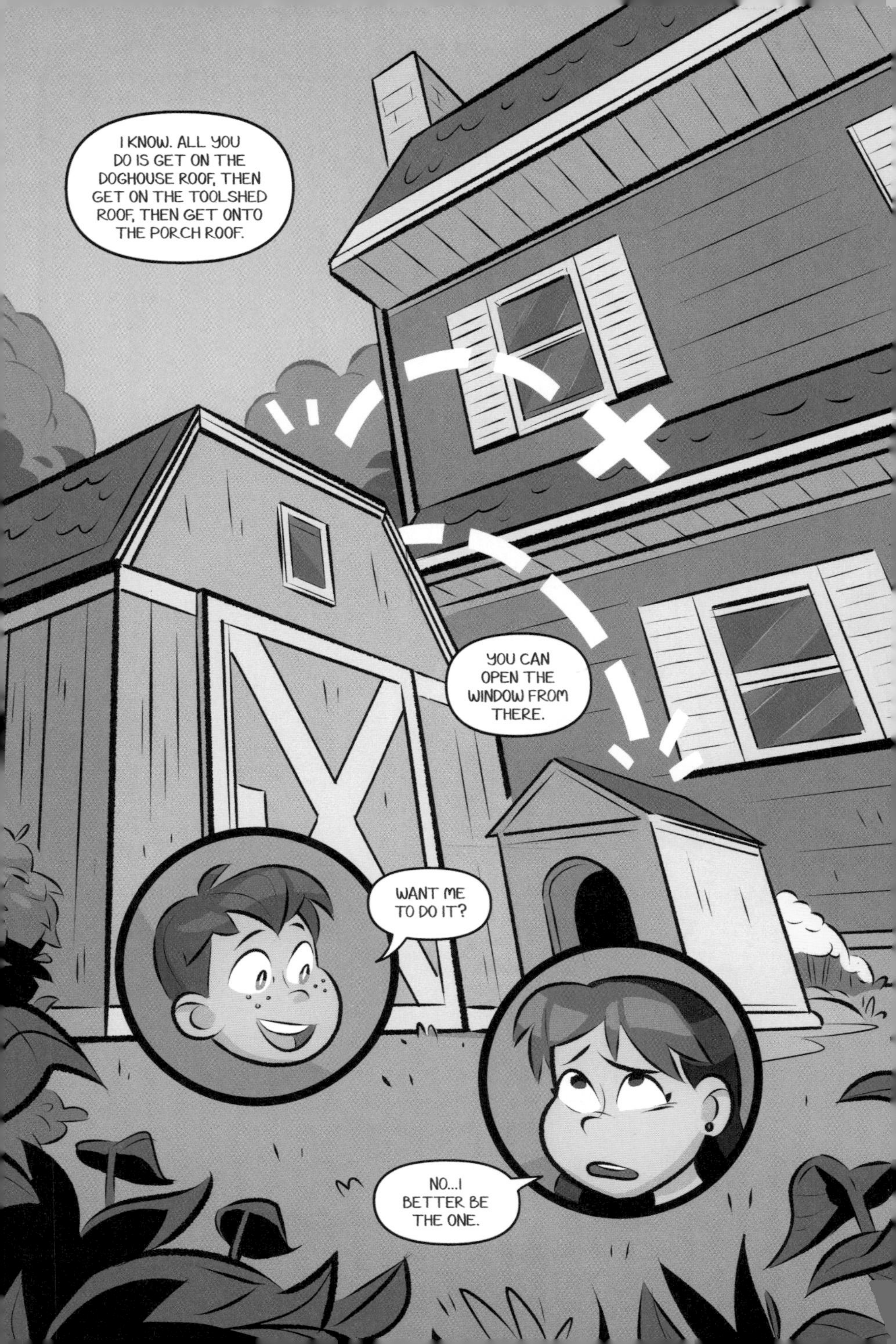
I KNOW. ALL YOU DO IS GET ON THE DOGHOUSE ROOF, THEN GET ON THE TOOLSHED ROOF, THEN GET ONTO THE PORCH ROOF.
YOU CAN OPEN THE WINDOW FROM THERE.
WANT ME TO DO IT?
NO...I BETTER BE THE ONE.

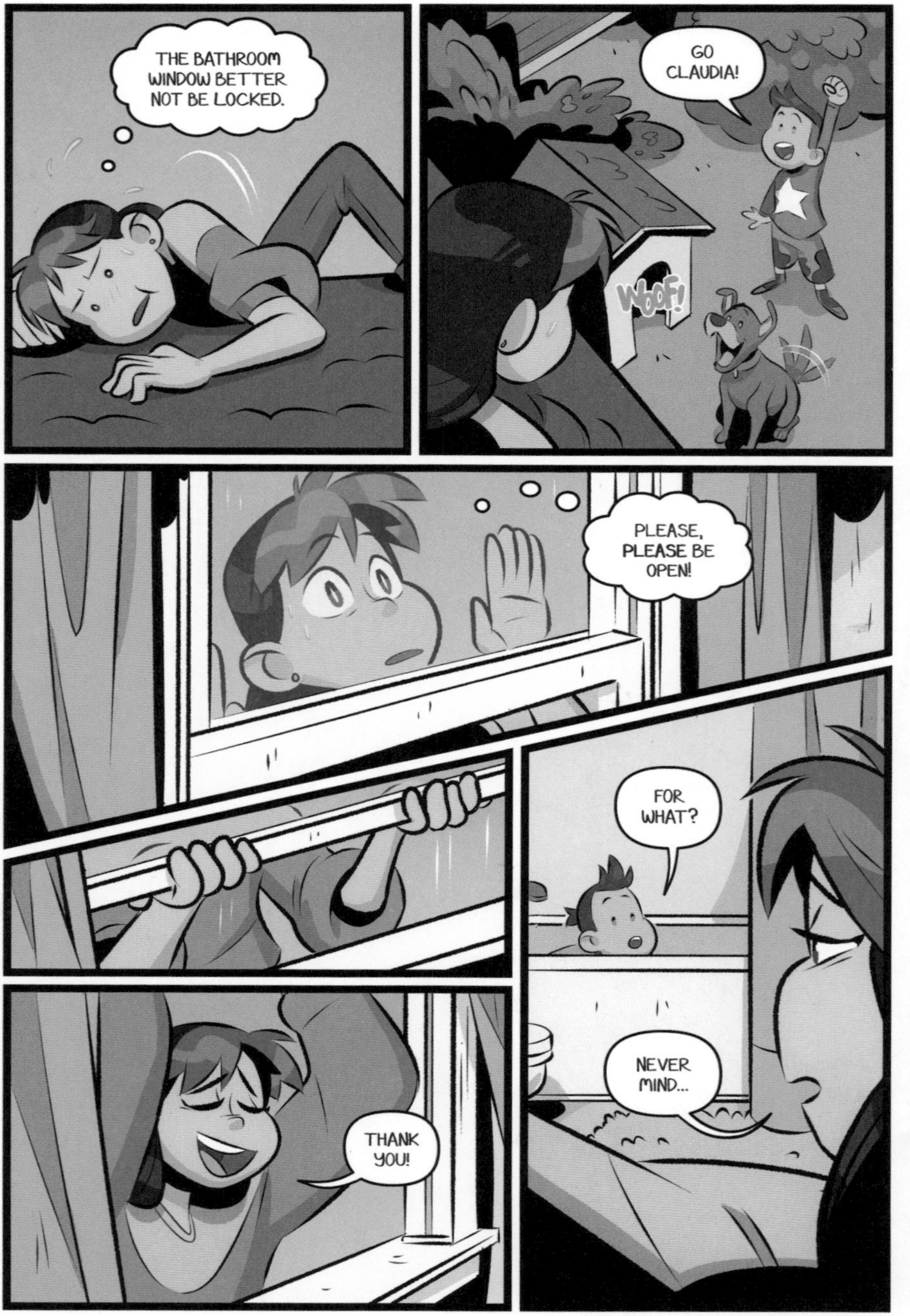
THE BATHROOM WINDOW BETTER NOT BE LOCKED.
GO CLAUDIA!
WOOF!
PLEASE, PLEASE BE OPEN!
FOR WHAT?
THANK YOU!
NEVER MIND...

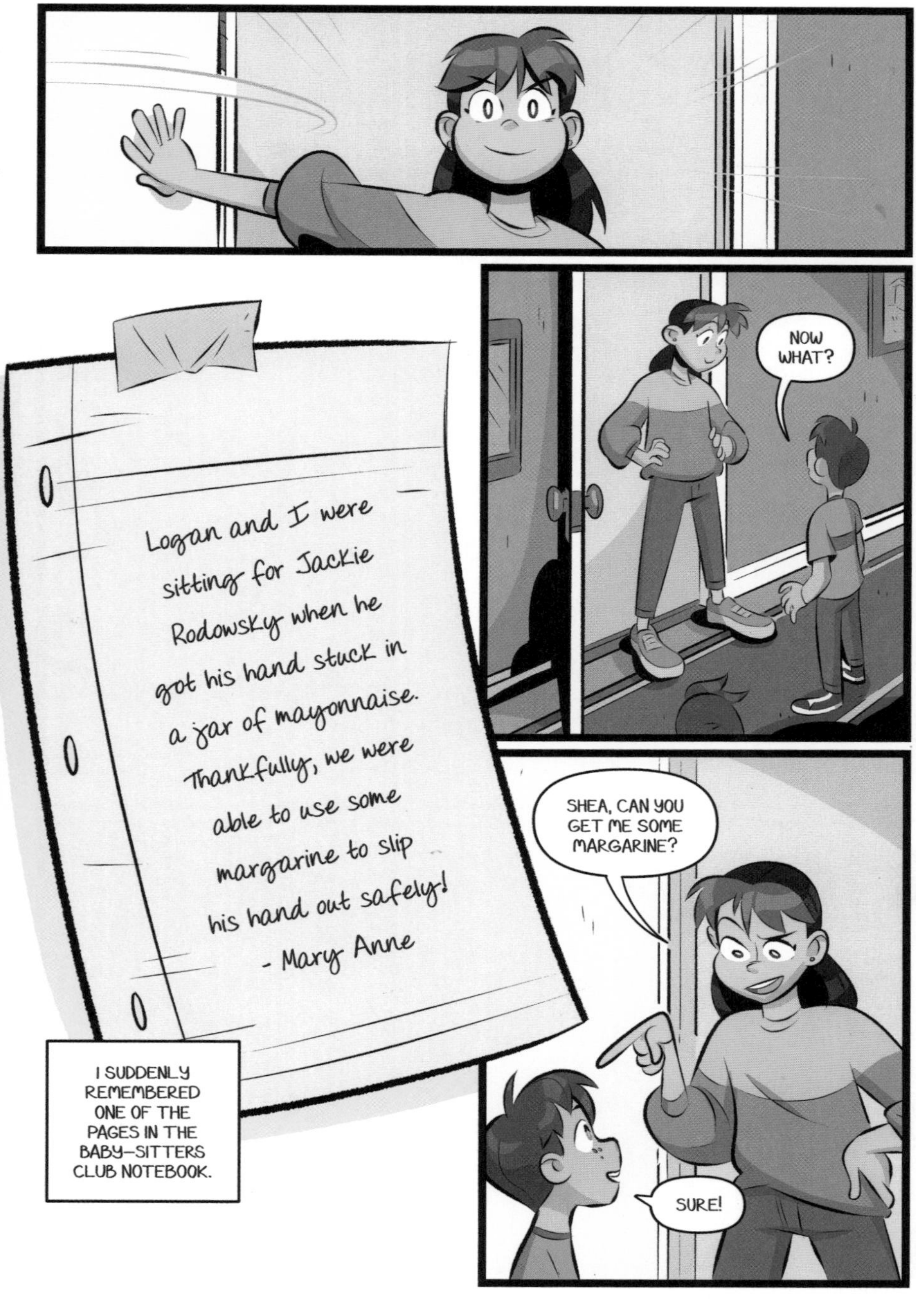
NOW WHAT?
Logan and I were sitting for Jackie Rodowsky when he got his hand stuck in a jar of mayonnaise. Thankfully, we were able to use some margarine to slip his hand out safely! - Mary Anne
SHEA, CAN YOU GET ME SOME MARGARINE?
I SUDDENLY REMEMBERED ONE OF THE PAGES IN THE BABY-SITTERS CLUB NOTEBOOK.
SURE!

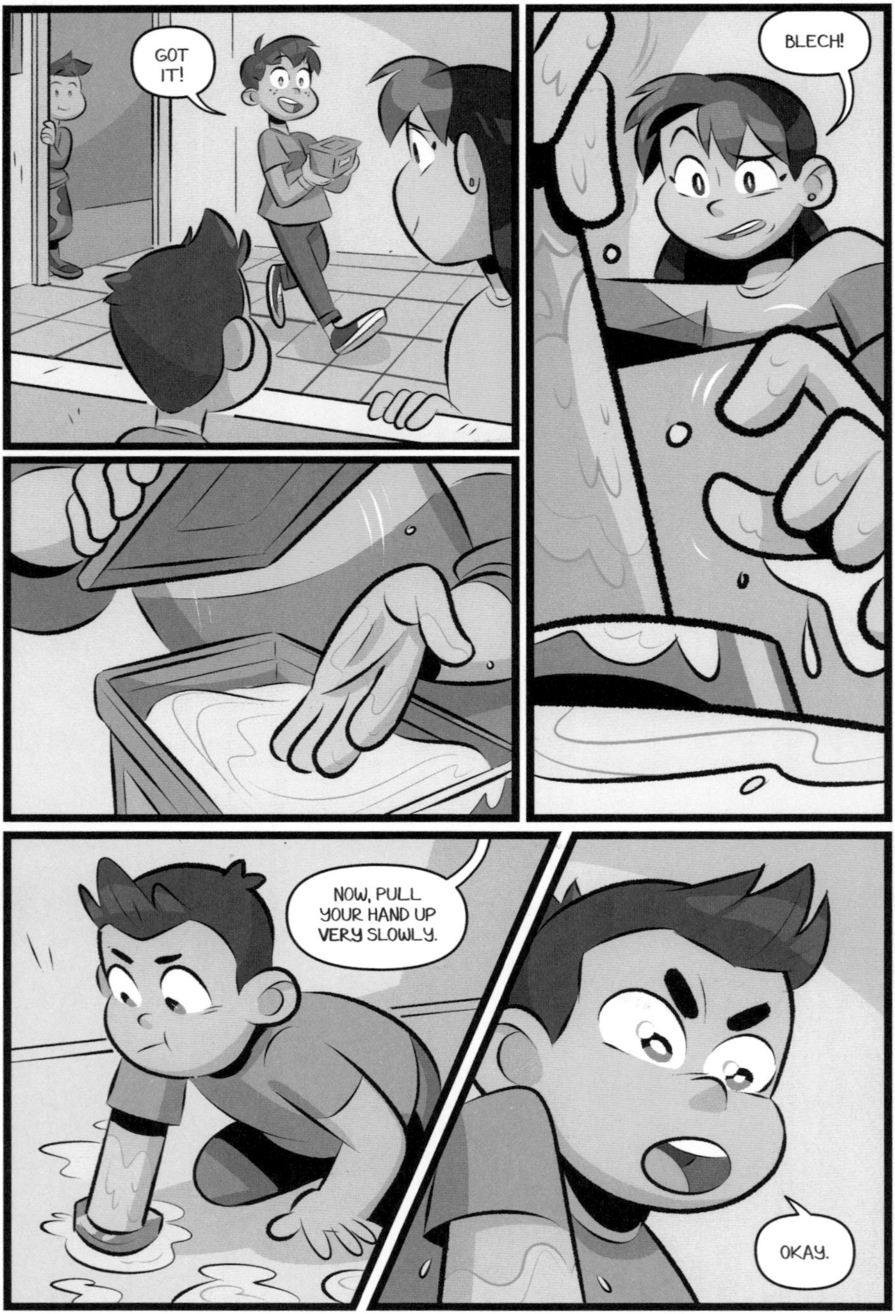
GOT IT!
BLECH!
NOW, PULL YOUR HAND UP VERY SLOWLY.
OKAY.

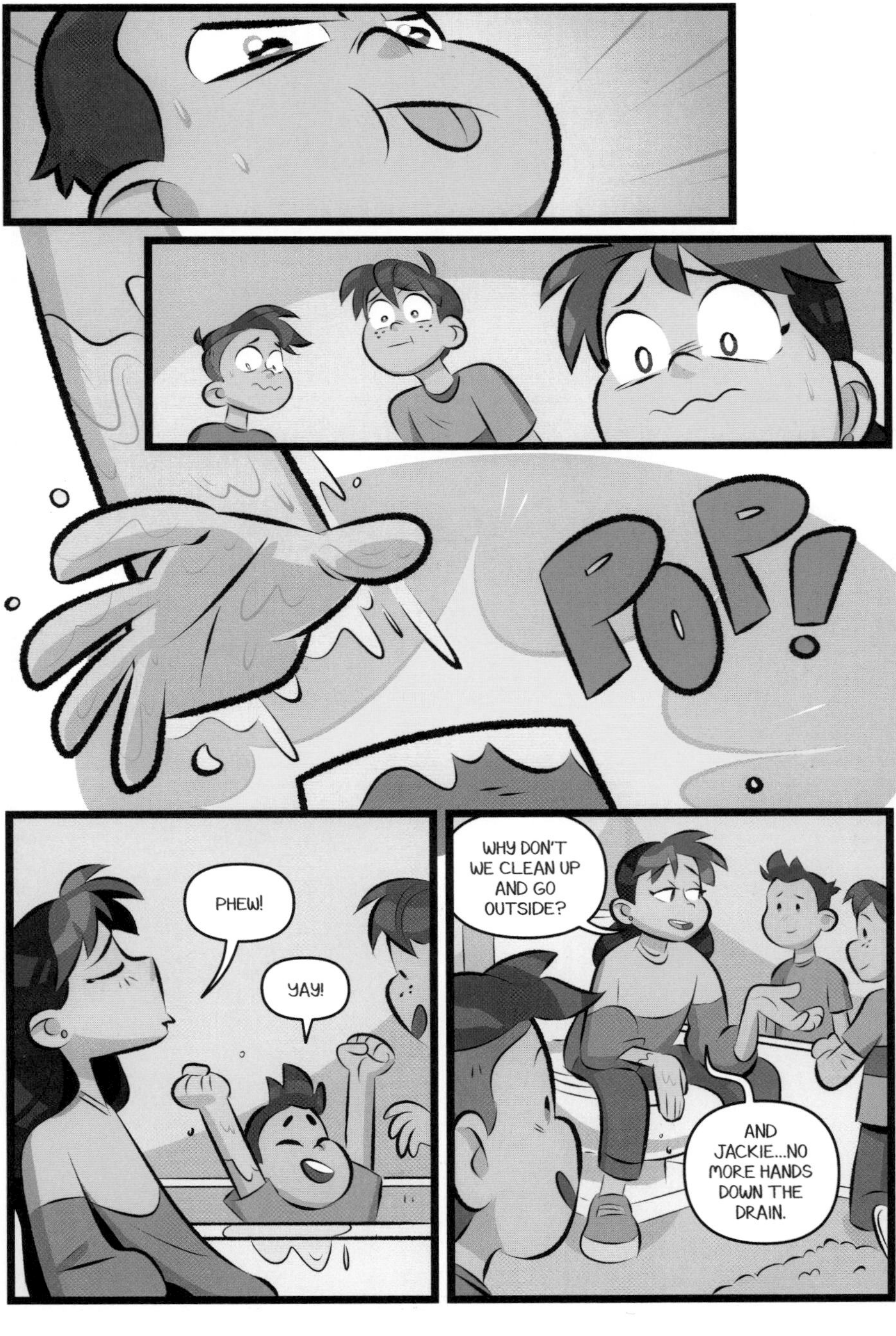
POP!
PHEW!
YAY!
WHY DON'T WE CLEAN UP AND GO OUTSIDE?
AND JACKIE...NO MORE HANDS DOWN THE DRAIN.

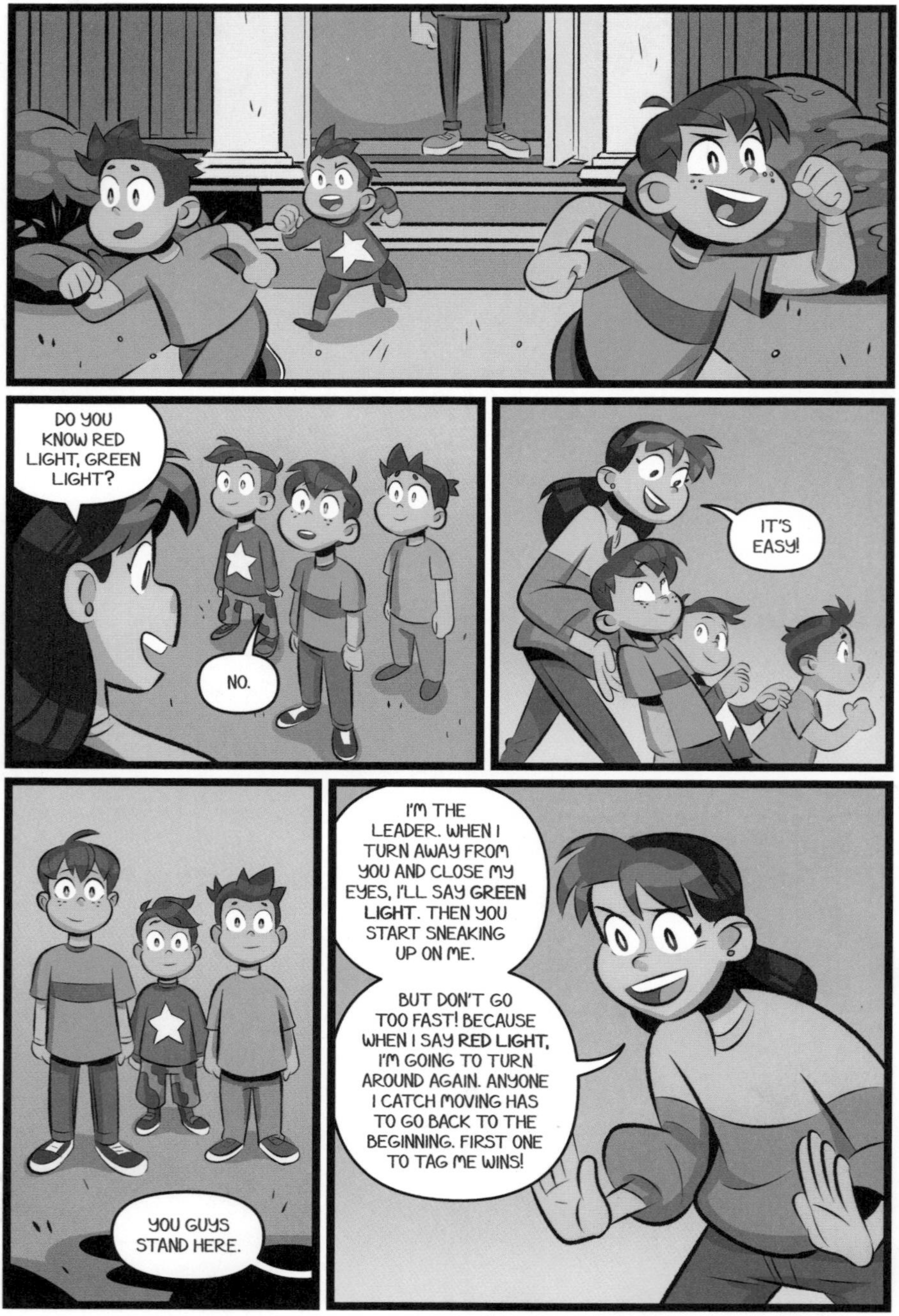
DO YOU KNOW RED LIGHT, GREEN LIGHT?
NO.
IT'S EASY!
YOU GUYS STAND HERE.
I'M THE LEADER. WHEN I TURN AWAY FROM YOU AND CLOSE MY EYES, I'LL SAY **GREEN LIGHT**. THEN YOU START SNEAKING UP ON ME.
BUT DON'T GO TOO FAST! BECAUSE WHEN I SAY **RED LIGHT**, I'M GOING TO TURN AROUND AGAIN. ANYONE I CATCH MOVING HAS TO GO BACK TO THE BEGINNING. FIRST ONE TO TAG ME WINS!

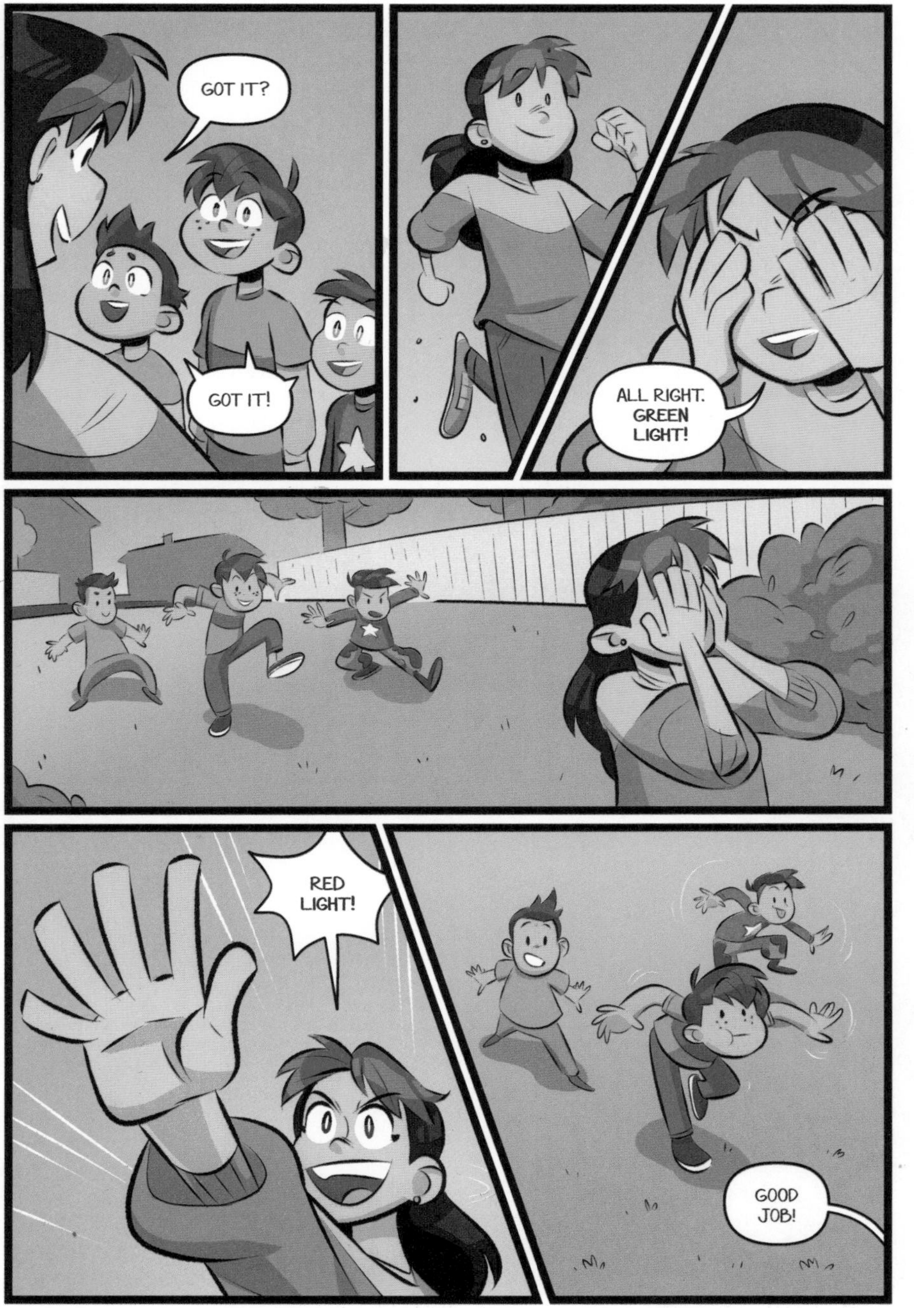
GOT IT?
GOT IT!
ALL RIGHT. GREEN LIGHT!
RED LIGHT!
GOOD JOB!

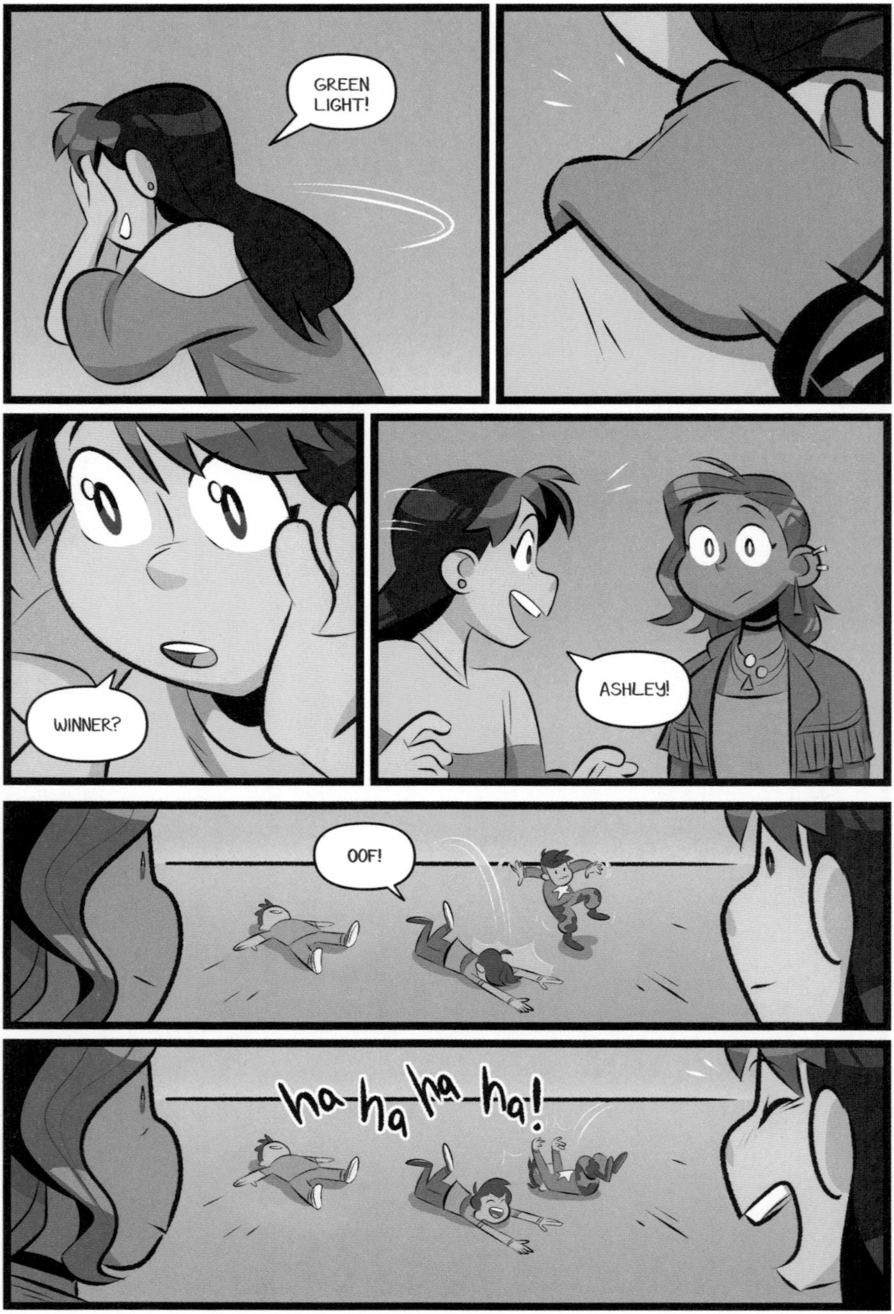
GREEN LIGHT!
WINNER?
ASHLEY!
OOF!
ha ha ha ha!

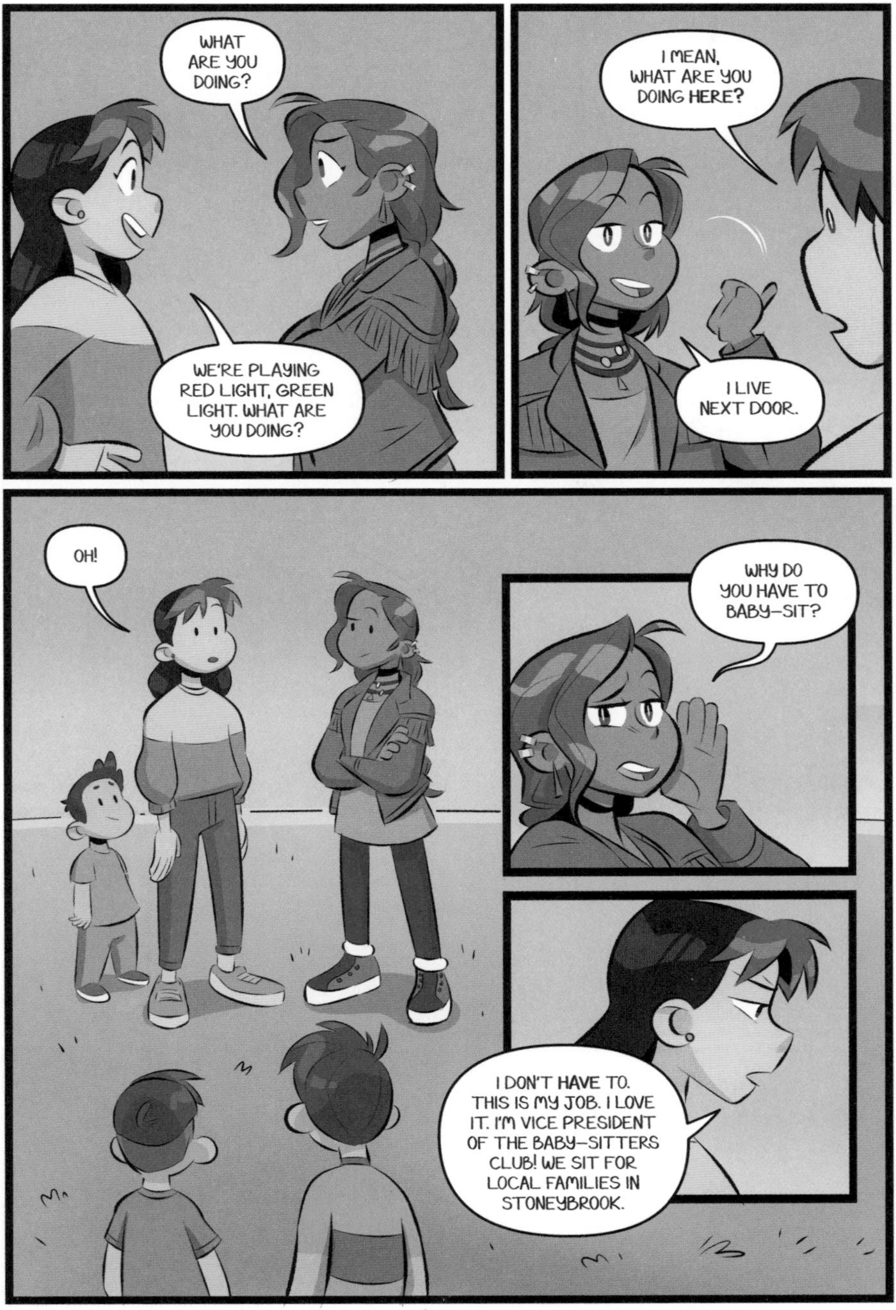
WHAT ARE YOU DOING?
WE'RE PLAYING RED LIGHT, GREEN LIGHT. WHAT ARE YOU DOING?
I MEAN, WHAT ARE YOU DOING HERE?
I LIVE NEXT DOOR.
OH!
WHY DO YOU HAVE TO BABY-SIT?
I DON'T **HAVE** TO. THIS IS MY JOB. I LOVE IT. I'M VICE PRESIDENT OF THE BABY-SITTERS CLUB! WE SIT FOR LOCAL FAMILIES IN STONEYBROOK.

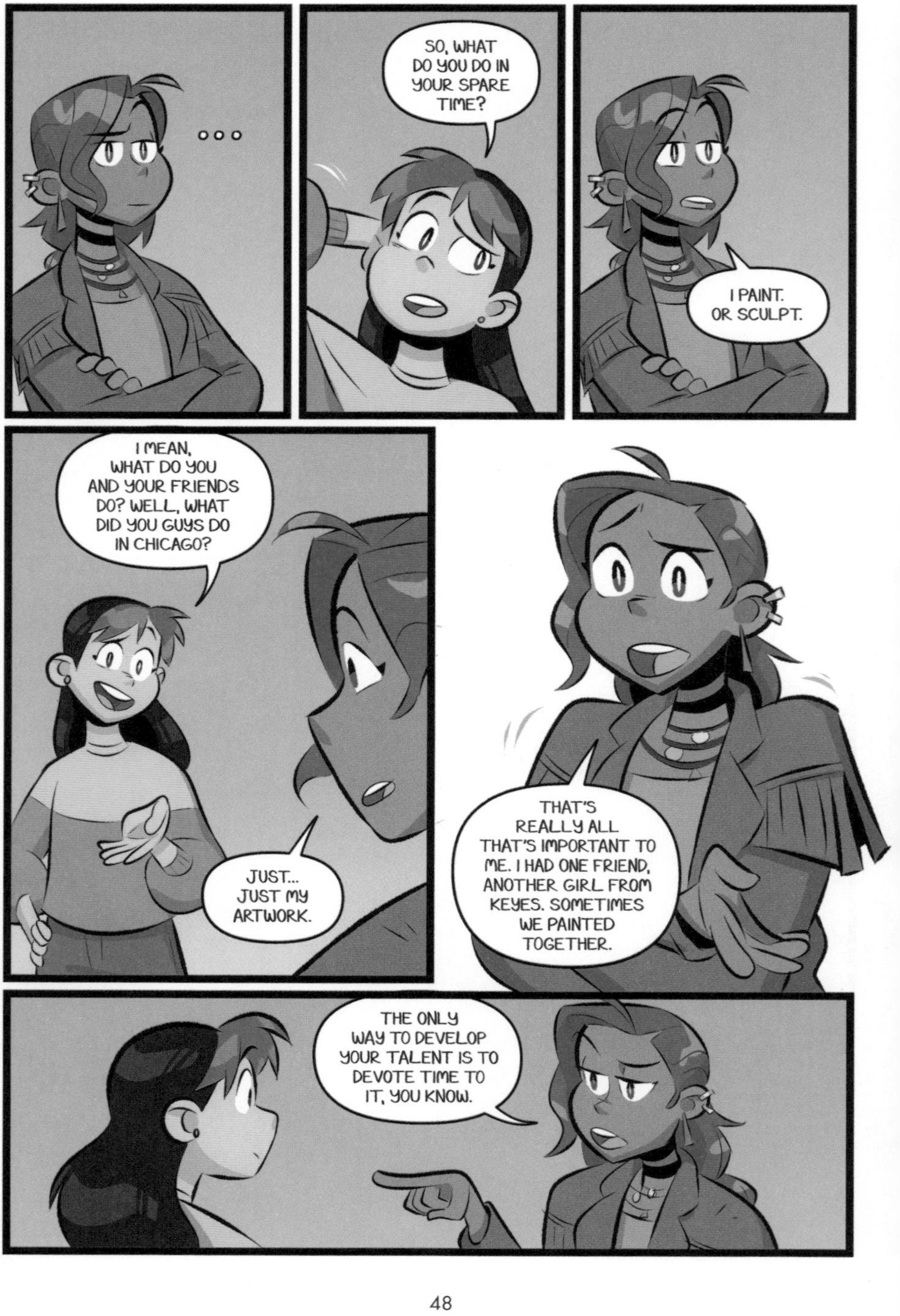
...
SO, WHAT DO YOU DO IN YOUR SPARE TIME?
I PAINT. OR SCULPT.
I MEAN, WHAT DO YOU AND YOUR FRIENDS DO? WELL, WHAT DID YOU GUYS DO IN CHICAGO?
JUST... JUST MY ARTWORK.
THAT'S REALLY ALL THAT'S IMPORTANT TO ME. I HAD ONE FRIEND, ANOTHER GIRL FROM KEYES. SOMETIMES WE PAINTED TOGETHER.
THE ONLY WAY TO DEVELOP YOUR TALENT IS TO DEVOTE TIME TO IT, YOU KNOW.

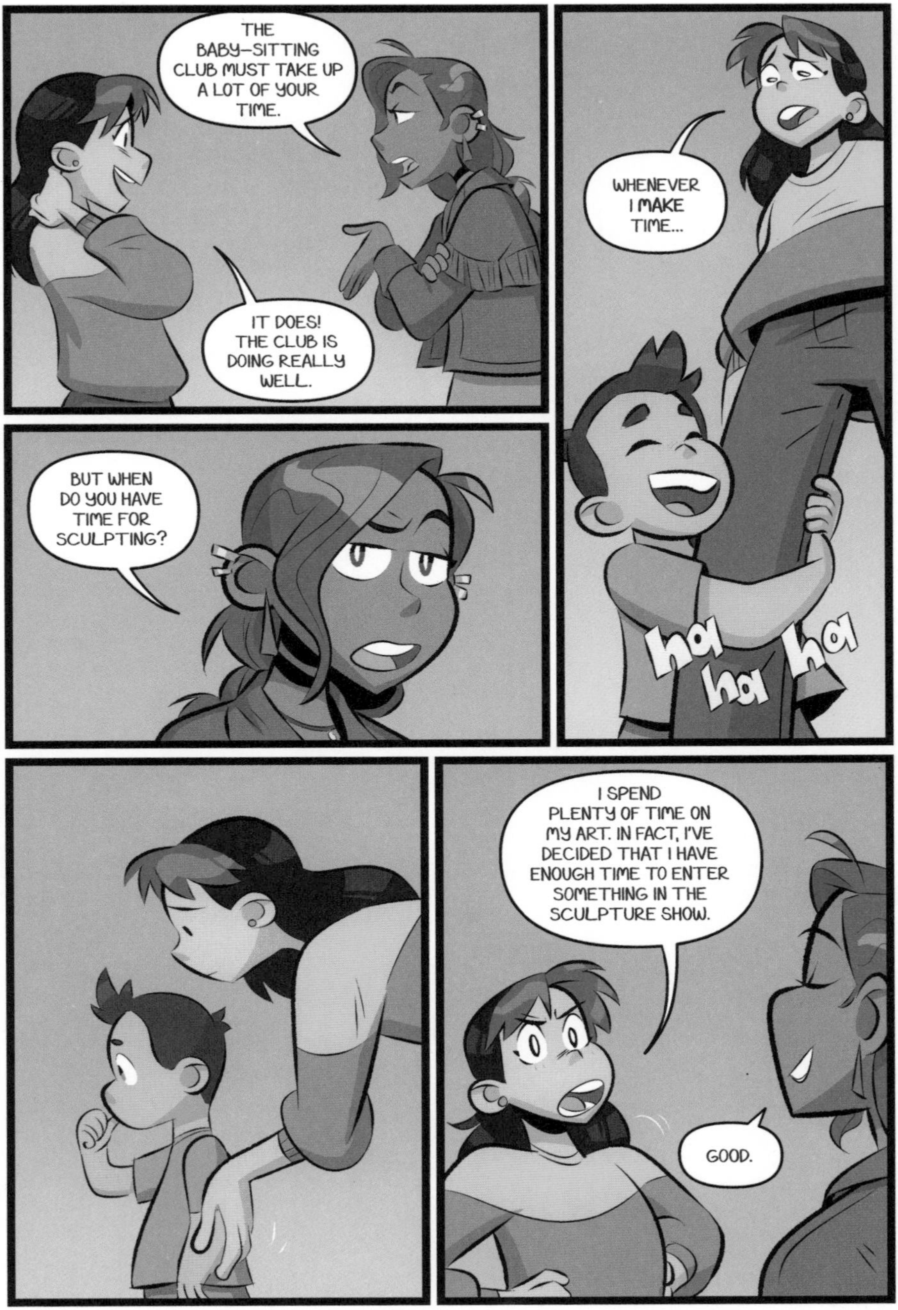
THE BABY-SITTING CLUB MUST TAKE UP A LOT OF YOUR TIME.
IT DOES! THE CLUB IS DOING REALLY WELL.
WHENEVER I MAKE TIME...
BUT WHEN DO YOU HAVE TIME FOR SCULPTING?
ha ha ha
I SPEND PLENTY OF TIME ON MY ART. IN FACT, I'VE DECIDED THAT I HAVE ENOUGH TIME TO ENTER SOMETHING IN THE SCULPTURE SHOW.
GOOD.

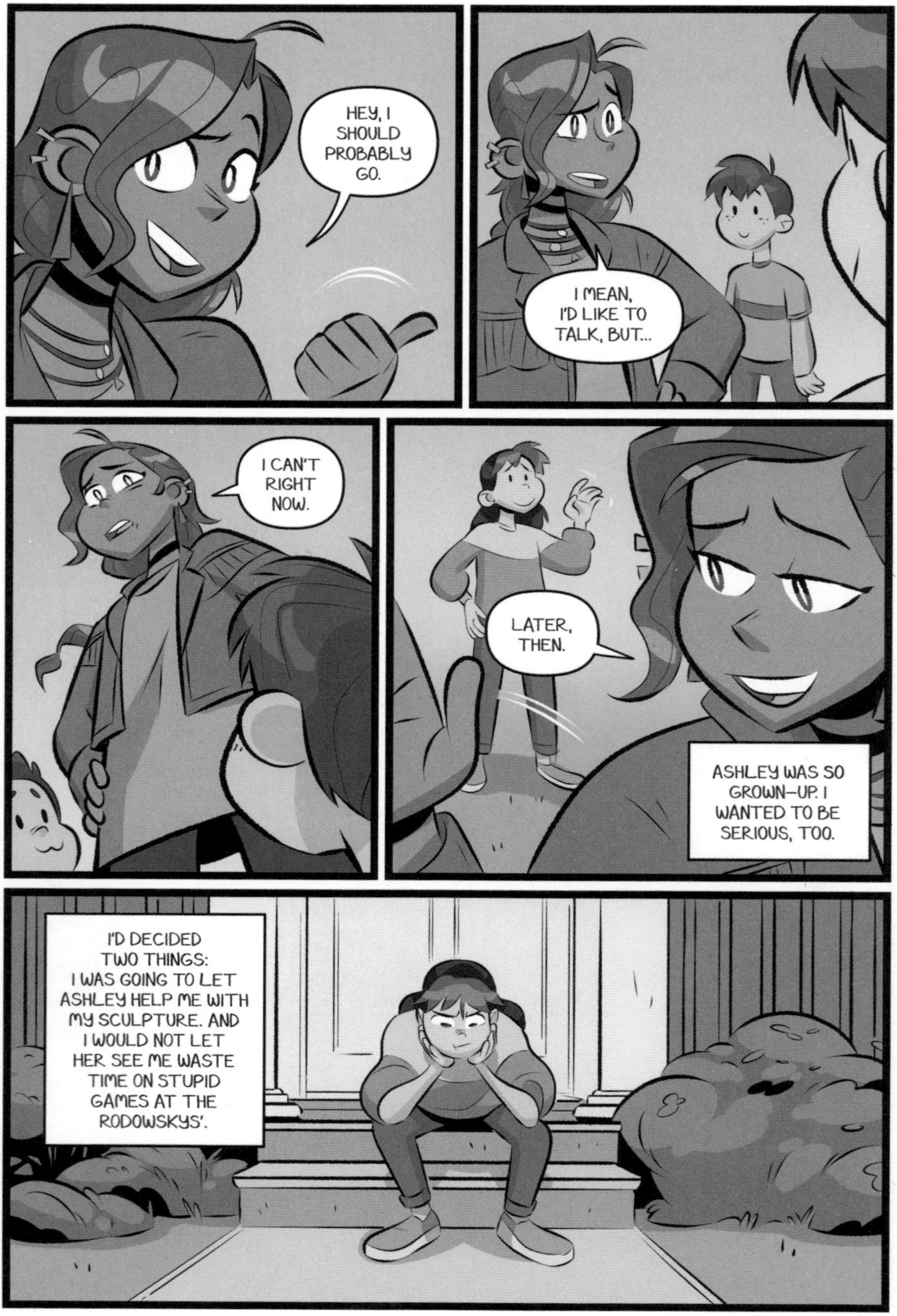
HEY, I SHOULD PROBABLY GO.
I MEAN, I'D LIKE TO TALK, BUT...
I CAN'T RIGHT NOW.
LATER, THEN.
ASHLEY WAS SO GROWN-UP. I WANTED TO BE SERIOUS, TOO.
I'D DECIDED TWO THINGS: I WAS GOING TO LET ASHLEY HELP ME WITH MY SCULPTURE. AND I WOULD NOT LET HER SEE ME WASTE TIME ON STUPID GAMES AT THE RODOWSKYS'.

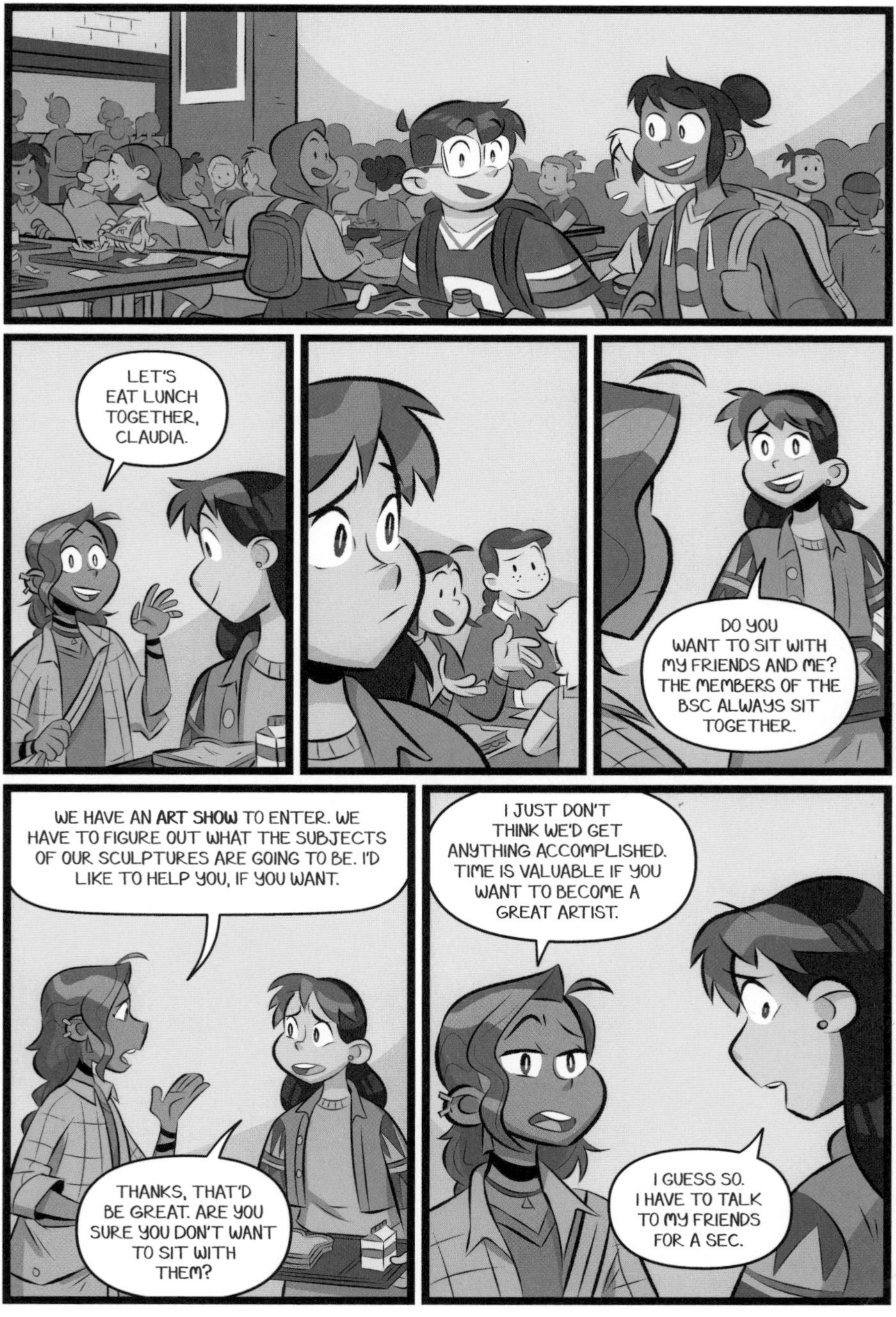
LET'S EAT LUNCH TOGETHER, CLAUDIA.
DO YOU WANT TO SIT WITH MY FRIENDS AND ME? THE MEMBERS OF THE BSC ALWAYS SIT TOGETHER.
WE HAVE AN ART SHOW TO ENTER. WE HAVE TO FIGURE OUT WHAT THE SUBJECTS OF OUR SCULPTURES ARE GOING TO BE. I'D LIKE TO HELP YOU, IF YOU WANT.
THANKS, THAT'D BE GREAT. ARE YOU SURE YOU DON'T WANT TO SIT WITH THEM?
I JUST DON'T THINK WE'D GET ANYTHING ACCOMPLISHED. TIME IS VALUABLE IF YOU WANT TO BECOME A GREAT ARTIST.
I GUESS SO. I HAVE TO TALK TO MY FRIENDS FOR A SEC.

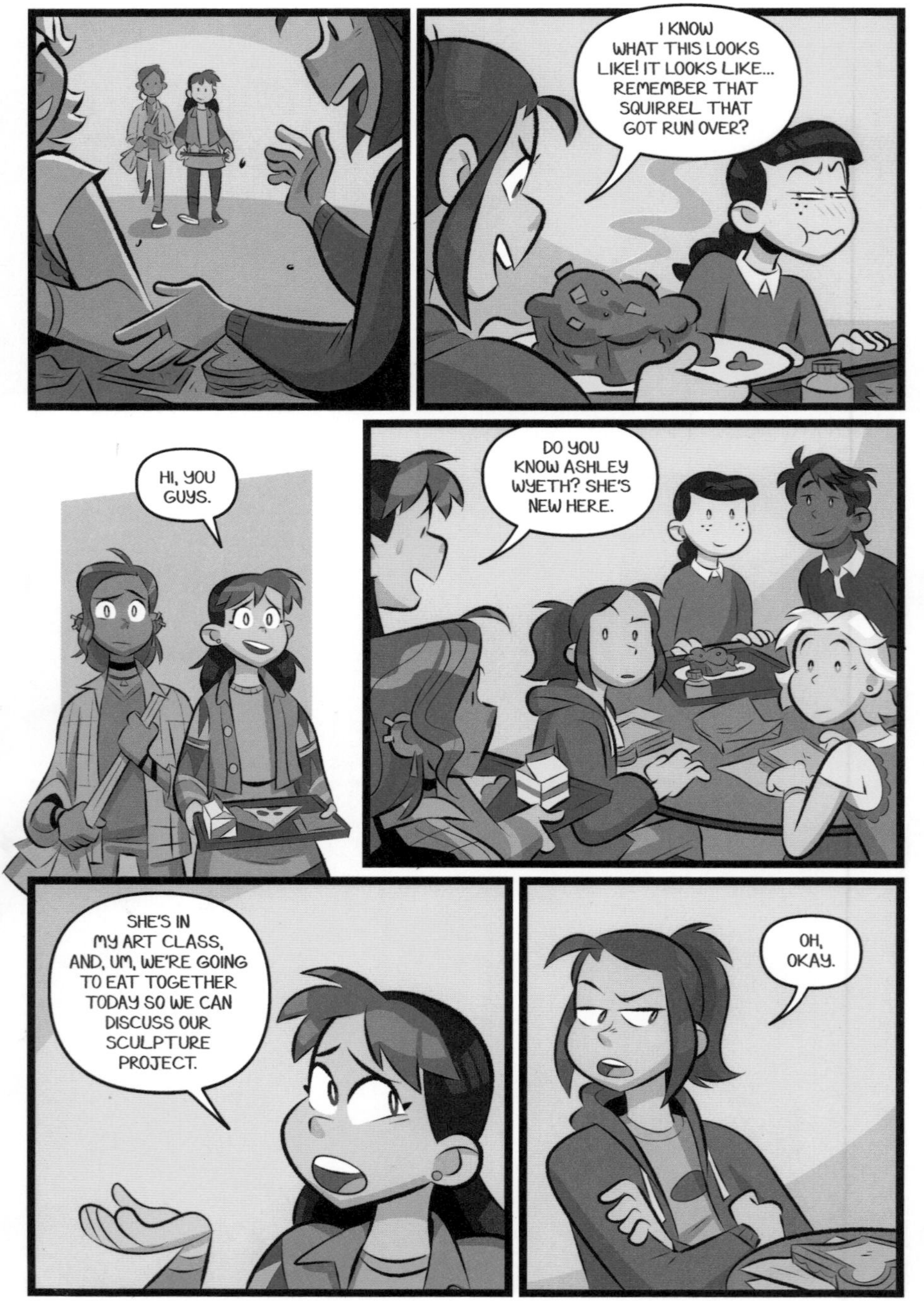
I KNOW WHAT THIS LOOKS LIKE! IT LOOKS LIKE... REMEMBER THAT SQUIRREL THAT GOT RUN OVER?
HI, YOU GUYS.
DO YOU KNOW ASHLEY WYETH? SHE'S NEW HERE.
SHE'S IN MY ART CLASS, AND, UM, WE'RE GOING TO EAT TOGETHER TODAY SO WE CAN DISCUSS OUR SCULPTURE PROJECT.
OH, OKAY.

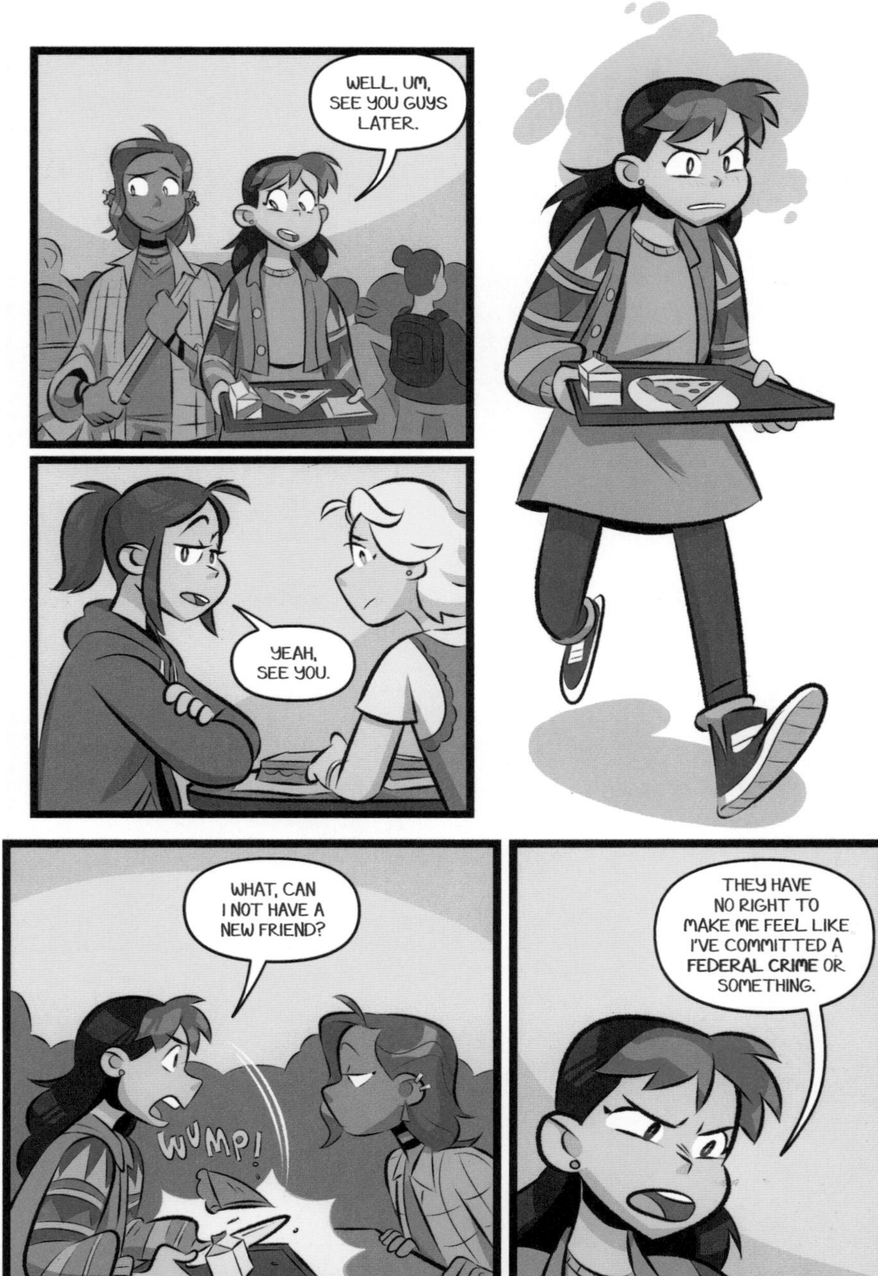
WELL, UM, SEE YOU GUYS LATER.
YEAH, SEE YOU.
WHAT, CAN I NOT HAVE A NEW FRIEND?
WUMP!
THEY HAVE NO RIGHT TO MAKE ME FEEL LIKE I'VE COMMITTED A FEDERAL CRIME OR SOMETHING.

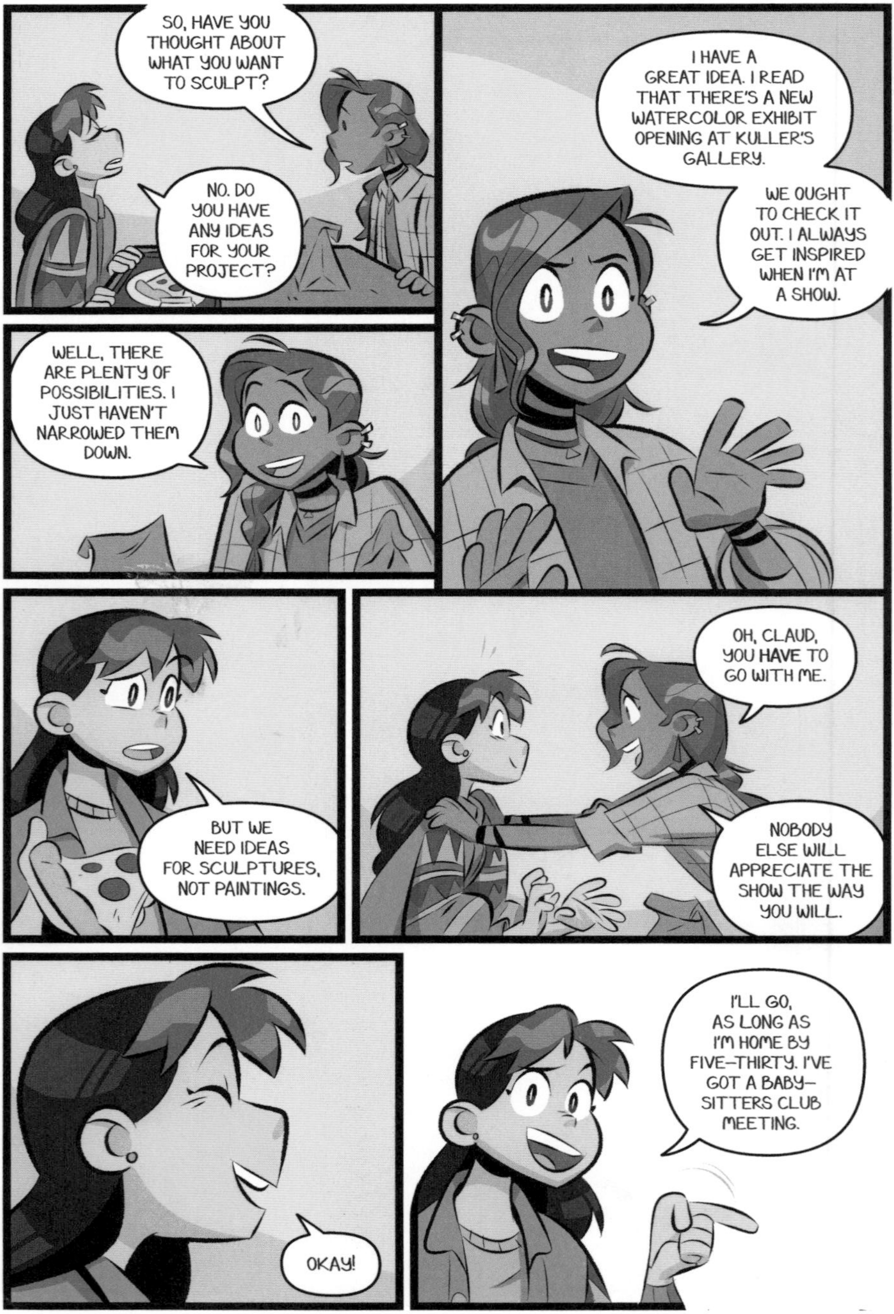
SO, HAVE YOU THOUGHT ABOUT WHAT YOU WANT TO SCULPT?
NO. DO YOU HAVE ANY IDEAS FOR YOUR PROJECT?
I HAVE A GREAT IDEA. I READ THAT THERE'S A NEW WATERCOLOR EXHIBIT OPENING AT KULLER'S GALLERY.
WE OUGHT TO CHECK IT OUT. I ALWAYS GET INSPIRED WHEN I'M AT A SHOW.
WELL, THERE ARE PLENTY OF POSSIBILITIES. I JUST HAVEN'T NARROWED THEM DOWN.
BUT WE NEED IDEAS FOR SCULPTURES, NOT PAINTINGS.
OH, CLAUD, YOU HAVE TO GO WITH ME.
NOBODY ELSE WILL APPRECIATE THE SHOW THE WAY YOU WILL.
OKAY!
I'LL GO, AS LONG AS I'M HOME BY FIVE-THIRTY. I'VE GOT A BABY-SITTERS CLUB MEETING.

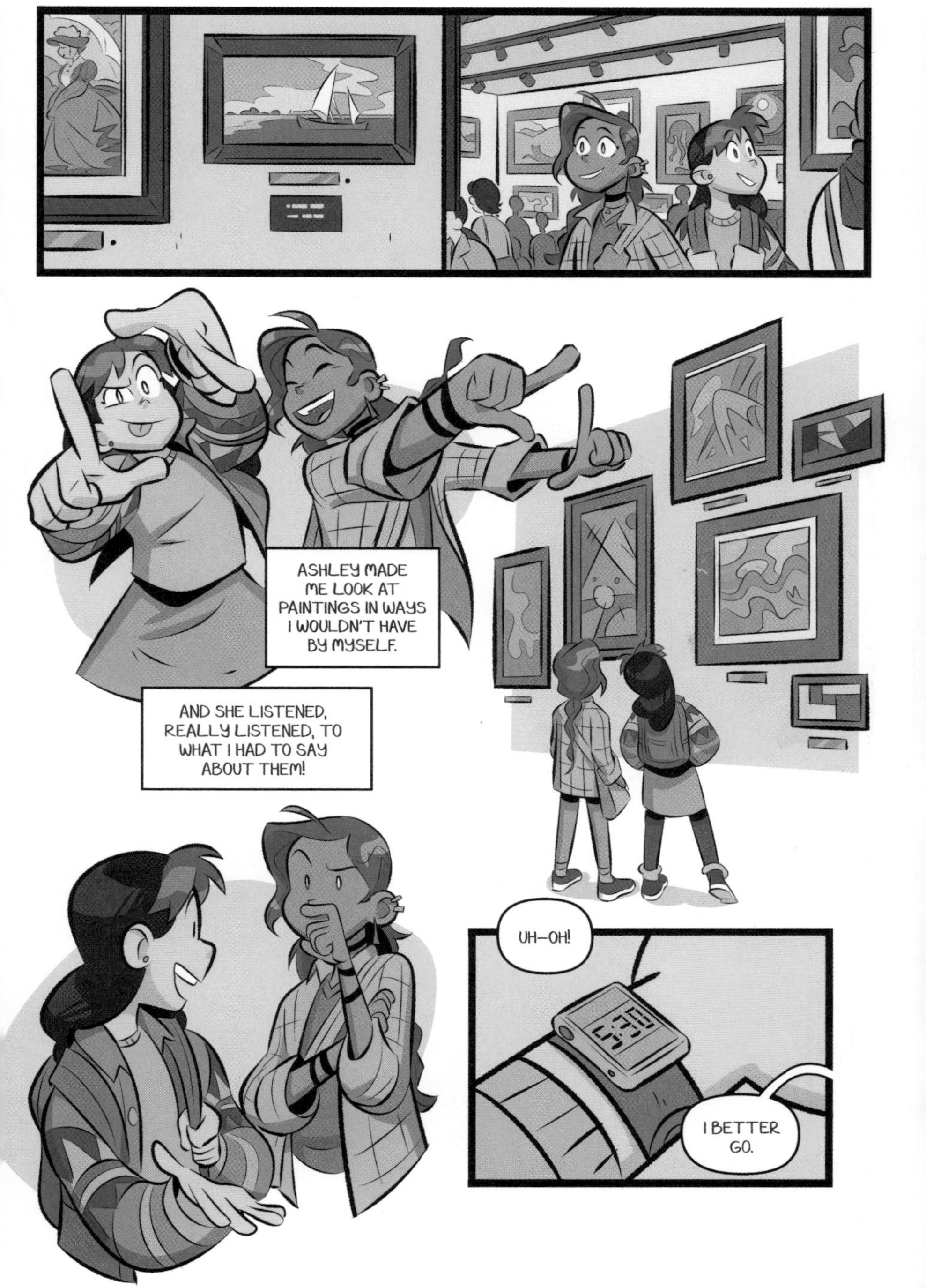
ASHLEY MADE ME LOOK AT PAINTINGS IN WAYS I WOULDN'T HAVE BY MYSELF.
AND SHE LISTENED, REALLY LISTENED, TO WHAT I HAD TO SAY ABOUT THEM!
UH-OH!
I BETTER GO.

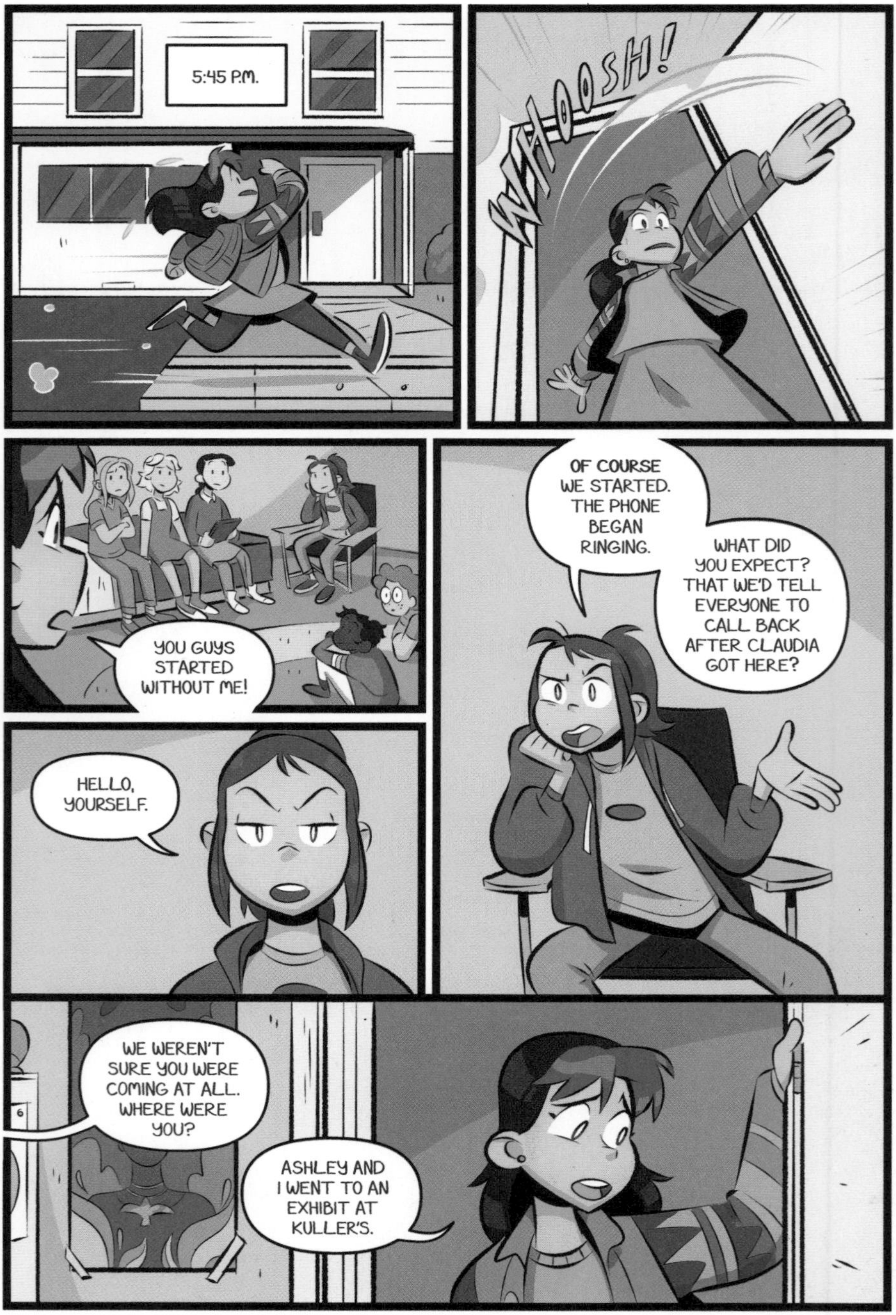
5:45 P.M.
WHOOSH!
YOU GUYS STARTED WITHOUT ME!
OF COURSE WE STARTED. THE PHONE BEGAN RINGING.
WHAT DID YOU EXPECT? THAT WE'D TELL EVERYONE TO CALL BACK AFTER CLAUDIA GOT HERE?
HELLO, YOURSELF.
WE WEREN'T SURE YOU WERE COMING AT ALL. WHERE WERE YOU?
ASHLEY AND I WENT TO AN EXHIBIT AT KULLER'S.

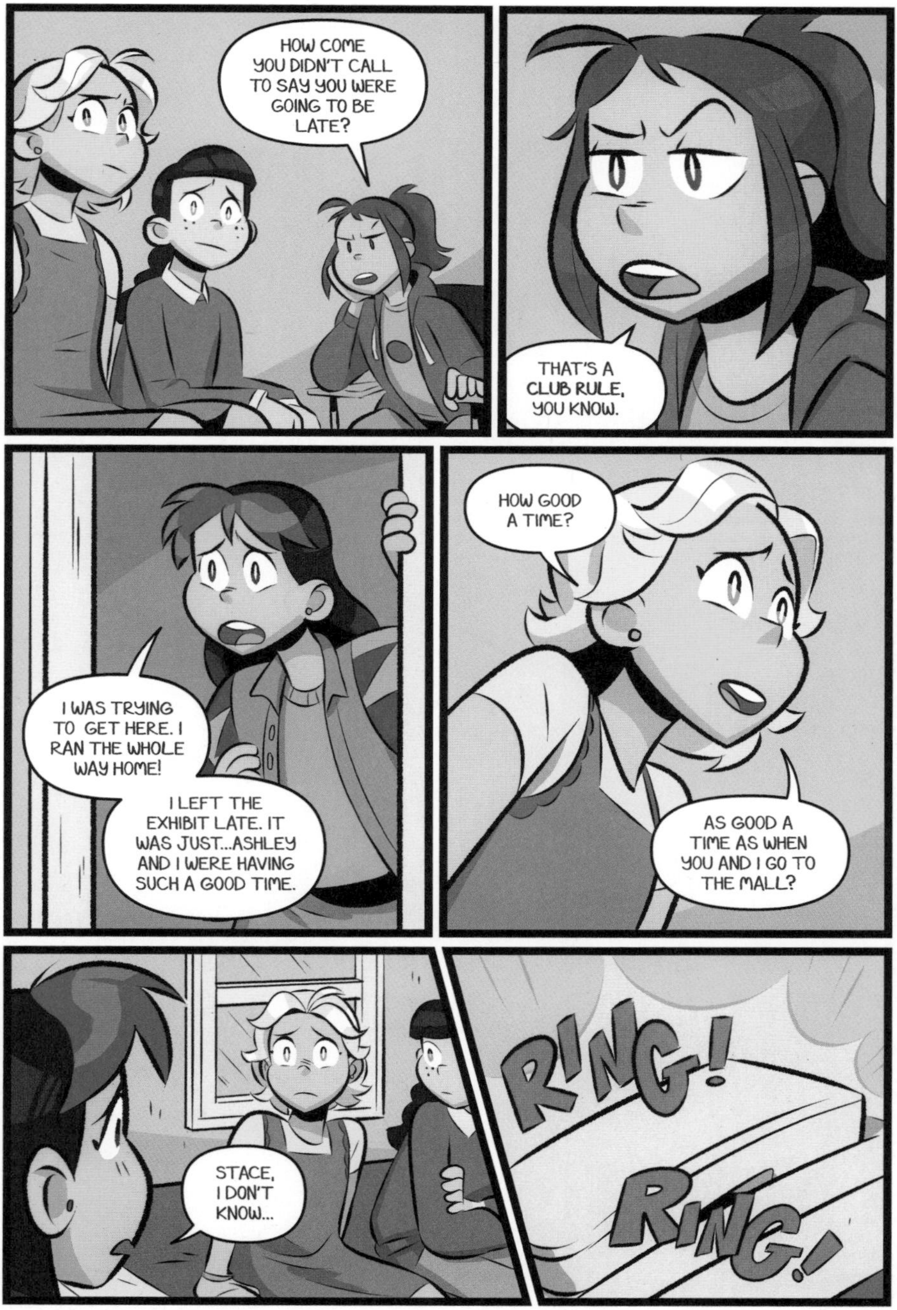
HOW COME YOU DIDN'T CALL TO SAY YOU WERE GOING TO BE LATE?
THAT'S A CLUB RULE, YOU KNOW.
I WAS TRYING TO GET HERE. I RAN THE WHOLE WAY HOME!
I LEFT THE EXHIBIT LATE. IT WAS JUST...ASHLEY AND I WERE HAVING SUCH A GOOD TIME.
HOW GOOD A TIME?
AS GOOD A TIME AS WHEN YOU AND I GO TO THE MALL?
STACE, I DON'T KNOW...
RING!
RING!

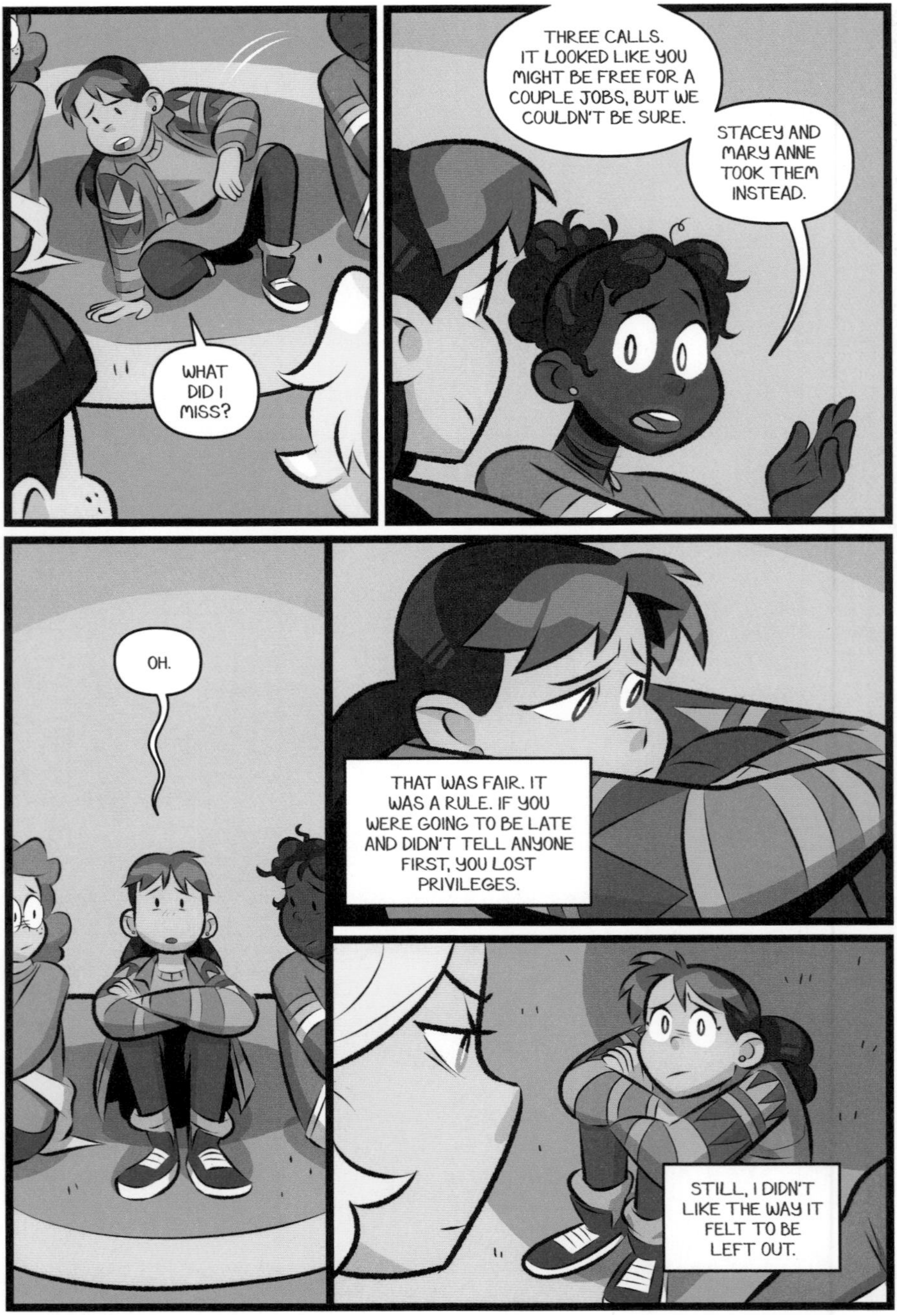
WHAT DID I MISS?
THREE CALLS. IT LOOKED LIKE YOU MIGHT BE FREE FOR A COUPLE JOBS, BUT WE COULDN'T BE SURE.
STACEY AND MARY ANNE TOOK THEM INSTEAD.
OH.
THAT WAS FAIR. IT WAS A RULE. IF YOU WERE GOING TO BE LATE AND DIDN'T TELL ANYONE FIRST, YOU LOST PRIVILEGES.
STILL, I DIDN'T LIKE THE WAY IT FELT TO BE LEFT OUT.

CHAPTER 6

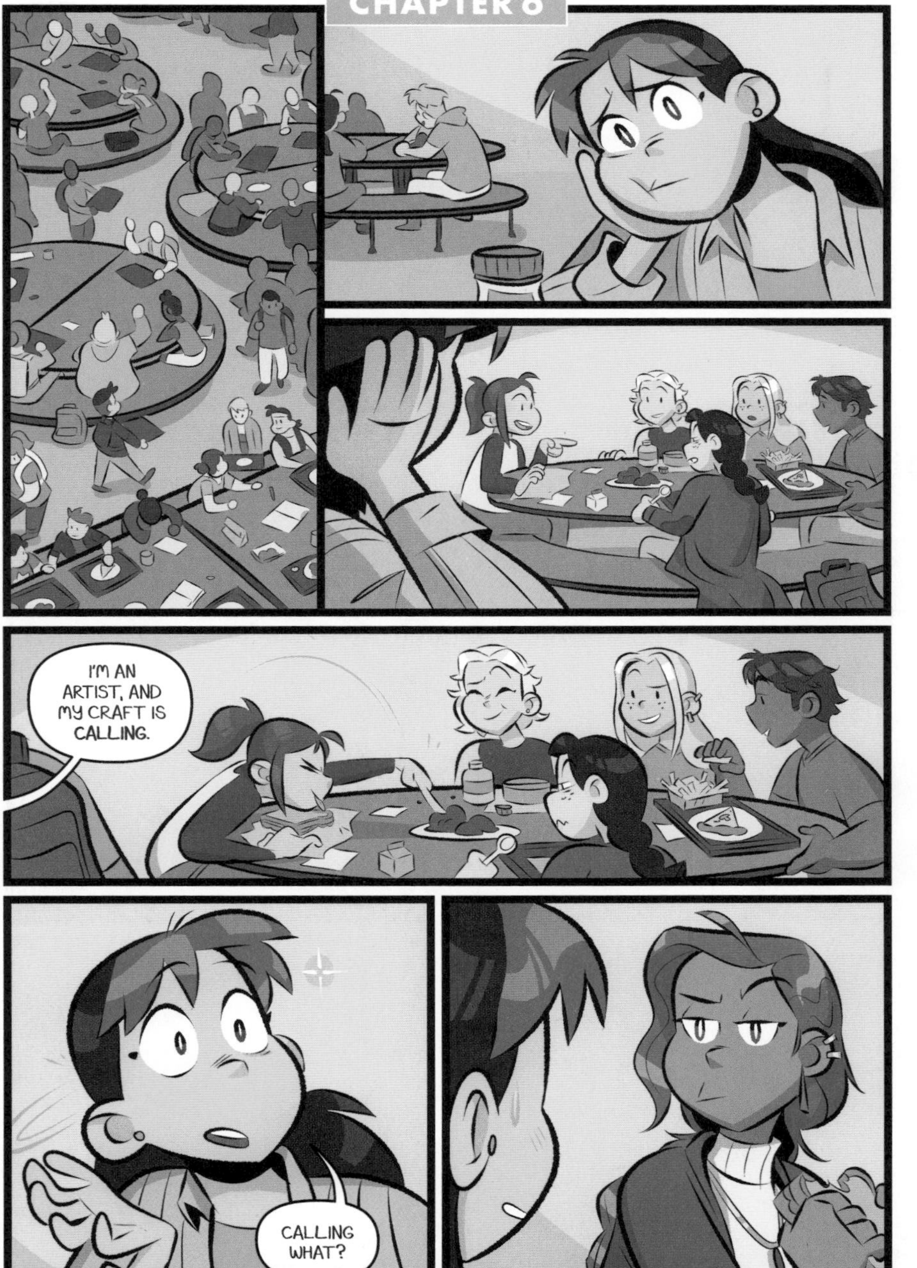
I'M AN ARTIST, AND MY CRAFT IS CALLING.
CALLING WHAT?

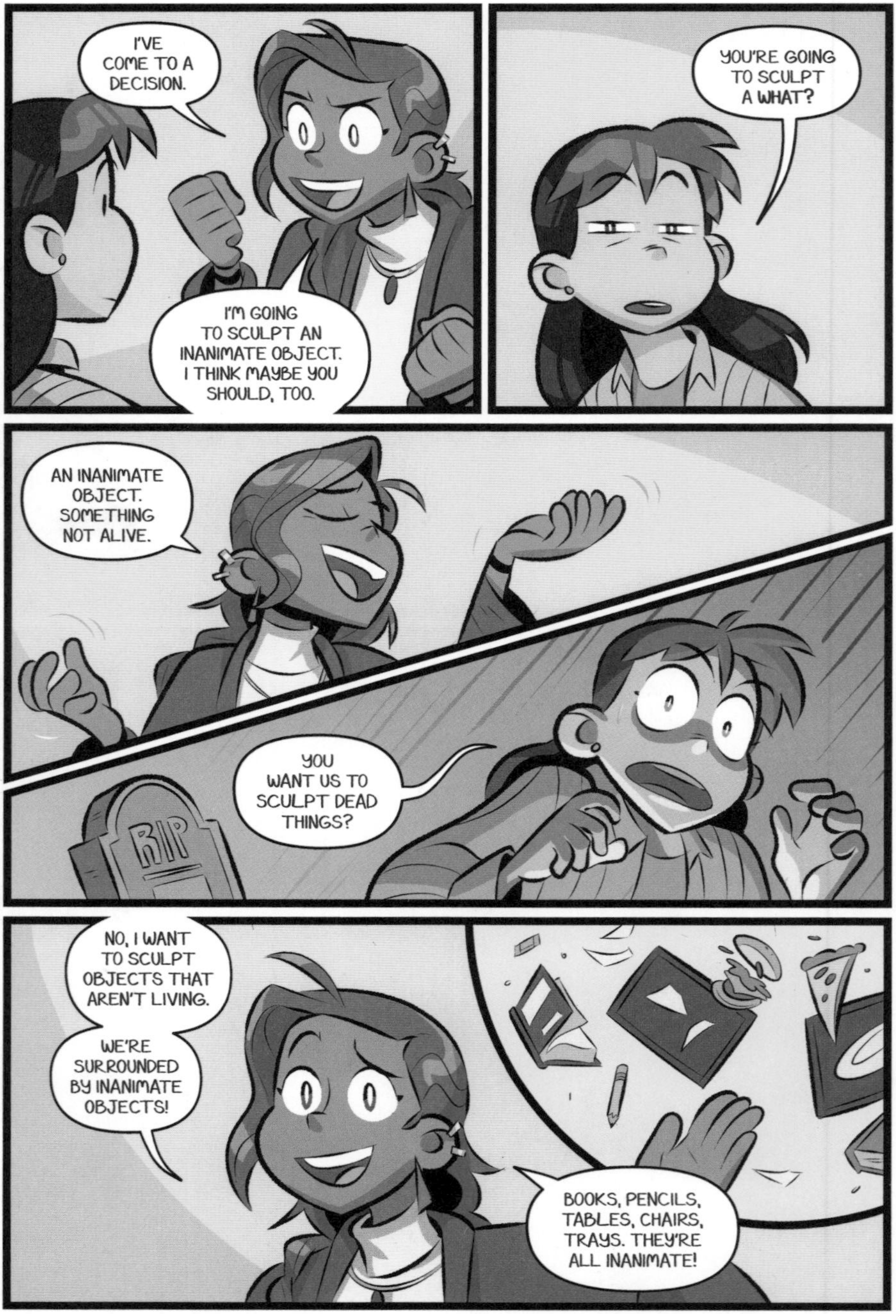
I'VE COME TO A DECISION.
I'M GOING TO SCULPT AN INANIMATE OBJECT. I THINK MAYBE YOU SHOULD, TOO.
YOU'RE GOING TO SCULPT A WHAT?
AN INANIMATE OBJECT. SOMETHING NOT ALIVE.
YOU WANT US TO SCULPT DEAD THINGS?
RIP
NO, I WANT TO SCULPT OBJECTS THAT AREN'T LIVING.
WE'RE SURROUNDED BY INANIMATE OBJECTS!
BOOKS, PENCILS, TABLES, CHAIRS, TRAYS. THEY'RE ALL INANIMATE!

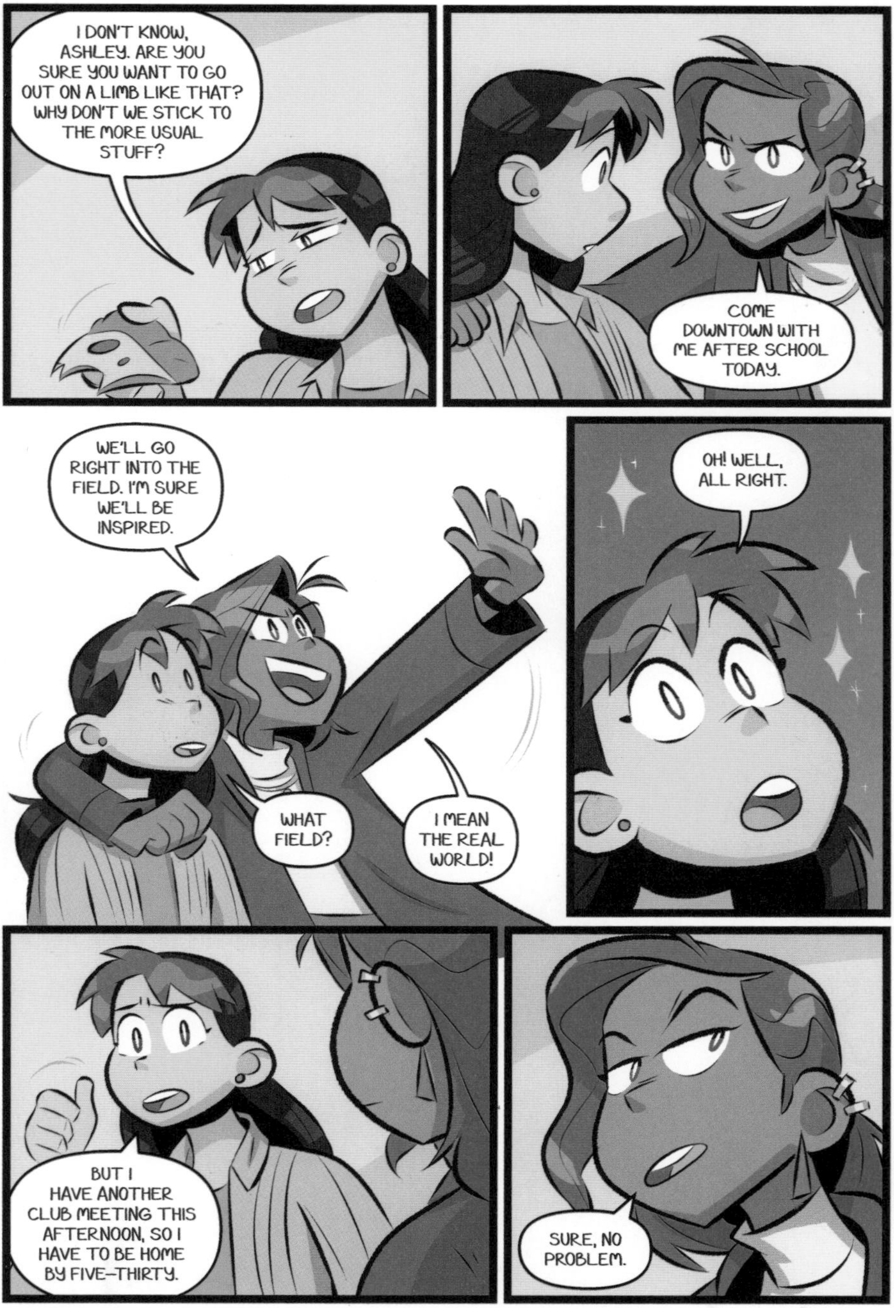
I DON'T KNOW, ASHLEY. ARE YOU SURE YOU WANT TO GO OUT ON A LIMB LIKE THAT? WHY DON'T WE STICK TO THE MORE USUAL STUFF?
COME DOWNTOWN WITH ME AFTER SCHOOL TODAY.
WE'LL GO RIGHT INTO THE FIELD. I'M SURE WE'LL BE INSPIRED.
WHAT FIELD?
I MEAN THE REAL WORLD!
OH! WELL, ALL RIGHT.
BUT I HAVE ANOTHER CLUB MEETING THIS AFTERNOON, SO I HAVE TO BE HOME BY FIVE-THIRTY.
SURE, NO PROBLEM.

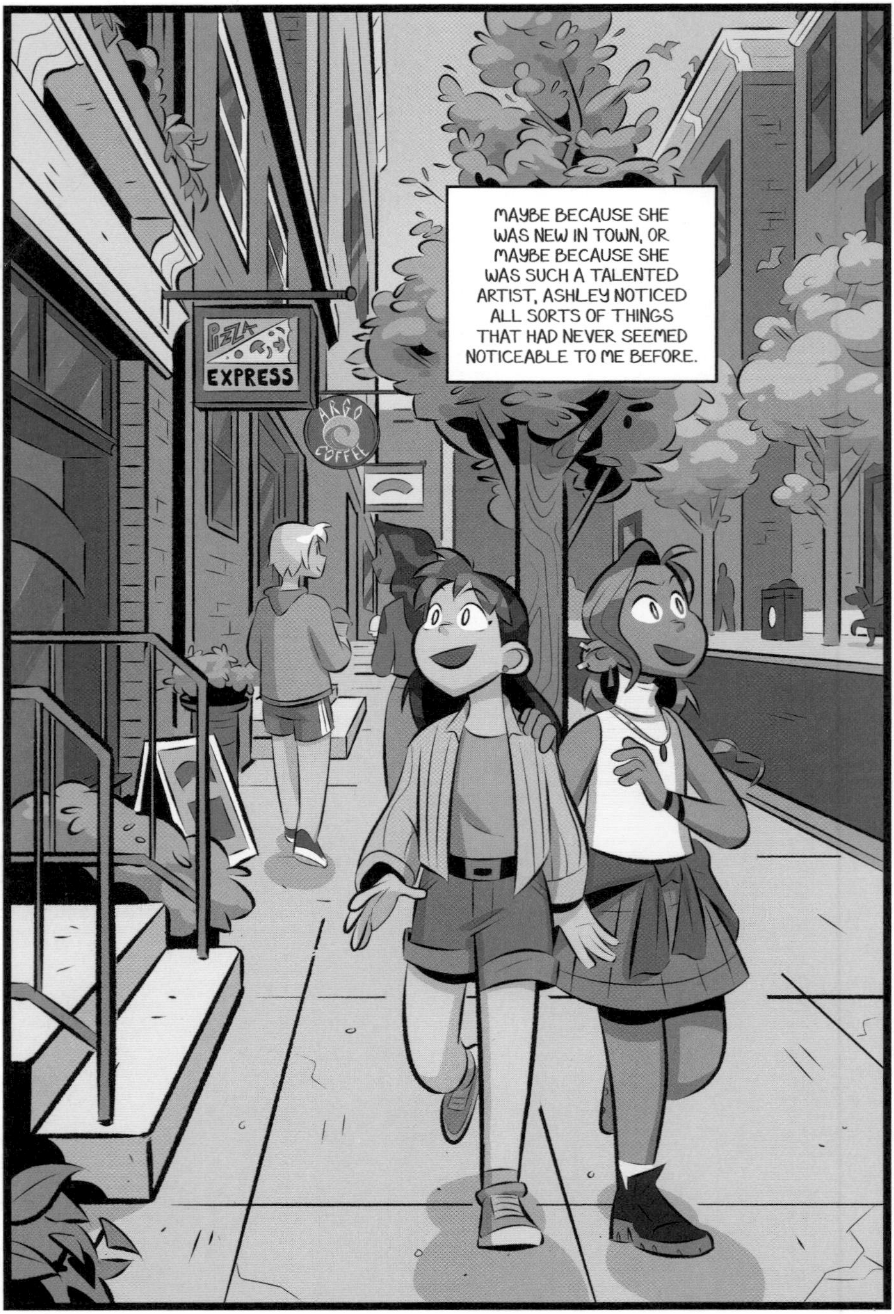
MAYBE BECAUSE SHE WAS NEW IN TOWN, OR MAYBE BECAUSE SHE WAS SUCH A TALENTED ARTIST, ASHLEY NOTICED ALL SORTS OF THINGS THAT HAD NEVER SEEMED NOTICEABLE TO ME BEFORE.
PIZZA EXPRESS
ARGO COFFEE

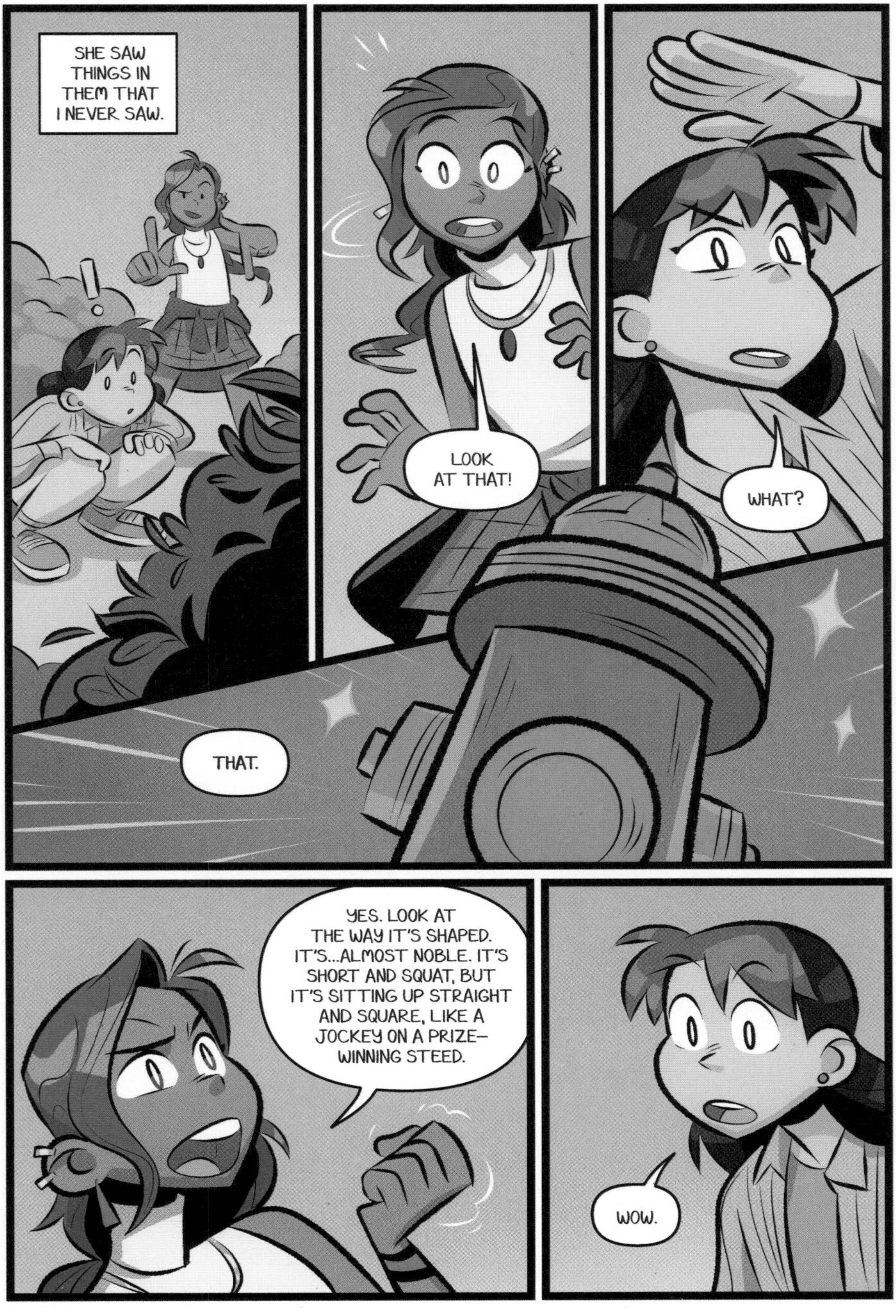
SHE SAW THINGS IN THEM THAT I NEVER SAW.
LOOK AT THAT!
WHAT?
THAT.
YES. LOOK AT THE WAY IT'S SHAPED. IT'S...ALMOST NOBLE. IT'S SHORT AND SQUAT, BUT IT'S SITTING UP STRAIGHT AND SQUARE, LIKE A JOCKEY ON A PRIZE-WINNING STEED.
WOW.

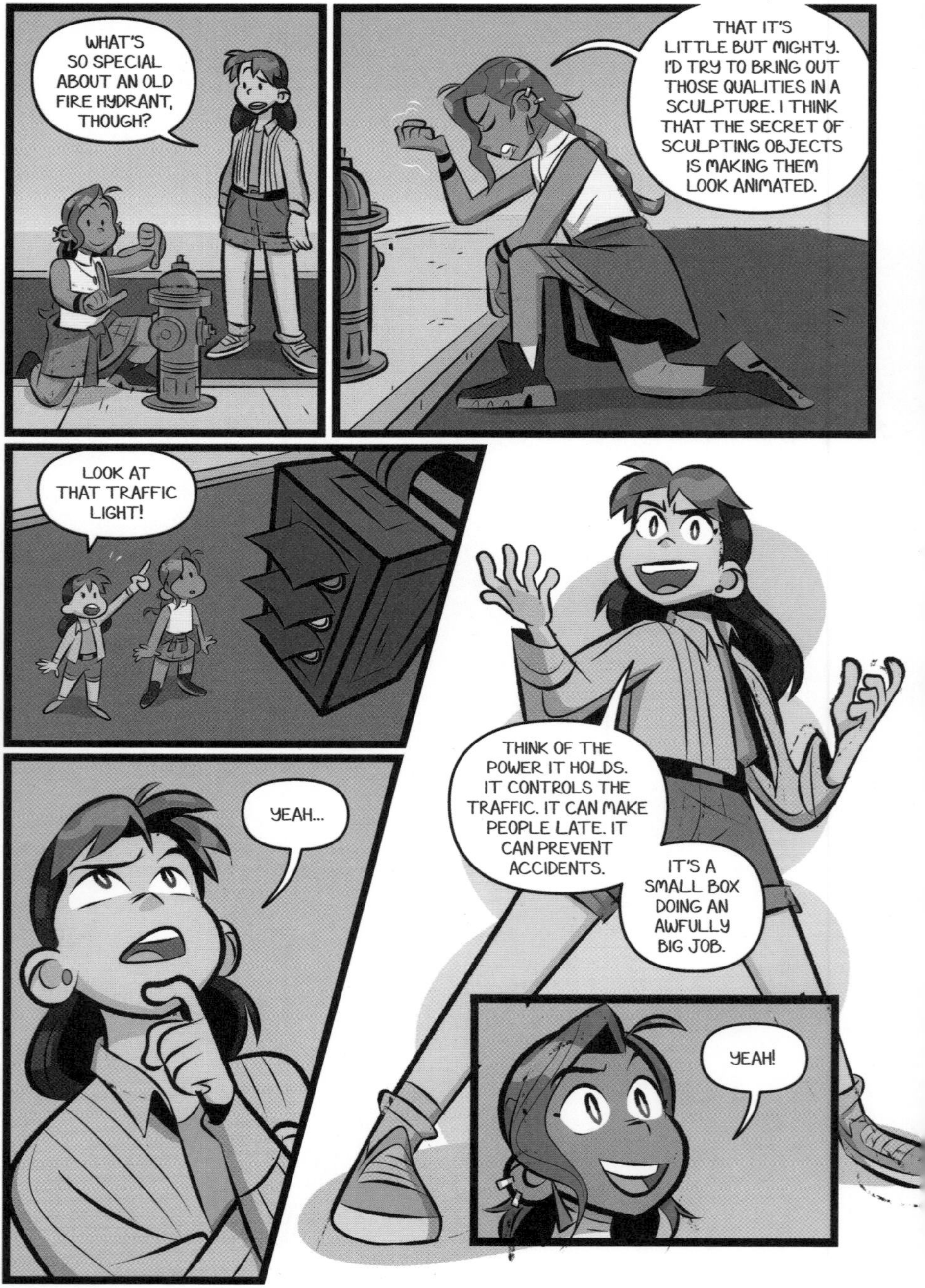
WHAT'S SO SPECIAL ABOUT AN OLD FIRE HYDRANT, THOUGH?
THAT IT'S LITTLE BUT MIGHTY. I'D TRY TO BRING OUT THOSE QUALITIES IN A SCULPTURE. I THINK THAT THE SECRET OF SCULPTING OBJECTS IS MAKING THEM LOOK ANIMATED.
LOOK AT THAT TRAFFIC LIGHT!
THINK OF THE POWER IT HOLDS. IT CONTROLS THE TRAFFIC. IT CAN MAKE PEOPLE LATE. IT CAN PREVENT ACCIDENTS.
IT'S A SMALL BOX DOING AN AWFULLY BIG JOB.
YEAH...
YEAH!

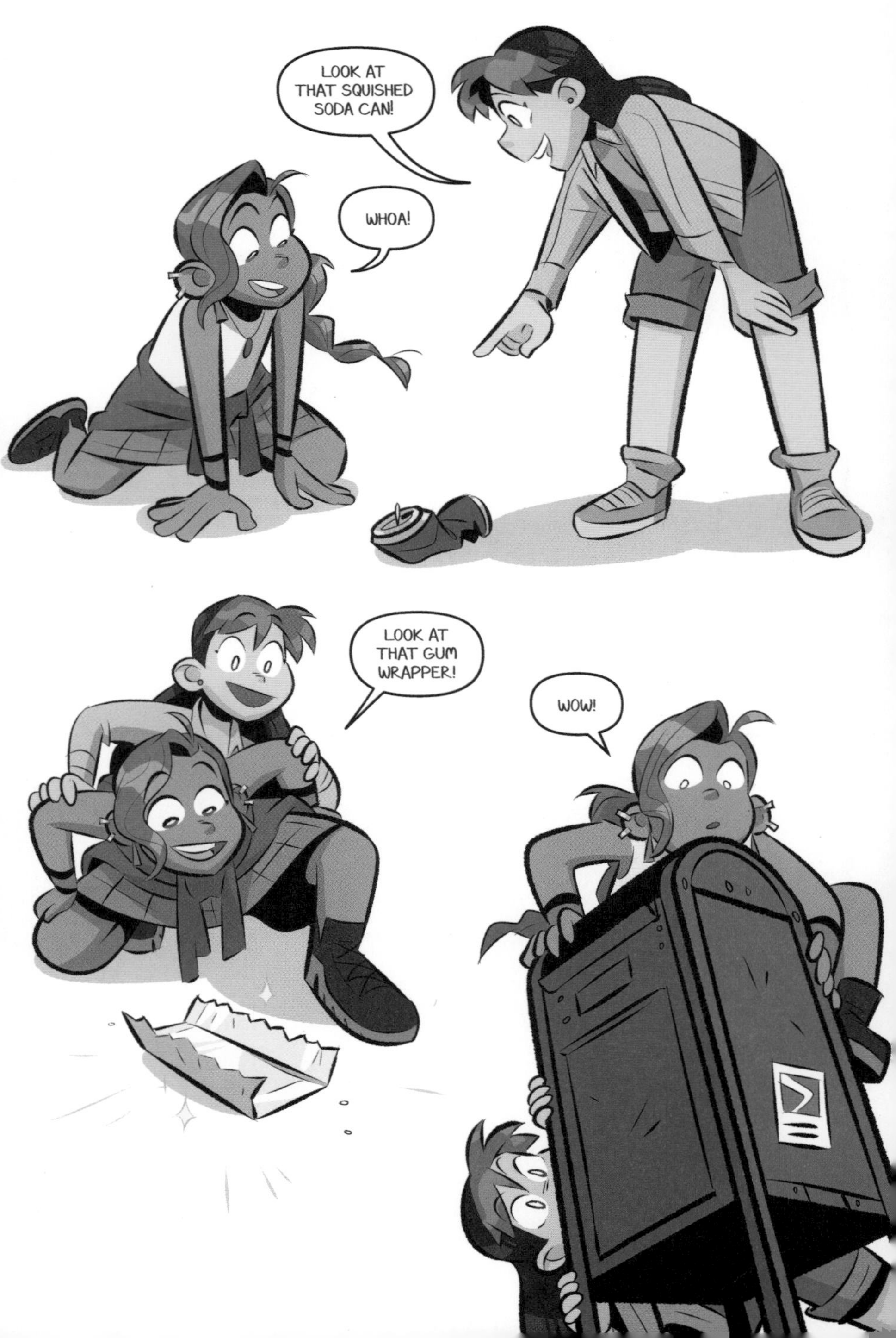
LOOK AT THAT SQUISHED SODA CAN!
WHOA!
LOOK AT THAT GUM WRAPPER!
WOW!

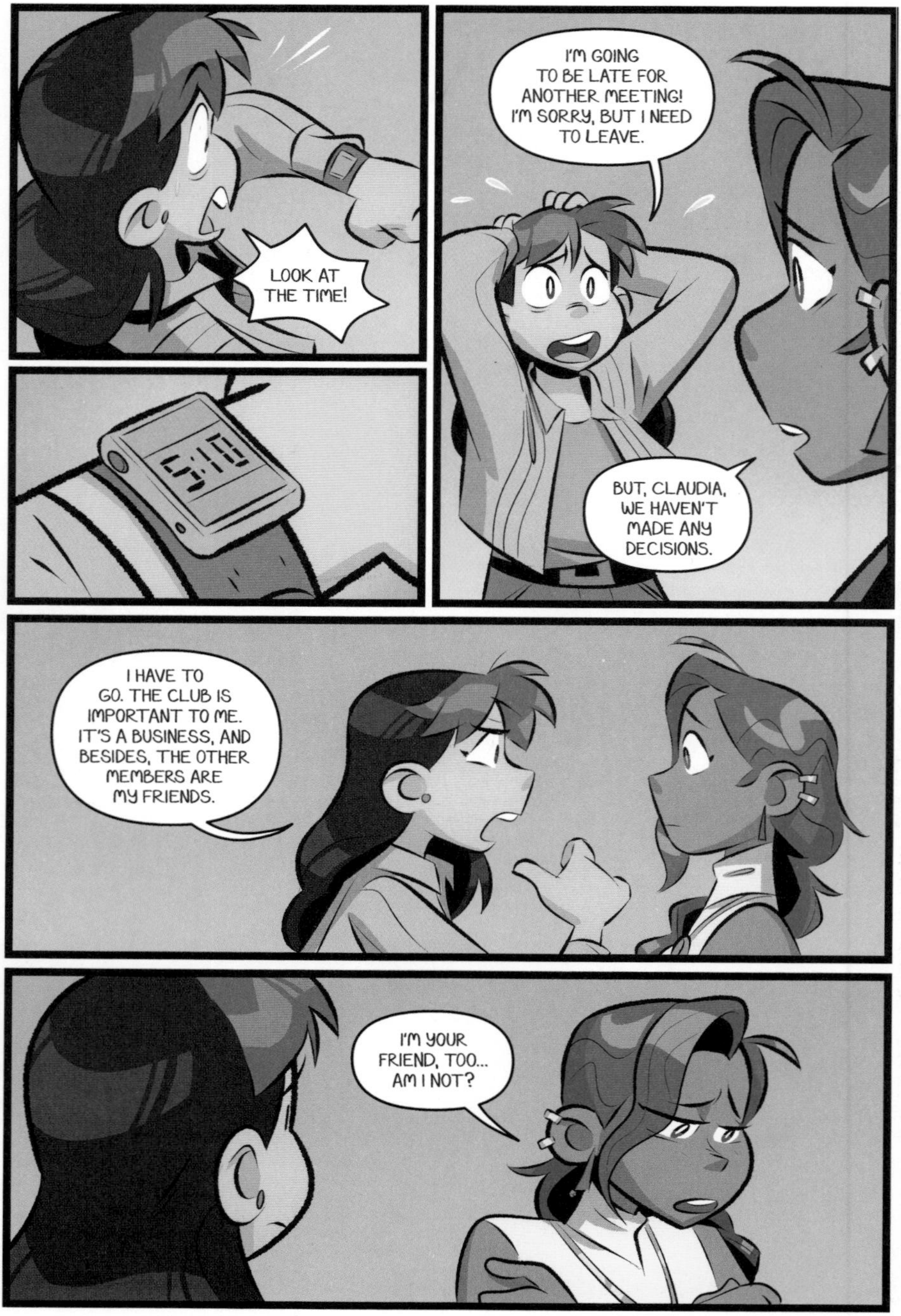
LOOK AT THE TIME!
5:10
I'M GOING TO BE LATE FOR ANOTHER MEETING! I'M SORRY, BUT I NEED TO LEAVE.
BUT, CLAUDIA, WE HAVEN'T MADE ANY DECISIONS.
I HAVE TO GO. THE CLUB IS IMPORTANT TO ME. IT'S A BUSINESS, AND BESIDES, THE OTHER MEMBERS ARE MY FRIENDS.
I'M YOUR FRIEND, TOO... AM I NOT?

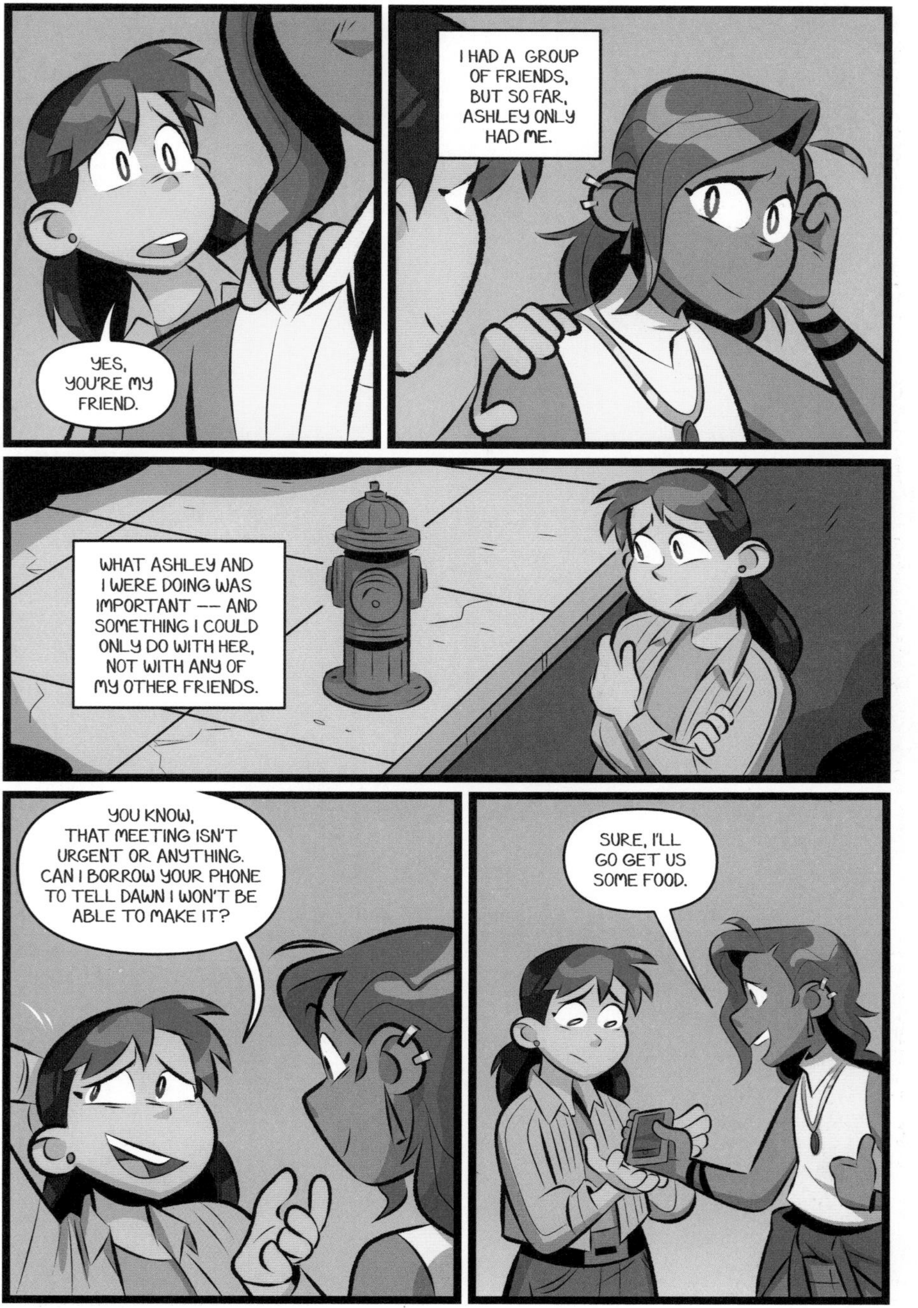
YES, YOU'RE MY FRIEND.
I HAD A GROUP OF FRIENDS, BUT SO FAR, ASHLEY ONLY HAD ME.
WHAT ASHLEY AND I WERE DOING WAS IMPORTANT -- AND SOMETHING I COULD ONLY DO WITH HER, NOT WITH ANY OF MY OTHER FRIENDS.
YOU KNOW, THAT MEETING ISN'T URGENT OR ANYTHING. CAN I BORROW YOUR PHONE TO TELL DAWN I WON'T BE ABLE TO MAKE IT?
SURE, I'LL GO GET US SOME FOOD.

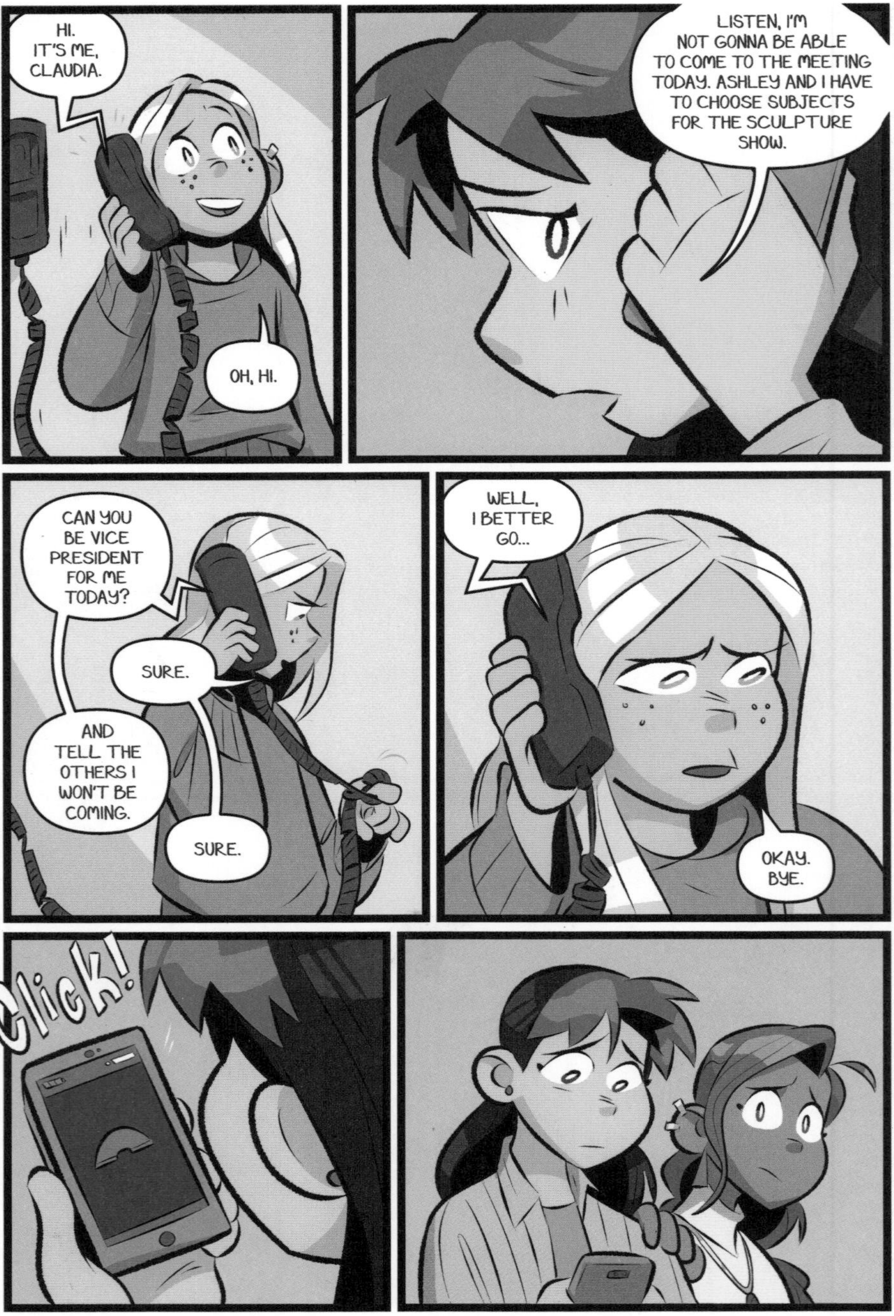
HI. IT'S ME, CLAUDIA.
OH, HI.
LISTEN, I'M NOT GONNA BE ABLE TO COME TO THE MEETING TODAY. ASHLEY AND I HAVE TO CHOOSE SUBJECTS FOR THE SCULPTURE SHOW.
CAN YOU BE VICE PRESIDENT FOR ME TODAY?
SURE.
AND TELL THE OTHERS I WON'T BE COMING.
SURE.
WELL, I BETTER GO...
OKAY. BYE.
CLICK!

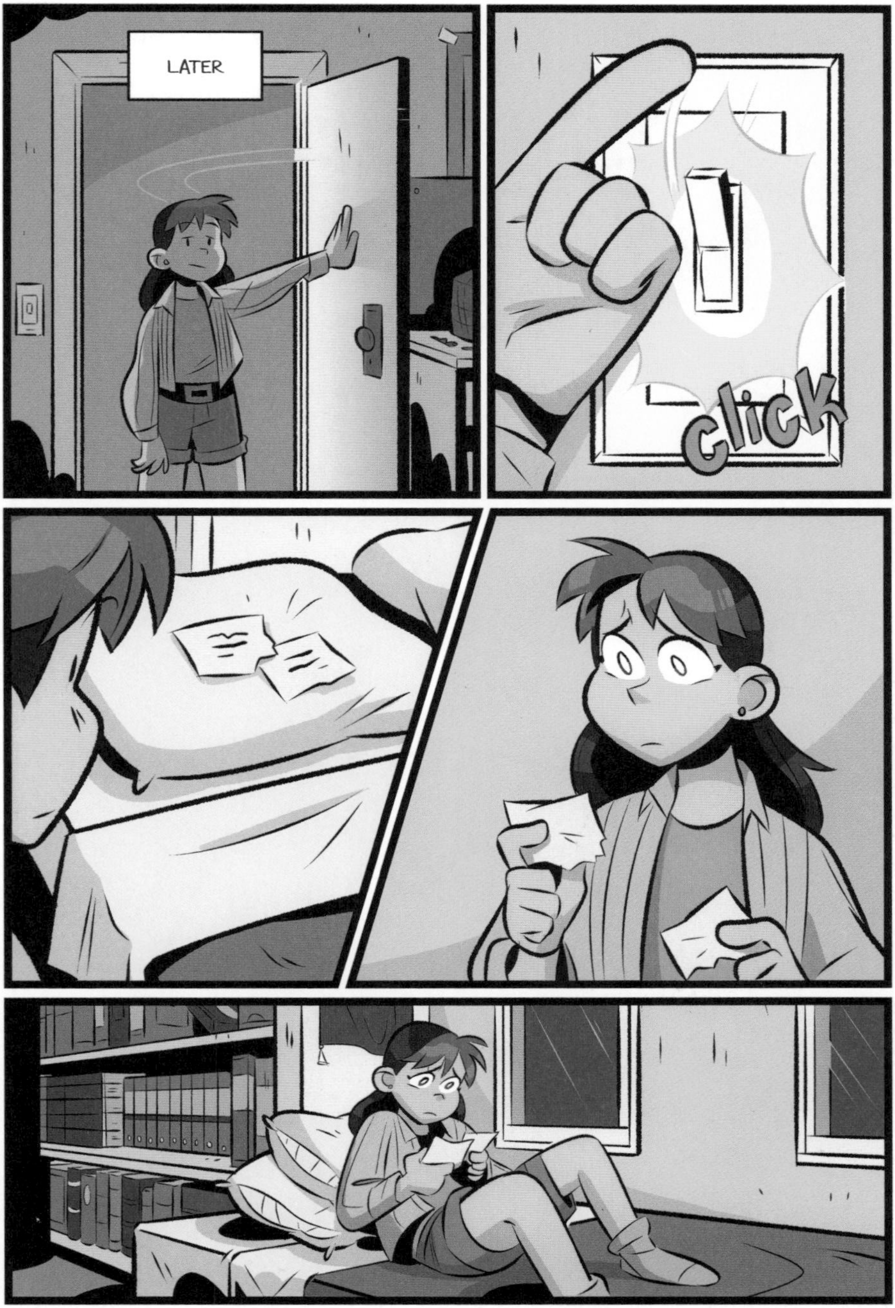
LATER
click

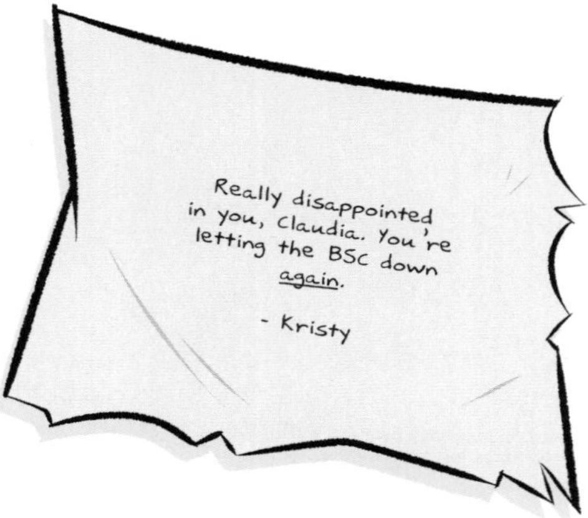
Really disappointed in you, Claudia. You're letting the BSC down again.
- Kristy

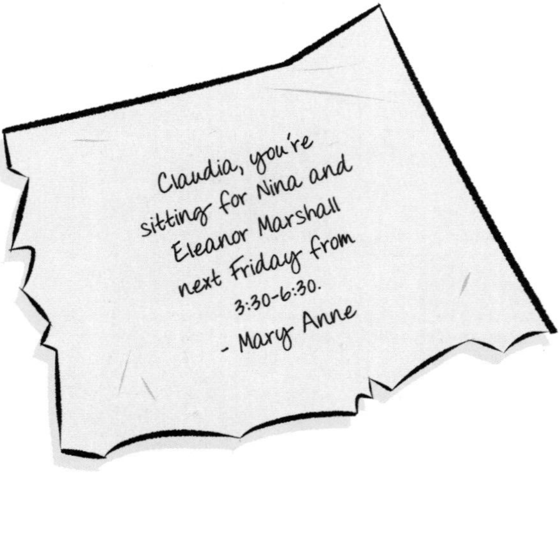
Claudia, you're sitting for Nina and Eleanor Marshall next Friday from 3:30-6:30.
- Mary Anne

CHAPTER 7

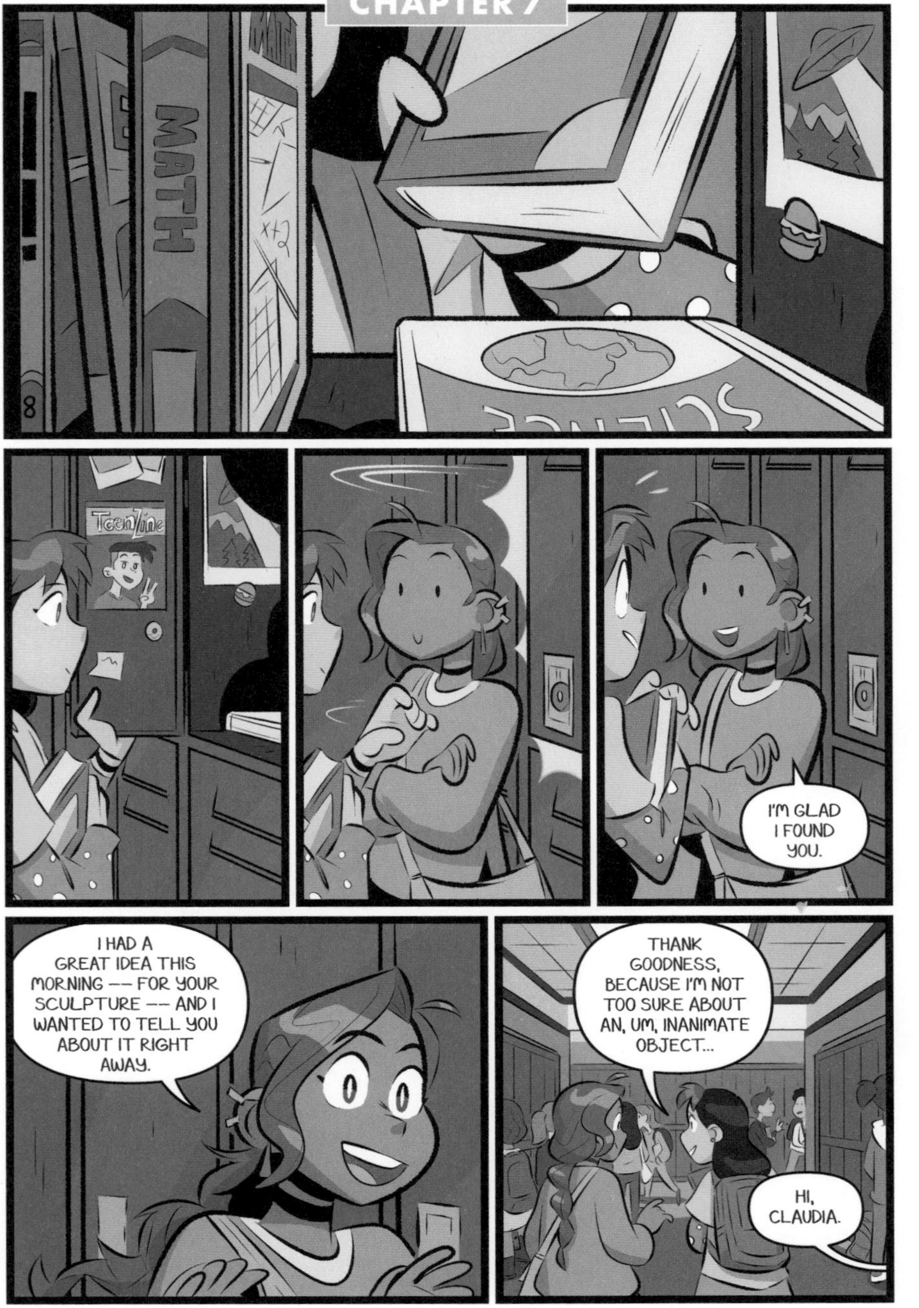
MATH
MATH
SCIENCE
TeenZine
I'M GLAD I FOUND YOU.
I HAD A GREAT IDEA THIS MORNING -- FOR YOUR SCULPTURE -- AND I WANTED TO TELL YOU ABOUT IT RIGHT AWAY.
THANK GOODNESS, BECAUSE I'M NOT TOO SURE ABOUT AN, UM, INANIMATE OBJECT...
HI, CLAUDIA.

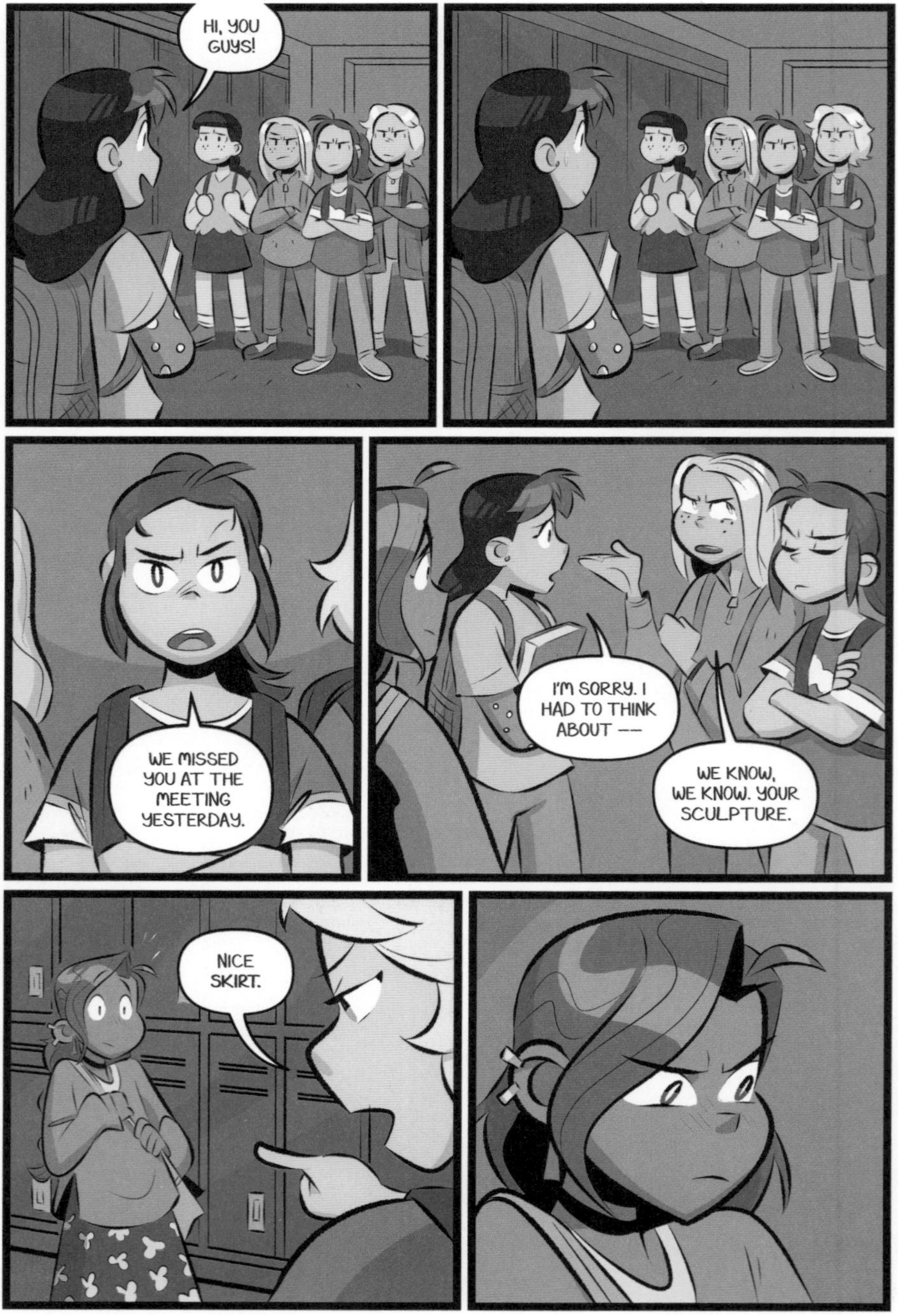
HI, YOU GUYS!
WE MISSED YOU AT THE MEETING YESTERDAY.
I'M SORRY. I HAD TO THINK ABOUT --
WE KNOW, WE KNOW. YOUR SCULPTURE.
NICE SKIRT.

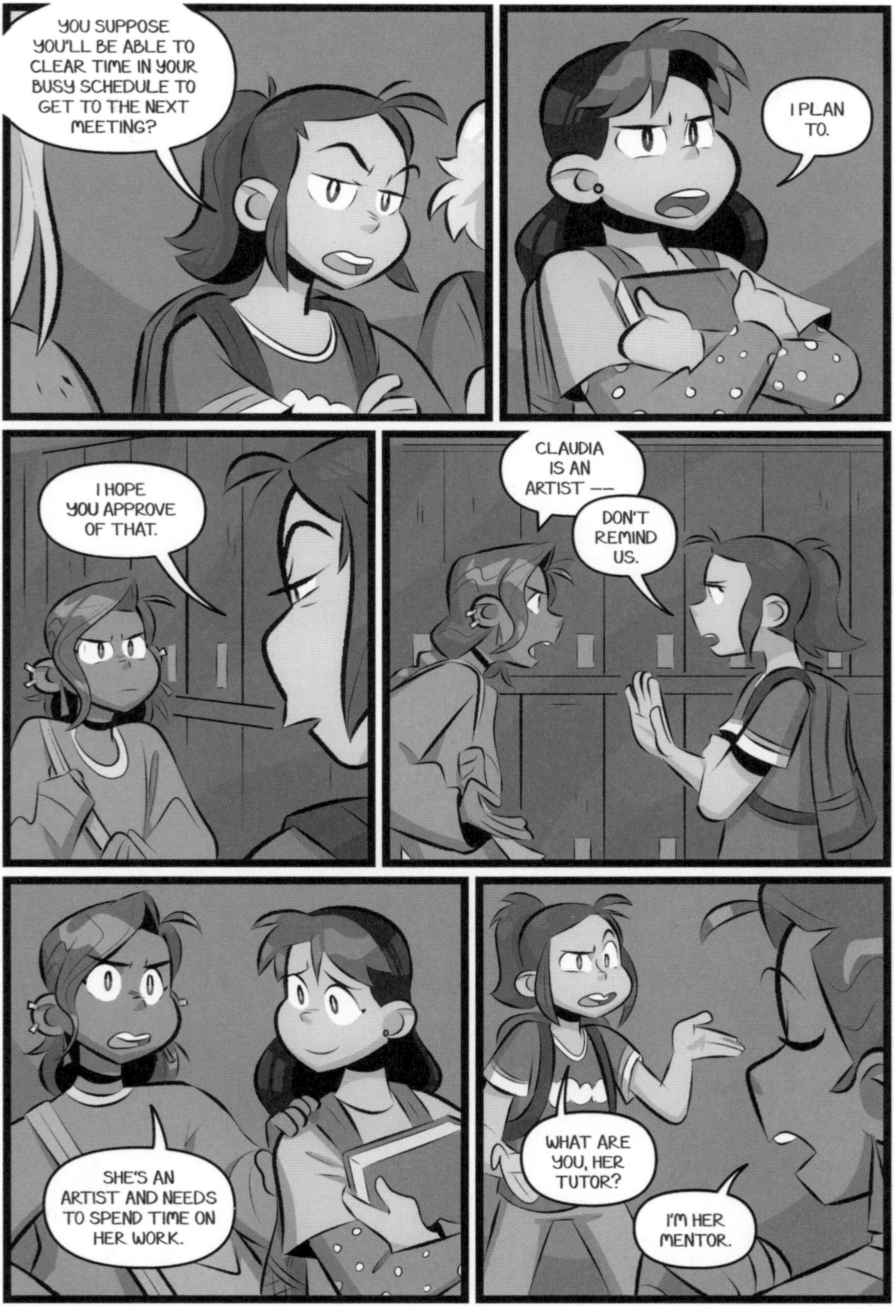
YOU SUPPOSE YOU'LL BE ABLE TO CLEAR TIME IN YOUR BUSY SCHEDULE TO GET TO THE NEXT MEETING?
I PLAN TO.
I HOPE YOU APPROVE OF THAT.
CLAUDIA IS AN ARTIST --
DON'T REMIND US.
SHE'S AN ARTIST AND NEEDS TO SPEND TIME ON HER WORK.
WHAT ARE YOU, HER TUTOR?
I'M HER MENTOR.

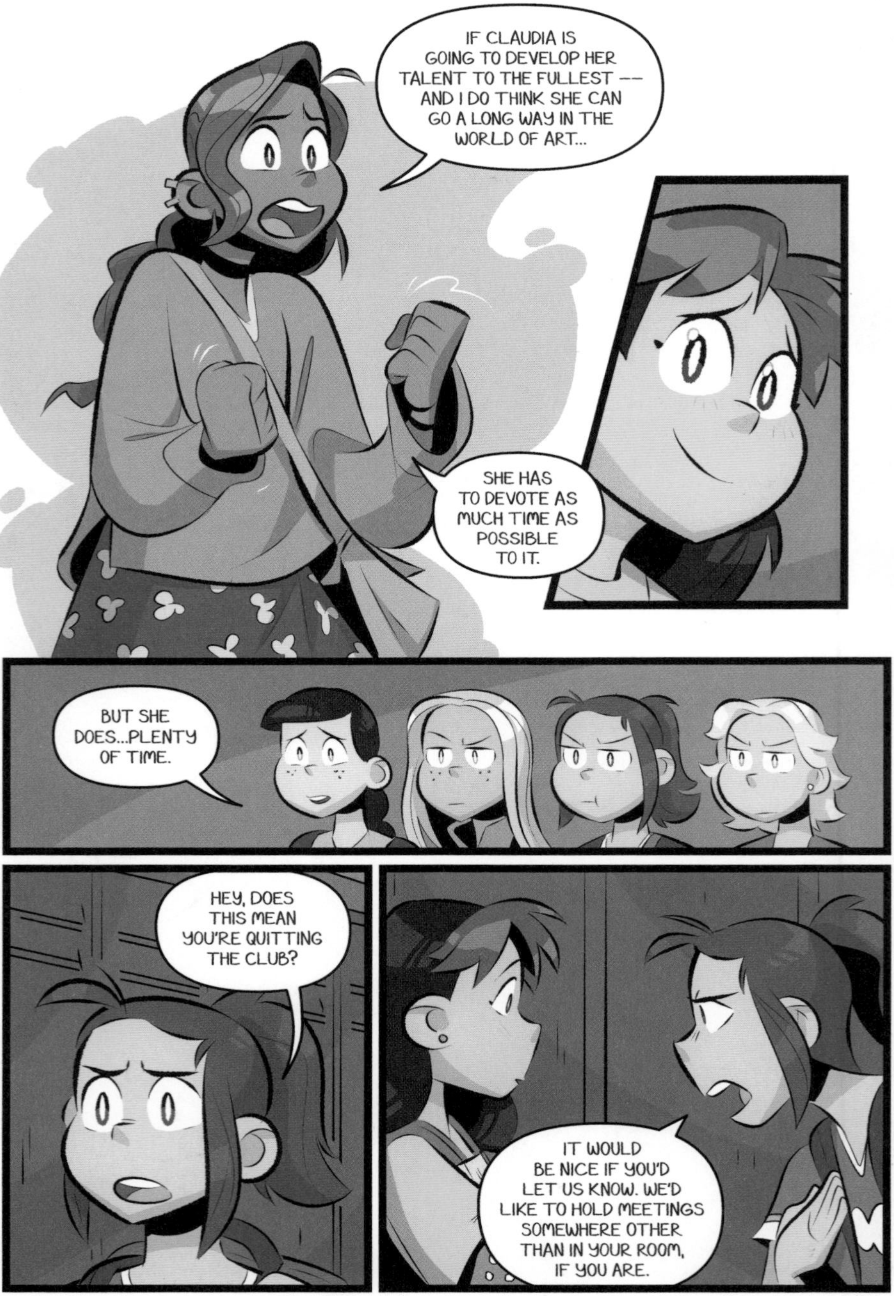

IF CLAUDIA IS GOING TO DEVELOP HER TALENT TO THE FULLEST -- AND I DO THINK SHE CAN GO A LONG WAY IN THE WORLD OF ART...
SHE HAS TO DEVOTE AS MUCH TIME AS POSSIBLE TO IT.
BUT SHE DOES...PLENTY OF TIME.
HEY, DOES THIS MEAN YOU'RE QUITTING THE CLUB?
IT WOULD BE NICE IF YOU'D LET US KNOW. WE'D LIKE TO HOLD MEETINGS SOMEWHERE OTHER THAN IN YOUR ROOM, IF YOU ARE.

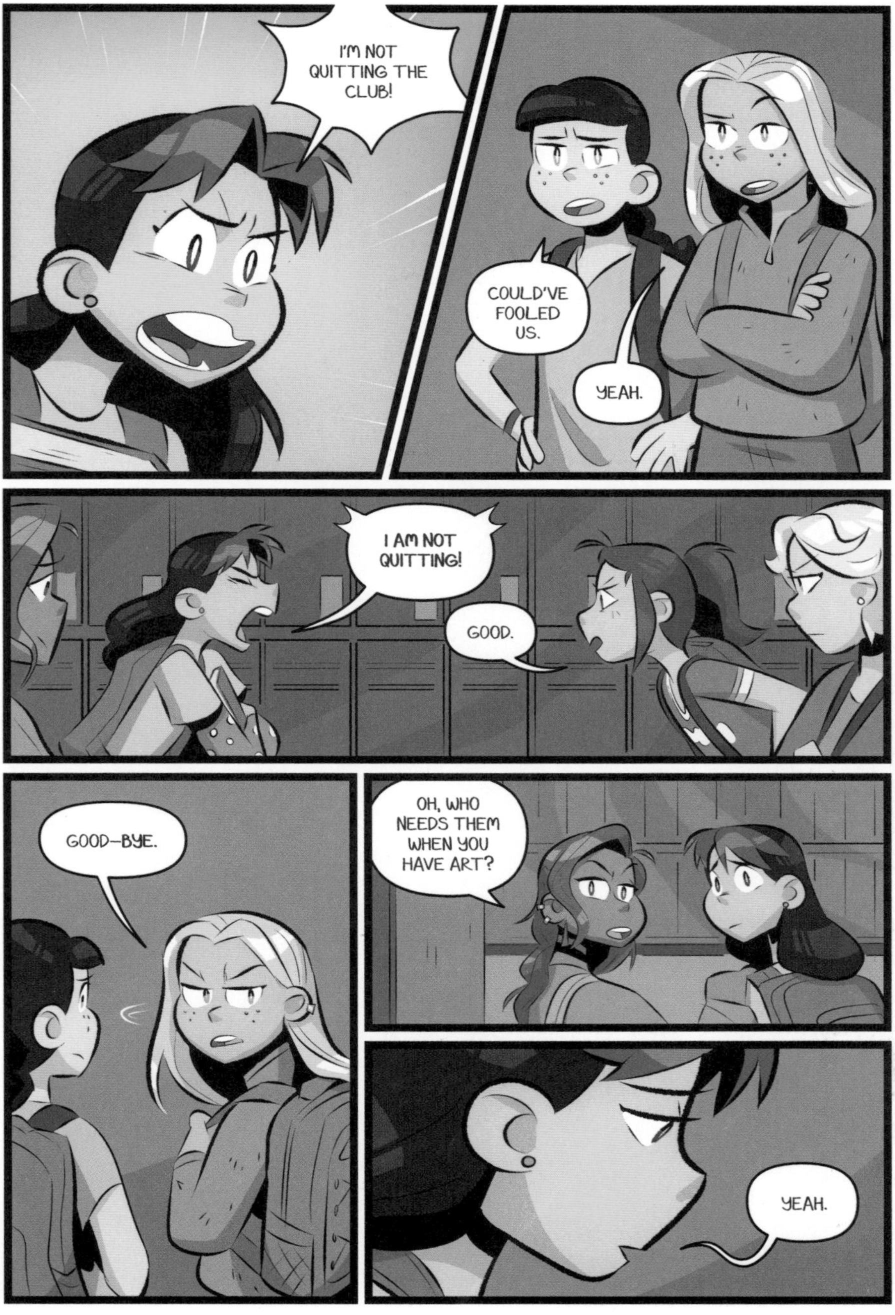
I'M NOT QUITTING THE CLUB!
COULD'VE FOOLED US.
YEAH.
I AM NOT QUITTING!
GOOD.
GOOD-BYE.
OH, WHO NEEDS THEM WHEN YOU HAVE ART?
YEAH.

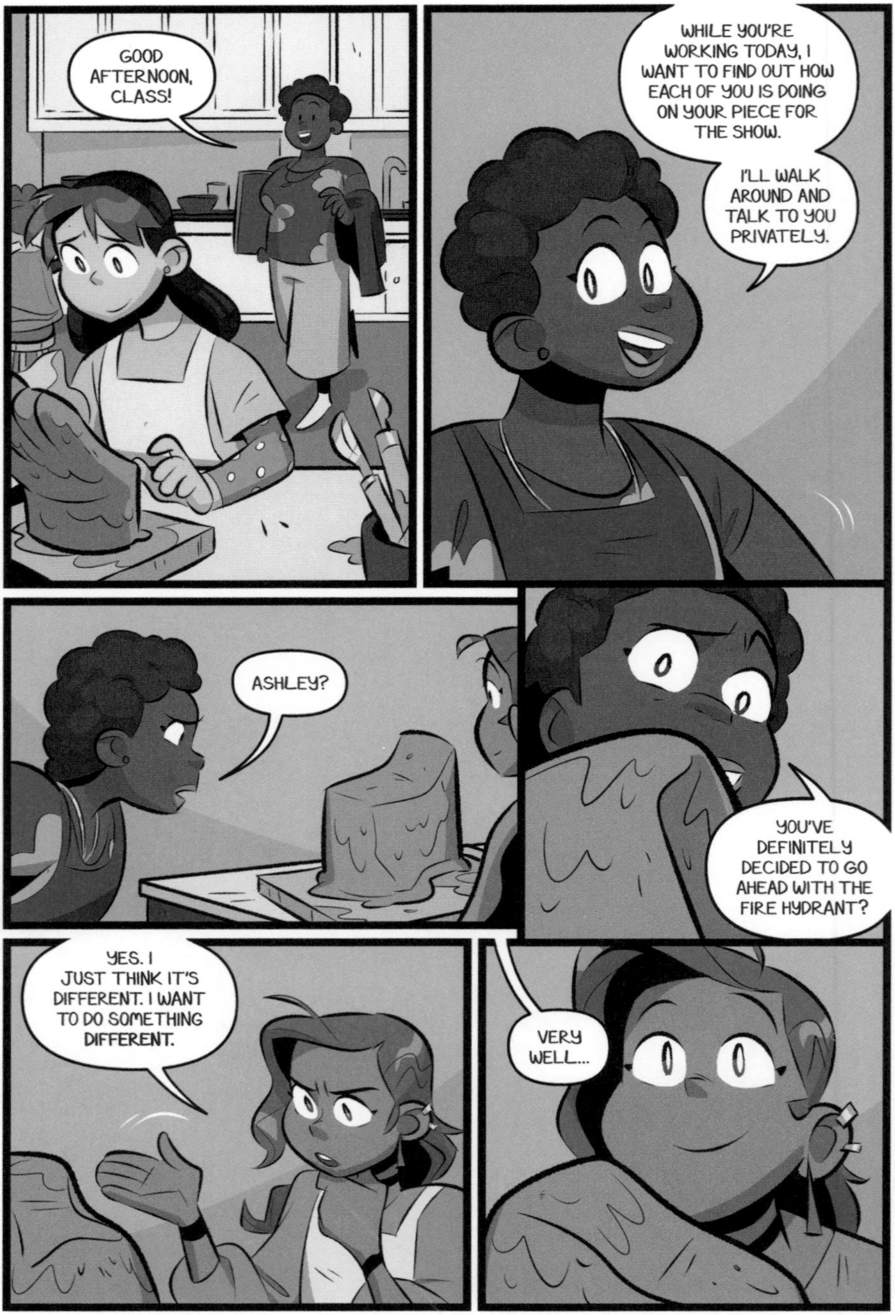
GOOD AFTERNOON, CLASS!
WHILE YOU'RE WORKING TODAY, I WANT TO FIND OUT HOW EACH OF YOU IS DOING ON YOUR PIECE FOR THE SHOW.
I'LL WALK AROUND AND TALK TO YOU PRIVATELY.
ASHLEY?
YOU'VE DEFINITELY DECIDED TO GO AHEAD WITH THE FIRE HYDRANT?
YES. I JUST THINK IT'S DIFFERENT. I WANT TO DO SOMETHING DIFFERENT.
VERY WELL...

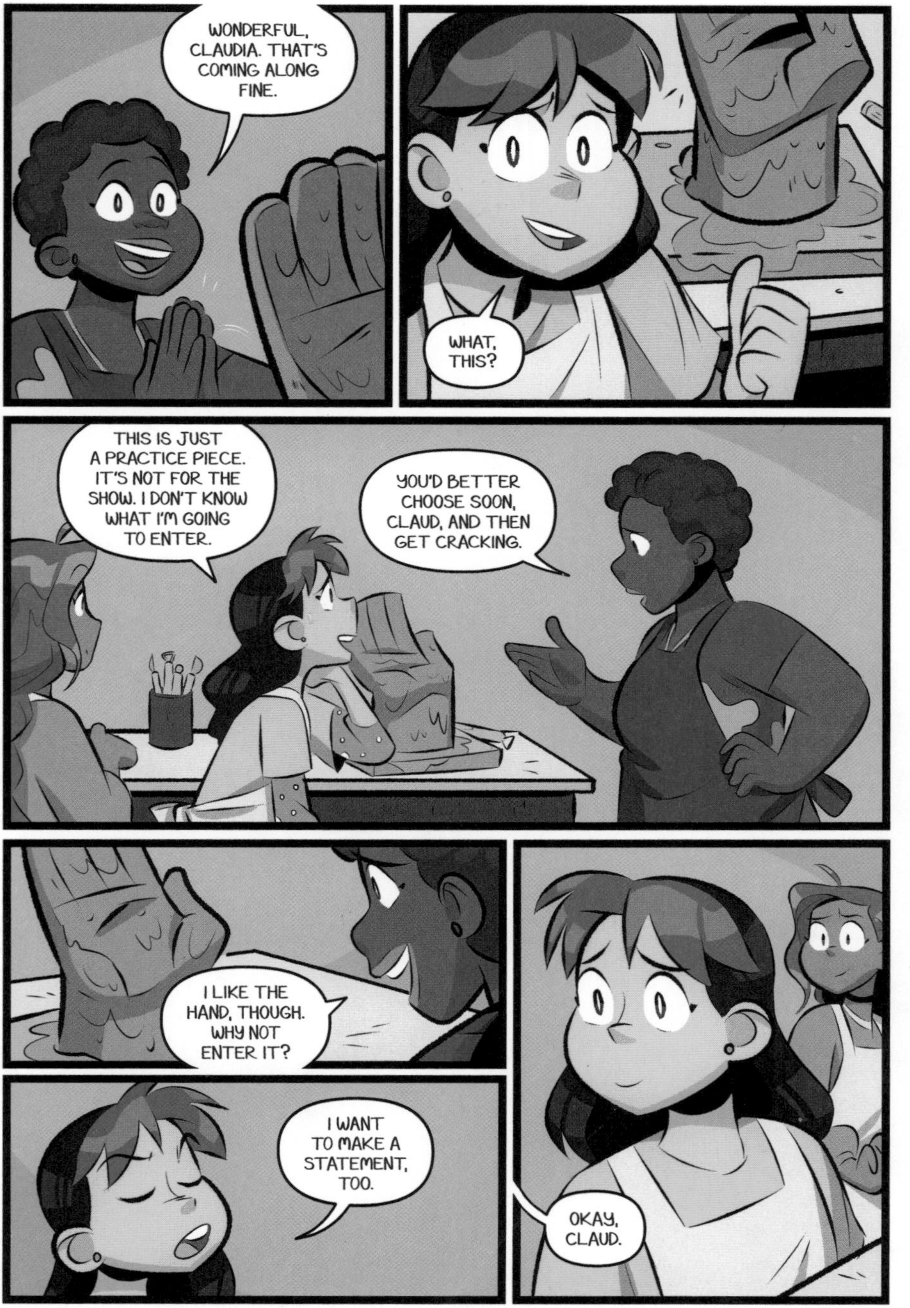
WONDERFUL, CLAUDIA. THAT'S COMING ALONG FINE.
WHAT, THIS?
THIS IS JUST A PRACTICE PIECE. IT'S NOT FOR THE SHOW. I DON'T KNOW WHAT I'M GOING TO ENTER.
YOU'D BETTER CHOOSE SOON, CLAUD, AND THEN GET CRACKING.
I LIKE THE HAND, THOUGH. WHY NOT ENTER IT?
I WANT TO MAKE A STATEMENT, TOO.
OKAY, CLAUD.

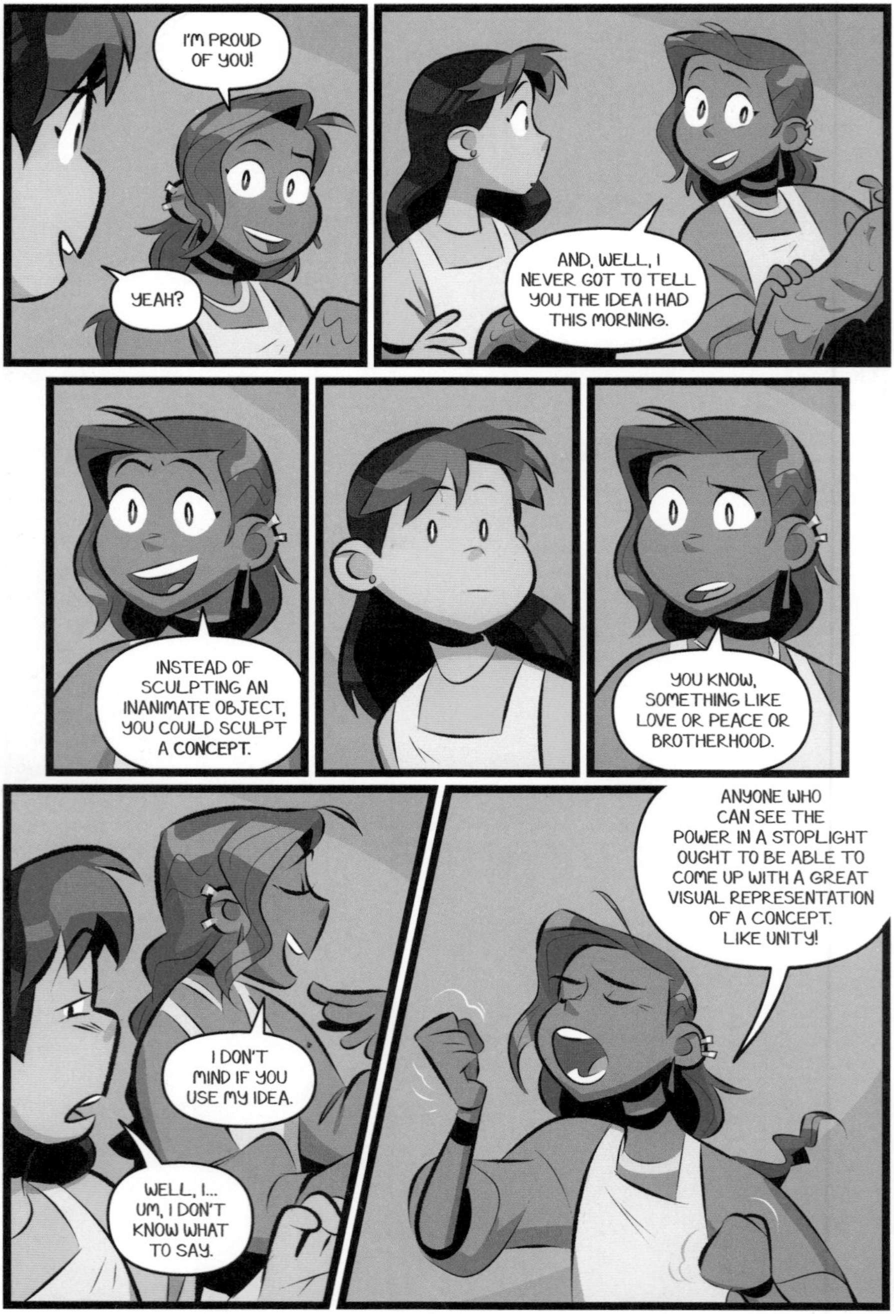
I'M PROUD OF YOU!
YEAH?
AND, WELL, I NEVER GOT TO TELL YOU THE IDEA I HAD THIS MORNING.
INSTEAD OF SCULPTING AN INANIMATE OBJECT, YOU COULD SCULPT A CONCEPT.
YOU KNOW, SOMETHING LIKE LOVE OR PEACE OR BROTHERHOOD.
I DON'T MIND IF YOU USE MY IDEA.
WELL, I... UM, I DON'T KNOW WHAT TO SAY.
ANYONE WHO CAN SEE THE POWER IN A STOPLIGHT OUGHT TO BE ABLE TO COME UP WITH A GREAT VISUAL REPRESENTATION OF A CONCEPT. LIKE UNITY!

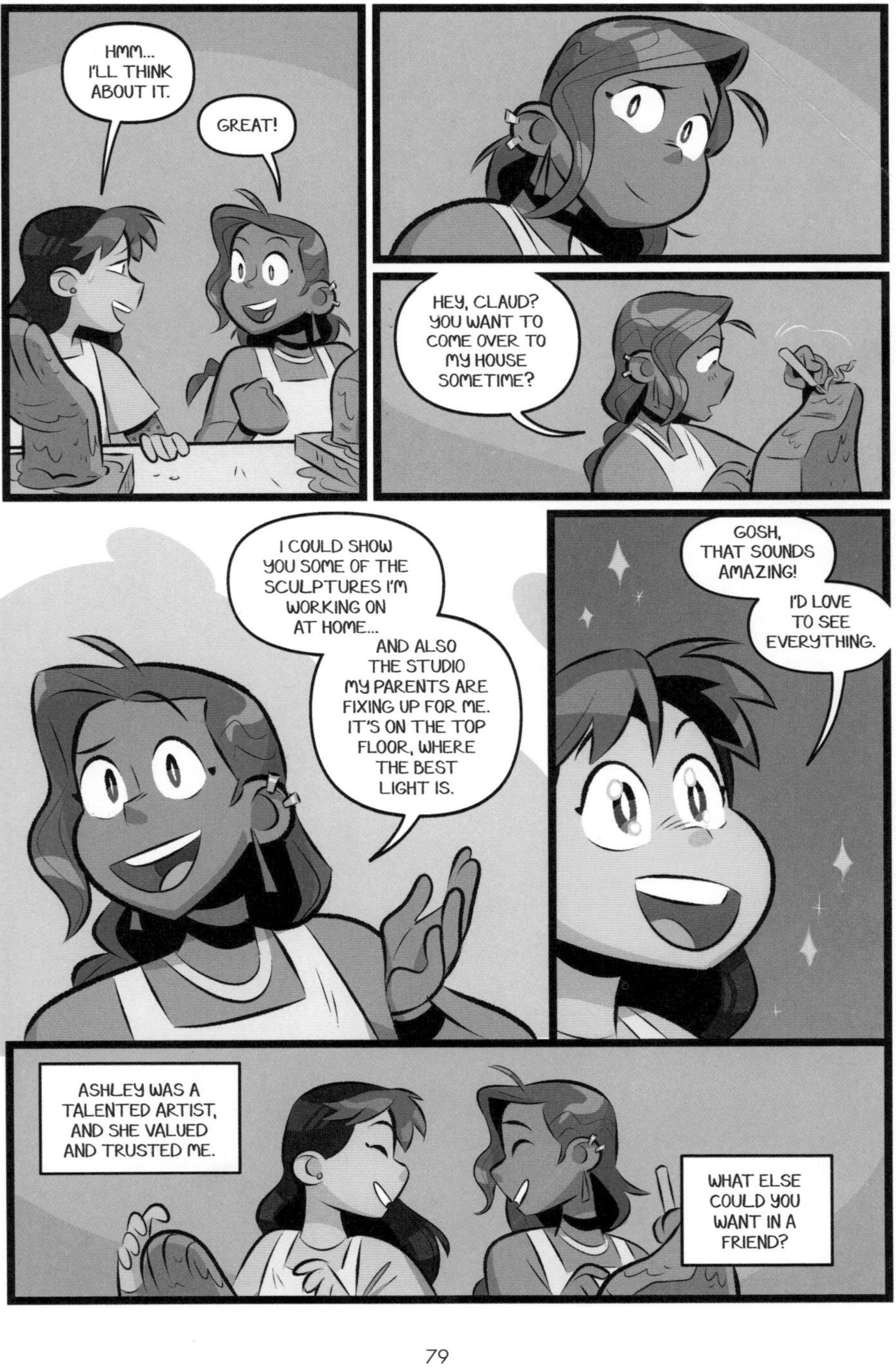
HMM...
I'LL THINK ABOUT IT.
GREAT!
HEY, CLAUD? YOU WANT TO COME OVER TO MY HOUSE SOMETIME?
I COULD SHOW YOU SOME OF THE SCULPTURES I'M WORKING ON AT HOME...
AND ALSO THE STUDIO MY PARENTS ARE FIXING UP FOR ME. IT'S ON THE TOP FLOOR, WHERE THE BEST LIGHT IS.
GOSH, THAT SOUNDS AMAZING!
I'D LOVE TO SEE EVERYTHING.
ASHLEY WAS A TALENTED ARTIST, AND SHE VALUED AND TRUSTED ME.
WHAT ELSE COULD YOU WANT IN A FRIEND?

Some people here are traitors. And you know who you are. Ordinarily, this notebook is used to record our baby-sitting jobs, but it's also for club problems, and we have a little problem right now. It's a certain person who keeps missing meetings. It's a good thing we have an alternate officer because Dawn sure has had to take over the duties of our vice president a lot lately.

BUT i DON'T MIND BEiNG ViCE PRESiDENT, YOU GUYS.

Okay, so Dawn doesn't mind, but we do mind having a VP who'd rather be an artist.

Yeah, our VP used to be very nice, but now she never shows up at meetings and she hangs around with a person who wears bell-bottom blue jeans to school.

CHAPTER 8

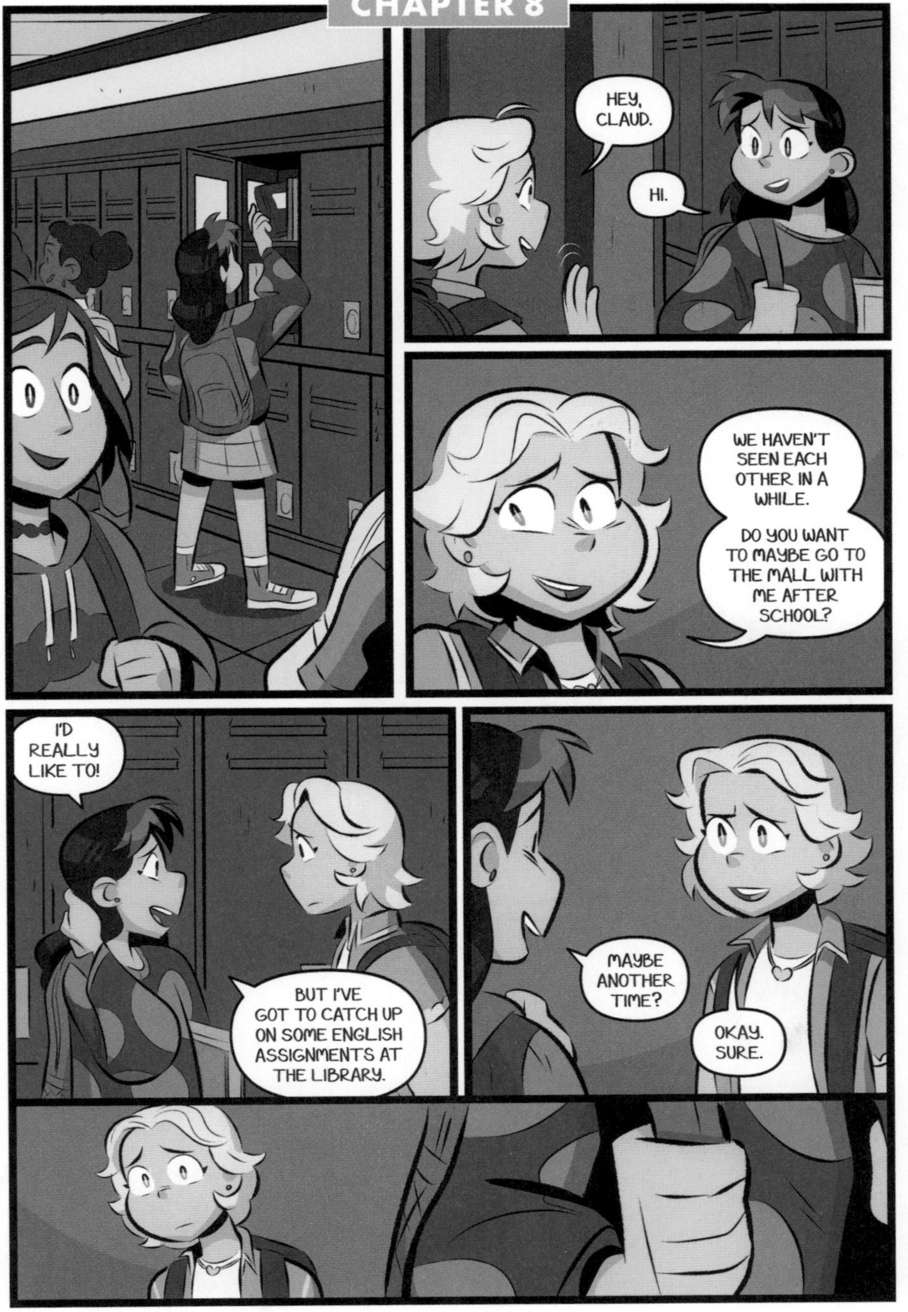
HEY, CLAUD.
HI.
WE HAVEN'T SEEN EACH OTHER IN A WHILE.
DO YOU WANT TO MAYBE GO TO THE MALL WITH ME AFTER SCHOOL?
I'D REALLY LIKE TO!
BUT I'VE GOT TO CATCH UP ON SOME ENGLISH ASSIGNMENTS AT THE LIBRARY.
MAYBE ANOTHER TIME?
OKAY. SURE.

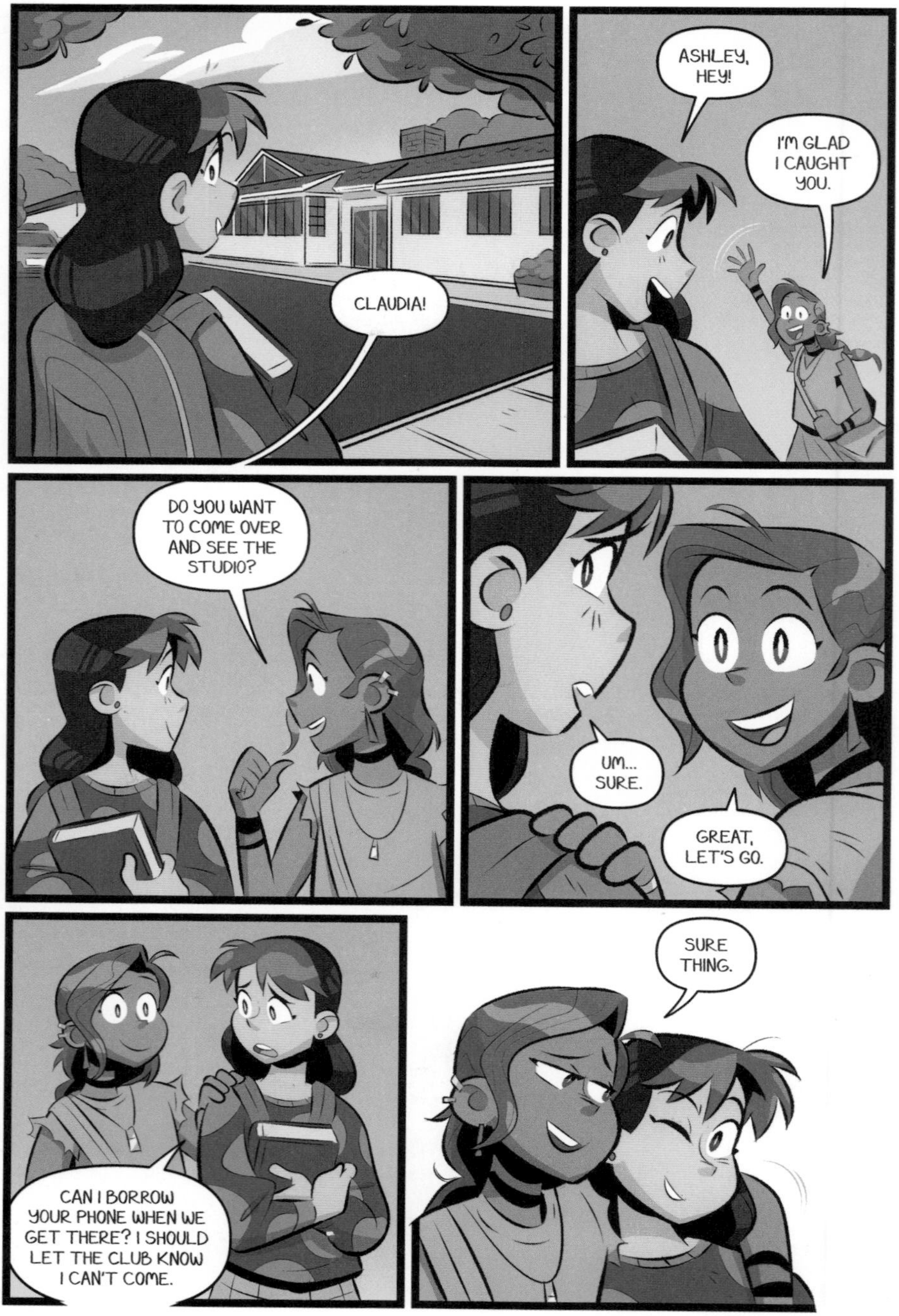
CLAUDIA!
ASHLEY, HEY!
I'M GLAD I CAUGHT YOU.
DO YOU WANT TO COME OVER AND SEE THE STUDIO?
UM... SURE.
GREAT, LET'S GO.
CAN I BORROW YOUR PHONE WHEN WE GET THERE? I SHOULD LET THE CLUB KNOW I CAN'T COME.
SURE THING.

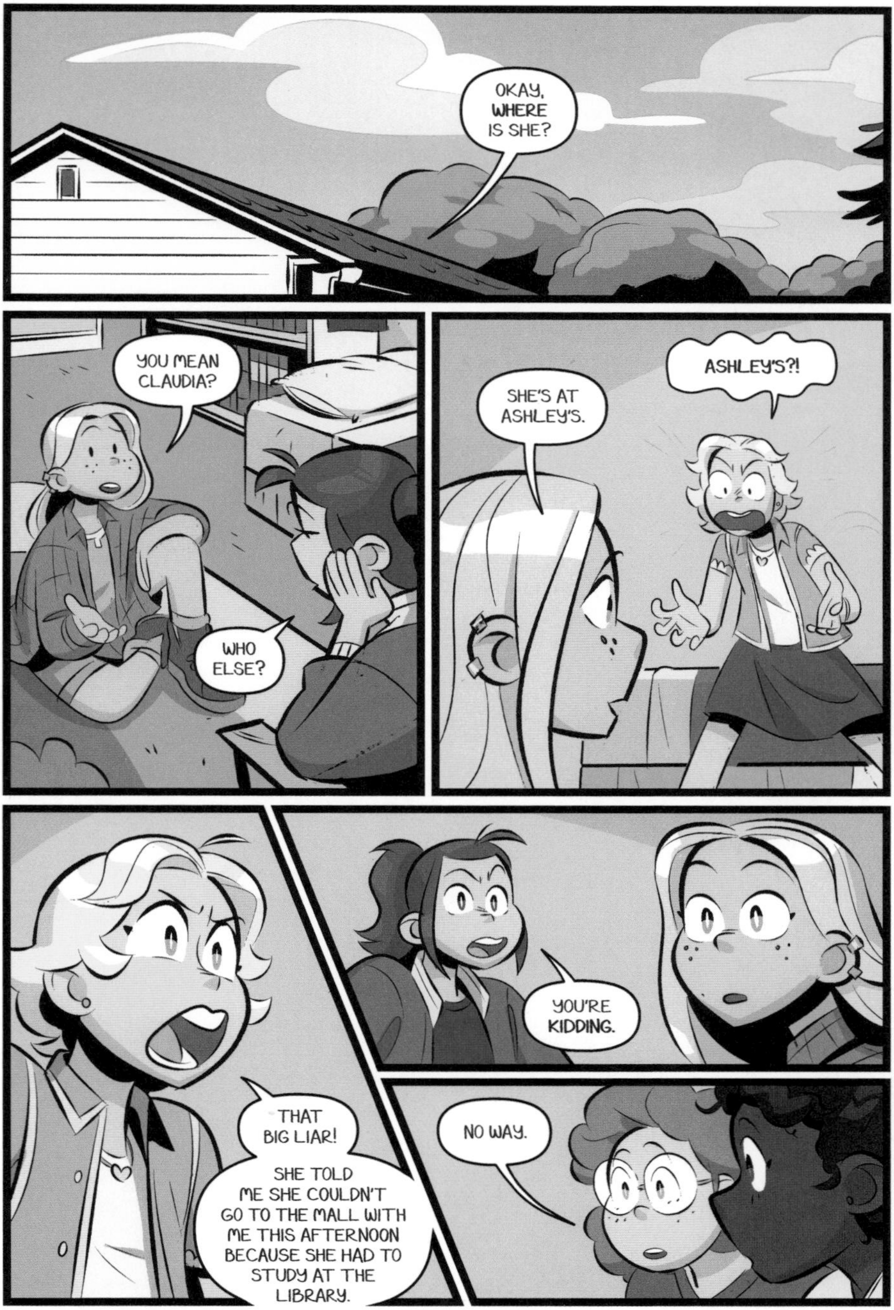
OKAY, WHERE IS SHE?
YOU MEAN CLAUDIA?
WHO ELSE?
SHE'S AT ASHLEY'S.
ASHLEY'S?!
THAT BIG LIAR!
SHE TOLD ME SHE COULDN'T GO TO THE MALL WITH ME THIS AFTERNOON BECAUSE SHE HAD TO STUDY AT THE LIBRARY.
YOU'RE KIDDING.
NO WAY.

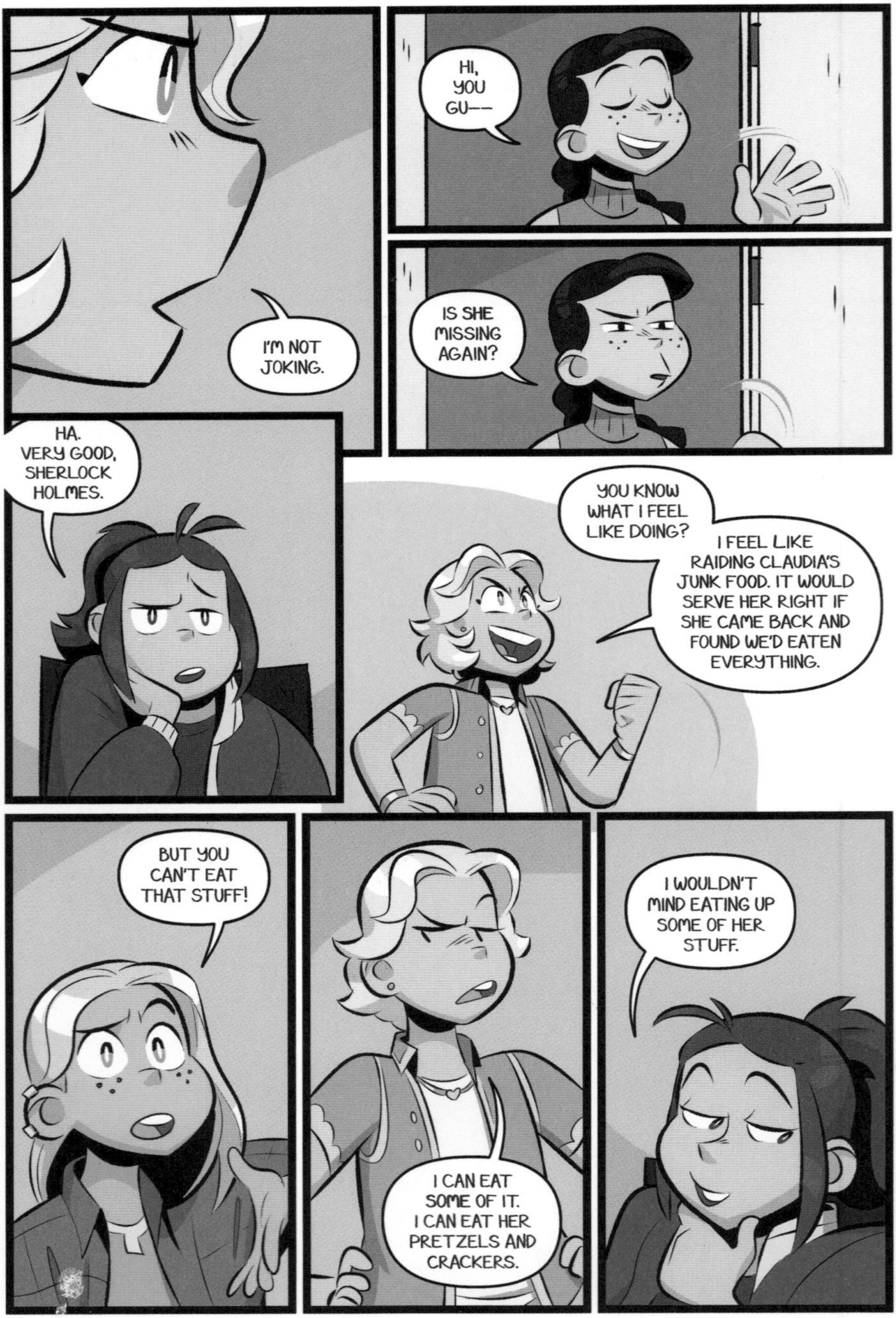
HI, YOU GU--
I'M NOT JOKING.
IS SHE MISSING AGAIN?
HA. VERY GOOD, SHERLOCK HOLMES.
YOU KNOW WHAT I FEEL LIKE DOING?
I FEEL LIKE RAIDING CLAUDIA'S JUNK FOOD. IT WOULD SERVE HER RIGHT IF SHE CAME BACK AND FOUND WE'D EATEN EVERYTHING.
BUT YOU CAN'T EAT THAT STUFF!
I CAN EAT SOME OF IT. I CAN EAT HER PRETZELS AND CRACKERS.
I WOULDN'T MIND EATING UP SOME OF HER STUFF.

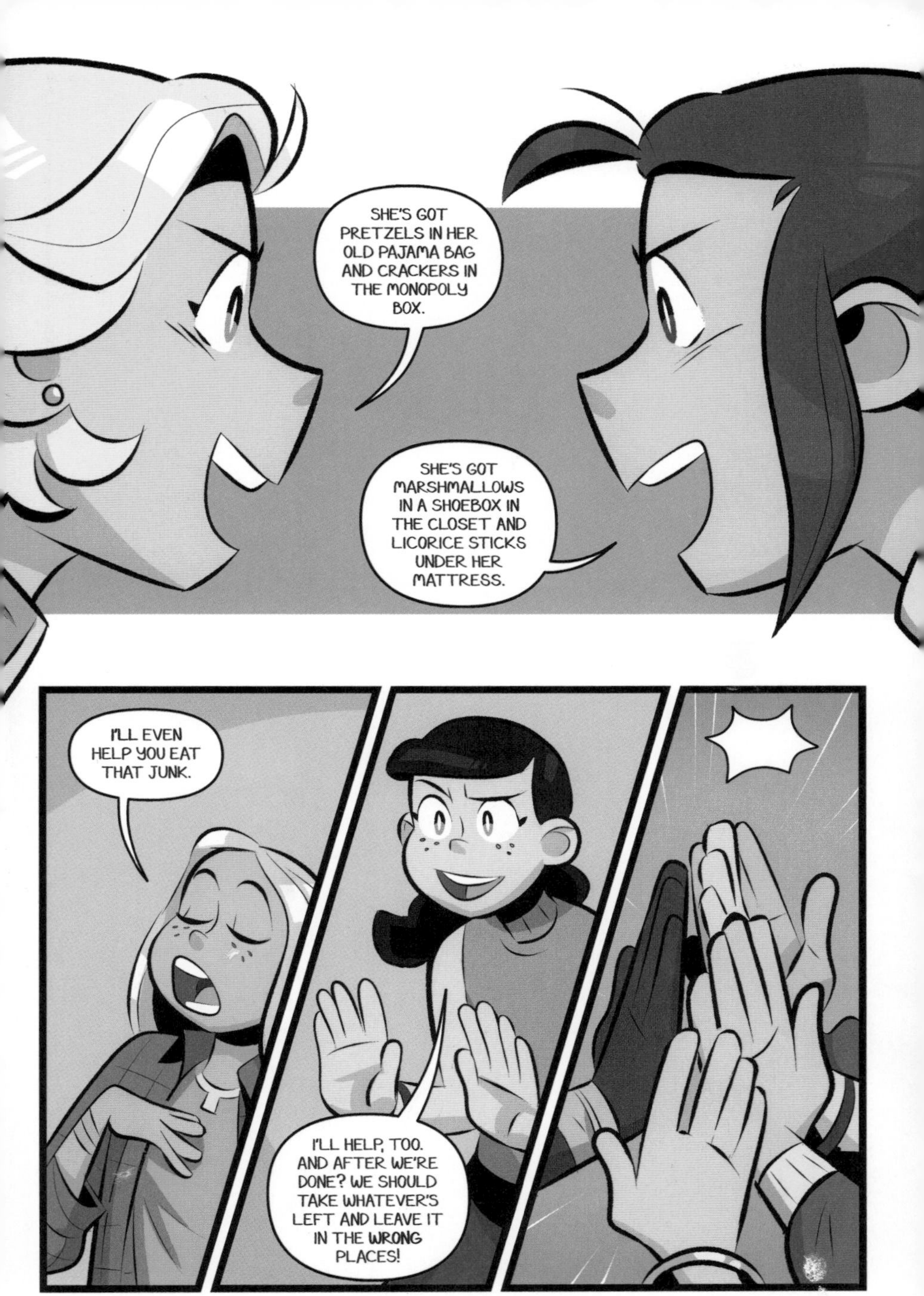
SHE'S GOT PRETZELS IN HER OLD PAJAMA BAG AND CRACKERS IN THE MONOPOLY BOX.
SHE'S GOT MARSHMALLOWS IN A SHOEBOX IN THE CLOSET AND LICORICE STICKS UNDER HER MATTRESS.
I'LL EVEN HELP YOU EAT THAT JUNK.
I'LL HELP, TOO. AND AFTER WE'RE DONE? WE SHOULD TAKE WHATEVER'S LEFT AND LEAVE IT IN THE WRONG PLACES!

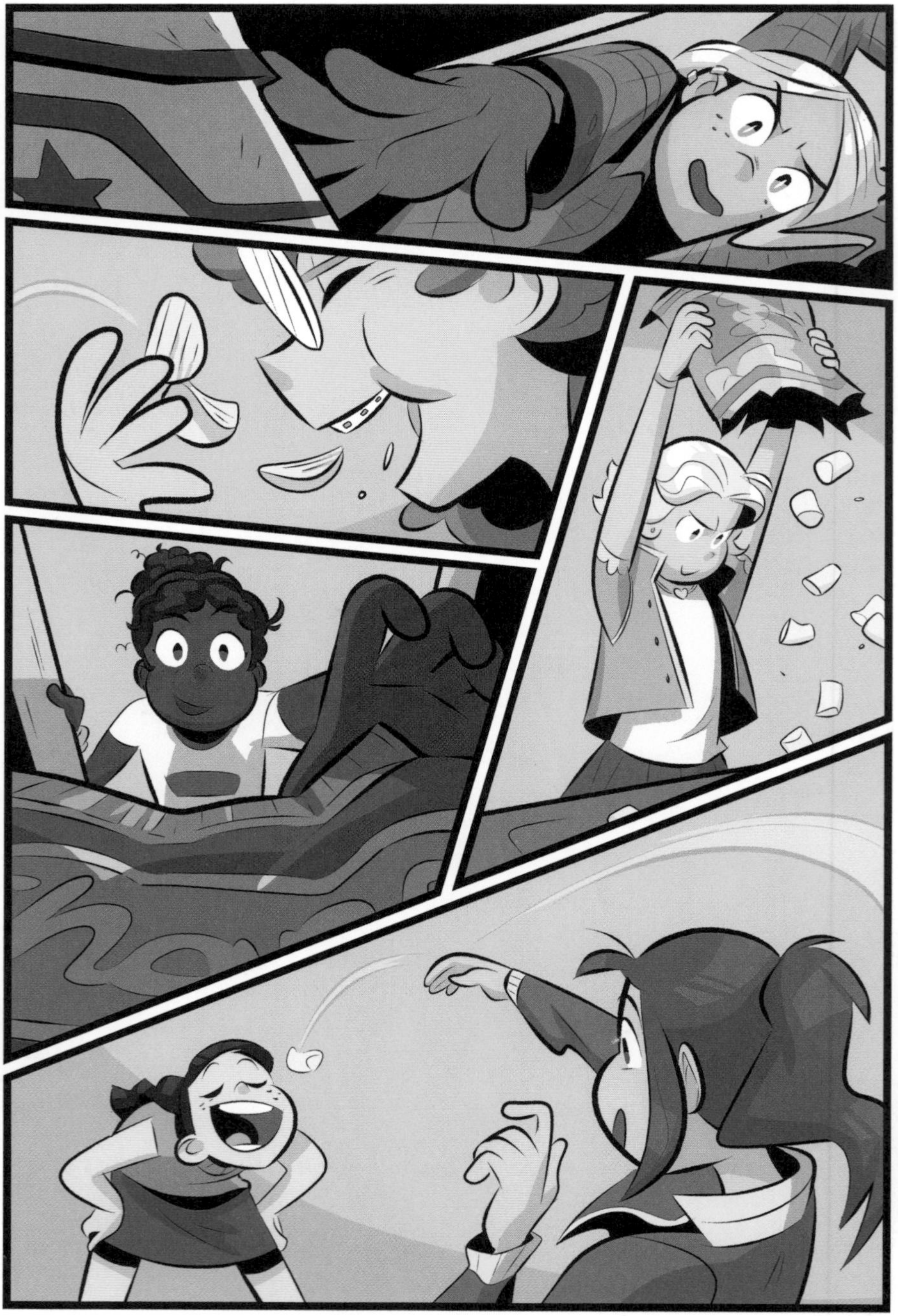

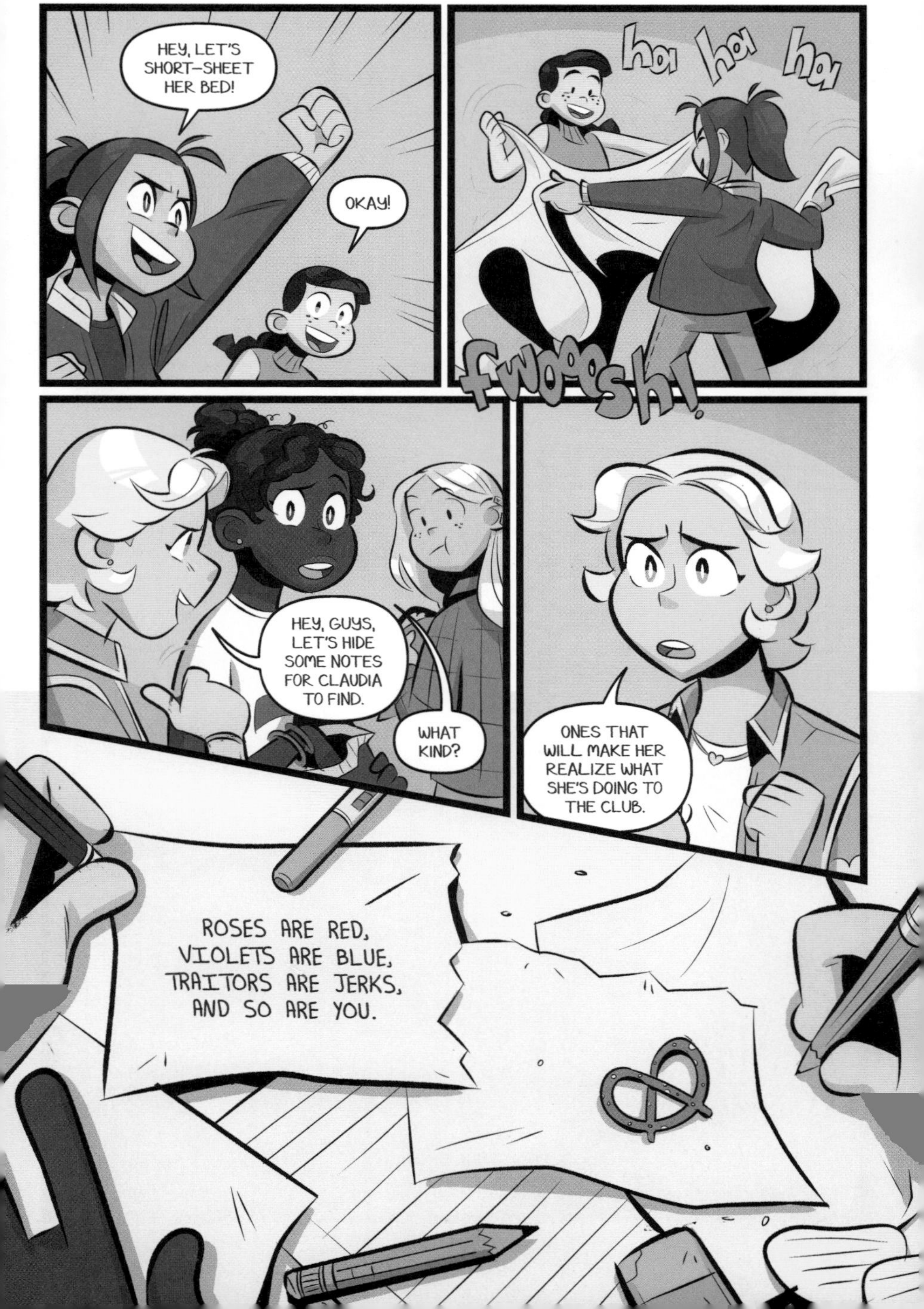
HEY, LET'S SHORT-SHEET HER BED!
OKAY!
ha ha ha
fwoosh!
HEY, GUYS, LET'S HIDE SOME NOTES FOR CLAUDIA TO FIND.
WHAT KIND?
ONES THAT WILL MAKE HER REALIZE WHAT SHE'S DOING TO THE CLUB.
ROSES ARE RED,
VIOLETS ARE BLUE,
TRAITORS ARE JERKS,
AND SO ARE YOU.

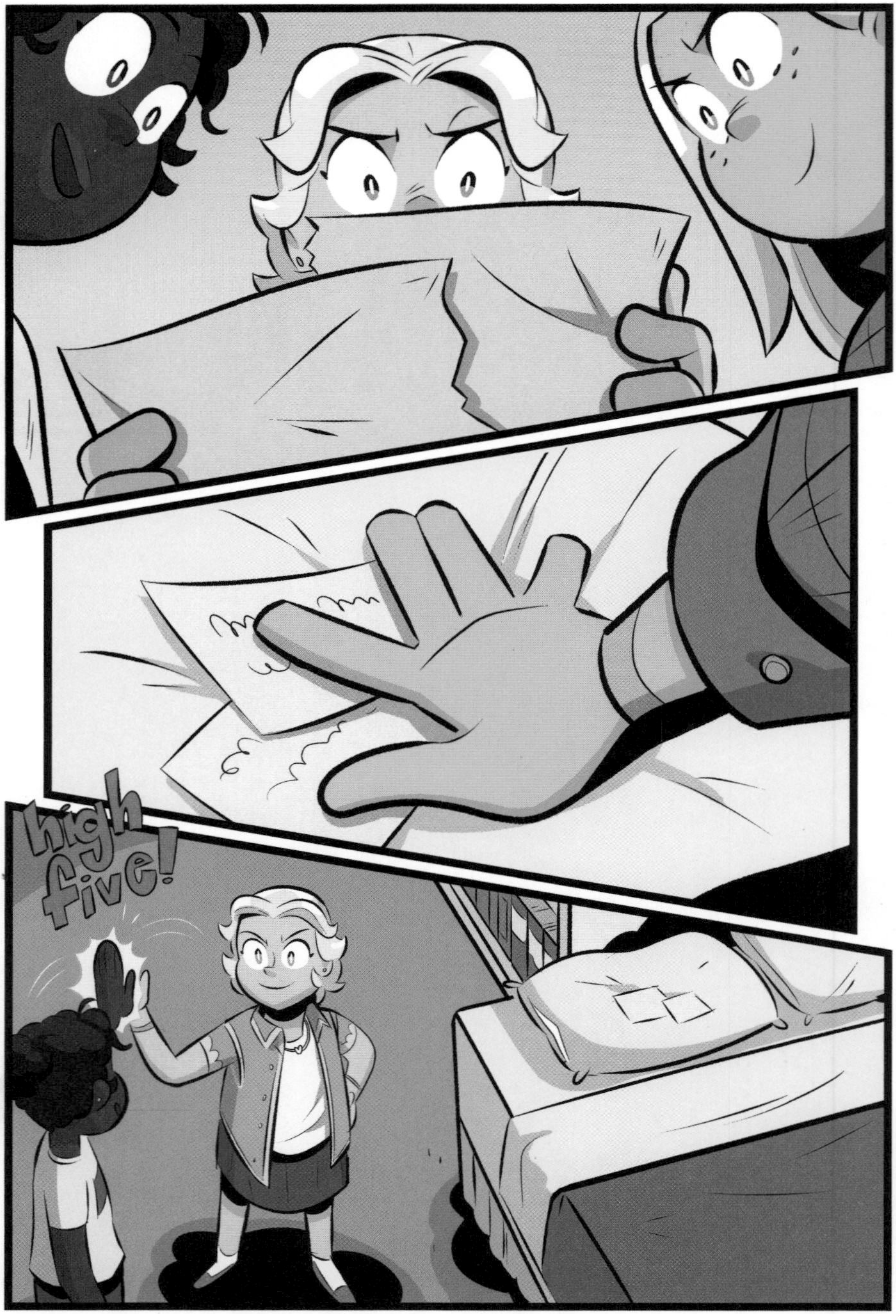
high five!

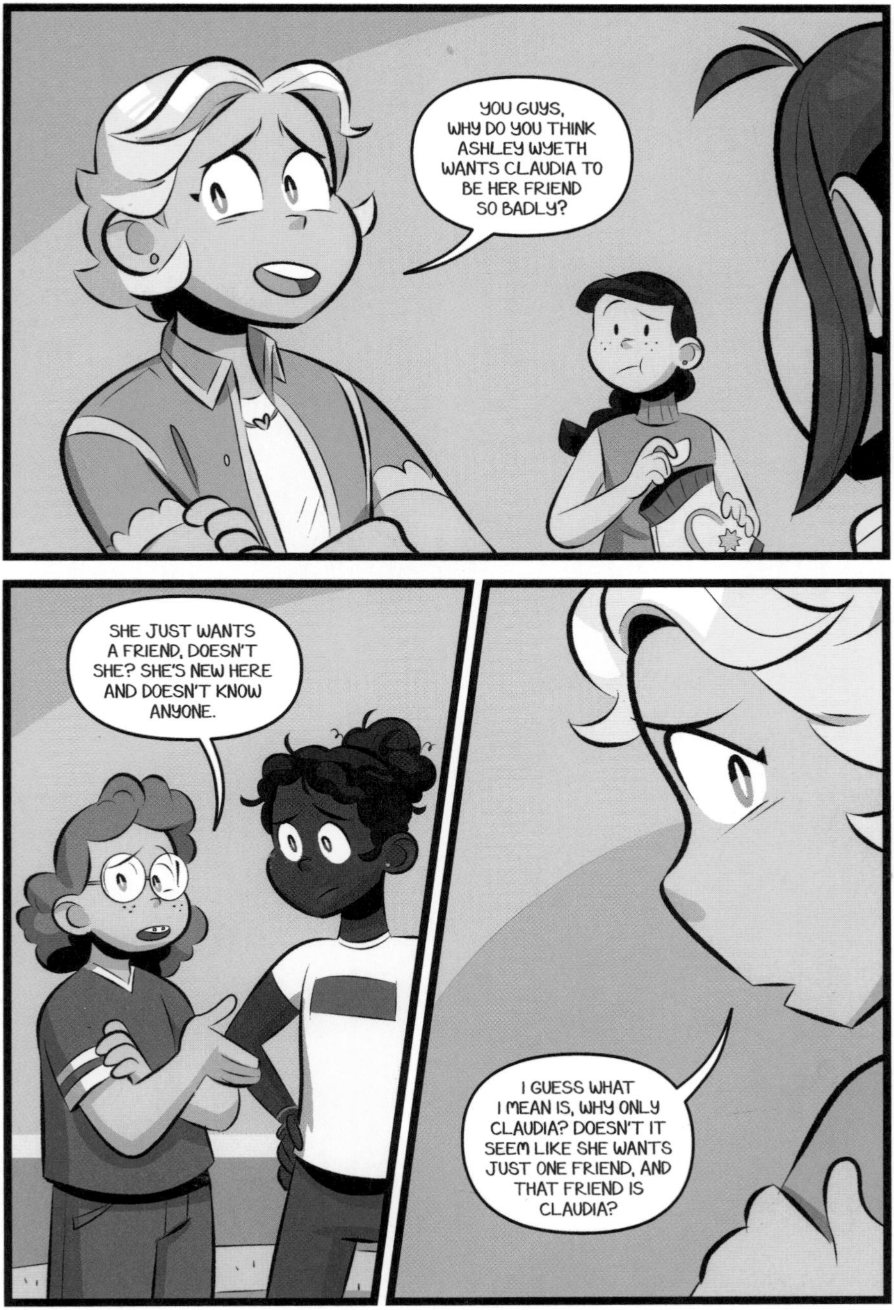
YOU GUYS, WHY DO YOU THINK ASHLEY WYETH WANTS CLAUDIA TO BE HER FRIEND SO BADLY?
SHE JUST WANTS A FRIEND, DOESN'T SHE? SHE'S NEW HERE AND DOESN'T KNOW ANYONE.
I GUESS WHAT I MEAN IS, WHY ONLY CLAUDIA? DOESN'T IT SEEM LIKE SHE WANTS JUST ONE FRIEND, AND THAT FRIEND IS CLAUDIA?

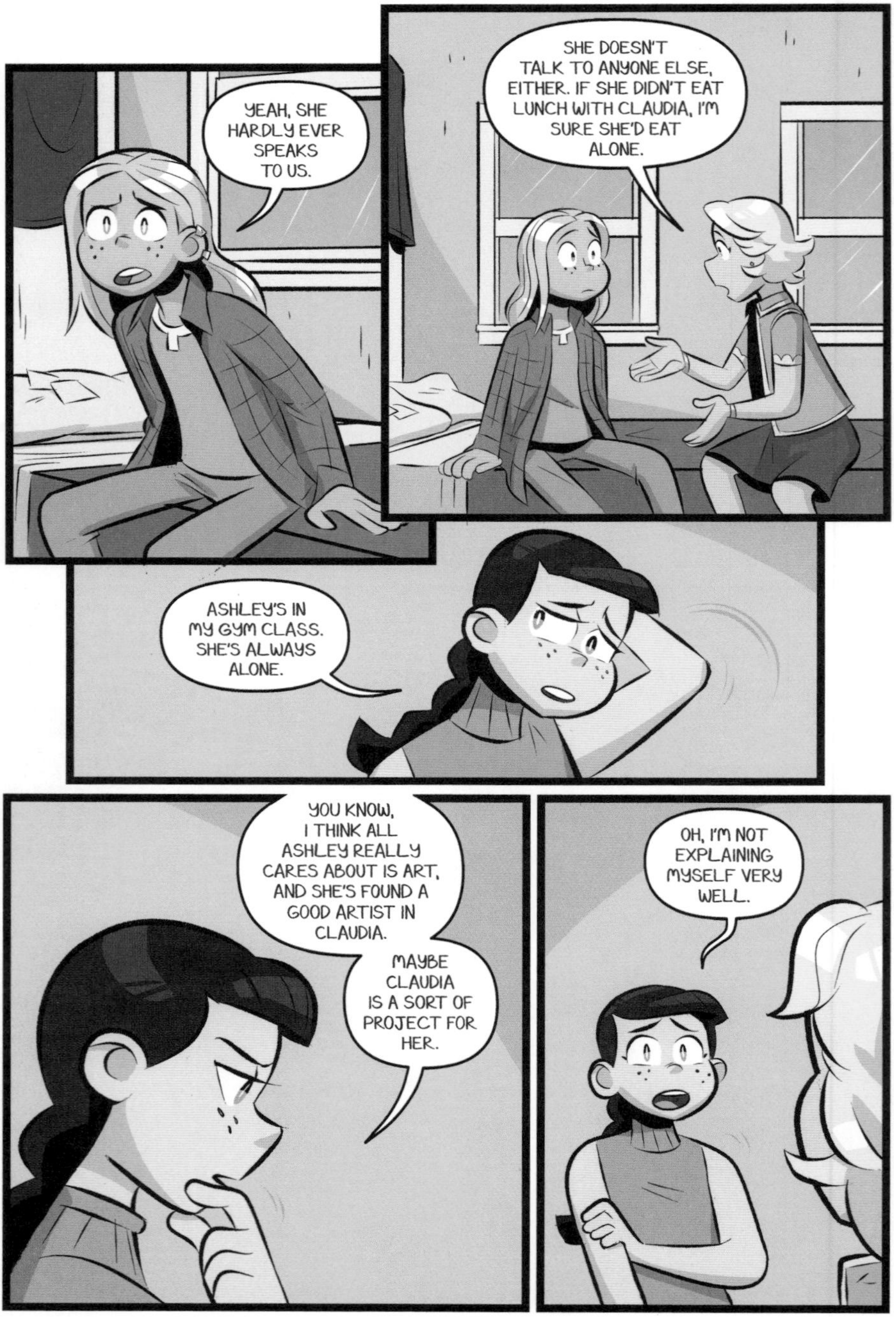
YEAH, SHE HARDLY EVER SPEAKS TO US.
SHE DOESN'T TALK TO ANYONE ELSE, EITHER. IF SHE DIDN'T EAT LUNCH WITH CLAUDIA, I'M SURE SHE'D EAT ALONE.
ASHLEY'S IN MY GYM CLASS. SHE'S ALWAYS ALONE.
YOU KNOW, I THINK ALL ASHLEY REALLY CARES ABOUT IS ART, AND SHE'S FOUND A GOOD ARTIST IN CLAUDIA.
MAYBE CLAUDIA IS A SORT OF PROJECT FOR HER.
OH, I'M NOT EXPLAINING MYSELF VERY WELL.

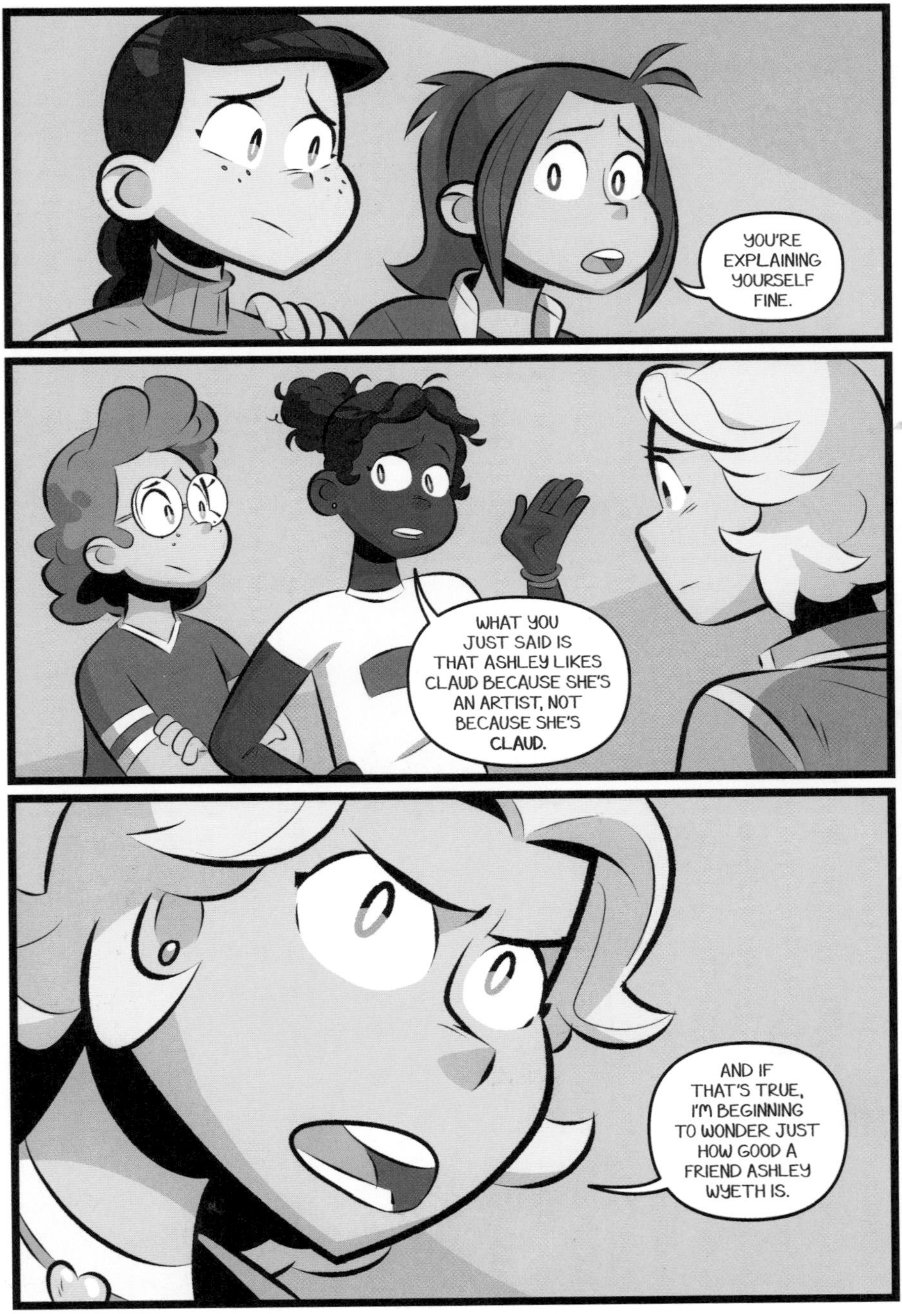
YOU'RE EXPLAINING YOURSELF FINE.
WHAT YOU JUST SAID IS THAT ASHLEY LIKES CLAUD BECAUSE SHE'S AN ARTIST, NOT BECAUSE SHE'S **CLAUD.**
AND IF THAT'S TRUE, I'M BEGINNING TO WONDER JUST HOW GOOD A FRIEND ASHLEY WYETH IS.

CHAPTER 9

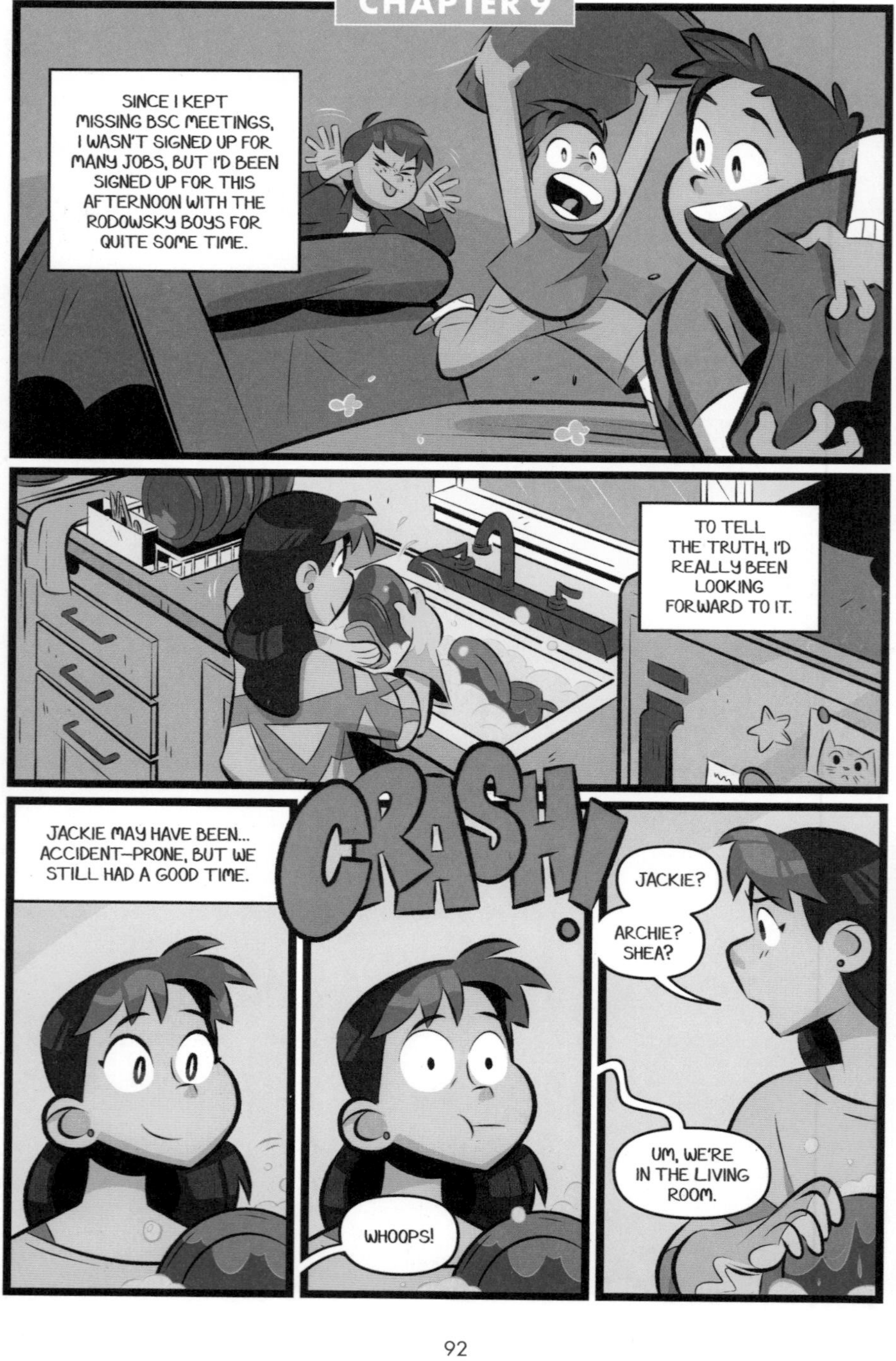

SINCE I KEPT MISSING BSC MEETINGS, I WASN'T SIGNED UP FOR MANY JOBS, BUT I'D BEEN SIGNED UP FOR THIS AFTERNOON WITH THE RODOWSKY BOYS FOR QUITE SOME TIME.
TO TELL THE TRUTH, I'D REALLY BEEN LOOKING FORWARD TO IT.
JACKIE MAY HAVE BEEN... ACCIDENT-PRONE, BUT WE STILL HAD A GOOD TIME.
CRASH!
WHOOPS!
JACKIE?
ARCHIE? SHEA?
UM, WE'RE IN THE LIVING ROOM.

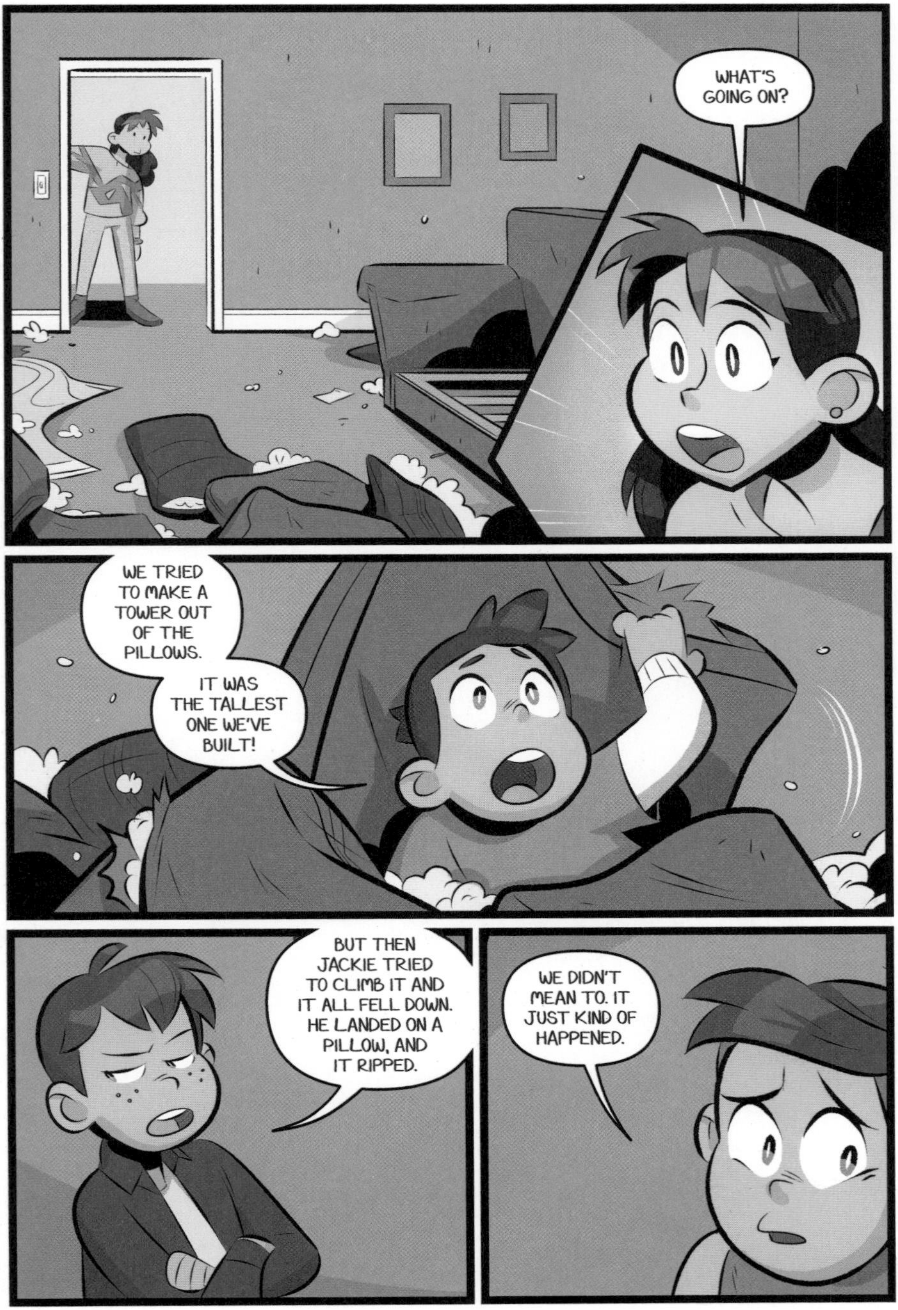
WHAT'S GOING ON?
WE TRIED TO MAKE A TOWER OUT OF THE PILLOWS.
IT WAS THE TALLEST ONE WE'VE BUILT!
BUT THEN JACKIE TRIED TO CLIMB IT AND IT ALL FELL DOWN. HE LANDED ON A PILLOW, AND IT RIPPED.
WE DIDN'T MEAN TO. IT JUST KIND OF HAPPENED.

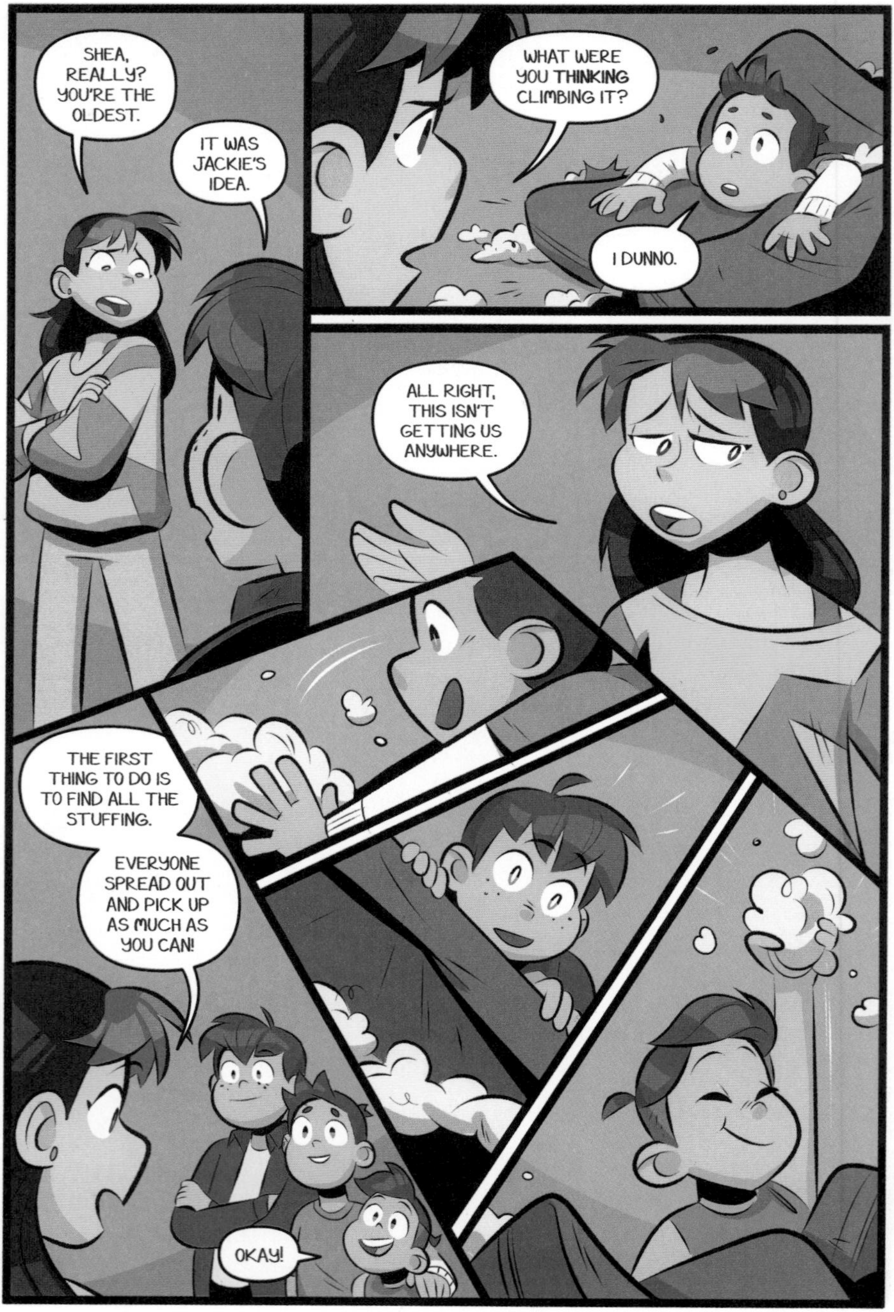
SHEA, REALLY? YOU'RE THE OLDEST.
IT WAS JACKIE'S IDEA.
WHAT WERE YOU THINKING CLIMBING IT?
I DUNNO.
ALL RIGHT, THIS ISN'T GETTING US ANYWHERE.
THE FIRST THING TO DO IS TO FIND ALL THE STUFFING.
EVERYONE SPREAD OUT AND PICK UP AS MUCH AS YOU CAN!
OKAY!

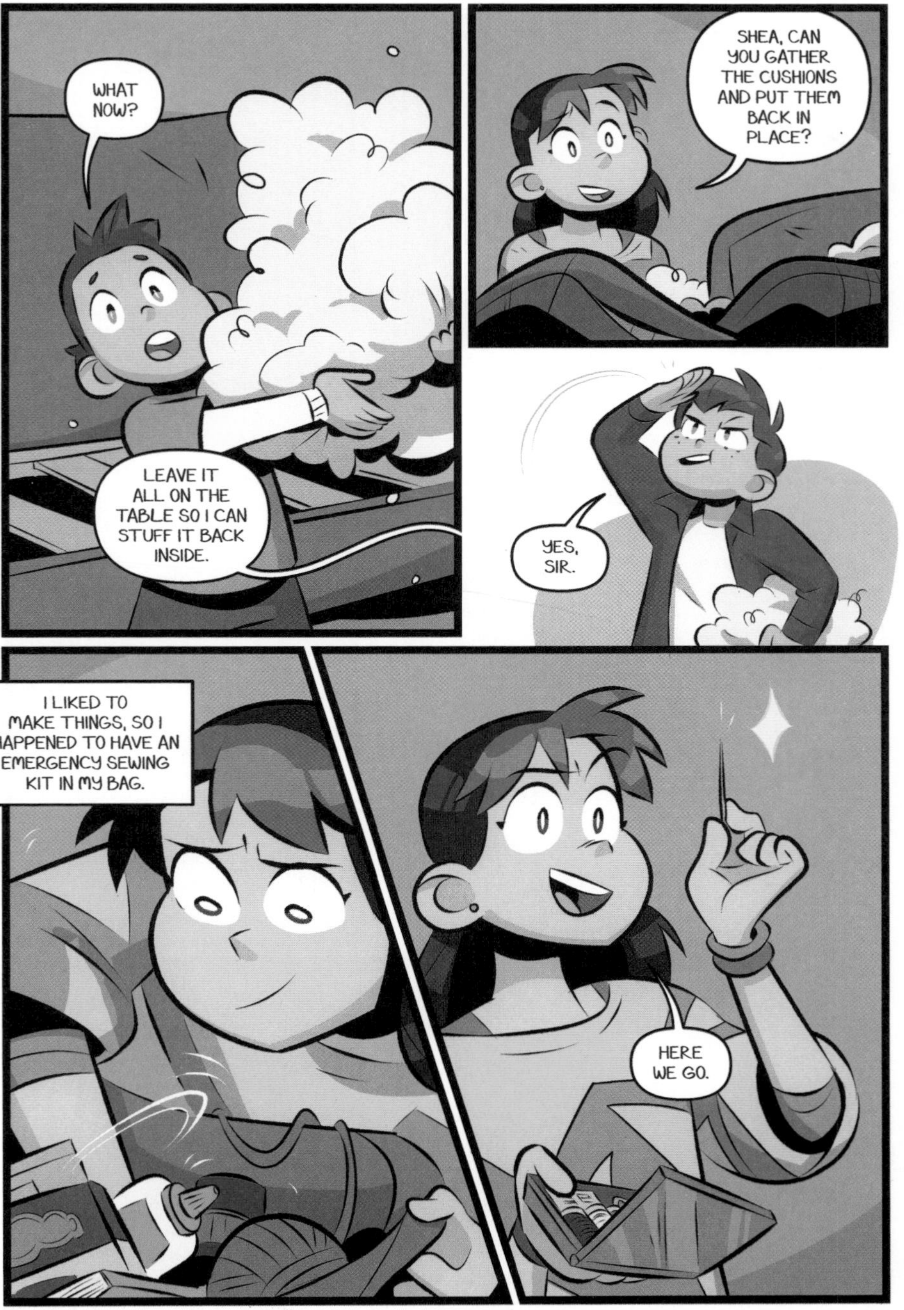
WHAT NOW?
LEAVE IT ALL ON THE TABLE SO I CAN STUFF IT BACK INSIDE.
SHEA, CAN YOU GATHER THE CUSHIONS AND PUT THEM BACK IN PLACE?
YES, SIR.
I LIKED TO MAKE THINGS, SO I HAPPENED TO HAVE AN EMERGENCY SEWING KIT IN MY BAG.
HERE WE GO.

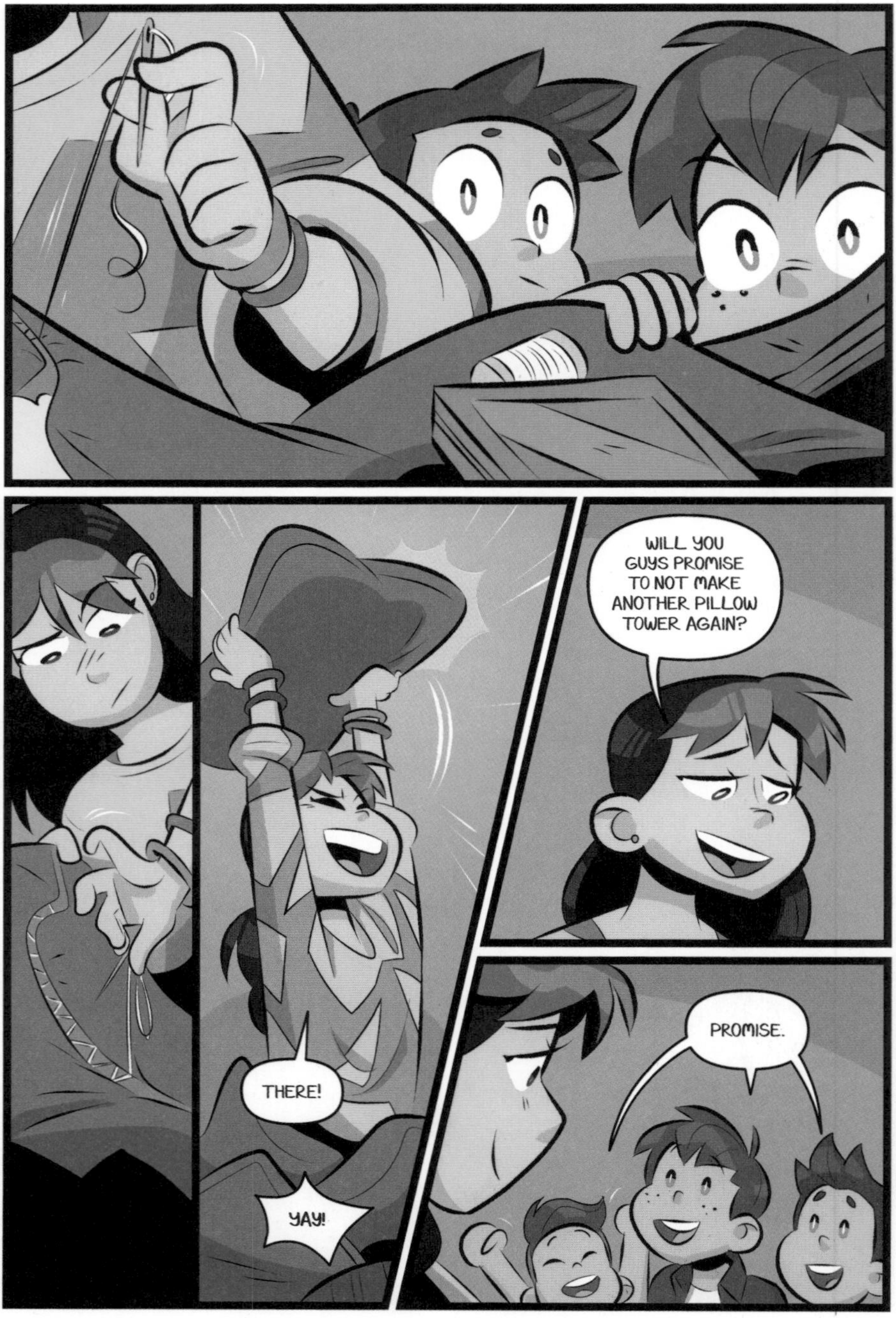
THERE!
YAY!
WILL YOU GUYS PROMISE TO NOT MAKE ANOTHER PILLOW TOWER AGAIN?
PROMISE.

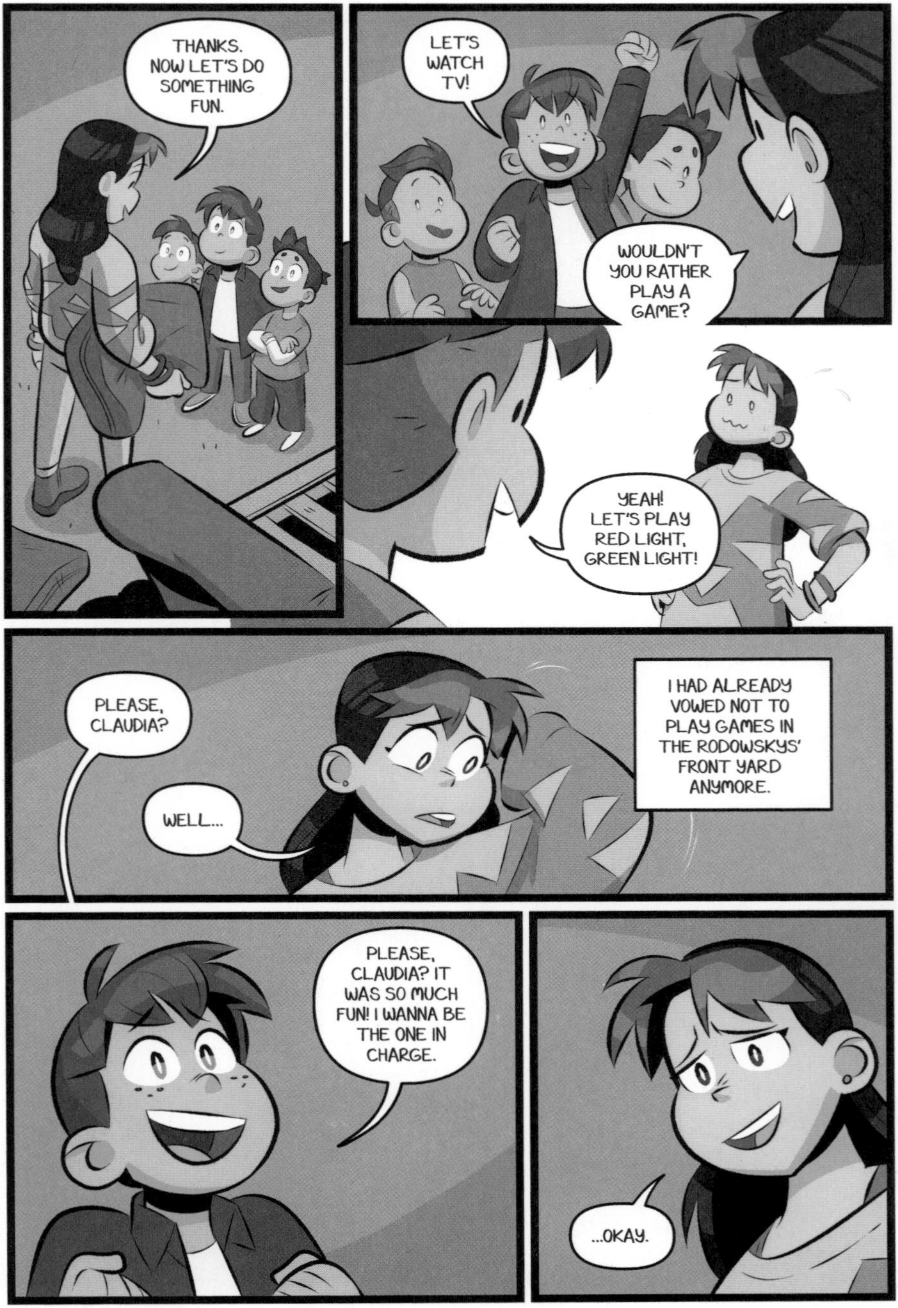
THANKS. NOW LET'S DO SOMETHING FUN.
LET'S WATCH TV!
WOULDN'T YOU RATHER PLAY A GAME?
YEAH! LET'S PLAY RED LIGHT, GREEN LIGHT!
PLEASE, CLAUDIA?
WELL...
I HAD ALREADY VOWED NOT TO PLAY GAMES IN THE RODOWSKYS' FRONT YARD ANYMORE.
PLEASE, CLAUDIA? IT WAS SO MUCH FUN! I WANNA BE THE ONE IN CHARGE.
...OKAY.

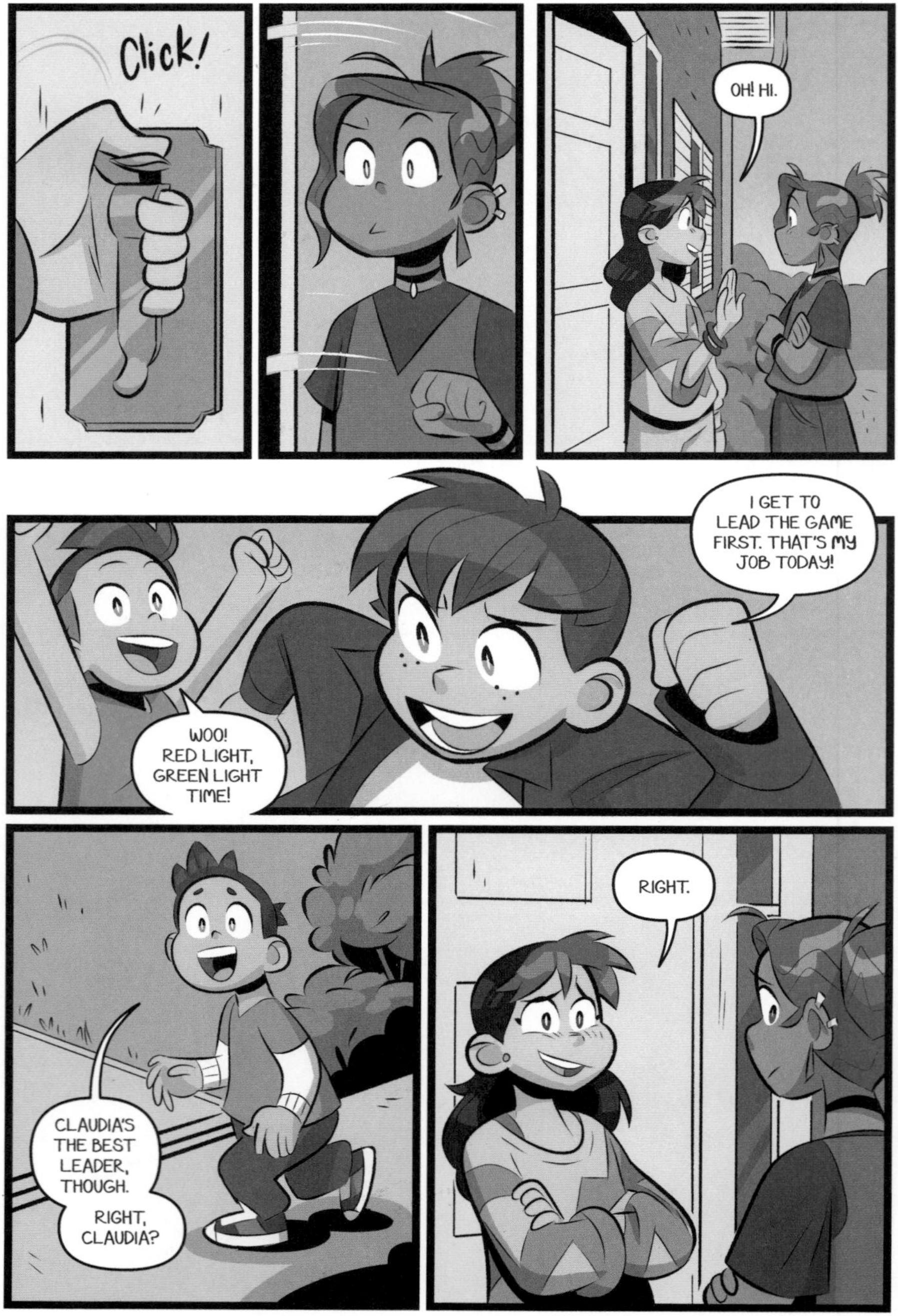
Click!
OH! HI.
I GET TO LEAD THE GAME FIRST. THAT'S MY JOB TODAY!
WOO! RED LIGHT, GREEN LIGHT TIME!
CLAUDIA'S THE BEST LEADER, THOUGH.
RIGHT, CLAUDIA?
RIGHT.

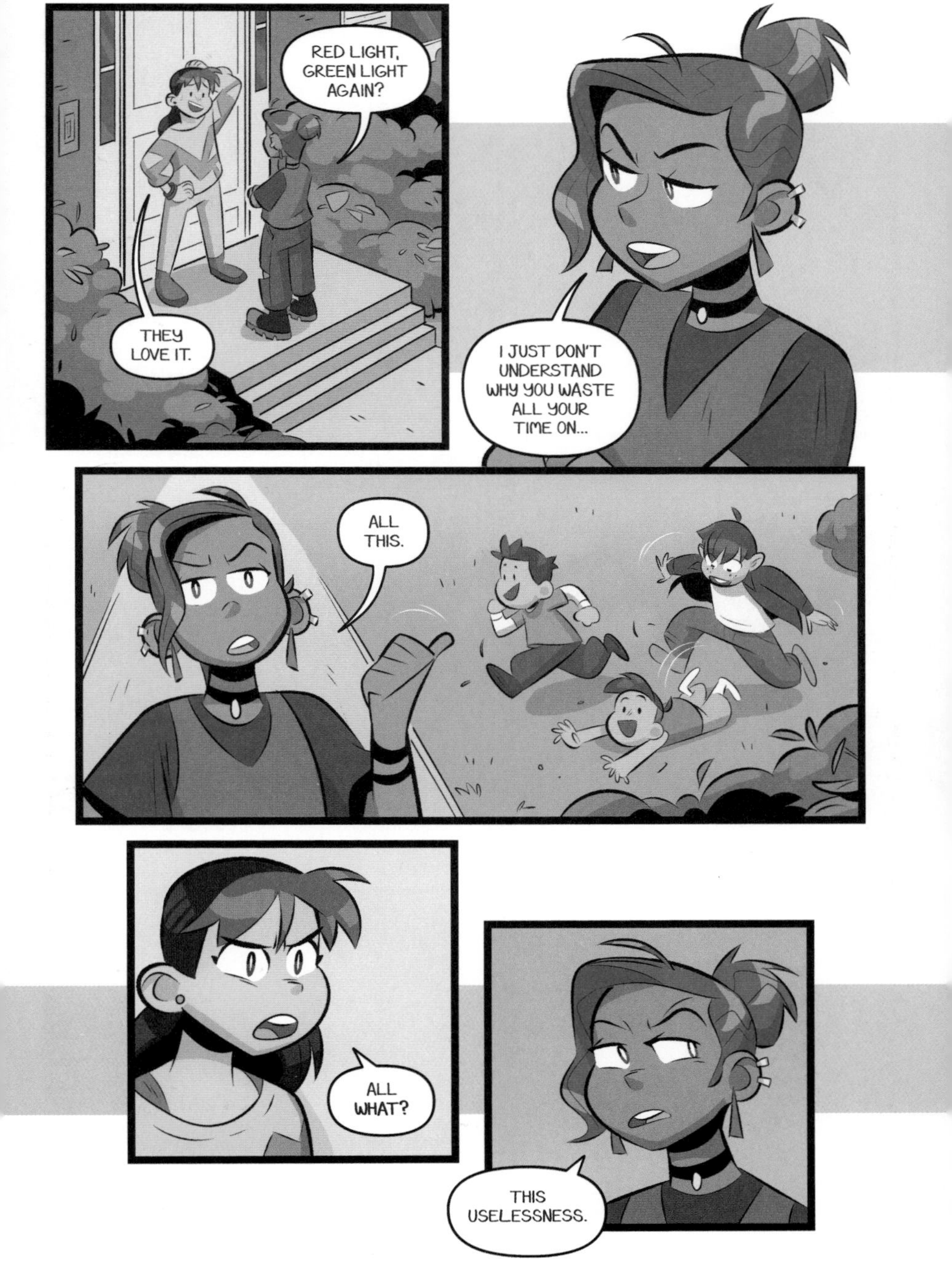
RED LIGHT, GREEN LIGHT AGAIN?
THEY LOVE IT.
I JUST DON'T UNDERSTAND WHY YOU WASTE ALL YOUR TIME ON...
ALL THIS.
ALL WHAT?
THIS USELESSNESS.

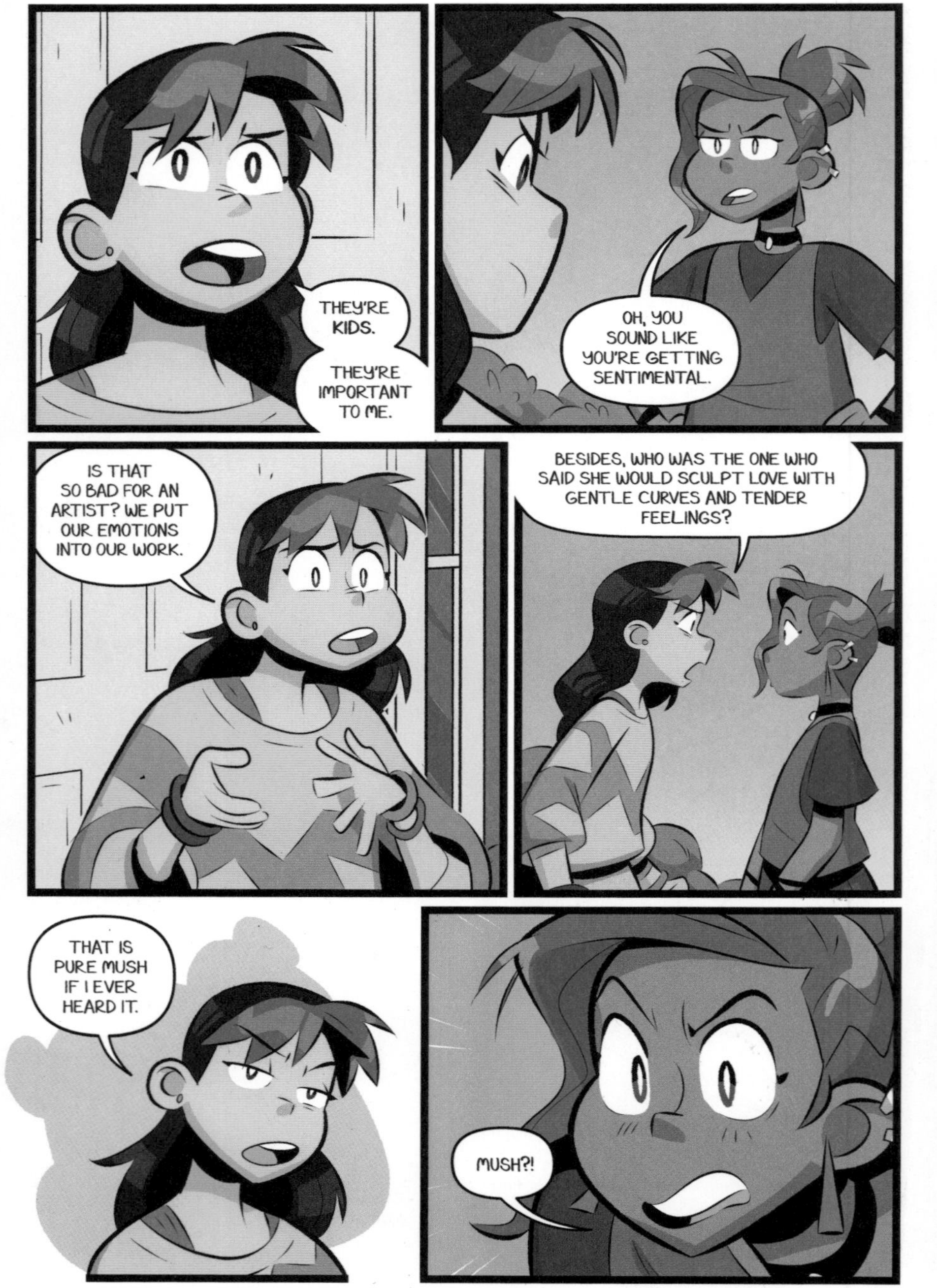
THEY'RE KIDS.
THEY'RE IMPORTANT TO ME.
OH, YOU SOUND LIKE YOU'RE GETTING SENTIMENTAL.
IS THAT SO BAD FOR AN ARTIST? WE PUT OUR EMOTIONS INTO OUR WORK.
BESIDES, WHO WAS THE ONE WHO SAID SHE WOULD SCULPT LOVE WITH GENTLE CURVES AND TENDER FEELINGS?
THAT IS PURE MUSH IF I EVER HEARD IT.
MUSH?!

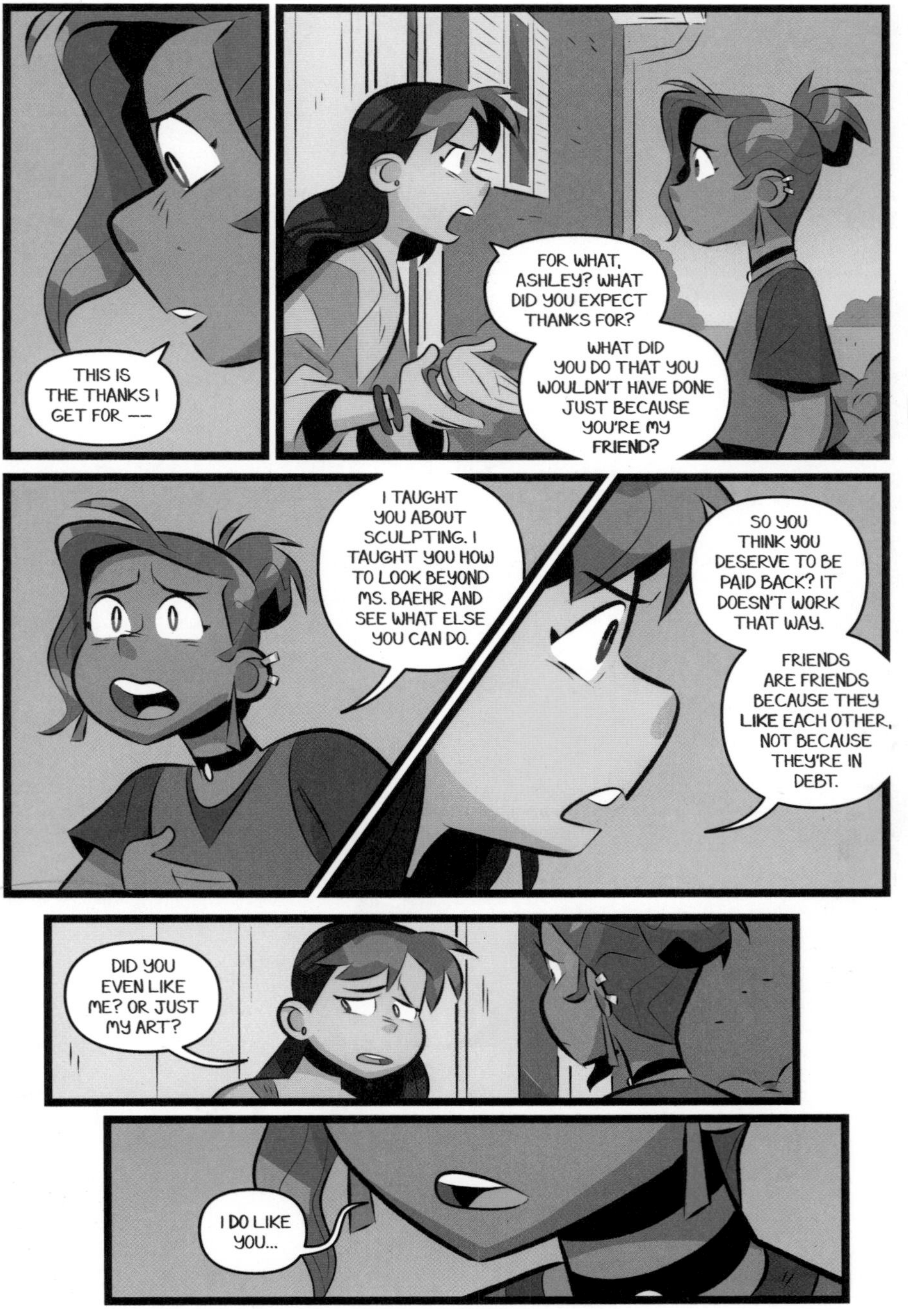
THIS IS THE THANKS I GET FOR --
FOR WHAT, ASHLEY? WHAT DID YOU EXPECT THANKS FOR?
WHAT DID YOU DO THAT YOU WOULDN'T HAVE DONE JUST BECAUSE YOU'RE MY FRIEND?
I TAUGHT YOU ABOUT SCULPTING. I TAUGHT YOU HOW TO LOOK BEYOND MS. BAEHR AND SEE WHAT ELSE YOU CAN DO.
SO YOU THINK YOU DESERVE TO BE PAID BACK? IT DOESN'T WORK THAT WAY.
FRIENDS ARE FRIENDS BECAUSE THEY LIKE EACH OTHER, NOT BECAUSE THEY'RE IN DEBT.
DID YOU EVEN LIKE ME? OR JUST MY ART?
I DO LIKE YOU...

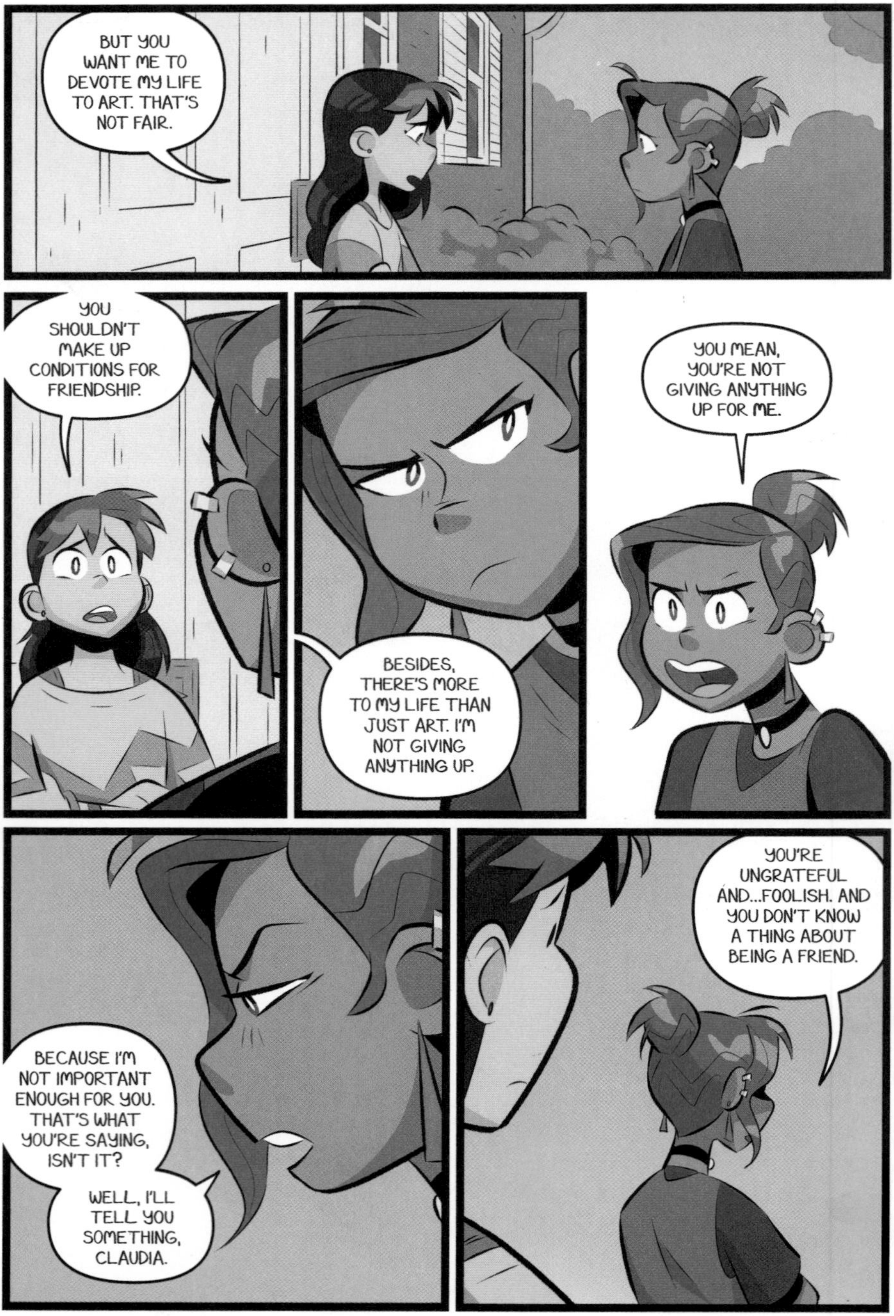
BUT YOU WANT ME TO DEVOTE MY LIFE TO ART. THAT'S NOT FAIR.
YOU SHOULDN'T MAKE UP CONDITIONS FOR FRIENDSHIP.
BESIDES, THERE'S MORE TO MY LIFE THAN JUST ART. I'M NOT GIVING ANYTHING UP.
YOU MEAN, YOU'RE NOT GIVING ANYTHING UP FOR ME.
BECAUSE I'M NOT IMPORTANT ENOUGH FOR YOU. THAT'S WHAT YOU'RE SAYING, ISN'T IT?
WELL, I'LL TELL YOU SOMETHING, CLAUDIA.
YOU'RE UNGRATEFUL AND...FOOLISH. AND YOU DON'T KNOW A THING ABOUT BEING A FRIEND.

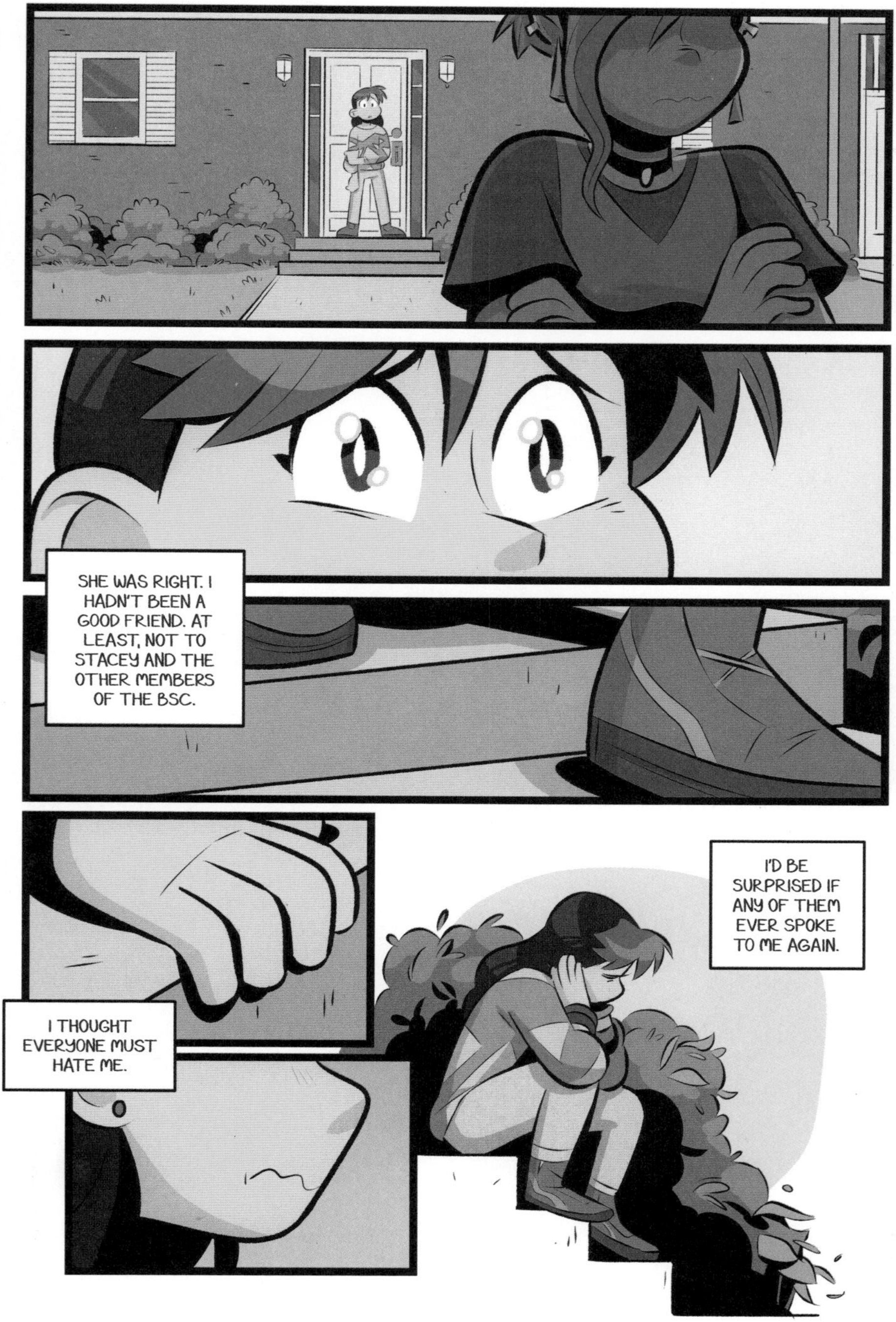
SHE WAS RIGHT. I HADN'T BEEN A GOOD FRIEND. AT LEAST, NOT TO STACEY AND THE OTHER MEMBERS OF THE BSC.
I THOUGHT EVERYONE MUST HATE ME.
I'D BE SURPRISED IF ANY OF THEM EVER SPOKE TO ME AGAIN.

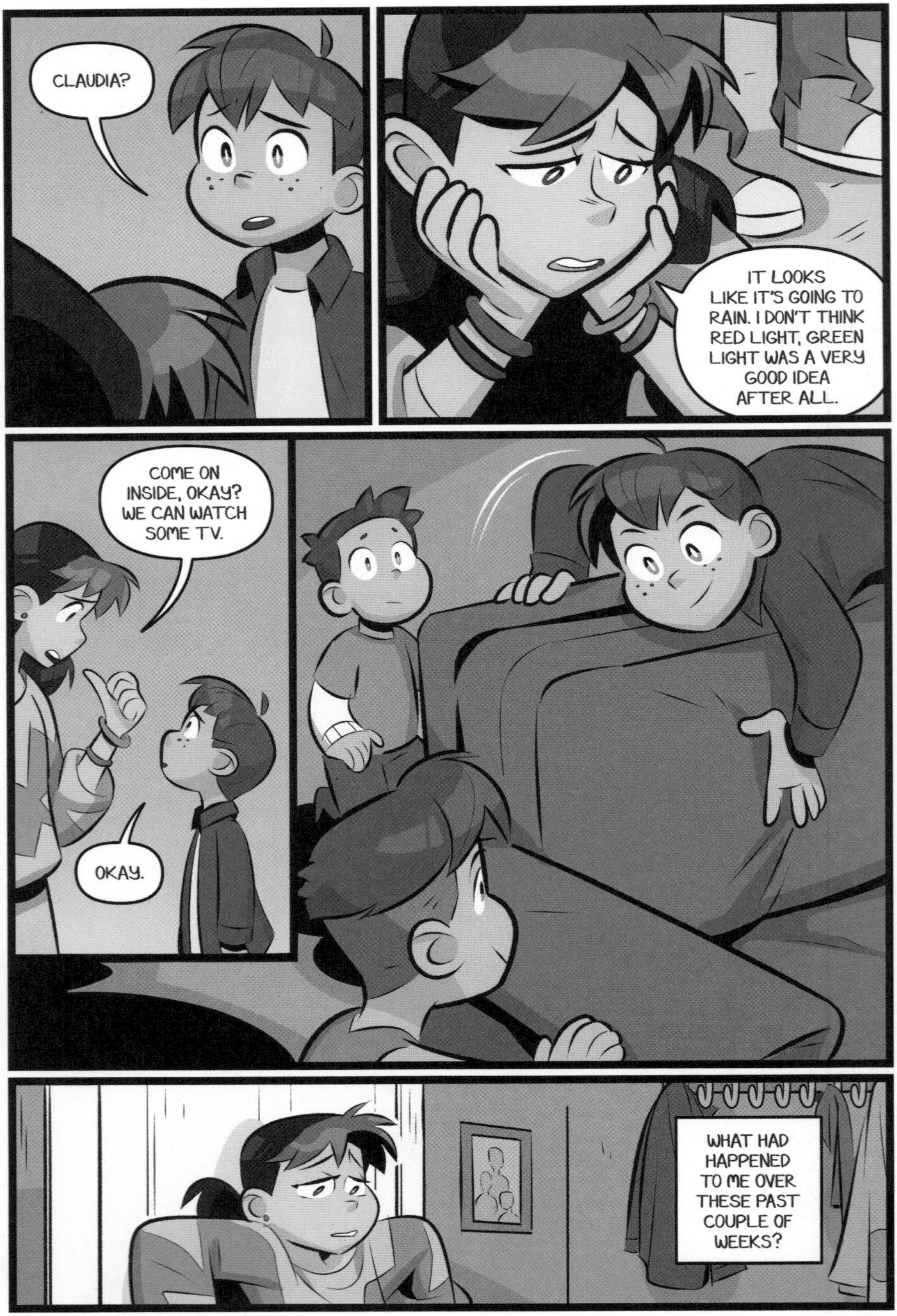
CLAUDIA?
IT LOOKS LIKE IT'S GOING TO RAIN. I DON'T THINK RED LIGHT, GREEN LIGHT WAS A VERY GOOD IDEA AFTER ALL.
COME ON INSIDE, OKAY? WE CAN WATCH SOME TV.
OKAY.
WHAT HAD HAPPENED TO ME OVER THESE PAST COUPLE OF WEEKS?

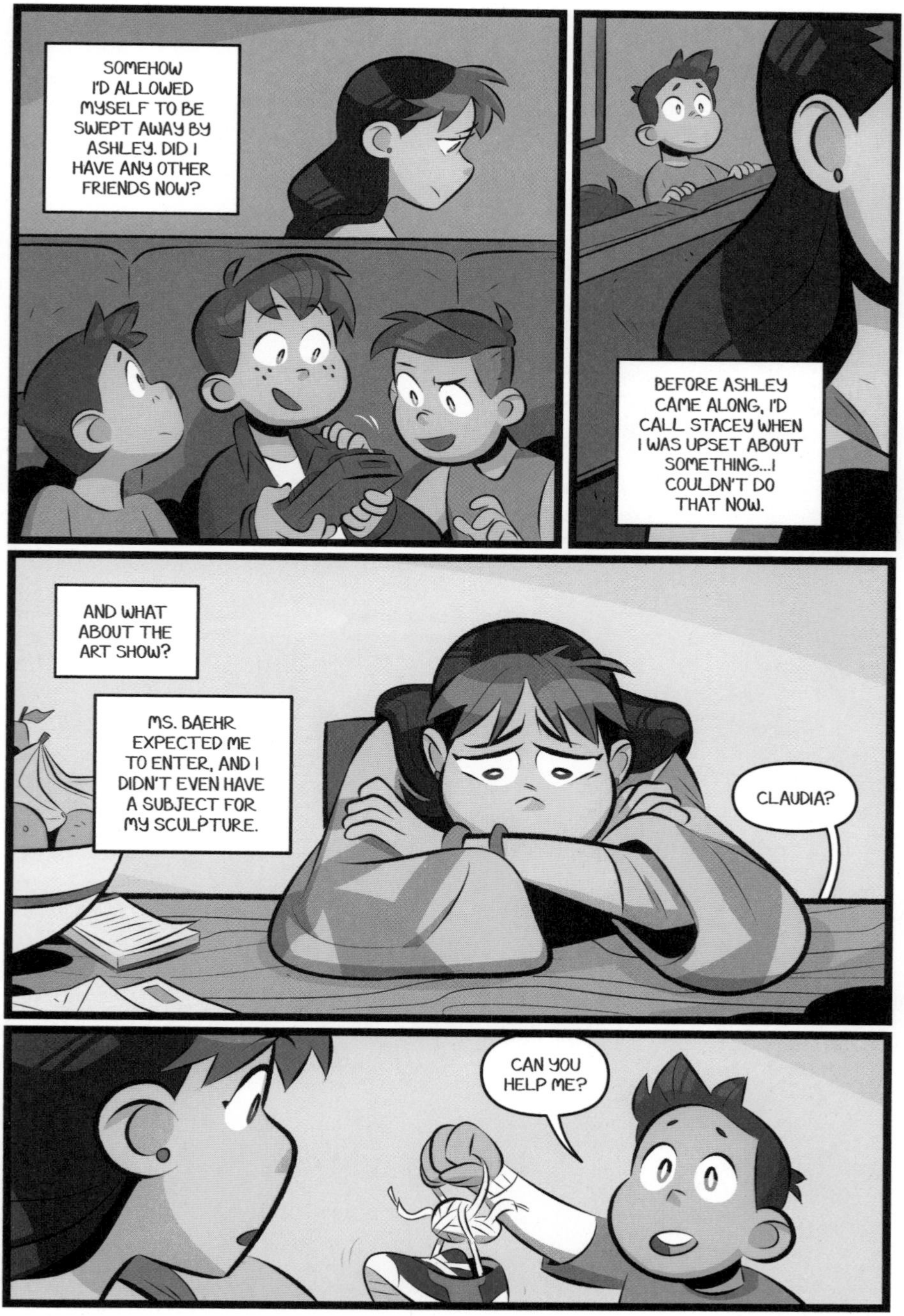
SOMEHOW I'D ALLOWED MYSELF TO BE SWEPT AWAY BY ASHLEY. DID I HAVE ANY OTHER FRIENDS NOW?
BEFORE ASHLEY CAME ALONG, I'D CALL STACEY WHEN I WAS UPSET ABOUT SOMETHING...I COULDN'T DO THAT NOW.
AND WHAT ABOUT THE ART SHOW?
MS. BAEHR EXPECTED ME TO ENTER, AND I DIDN'T EVEN HAVE A SUBJECT FOR MY SCULPTURE.
CLAUDIA?
CAN YOU HELP ME?

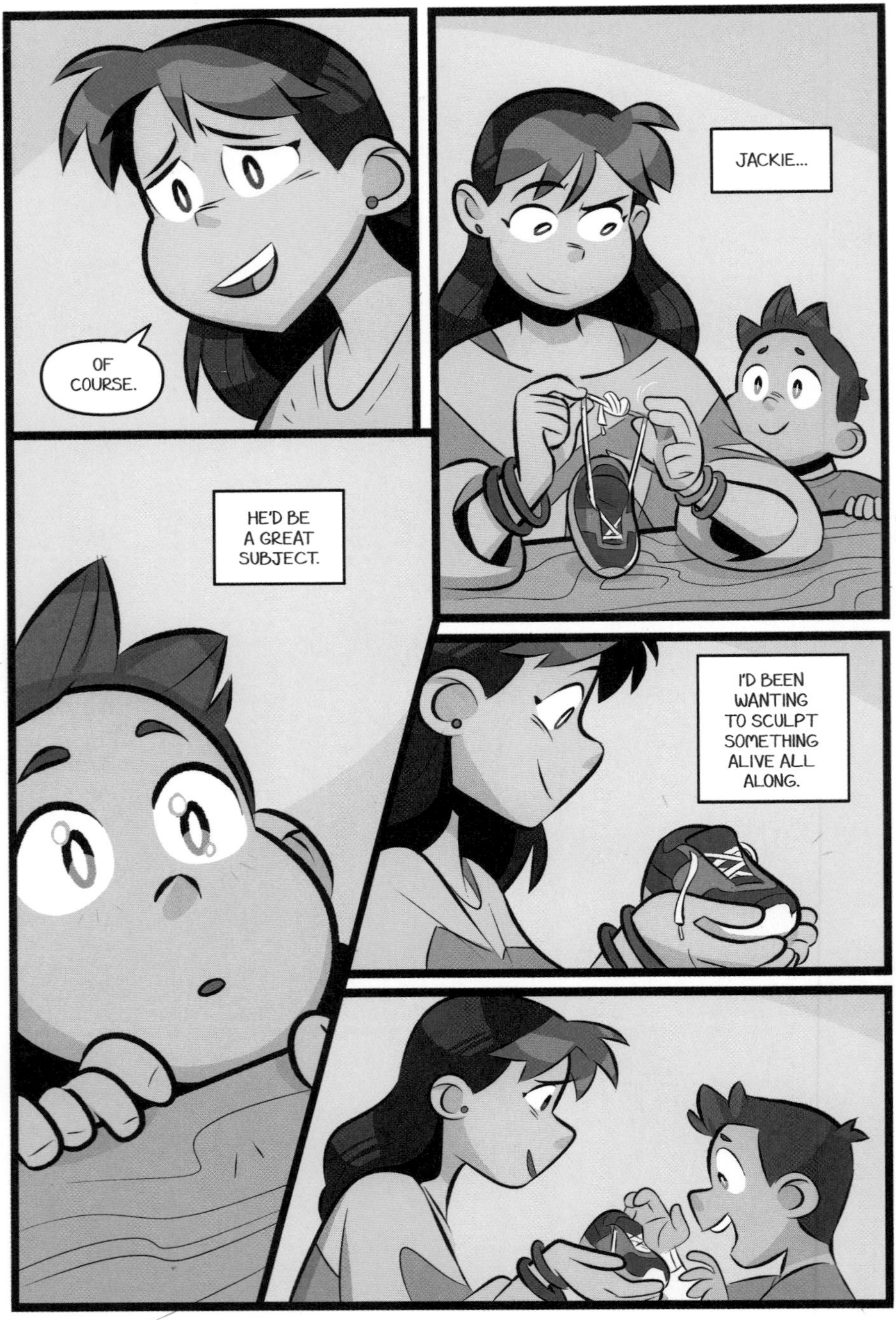
OF COURSE.
JACKIE...
HE'D BE A GREAT SUBJECT.
I'D BEEN WANTING TO SCULPT SOMETHING ALIVE ALL ALONG.

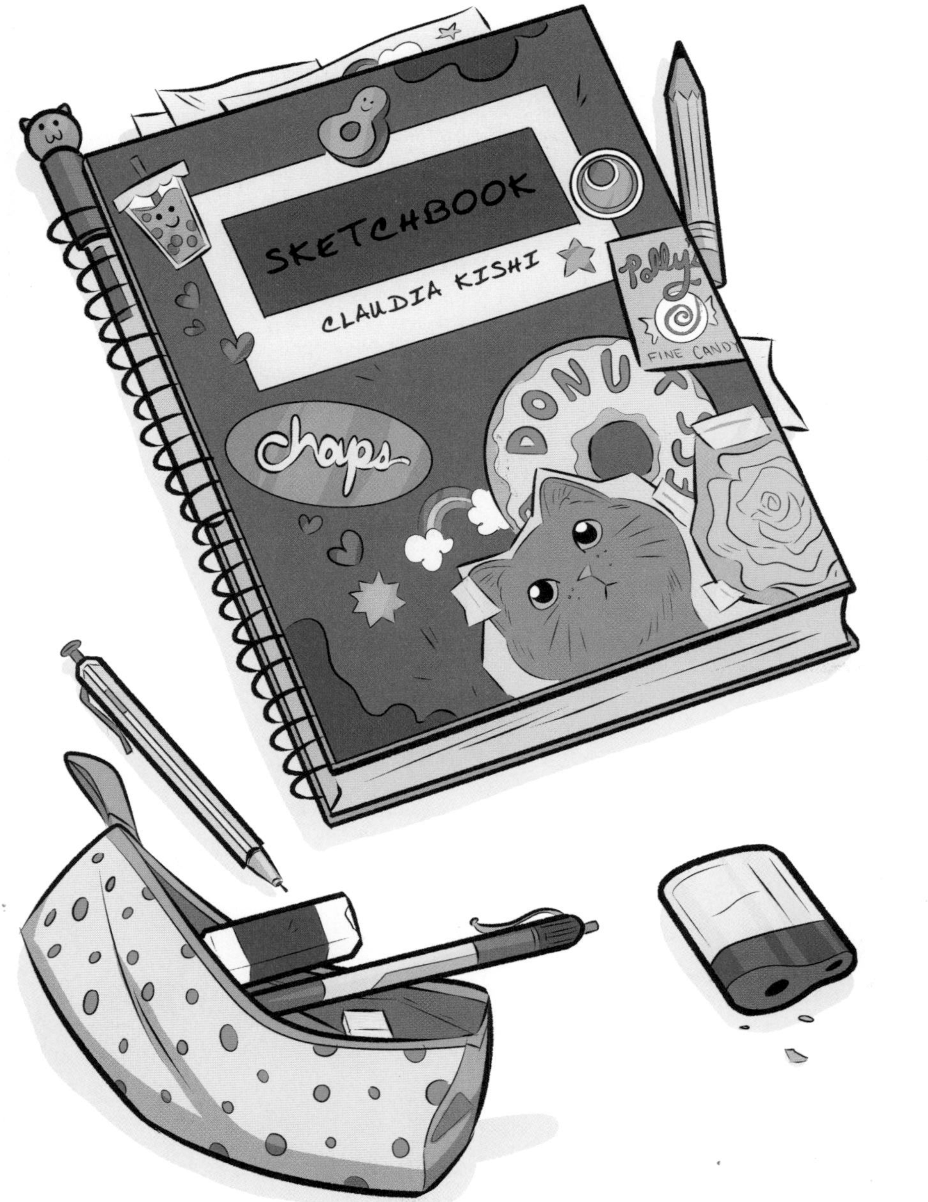
SKETCHBOOK
CLAUDIA KISHI
Polly's
FINE CANDY
DONUT
chaps

CHAPTER 10

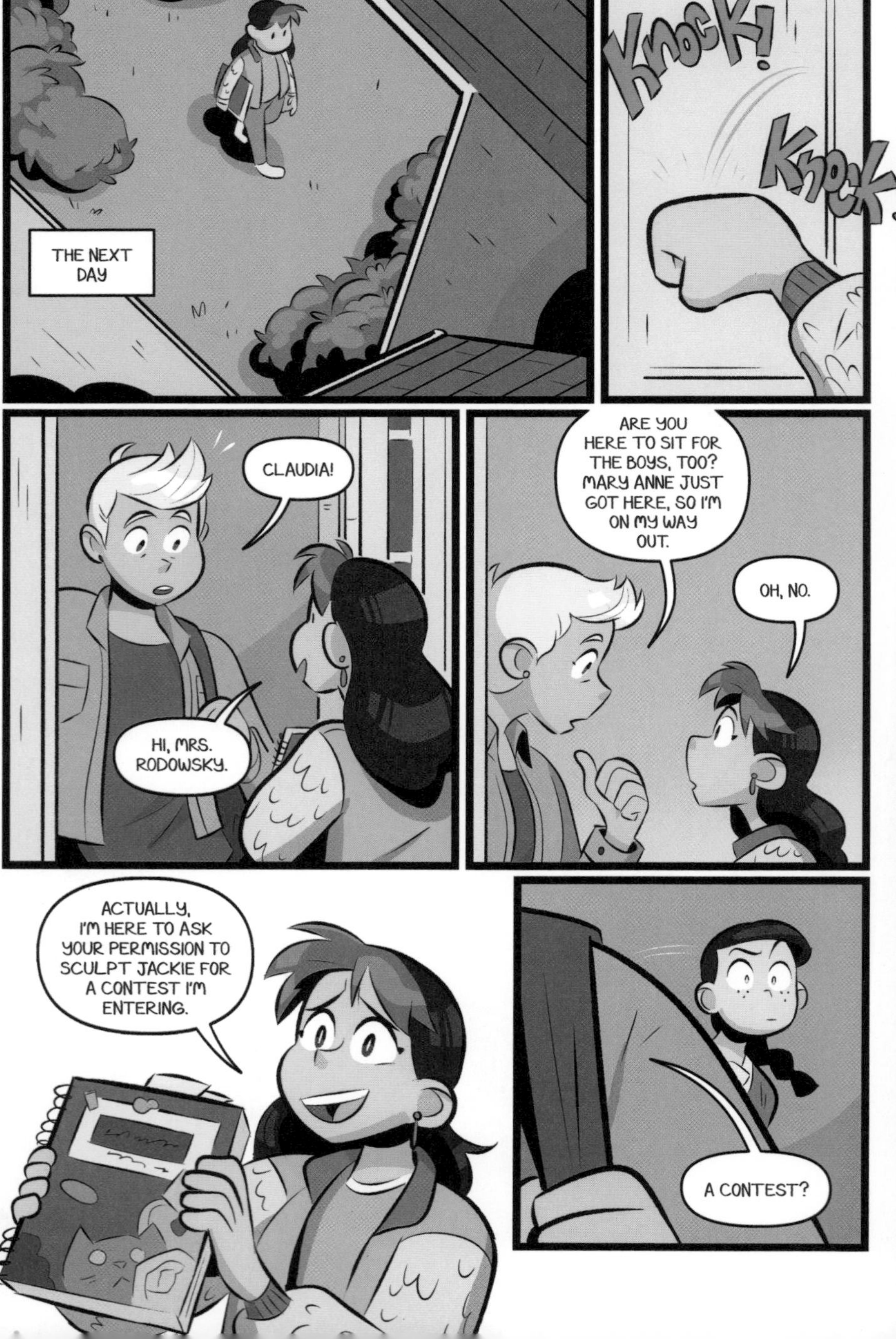
THE NEXT DAY
KNOCK!
KNOCK!
CLAUDIA!
HI, MRS. RODOWSKY.
ARE YOU HERE TO SIT FOR THE BOYS, TOO? MARY ANNE JUST GOT HERE, SO I'M ON MY WAY OUT.
OH, NO.
ACTUALLY, I'M HERE TO ASK YOUR PERMISSION TO SCULPT JACKIE FOR A CONTEST I'M ENTERING.
A CONTEST?

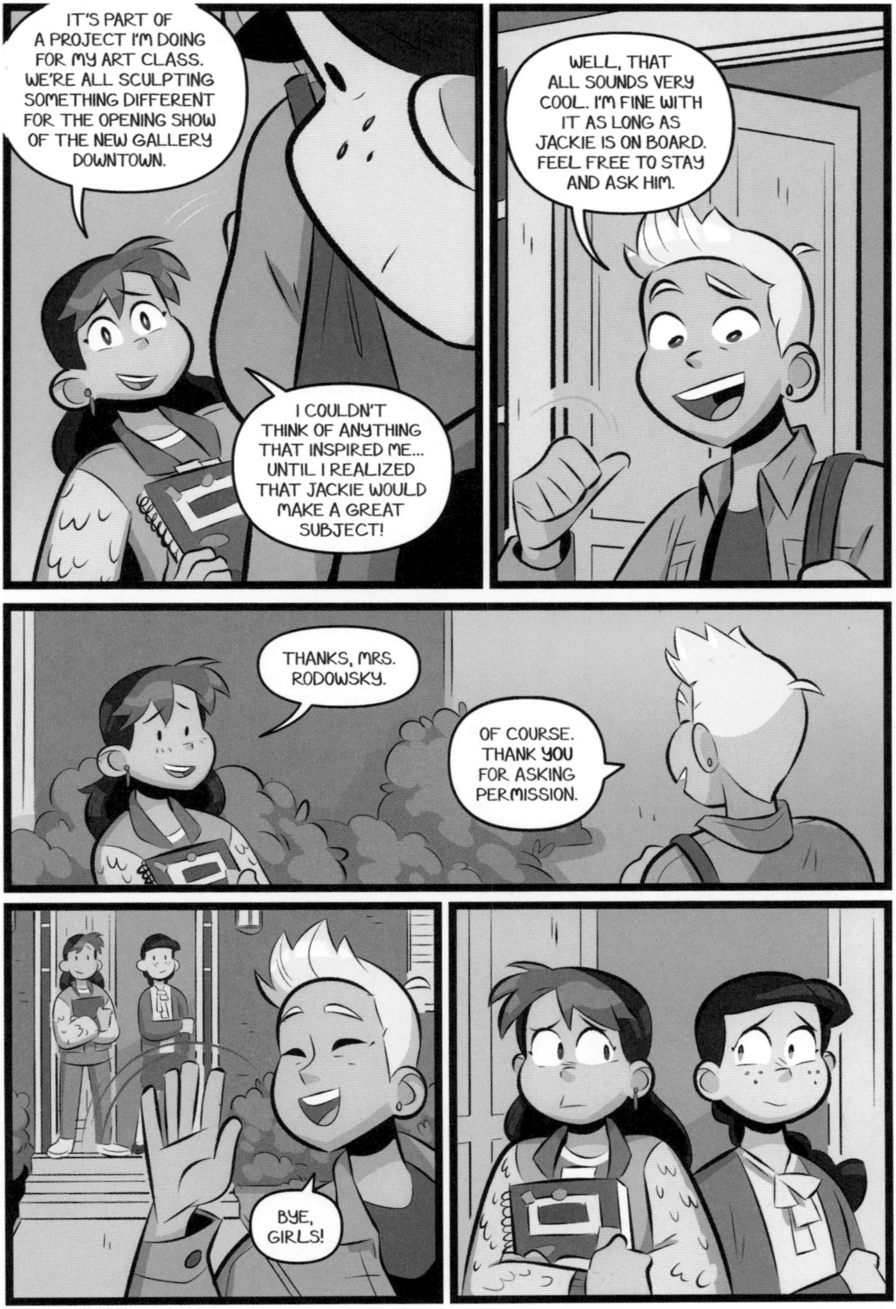
IT'S PART OF A PROJECT I'M DOING FOR MY ART CLASS. WE'RE ALL SCULPTING SOMETHING DIFFERENT FOR THE OPENING SHOW OF THE NEW GALLERY DOWNTOWN.
I COULDN'T THINK OF ANYTHING THAT INSPIRED ME... UNTIL I REALIZED THAT JACKIE WOULD MAKE A GREAT SUBJECT!
WELL, THAT ALL SOUNDS VERY COOL. I'M FINE WITH IT AS LONG AS JACKIE IS ON BOARD. FEEL FREE TO STAY AND ASK HIM.
THANKS, MRS. RODOWSKY.
OF COURSE. THANK YOU FOR ASKING PERMISSION.
BYE, GIRLS!

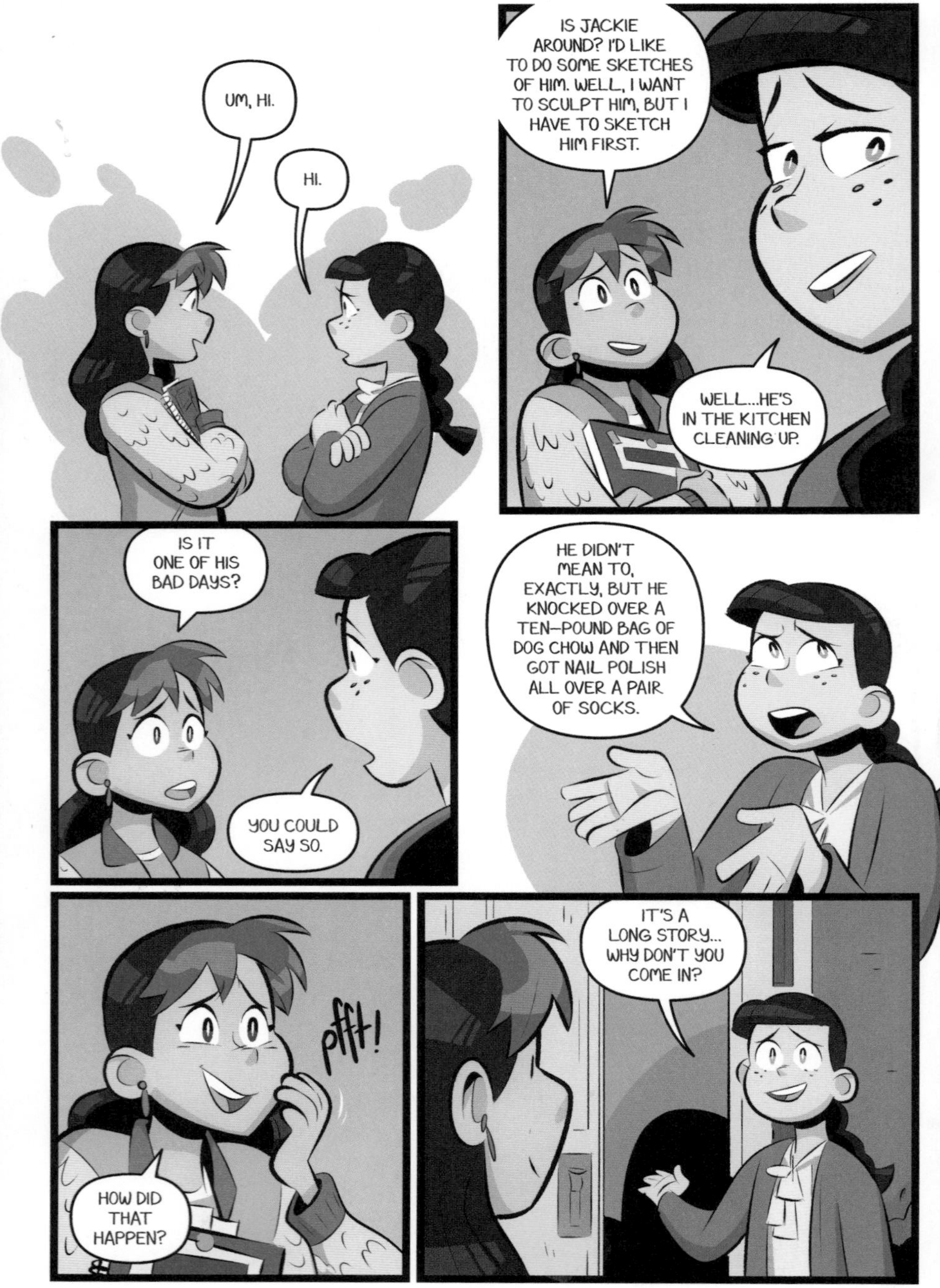
UM, HI.
HI.
IS JACKIE AROUND? I'D LIKE TO DO SOME SKETCHES OF HIM. WELL, I WANT TO SCULPT HIM, BUT I HAVE TO SKETCH HIM FIRST.
WELL...HE'S IN THE KITCHEN CLEANING UP.
IS IT ONE OF HIS BAD DAYS?
YOU COULD SAY SO.
HE DIDN'T MEAN TO, EXACTLY, BUT HE KNOCKED OVER A TEN-POUND BAG OF DOG CHOW AND THEN GOT NAIL POLISH ALL OVER A PAIR OF SOCKS.
pfft!
HOW DID THAT HAPPEN?
IT'S A LONG STORY... WHY DON'T YOU COME IN?

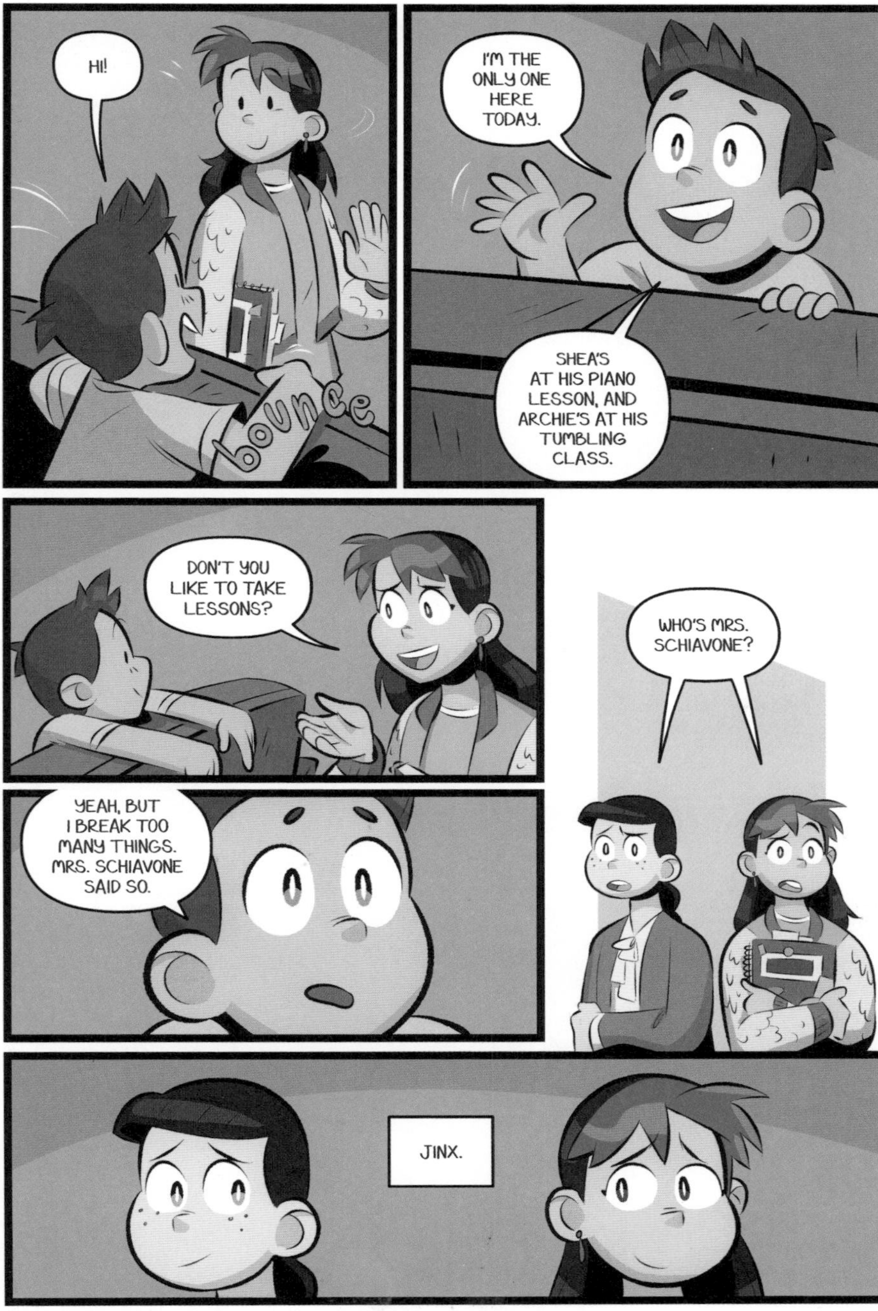
HI!
bounce
I'M THE ONLY ONE HERE TODAY.
SHEA'S AT HIS PIANO LESSON, AND ARCHIE'S AT HIS TUMBLING CLASS.
DON'T YOU LIKE TO TAKE LESSONS?
YEAH, BUT I BREAK TOO MANY THINGS. MRS. SCHIAVONE SAID SO.
WHO'S MRS. SCHIAVONE?
JINX.

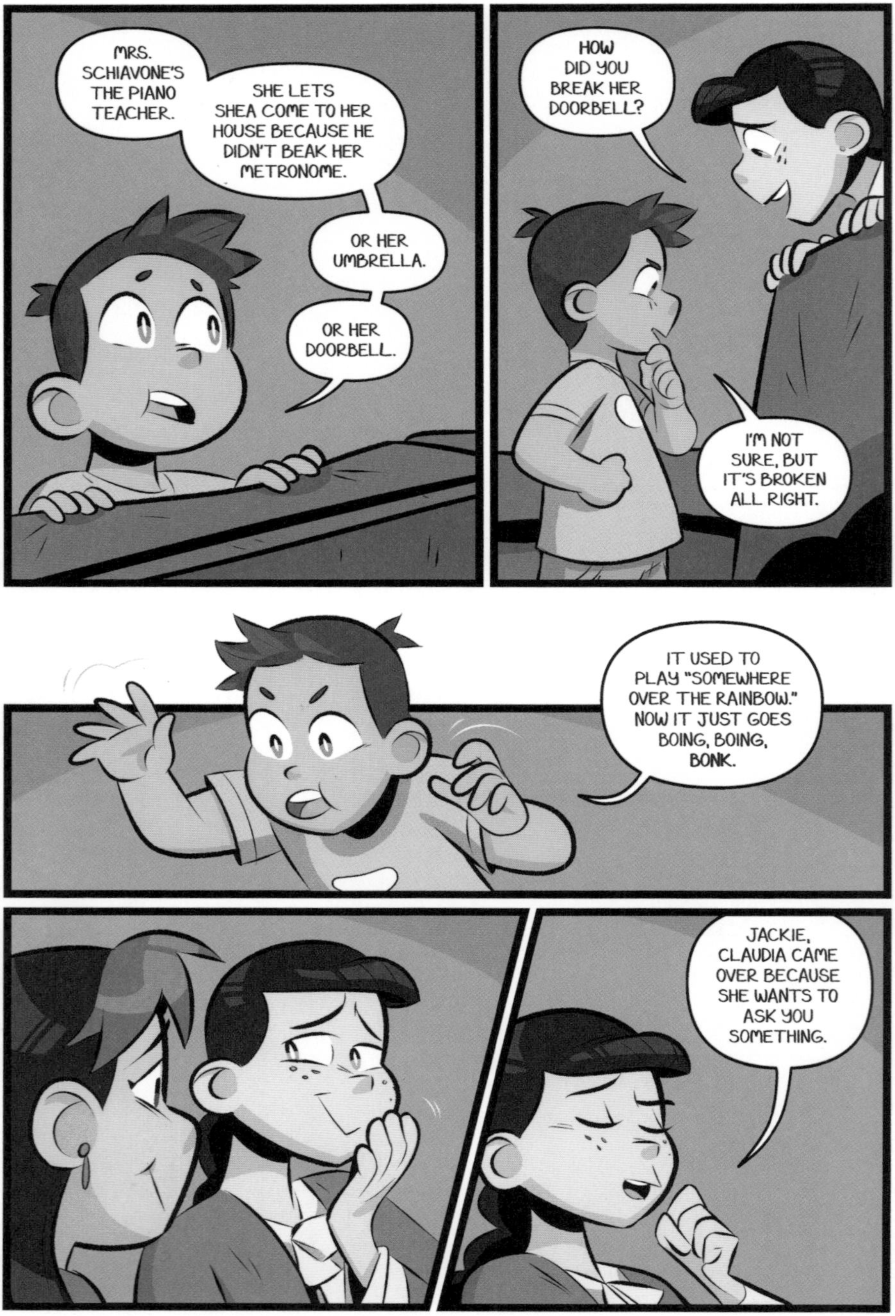
MRS. SCHIAVONE'S THE PIANO TEACHER.
SHE LETS SHEA COME TO HER HOUSE BECAUSE HE DIDN'T BEAK HER METRONOME.
OR HER UMBRELLA.
OR HER DOORBELL.
HOW DID YOU BREAK HER DOORBELL?
I'M NOT SURE, BUT IT'S BROKEN ALL RIGHT.
IT USED TO PLAY "SOMEWHERE OVER THE RAINBOW." NOW IT JUST GOES BOING, BOING, BONK.
JACKIE, CLAUDIA CAME OVER BECAUSE SHE WANTS TO ASK YOU SOMETHING.

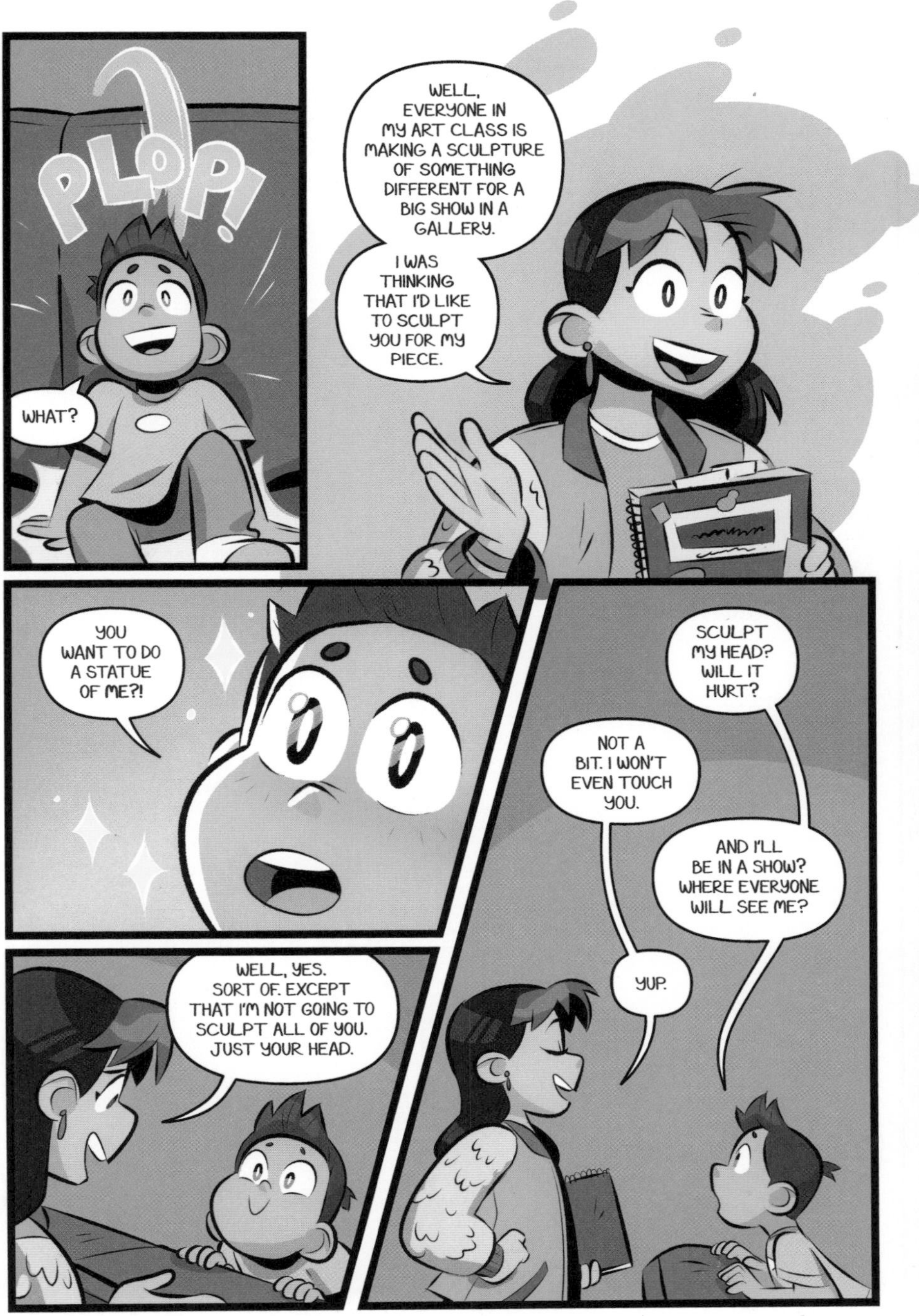
PLOP!
WHAT?
WELL, EVERYONE IN MY ART CLASS IS MAKING A SCULPTURE OF SOMETHING DIFFERENT FOR A BIG SHOW IN A GALLERY.
I WAS THINKING THAT I'D LIKE TO SCULPT YOU FOR MY PIECE.
YOU WANT TO DO A STATUE OF ME?!
WELL, YES. SORT OF. EXCEPT THAT I'M NOT GOING TO SCULPT ALL OF YOU. JUST YOUR HEAD.
SCULPT MY HEAD? WILL IT HURT?
NOT A BIT. I WON'T EVEN TOUCH YOU.
AND I'LL BE IN A SHOW? WHERE EVERYONE WILL SEE ME?
YUP.

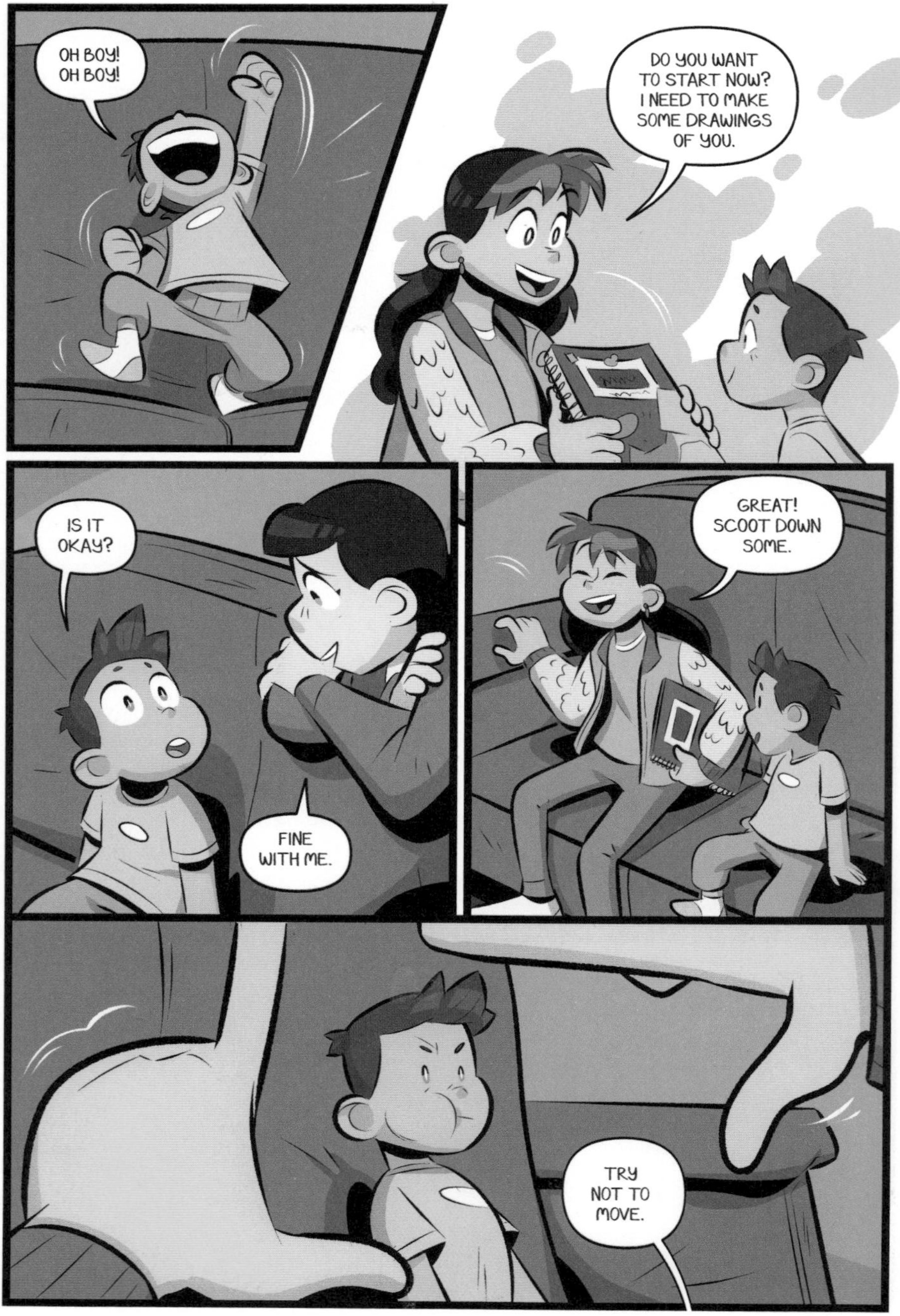
OH BOY!
OH BOY!
DO YOU WANT TO START NOW? I NEED TO MAKE SOME DRAWINGS OF YOU.
IS IT OKAY?
FINE WITH ME.
GREAT! SCOOT DOWN SOME.
TRY NOT TO MOVE.

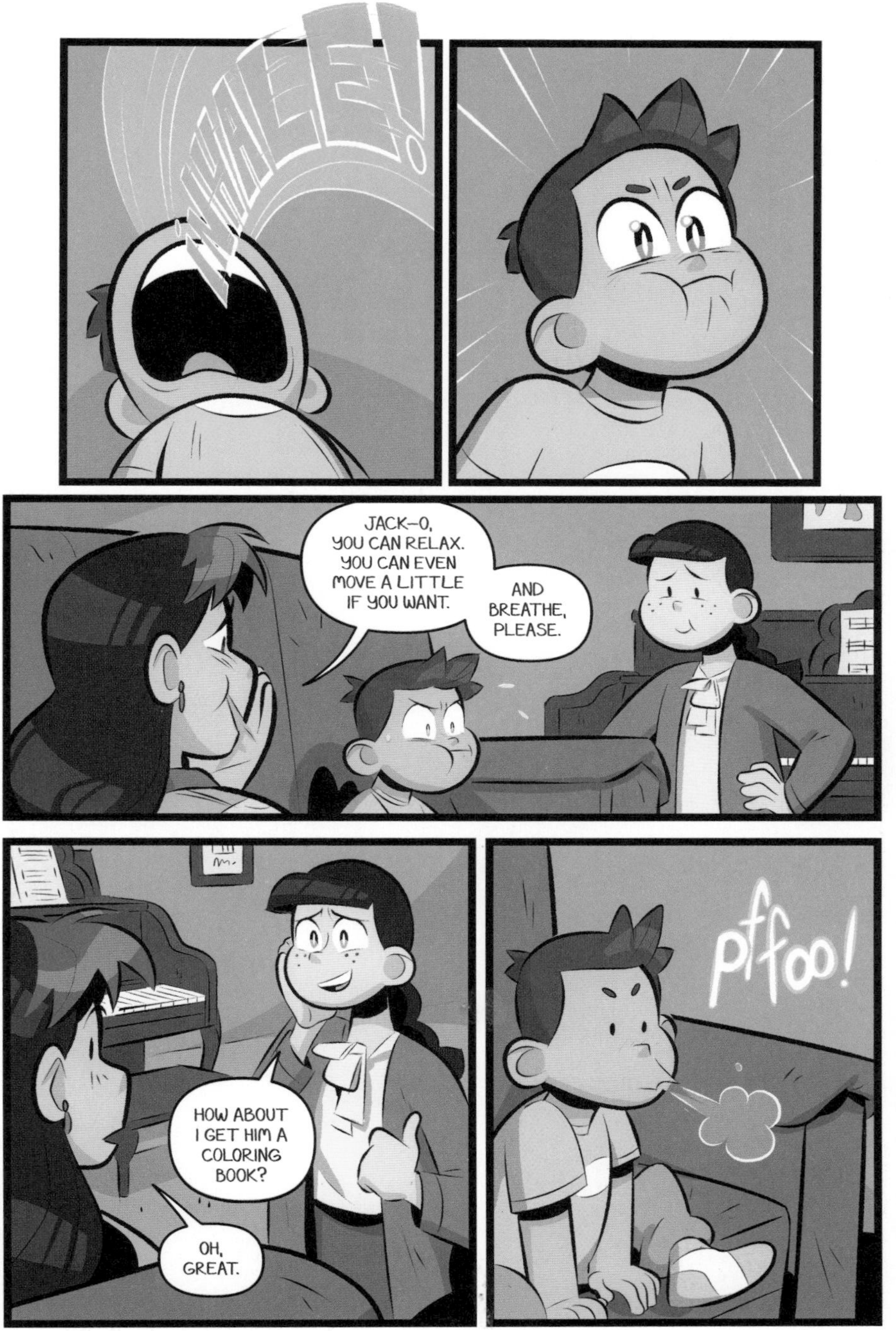
WHAEE!
JACK-O, YOU CAN RELAX. YOU CAN EVEN MOVE A LITTLE IF YOU WANT.
AND BREATHE, PLEASE.
HOW ABOUT I GET HIM A COLORING BOOK?
OH, GREAT.
pffoo!

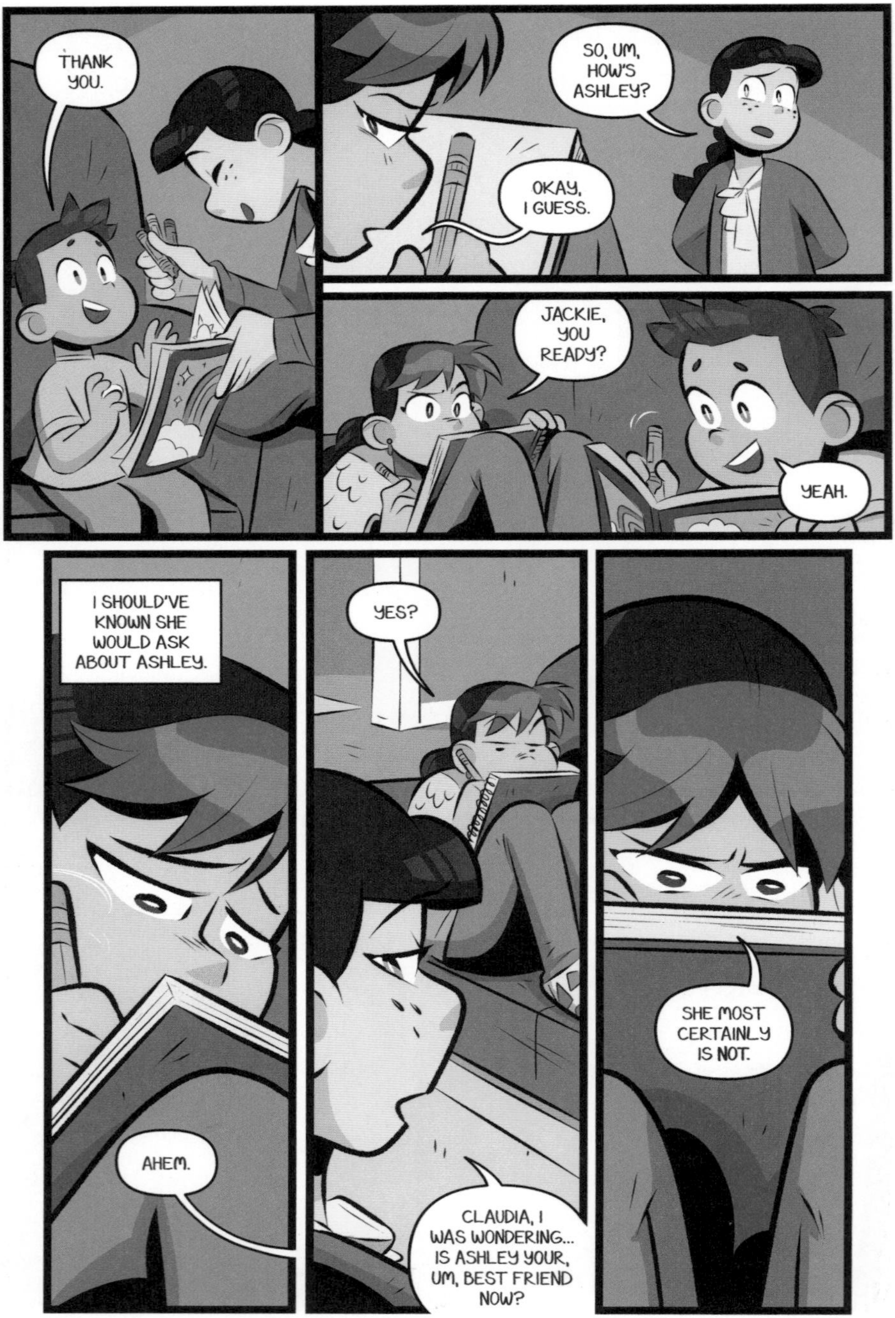
THANK YOU.
SO, UM, HOW'S ASHLEY?
OKAY, I GUESS.
JACKIE, YOU READY?
YEAH.
I SHOULD'VE KNOWN SHE WOULD ASK ABOUT ASHLEY.
AHEM.
YES?
CLAUDIA, I WAS WONDERING... IS ASHLEY YOUR, UM, BEST FRIEND NOW?
SHE MOST CERTAINLY IS NOT.

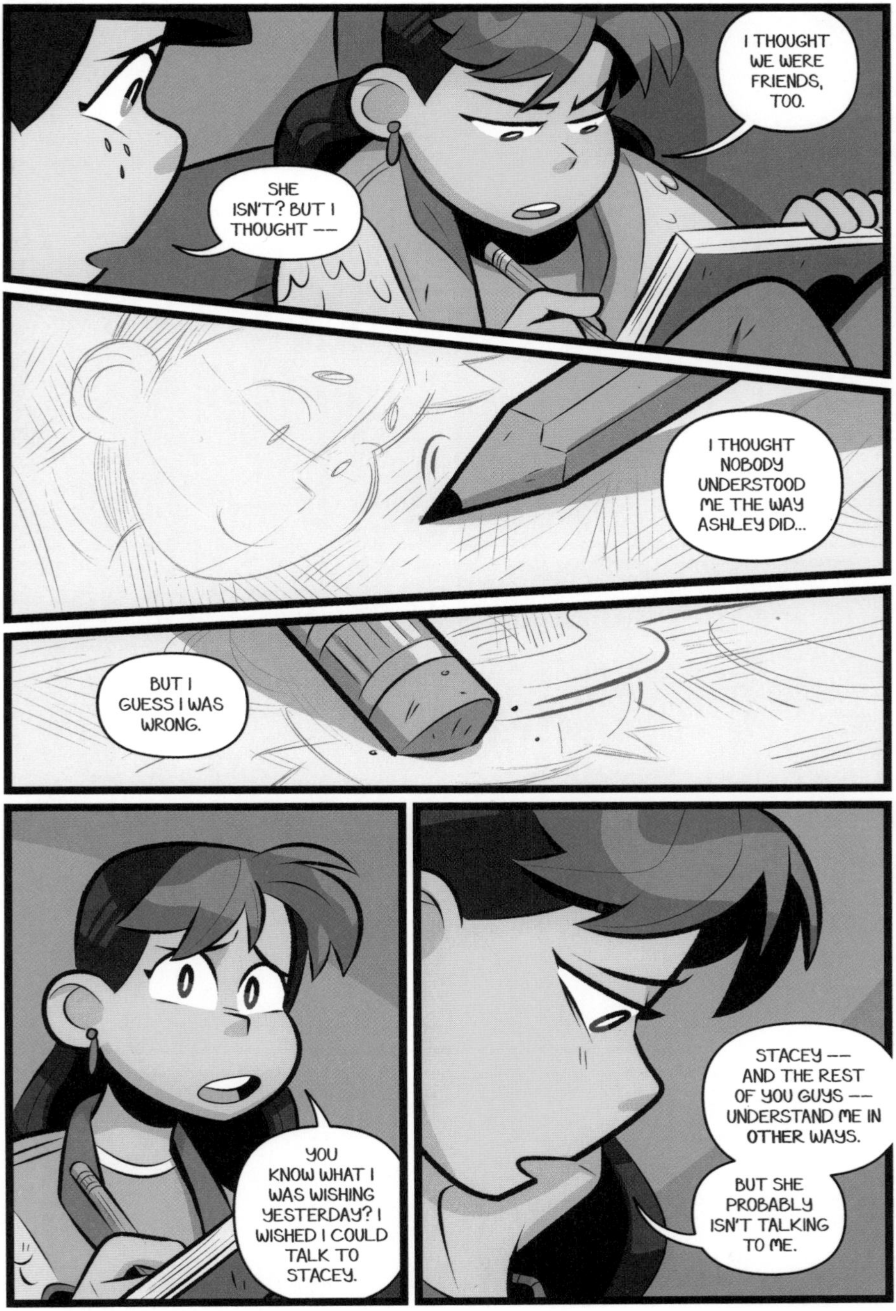
I THOUGHT WE WERE FRIENDS, TOO.
SHE ISN'T? BUT I THOUGHT --
I THOUGHT NOBODY UNDERSTOOD ME THE WAY ASHLEY DID...
BUT I GUESS I WAS WRONG.
YOU KNOW WHAT I WAS WISHING YESTERDAY? I WISHED I COULD TALK TO STACEY.
STACEY -- AND THE REST OF YOU GUYS -- UNDERSTAND ME IN OTHER WAYS.
BUT SHE PROBABLY ISN'T TALKING TO ME.

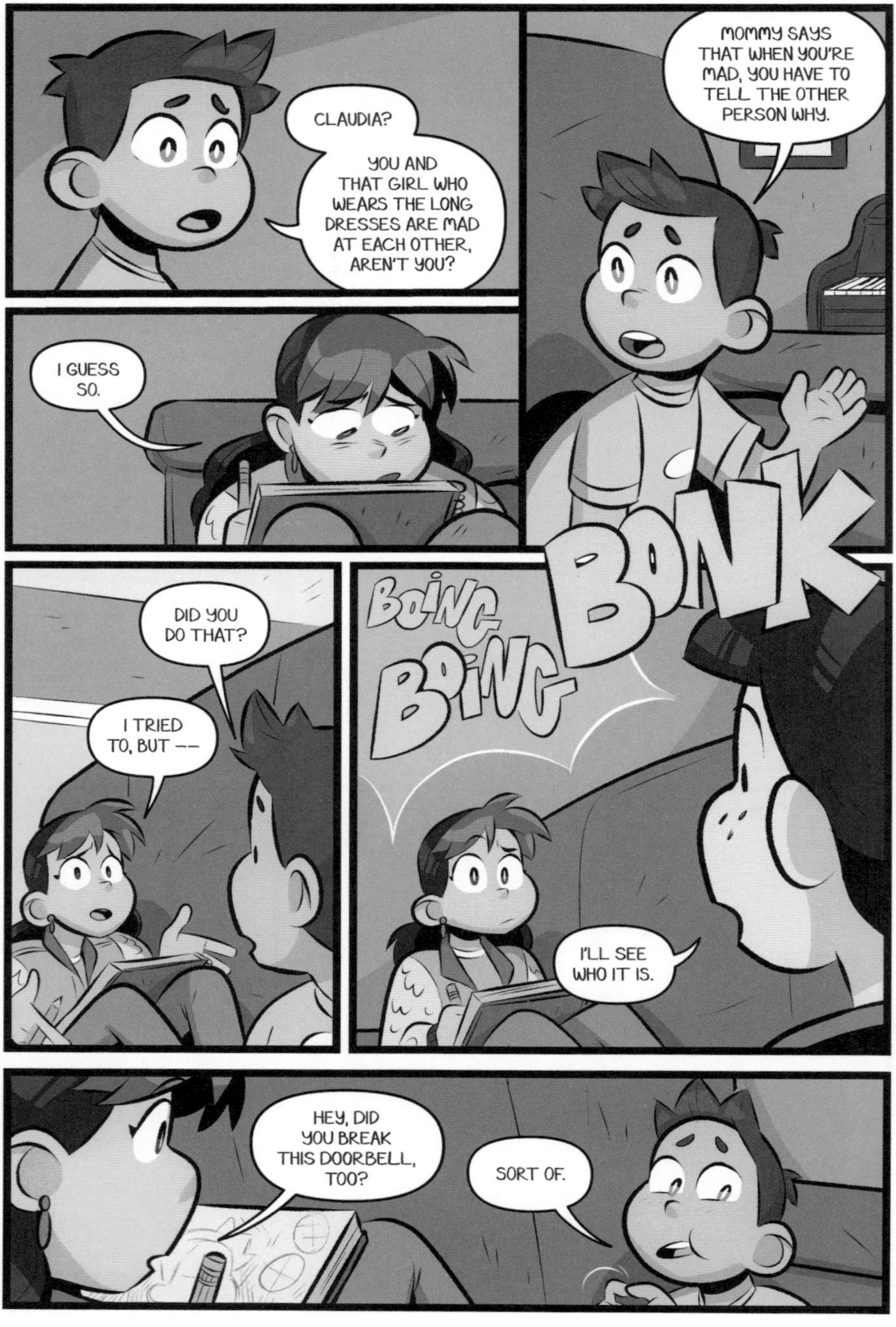
CLAUDIA?
YOU AND THAT GIRL WHO WEARS THE LONG DRESSES ARE MAD AT EACH OTHER, AREN'T YOU?
MOMMY SAYS THAT WHEN YOU'RE MAD, YOU HAVE TO TELL THE OTHER PERSON WHY.
I GUESS SO.
DID YOU DO THAT?
I TRIED TO, BUT --
BONK
BOING
BOING
I'LL SEE WHO IT IS.
HEY, DID YOU BREAK THIS DOORBELL, TOO?
SORT OF.

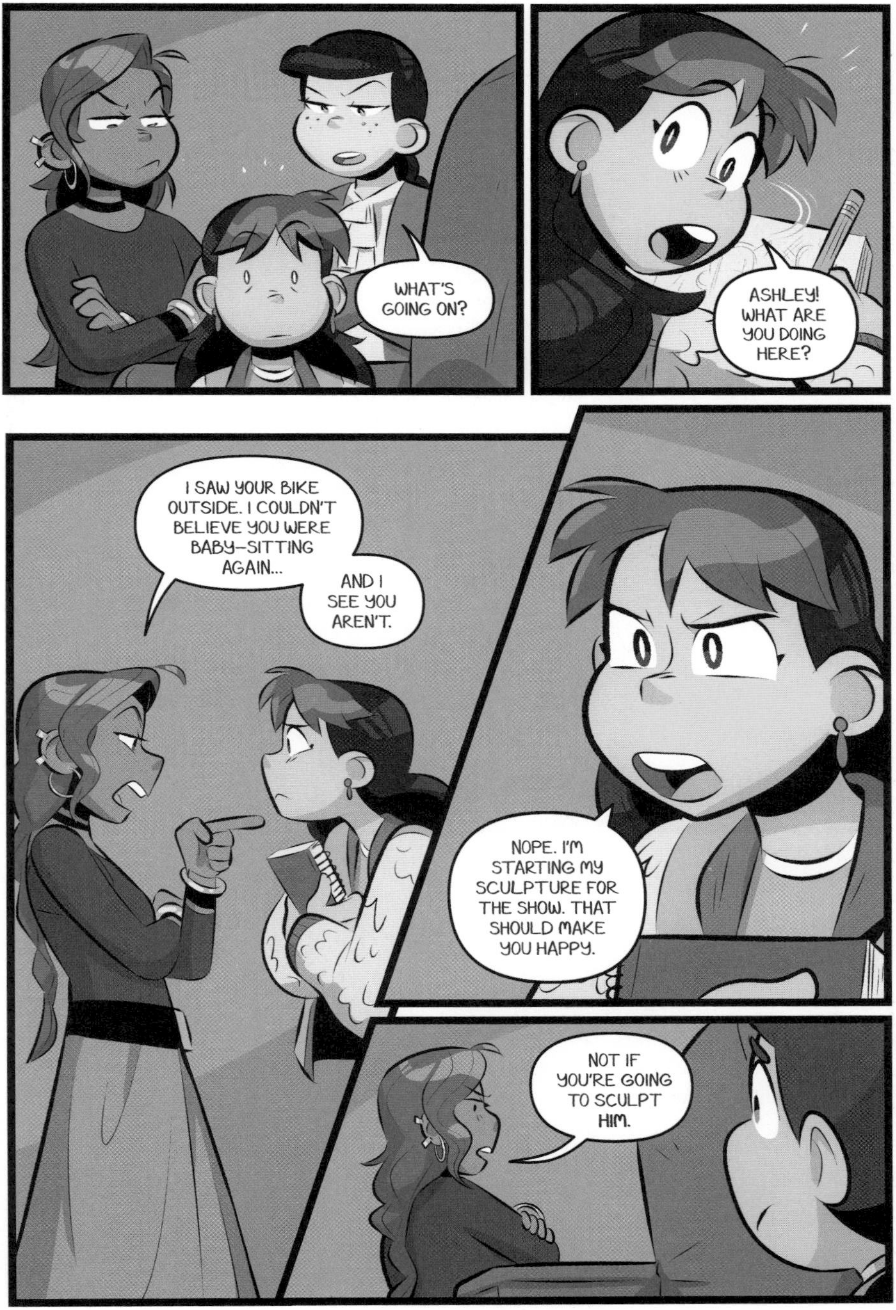
WHAT'S GOING ON?
ASHLEY! WHAT ARE YOU DOING HERE?
I SAW YOUR BIKE OUTSIDE. I COULDN'T BELIEVE YOU WERE BABY-SITTING AGAIN...
AND I SEE YOU AREN'T.
NOPE. I'M STARTING MY SCULPTURE FOR THE SHOW. THAT SHOULD MAKE YOU HAPPY.
NOT IF YOU'RE GOING TO SCULPT **HIM**.

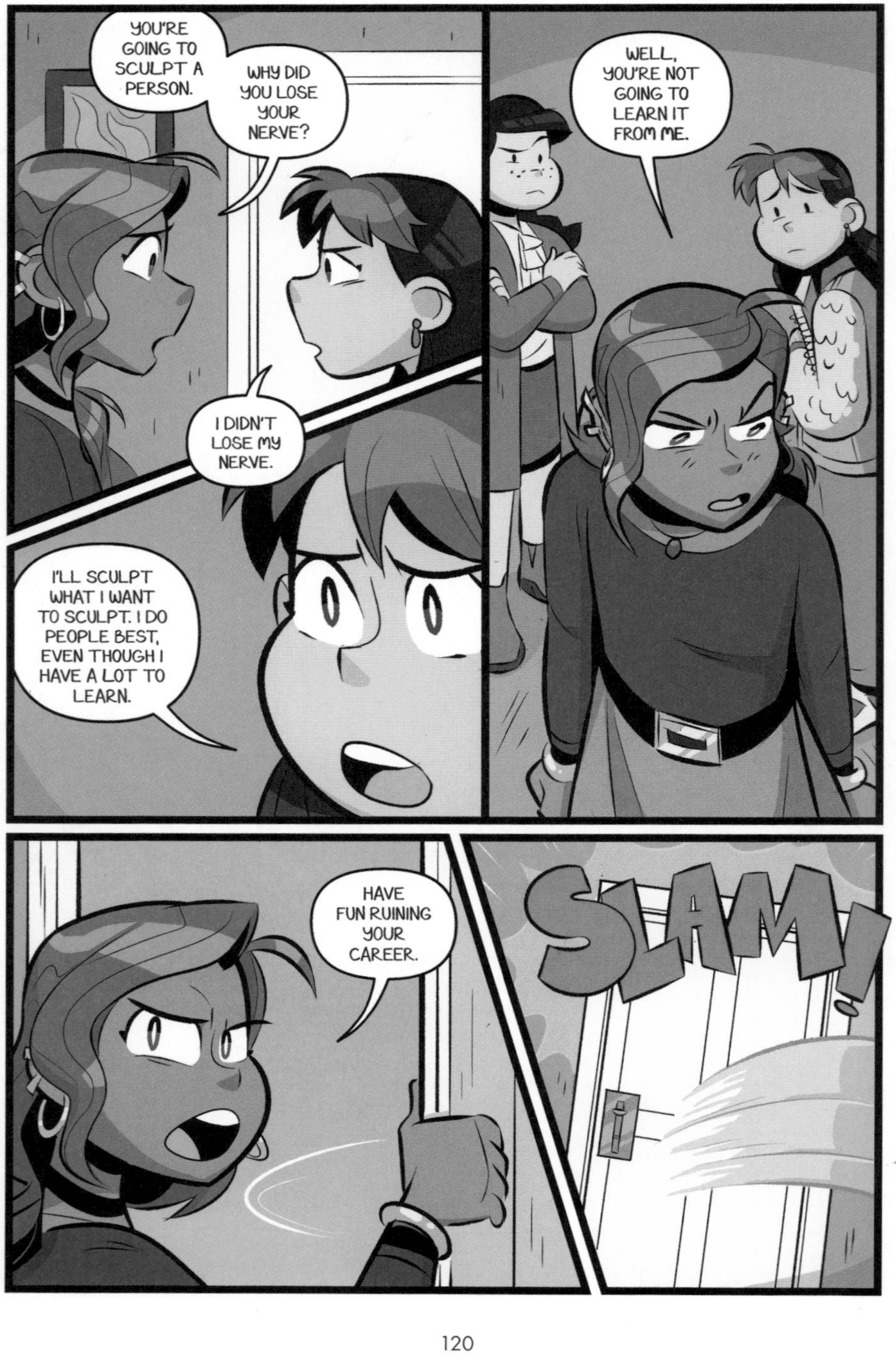
YOU'RE GOING TO SCULPT A PERSON.
WHY DID YOU LOSE YOUR NERVE?
I DIDN'T LOSE MY NERVE.
I'LL SCULPT WHAT I WANT TO SCULPT. I DO PEOPLE BEST, EVEN THOUGH I HAVE A LOT TO LEARN.
WELL, YOU'RE NOT GOING TO LEARN IT FROM ME.
HAVE FUN RUINING YOUR CAREER.
SLAM!

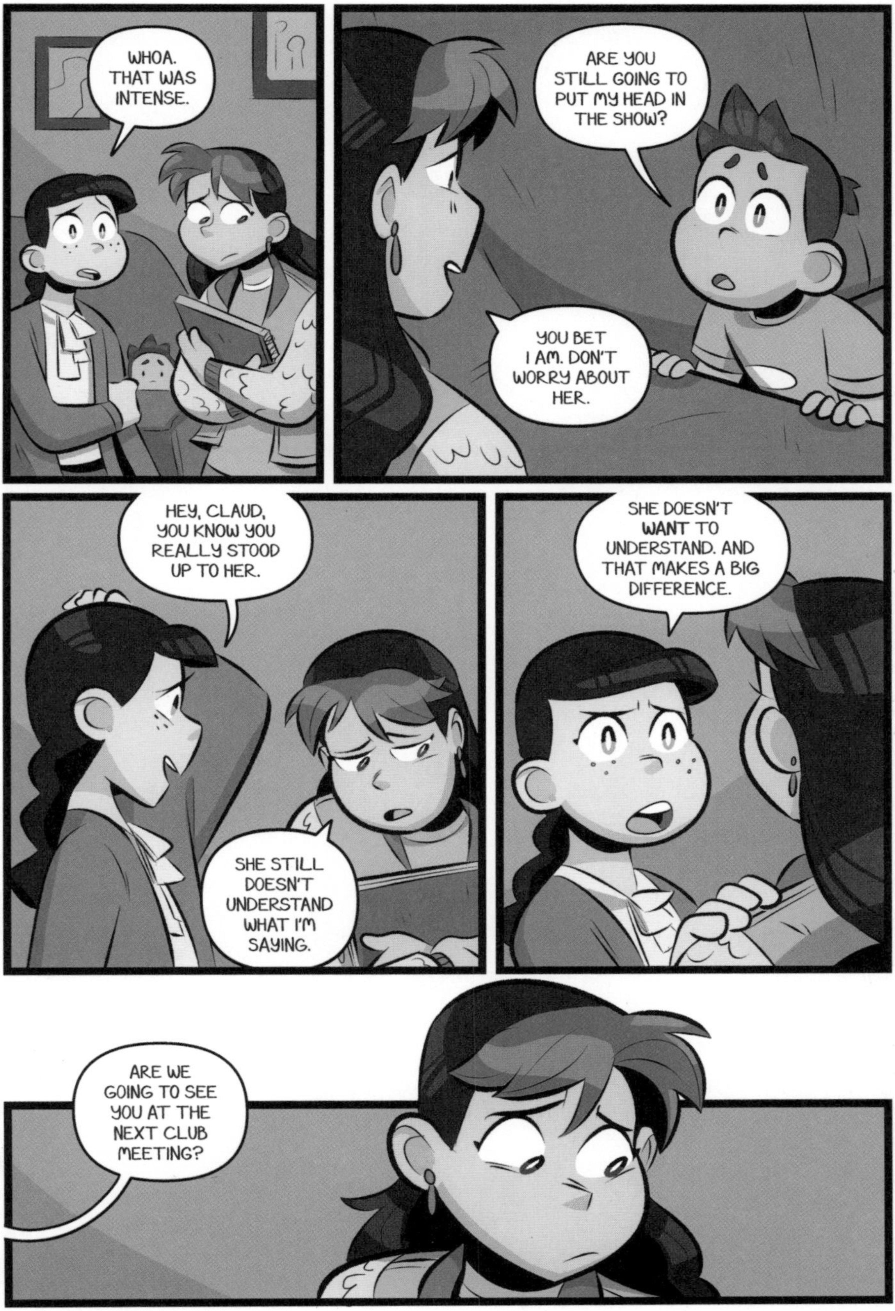
WHOA. THAT WAS INTENSE.
ARE YOU STILL GOING TO PUT MY HEAD IN THE SHOW?
YOU BET I AM. DON'T WORRY ABOUT HER.
HEY, CLAUD, YOU KNOW YOU REALLY STOOD UP TO HER.
SHE STILL DOESN'T UNDERSTAND WHAT I'M SAYING.
SHE DOESN'T **WANT** TO UNDERSTAND. AND THAT MAKES A BIG DIFFERENCE.
ARE WE GOING TO SEE YOU AT THE NEXT CLUB MEETING?

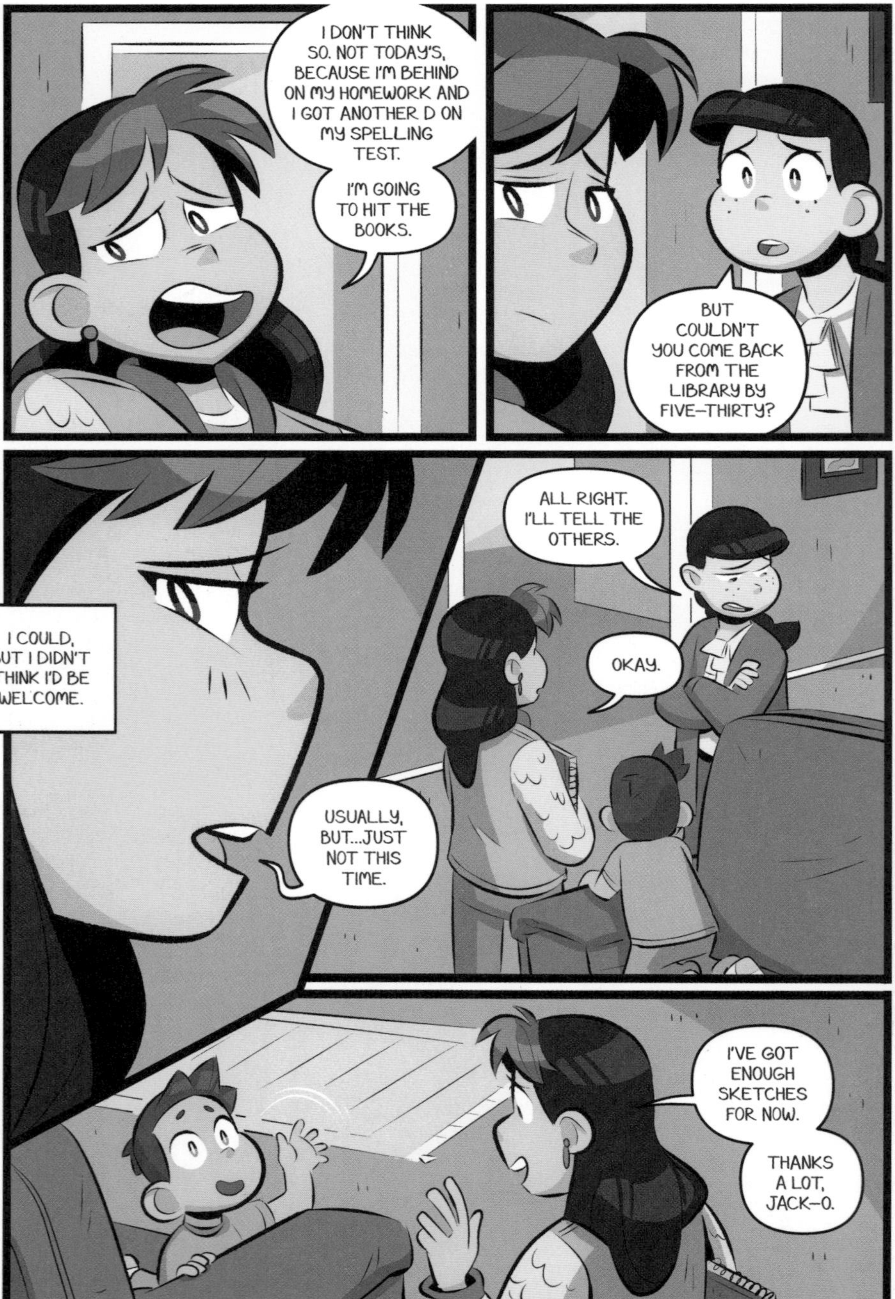
I DON'T THINK SO. NOT TODAY'S, BECAUSE I'M BEHIND ON MY HOMEWORK AND I GOT ANOTHER D ON MY SPELLING TEST.
I'M GOING TO HIT THE BOOKS.
BUT COULDN'T YOU COME BACK FROM THE LIBRARY BY FIVE-THIRTY?
I COULD, BUT I DIDN'T THINK I'D BE WELCOME.
ALL RIGHT. I'LL TELL THE OTHERS.
OKAY.
USUALLY, BUT...JUST NOT THIS TIME.
I'VE GOT ENOUGH SKETCHES FOR NOW.
THANKS A LOT, JACK-O.

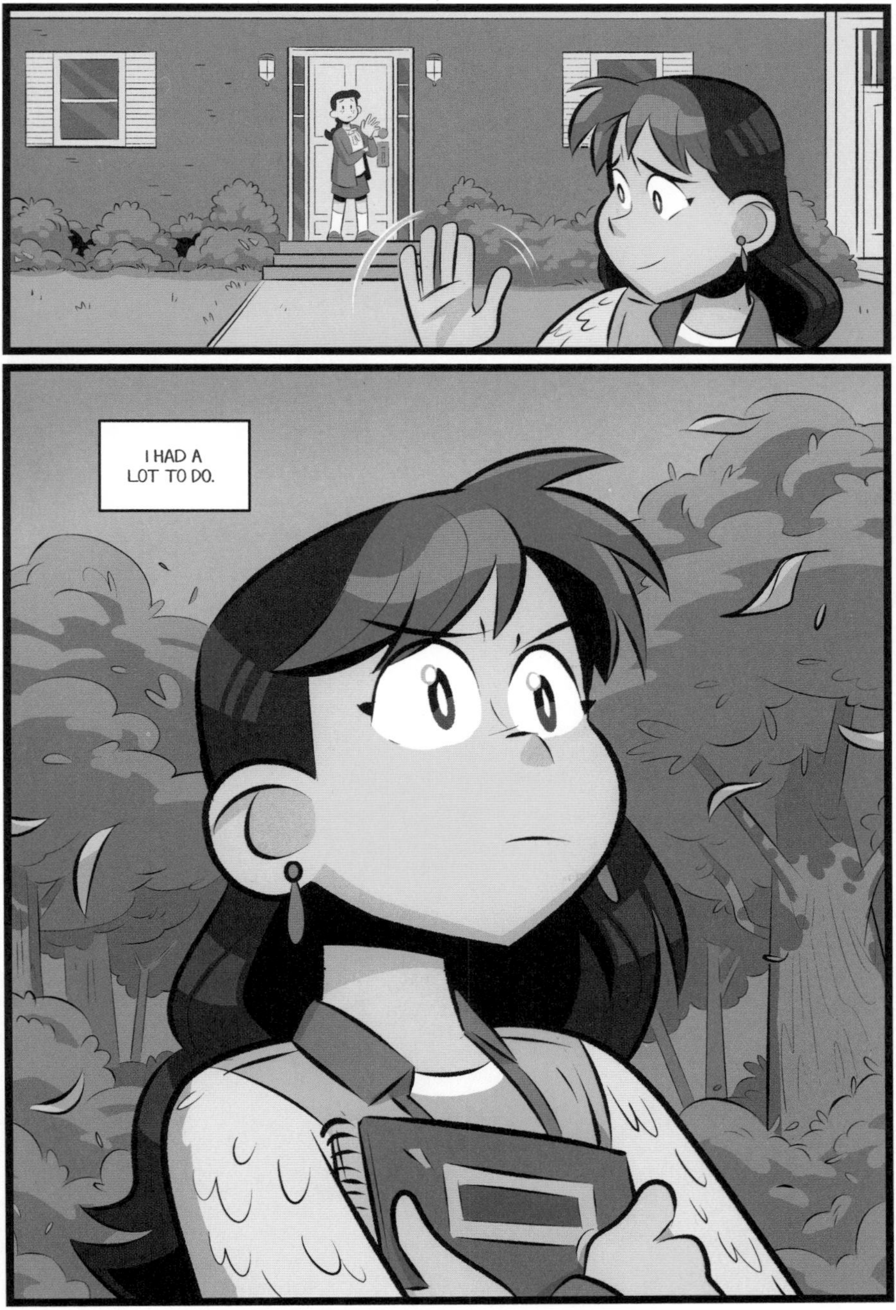
I HAD A
LOT TO DO.

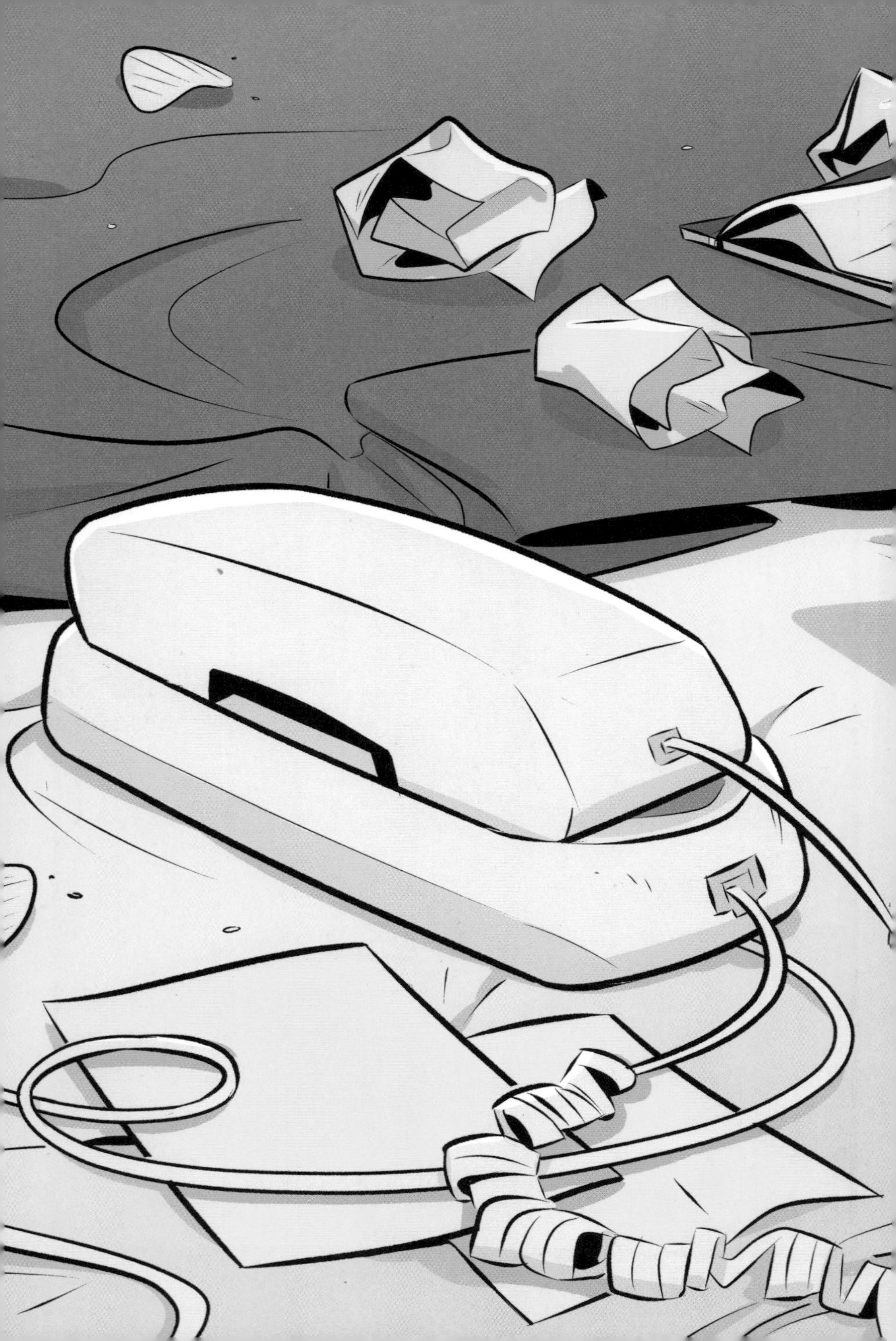

CHAPTER 11

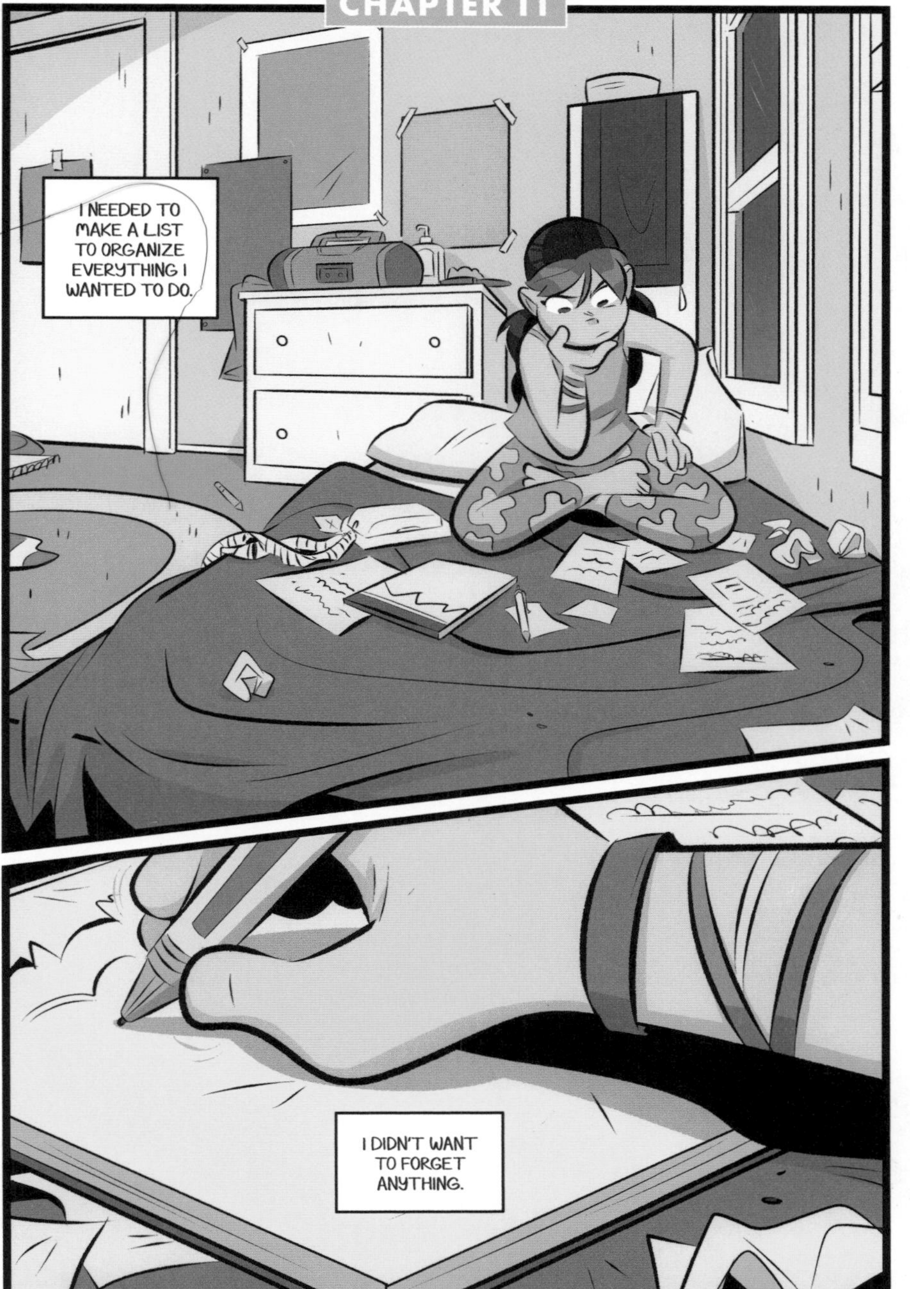
I NEEDED TO MAKE A LIST TO ORGANIZE EVERYTHING I WANTED TO DO.
I DIDN'T WANT TO FORGET ANYTHING.

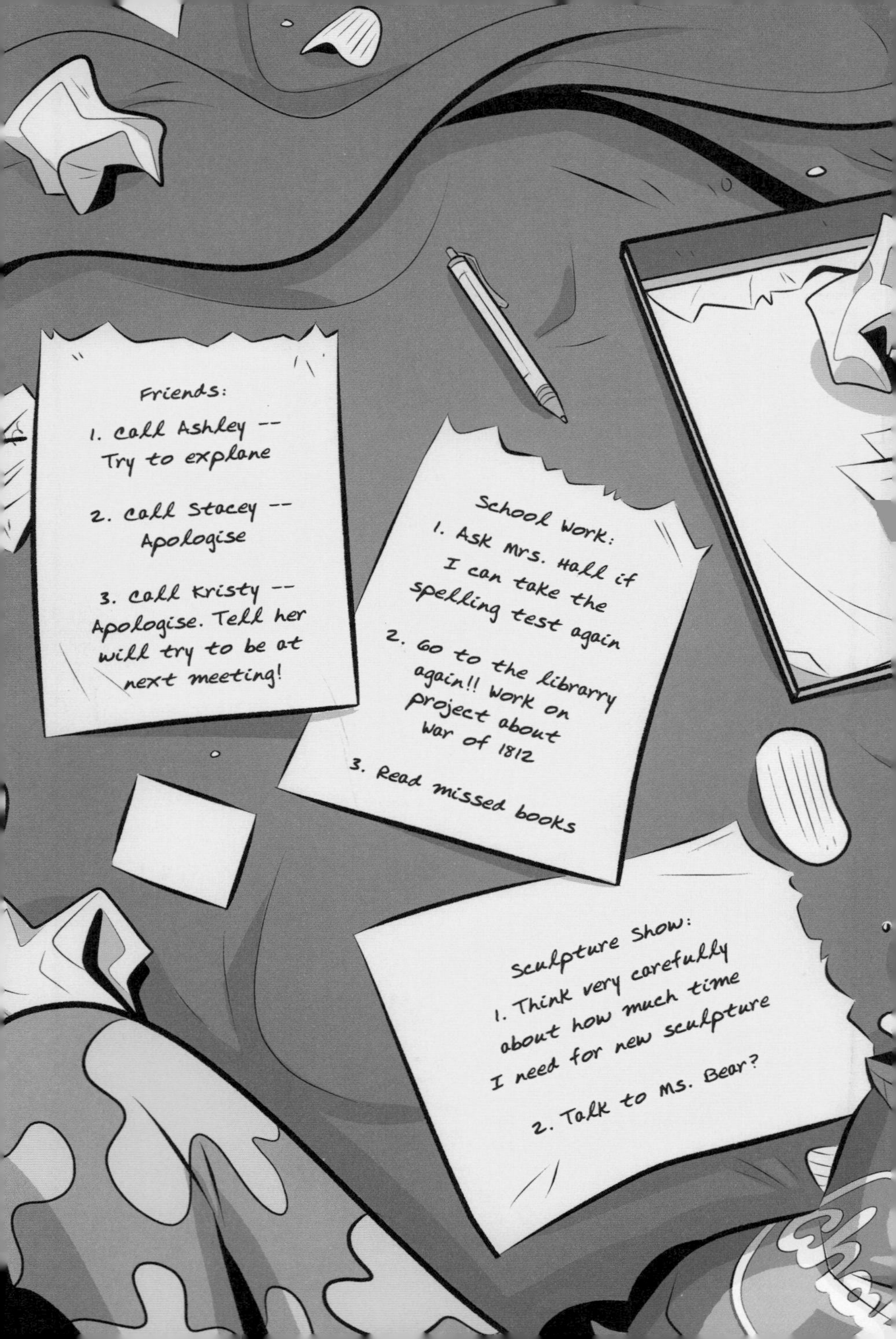
Friends:
1. Call Ashley -- Try to explane
2. Call Stacey -- Apologise
3. Call Kristy -- Apologise. Tell her will try to be at next meeting!
School Work:
1. Ask Mrs. Hall if I can take the spelling test again
2. Go to the librarry again!! Work on project about War of 1812
3. Read missed books
Sculpture Show:
1. Think very carefully about how much time I need for new sculpture
2. Talk to Ms. Bear?

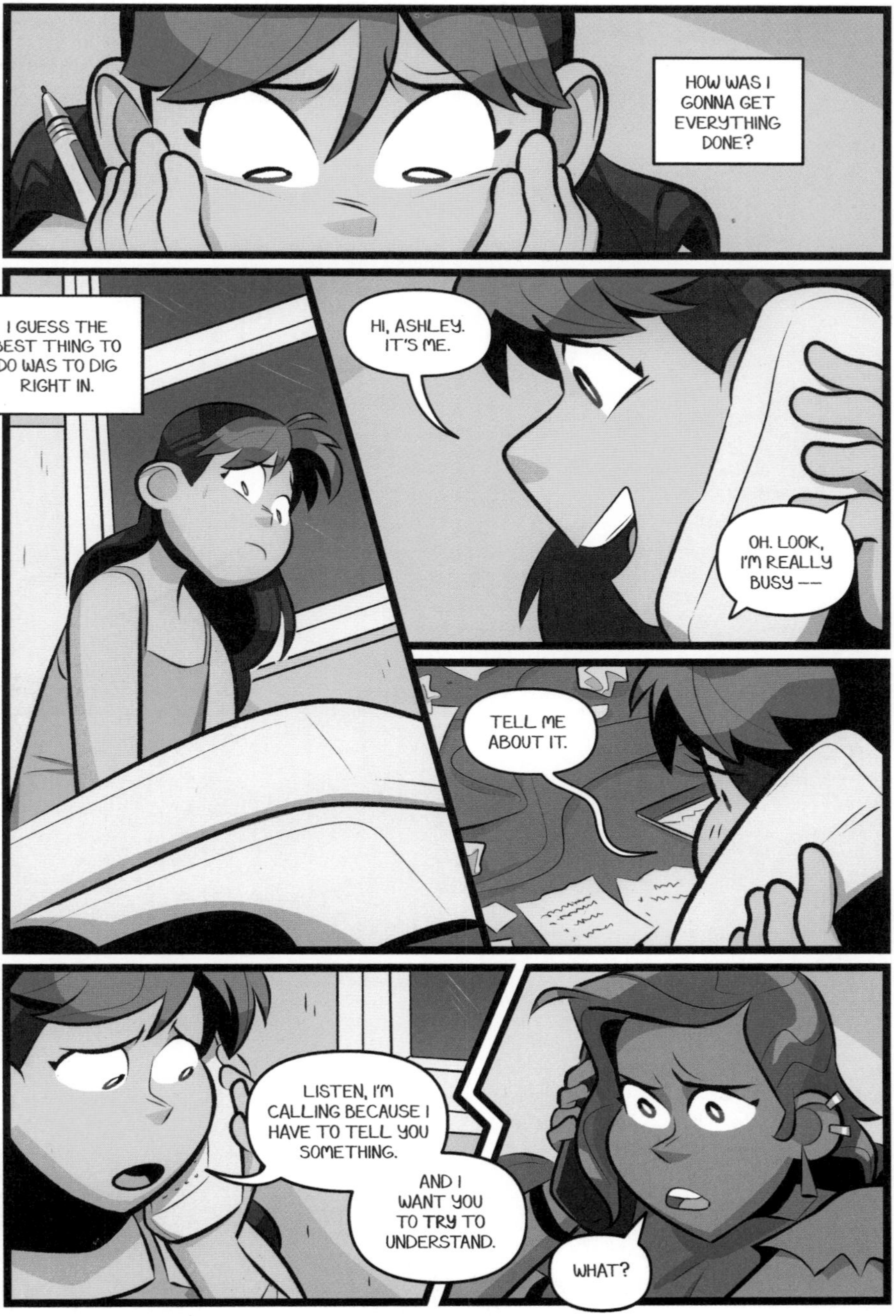
HOW WAS I GONNA GET EVERYTHING DONE?
I GUESS THE BEST THING TO DO WAS TO DIG RIGHT IN.
HI, ASHLEY. IT'S ME.
OH. LOOK, I'M REALLY BUSY --
TELL ME ABOUT IT.
LISTEN, I'M CALLING BECAUSE I HAVE TO TELL YOU SOMETHING.
AND I WANT YOU TO TRY TO UNDERSTAND.
WHAT?

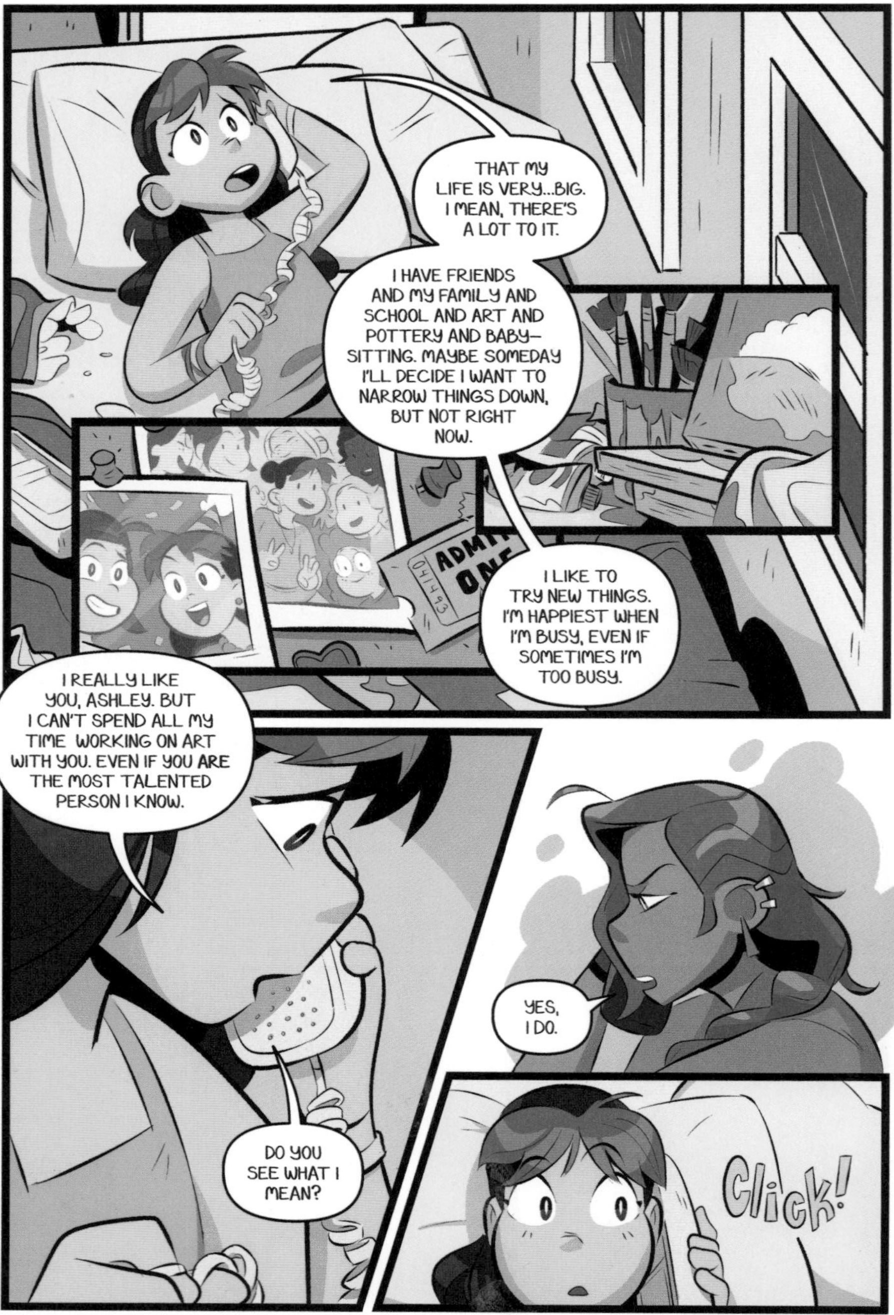
THAT MY LIFE IS VERY...BIG. I MEAN, THERE'S A LOT TO IT.
I HAVE FRIENDS AND MY FAMILY AND SCHOOL AND ART AND POTTERY AND BABY-SITTING. MAYBE SOMEDAY I'LL DECIDE I WANT TO NARROW THINGS DOWN, BUT NOT RIGHT NOW.
ADMIT ONE
I LIKE TO TRY NEW THINGS. I'M HAPPIEST WHEN I'M BUSY, EVEN IF SOMETIMES I'M TOO BUSY.
I REALLY LIKE YOU, ASHLEY. BUT I CAN'T SPEND ALL MY TIME WORKING ON ART WITH YOU. EVEN IF YOU ARE THE MOST TALENTED PERSON I KNOW.
DO YOU SEE WHAT I MEAN?
YES, I DO.
CLICK!

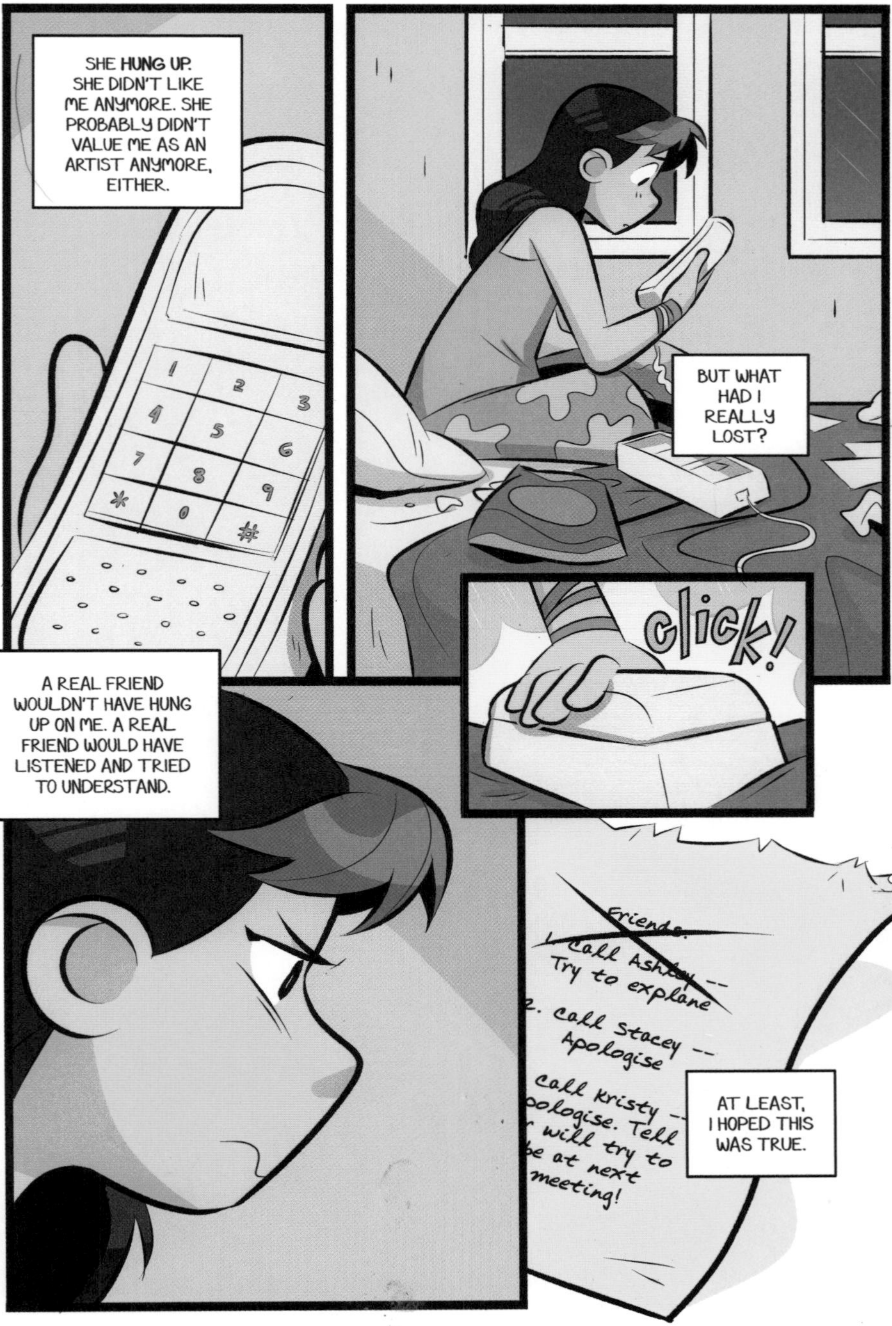
SHE **HUNG UP.** SHE DIDN'T LIKE ME ANYMORE. SHE PROBABLY DIDN'T VALUE ME AS AN ARTIST ANYMORE, EITHER.
1 2 3 4 5 6 7 8 9 * 0 #
BUT WHAT HAD I REALLY LOST?
click!
A REAL FRIEND WOULDN'T HAVE HUNG UP ON ME. A REAL FRIEND WOULD HAVE LISTENED AND TRIED TO UNDERSTAND.
Friends
Call Ashley -- Try to explane
2. Call Stacey -- Apologise
Call Kristy -- pologise. Tell r will try to be at next meeting!
AT LEAST, I HOPED THIS WAS TRUE.

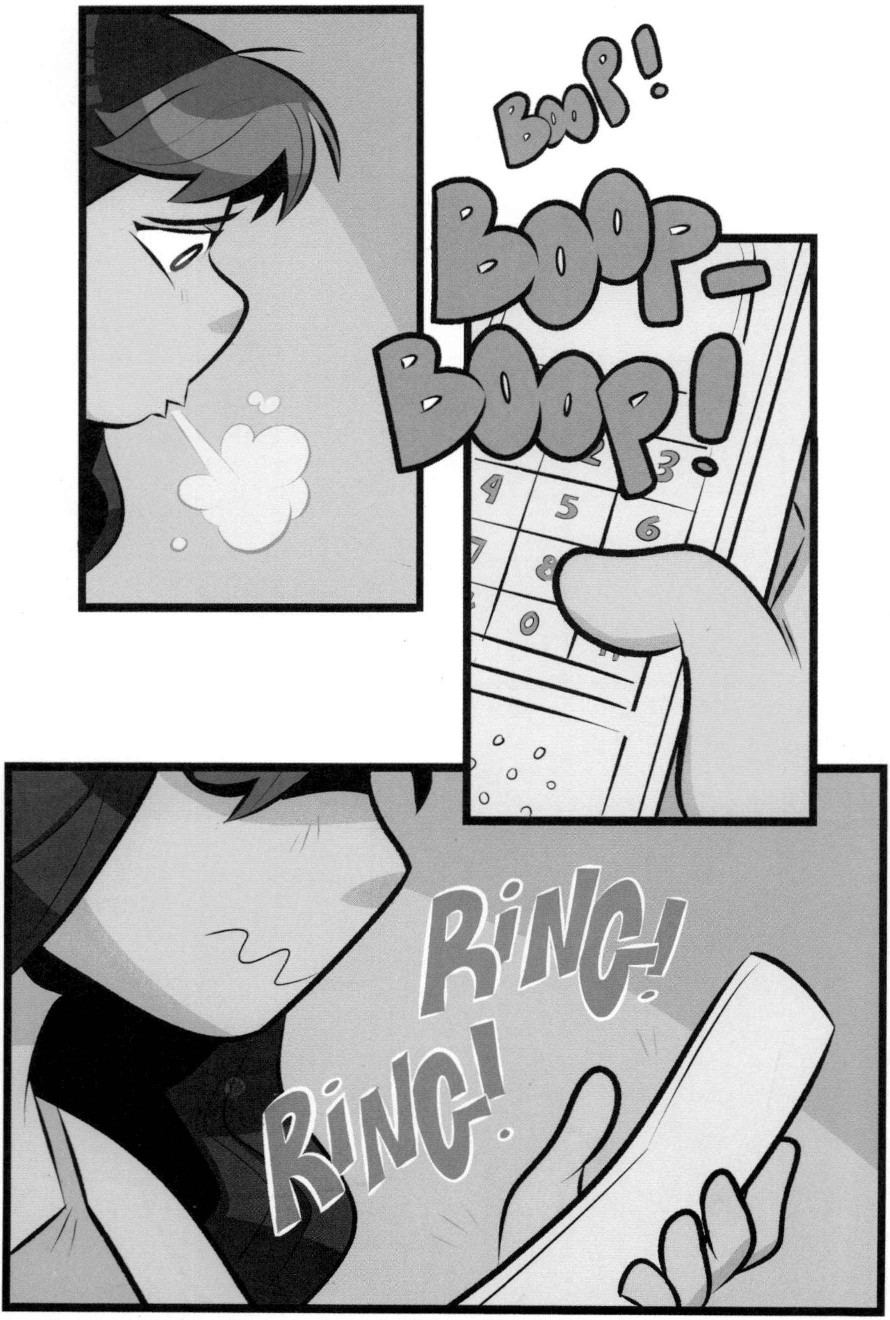
BOOP!
BOOP-BOOP!
RING!
RING!

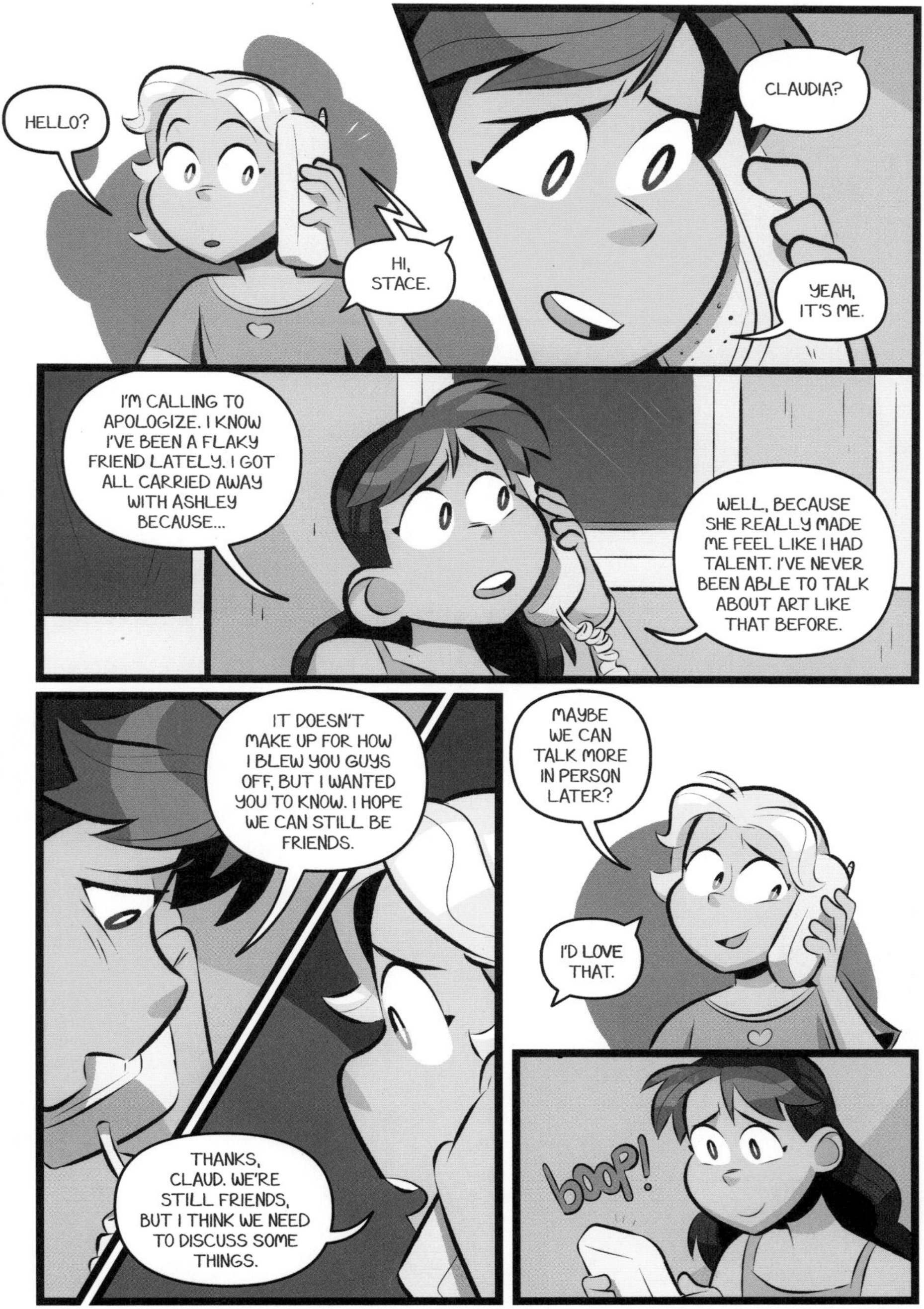
HELLO?
CLAUDIA?
HI, STACE.
YEAH, IT'S ME.
I'M CALLING TO APOLOGIZE. I KNOW I'VE BEEN A FLAKY FRIEND LATELY. I GOT ALL CARRIED AWAY WITH ASHLEY BECAUSE...
WELL, BECAUSE SHE REALLY MADE ME FEEL LIKE I HAD TALENT. I'VE NEVER BEEN ABLE TO TALK ABOUT ART LIKE THAT BEFORE.
IT DOESN'T MAKE UP FOR HOW I BLEW YOU GUYS OFF, BUT I WANTED YOU TO KNOW. I HOPE WE CAN STILL BE FRIENDS.
THANKS, CLAUD. WE'RE STILL FRIENDS, BUT I THINK WE NEED TO DISCUSS SOME THINGS.
MAYBE WE CAN TALK MORE IN PERSON LATER?
I'D LOVE THAT.
boop!

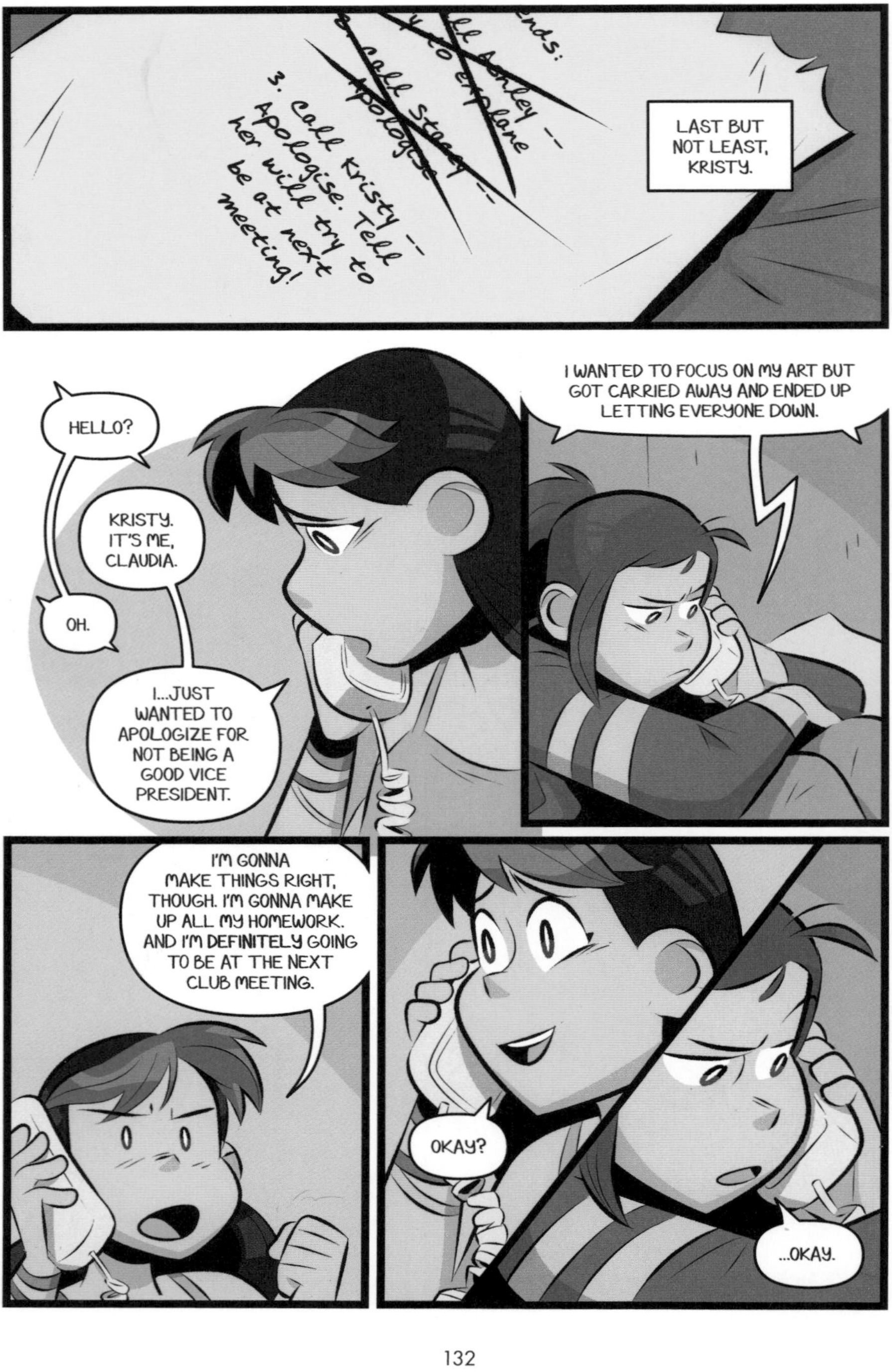
3. Call Kristy -- Apologise. Tell her will try to be at next meeting!
LAST BUT NOT LEAST, KRISTY.
HELLO?
KRISTY. IT'S ME, CLAUDIA.
OH.
I...JUST WANTED TO APOLOGIZE FOR NOT BEING A GOOD VICE PRESIDENT.
I WANTED TO FOCUS ON MY ART BUT GOT CARRIED AWAY AND ENDED UP LETTING EVERYONE DOWN.
I'M GONNA MAKE THINGS RIGHT, THOUGH. I'M GONNA MAKE UP ALL MY HOMEWORK. AND I'M DEFINITELY GOING TO BE AT THE NEXT CLUB MEETING.
OKAY?
...OKAY.

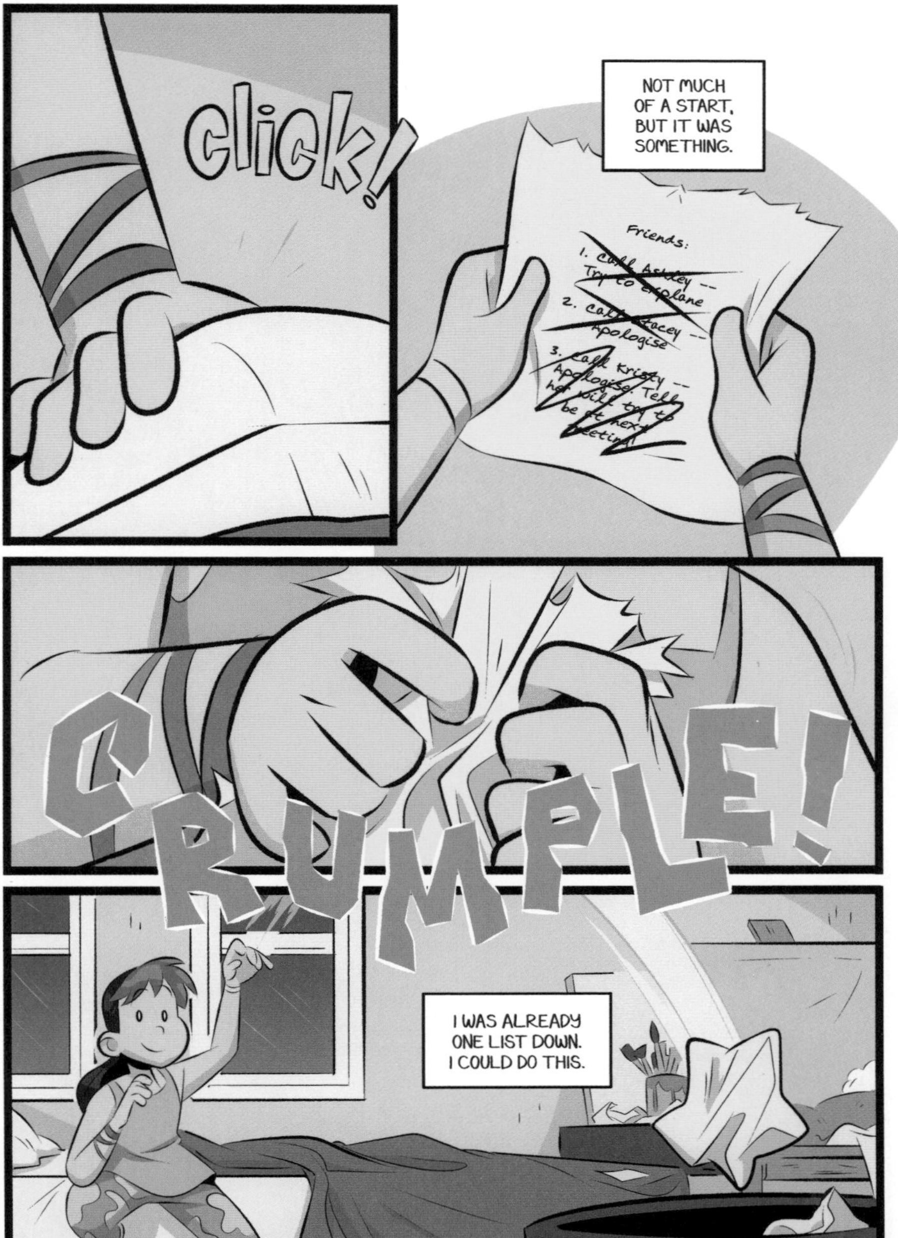
click!
NOT MUCH OF A START, BUT IT WAS SOMETHING.
Friends:
1. Call Ashley --
Try to explane
2. Call Stacey --
Apologise
3. Call Kristy --
Apologise. Tell
her I will try to
be at next
meeting!
CRUMPLE!
I WAS ALREADY ONE LIST DOWN. I COULD DO THIS.

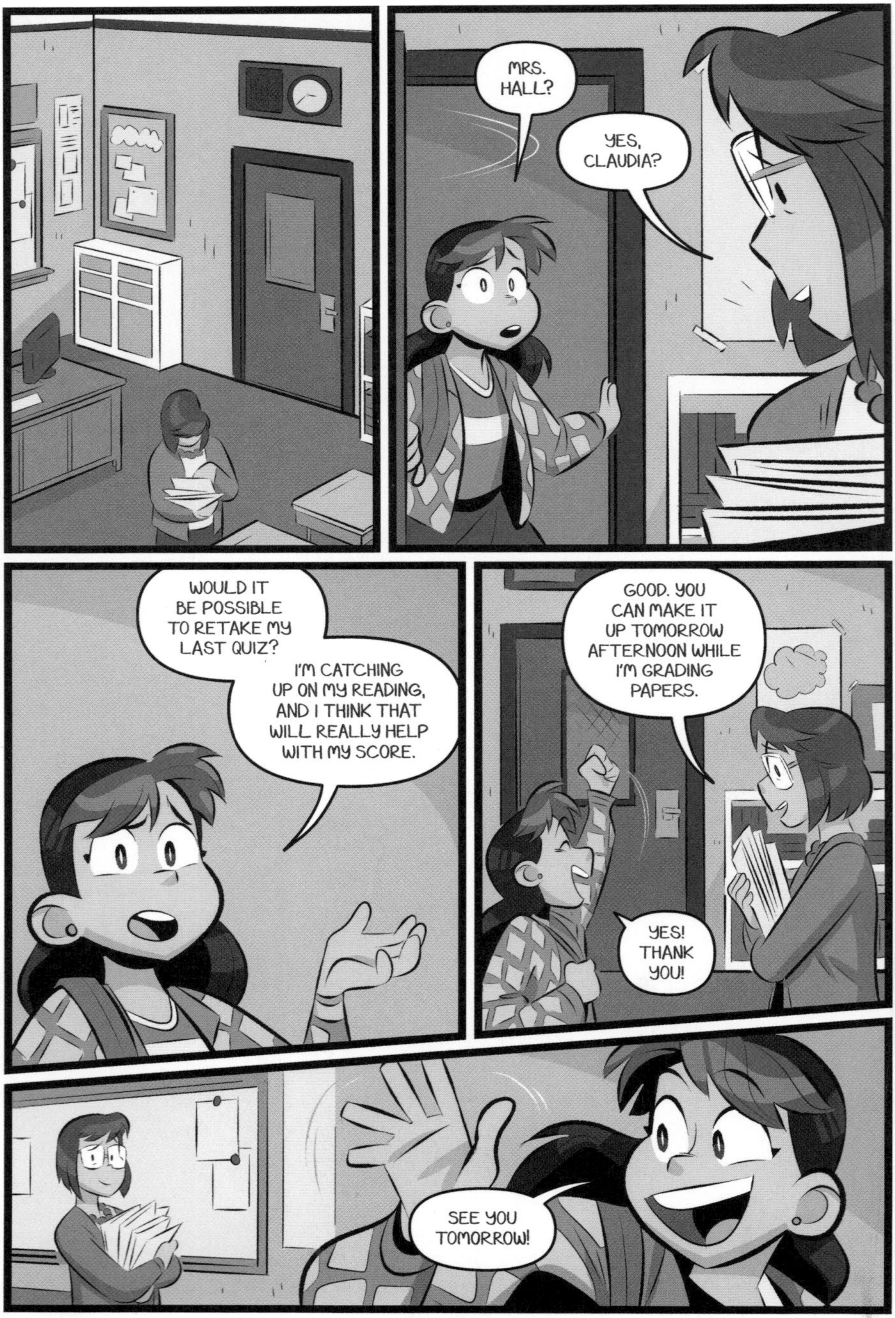
MRS. HALL?
YES, CLAUDIA?
WOULD IT BE POSSIBLE TO RETAKE MY LAST QUIZ?
I'M CATCHING UP ON MY READING, AND I THINK THAT WILL REALLY HELP WITH MY SCORE.
GOOD. YOU CAN MAKE IT UP TOMORROW AFTERNOON WHILE I'M GRADING PAPERS.
YES! THANK YOU!
SEE YOU TOMORROW!

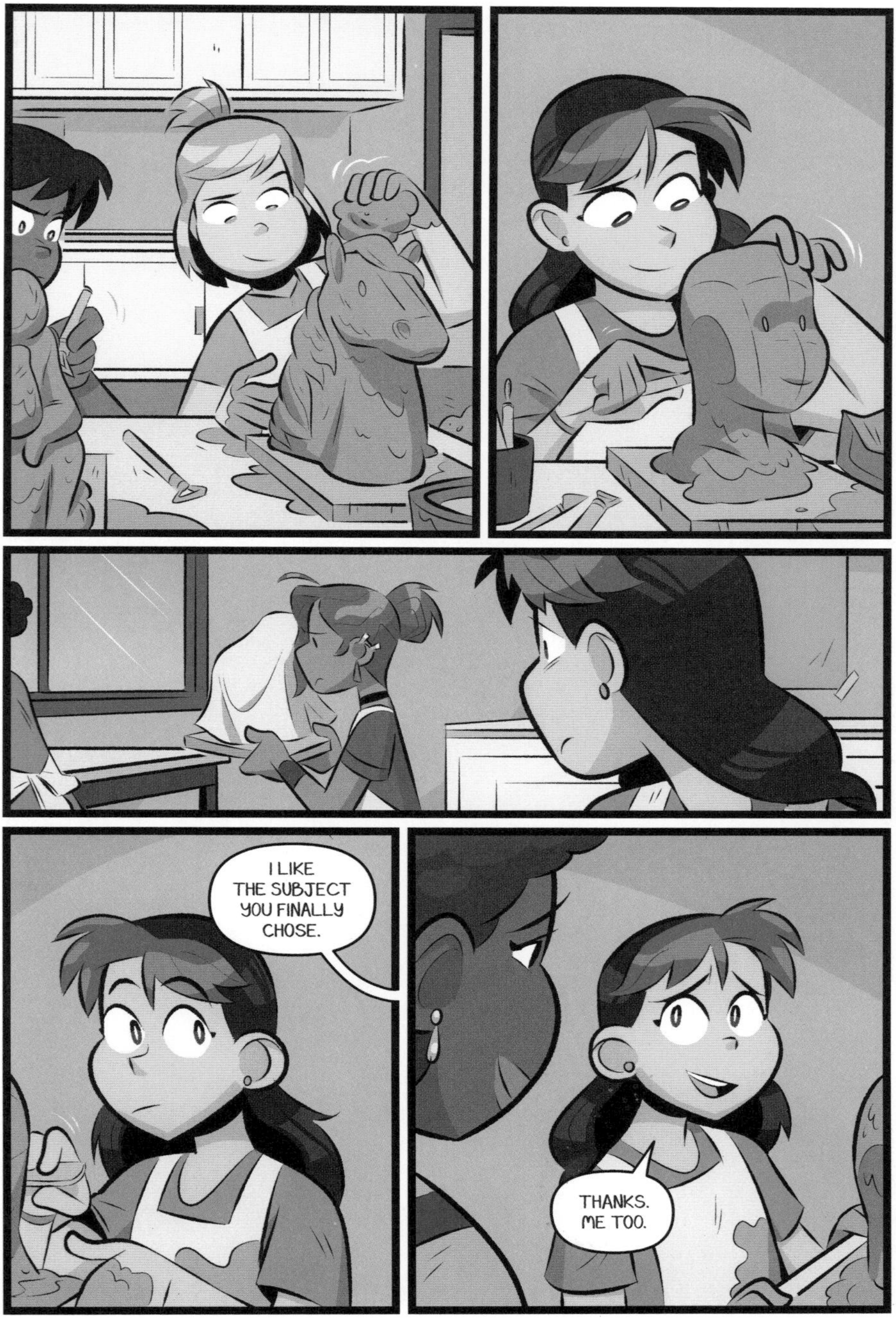
I LIKE THE SUBJECT YOU FINALLY CHOSE.
THANKS. ME TOO.

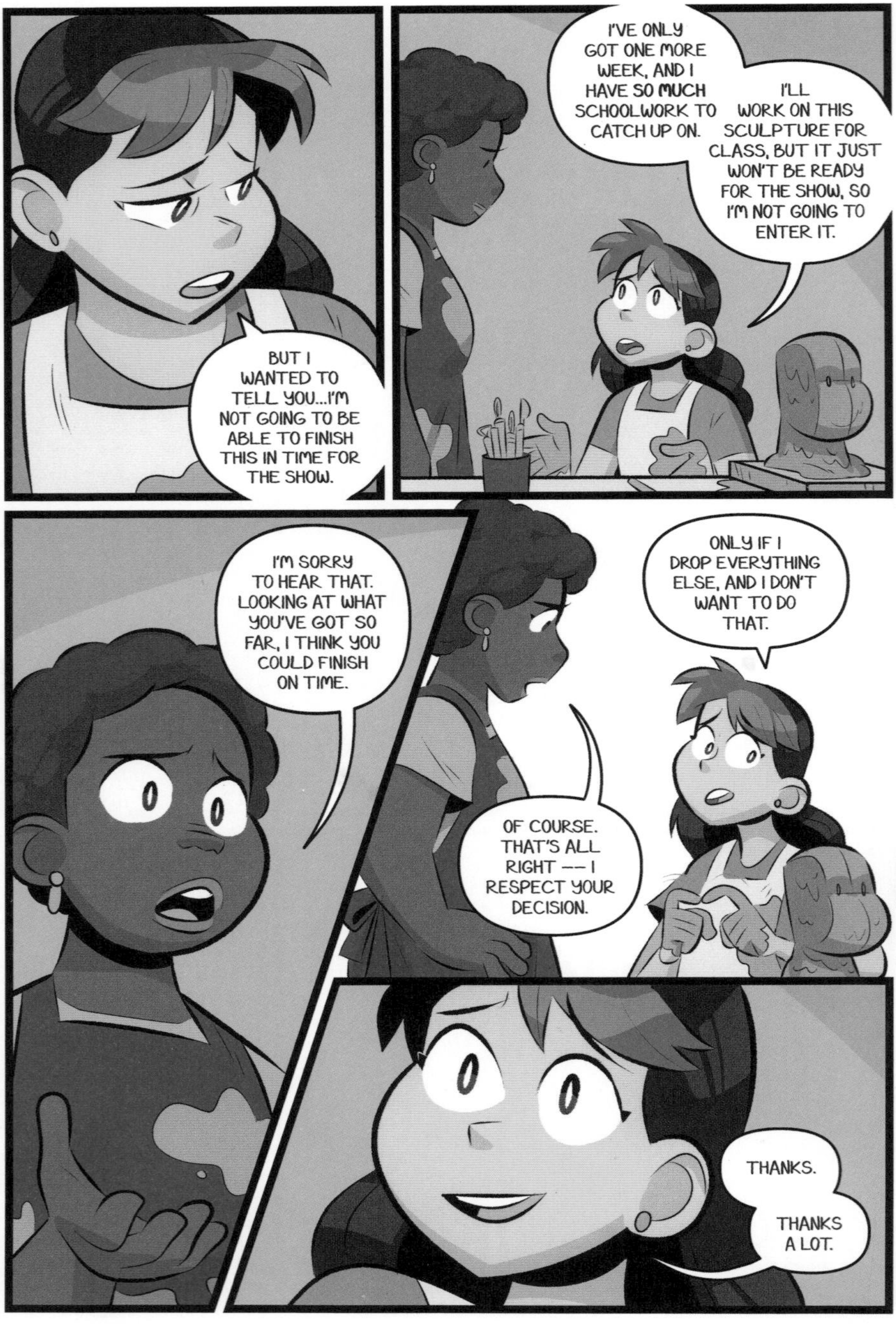
BUT I WANTED TO TELL YOU...I'M NOT GOING TO BE ABLE TO FINISH THIS IN TIME FOR THE SHOW.
I'VE ONLY GOT ONE MORE WEEK, AND I HAVE SO MUCH SCHOOLWORK TO CATCH UP ON.
I'LL WORK ON THIS SCULPTURE FOR CLASS, BUT IT JUST WON'T BE READY FOR THE SHOW, SO I'M NOT GOING TO ENTER IT.
I'M SORRY TO HEAR THAT. LOOKING AT WHAT YOU'VE GOT SO FAR, I THINK YOU COULD FINISH ON TIME.
ONLY IF I DROP EVERYTHING ELSE, AND I DON'T WANT TO DO THAT.
OF COURSE. THAT'S ALL RIGHT -- I RESPECT YOUR DECISION.
THANKS.
THANKS A LOT.

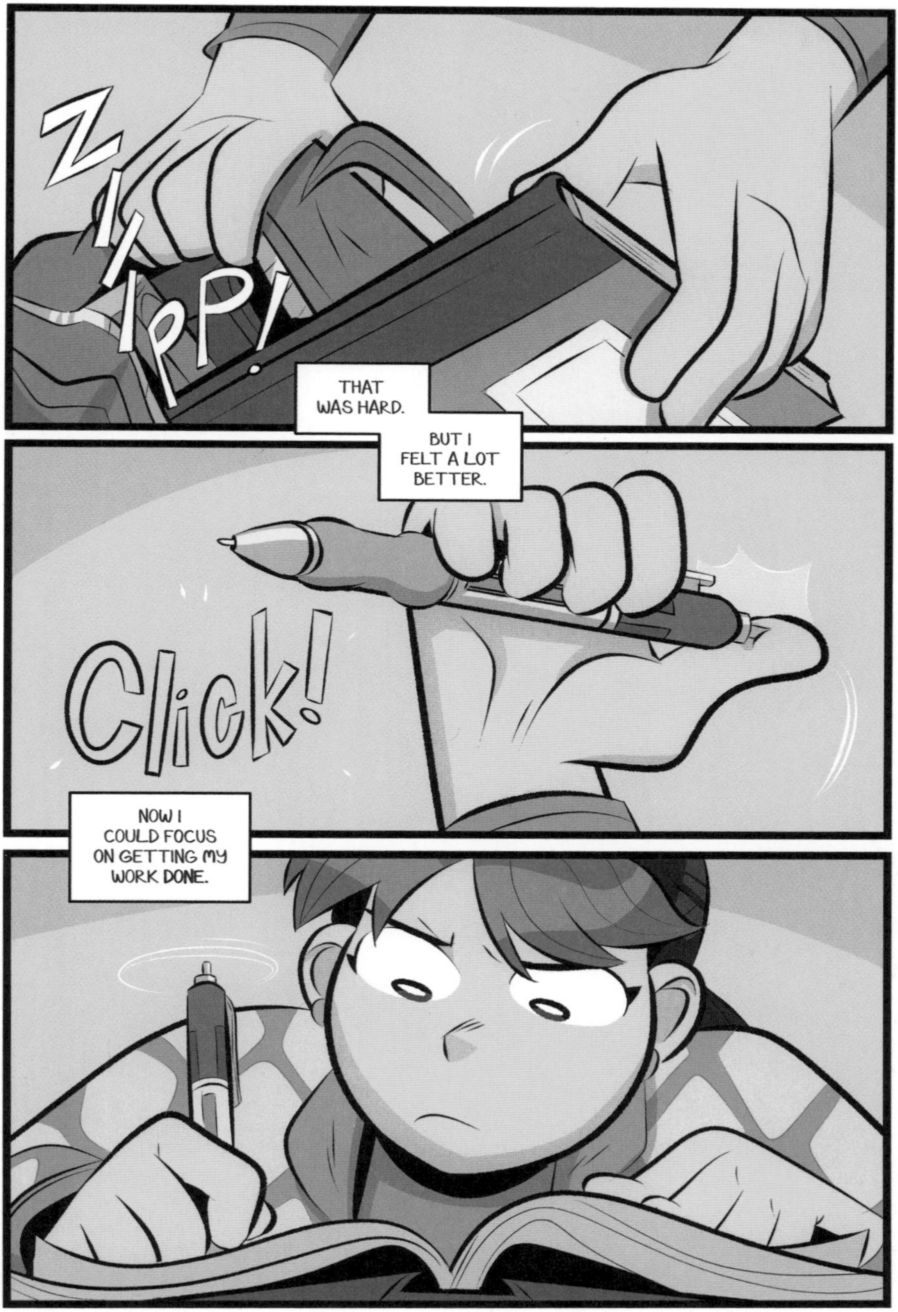
ZZIPP!
THAT WAS HARD.
BUT I FELT A LOT BETTER.
Click!
NOW I COULD FOCUS ON GETTING MY WORK DONE.

CHAPTER 12

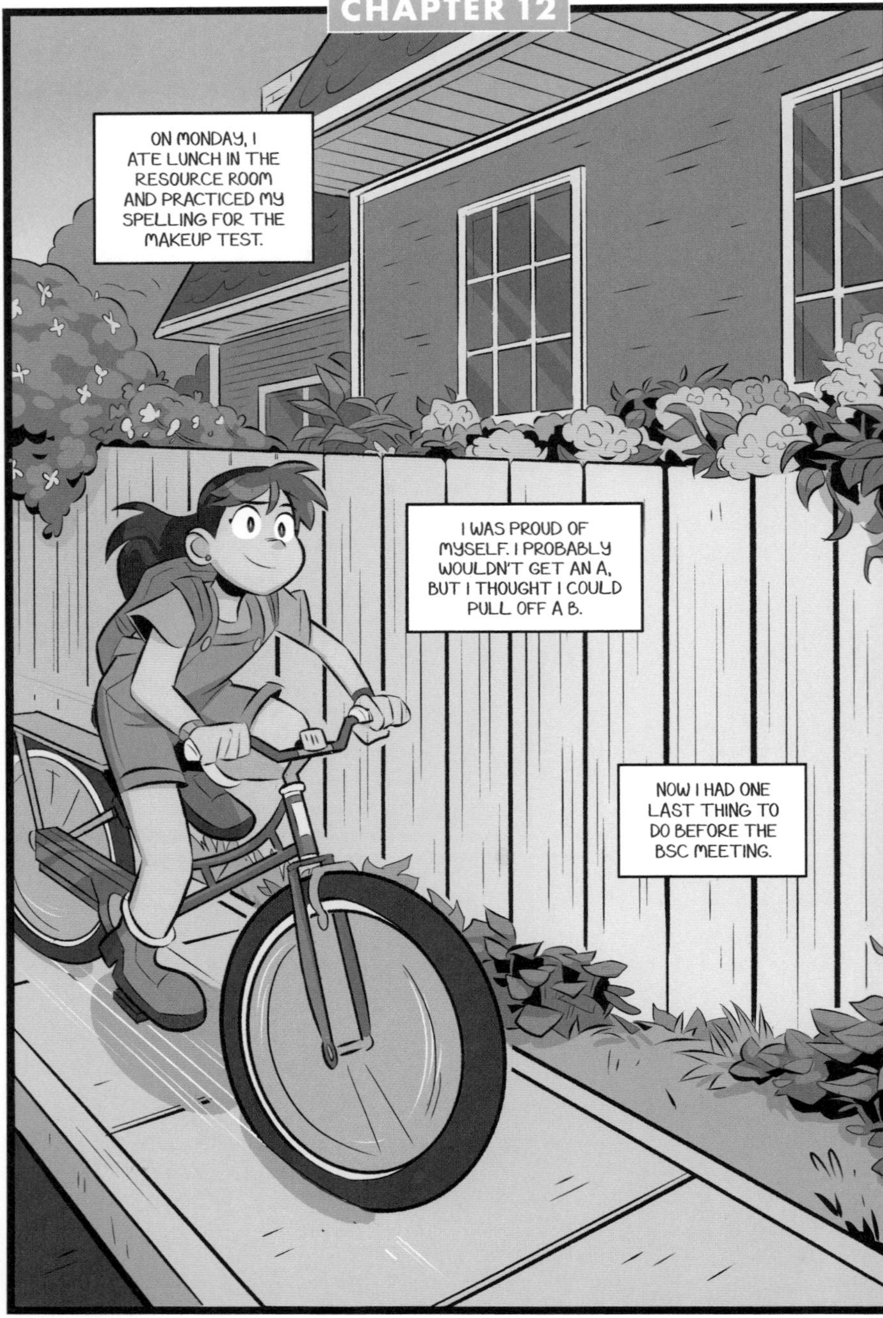
ON MONDAY, I ATE LUNCH IN THE RESOURCE ROOM AND PRACTICED MY SPELLING FOR THE MAKEUP TEST.
I WAS PROUD OF MYSELF. I PROBABLY WOULDN'T GET AN A, BUT I THOUGHT I COULD PULL OFF A B.
NOW I HAD ONE LAST THING TO DO BEFORE THE BSC MEETING.

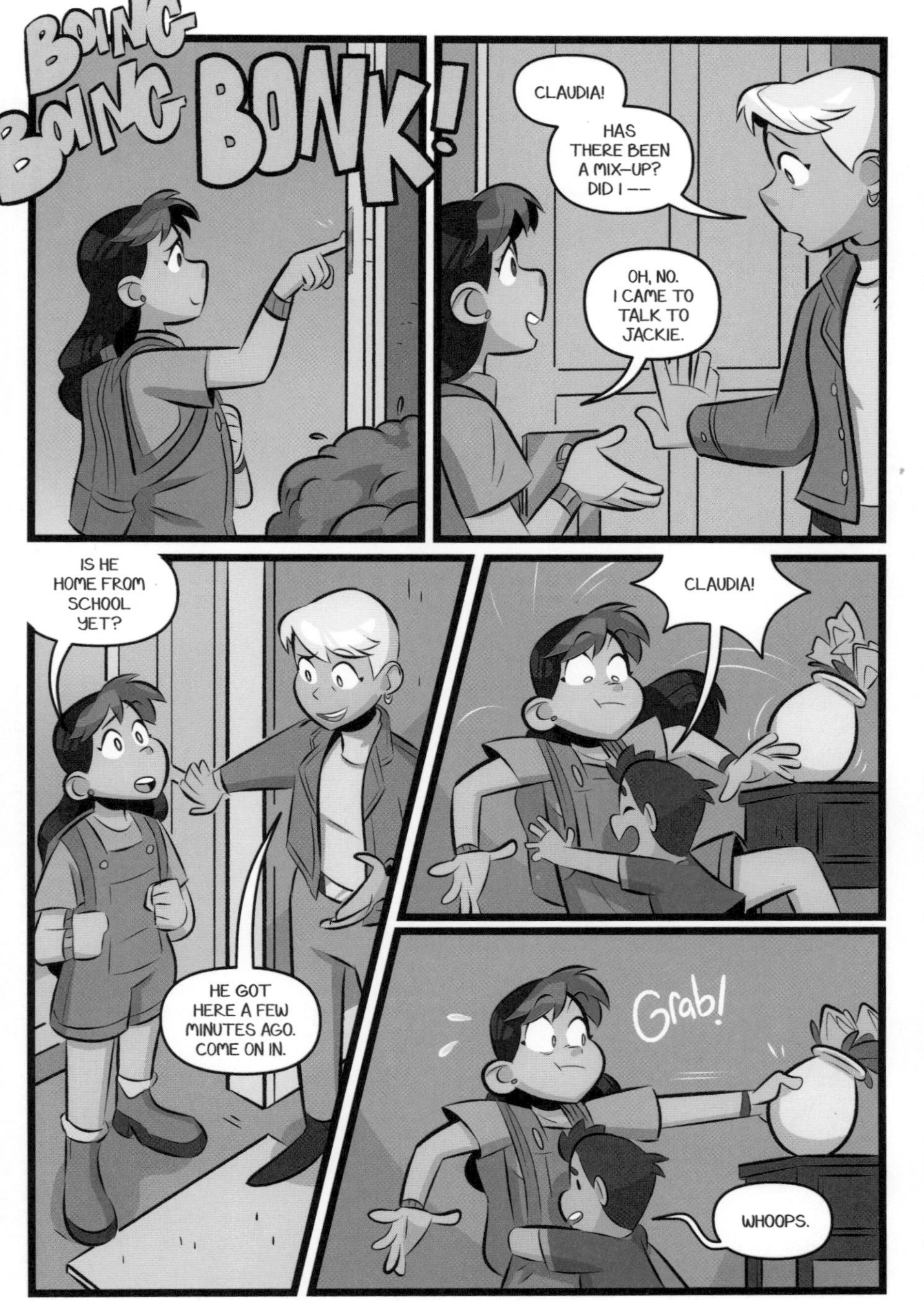
BOING
BOING
BONK!
CLAUDIA!
HAS THERE BEEN A MIX-UP? DID I --
OH, NO. I CAME TO TALK TO JACKIE.
IS HE HOME FROM SCHOOL YET?
HE GOT HERE A FEW MINUTES AGO. COME ON IN.
CLAUDIA!
Grab!
WHOOPS.

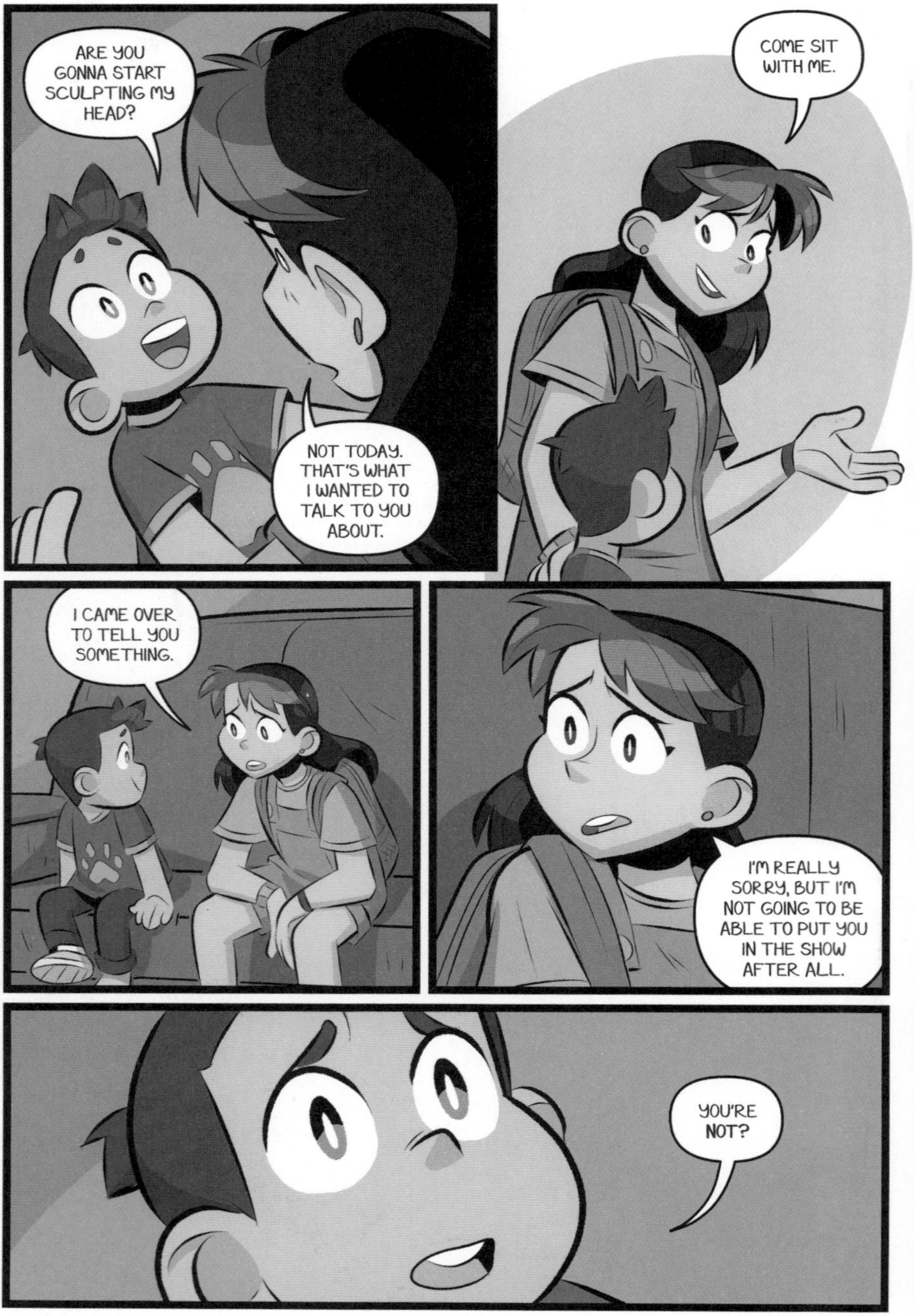
ARE YOU GONNA START SCULPTING MY HEAD?
NOT TODAY. THAT'S WHAT I WANTED TO TALK TO YOU ABOUT.
COME SIT WITH ME.
I CAME OVER TO TELL YOU SOMETHING.
I'M REALLY SORRY, BUT I'M NOT GOING TO BE ABLE TO PUT YOU IN THE SHOW AFTER ALL.
YOU'RE NOT?

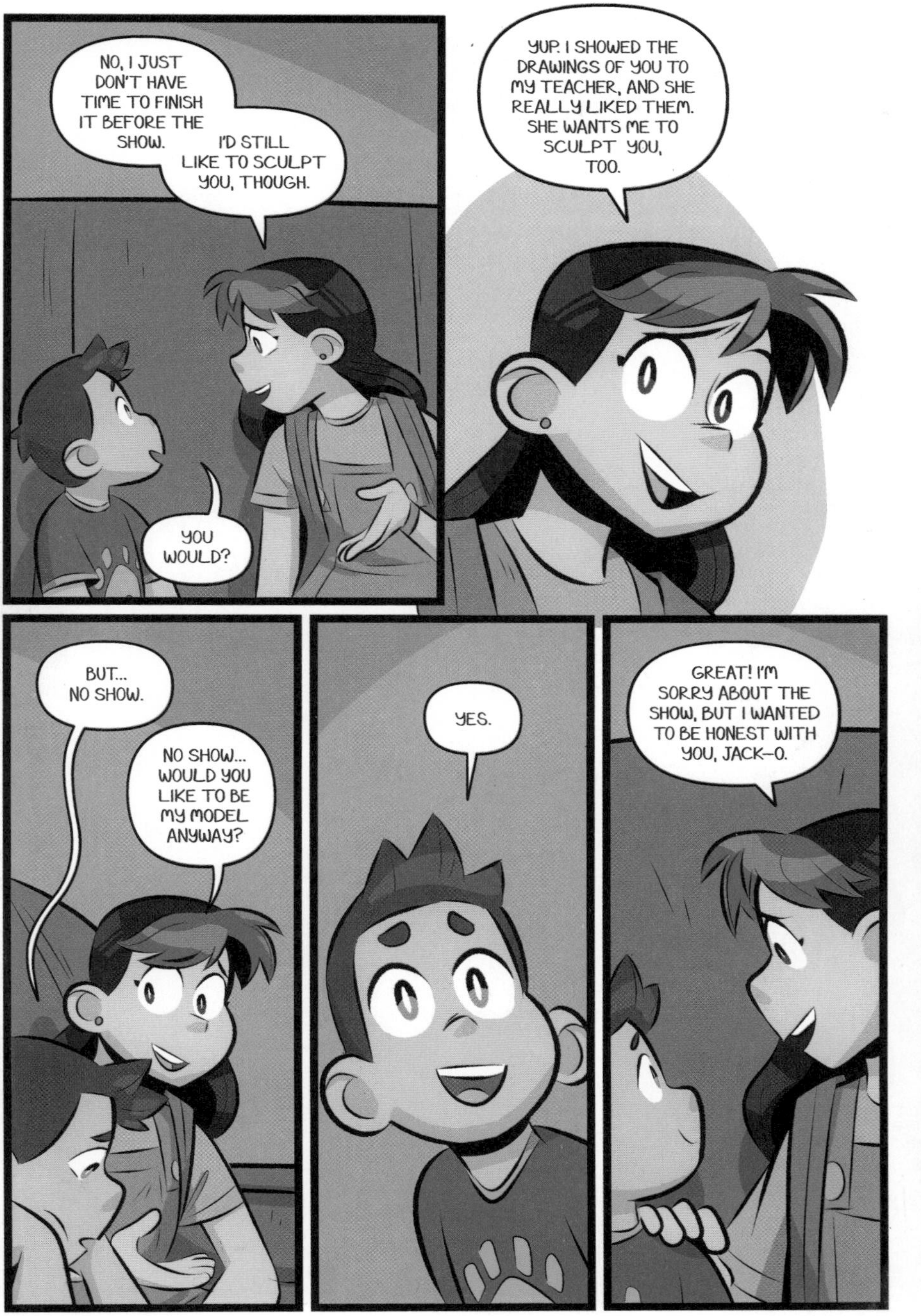
NO, I JUST DON'T HAVE TIME TO FINISH IT BEFORE THE SHOW.
I'D STILL LIKE TO SCULPT YOU, THOUGH.
YOU WOULD?
YUP. I SHOWED THE DRAWINGS OF YOU TO MY TEACHER, AND SHE REALLY LIKED THEM. SHE WANTS ME TO SCULPT YOU, TOO.
BUT... NO SHOW.
NO SHOW... WOULD YOU LIKE TO BE MY MODEL ANYWAY?
YES.
GREAT! I'M SORRY ABOUT THE SHOW, BUT I WANTED TO BE HONEST WITH YOU, JACK-O.

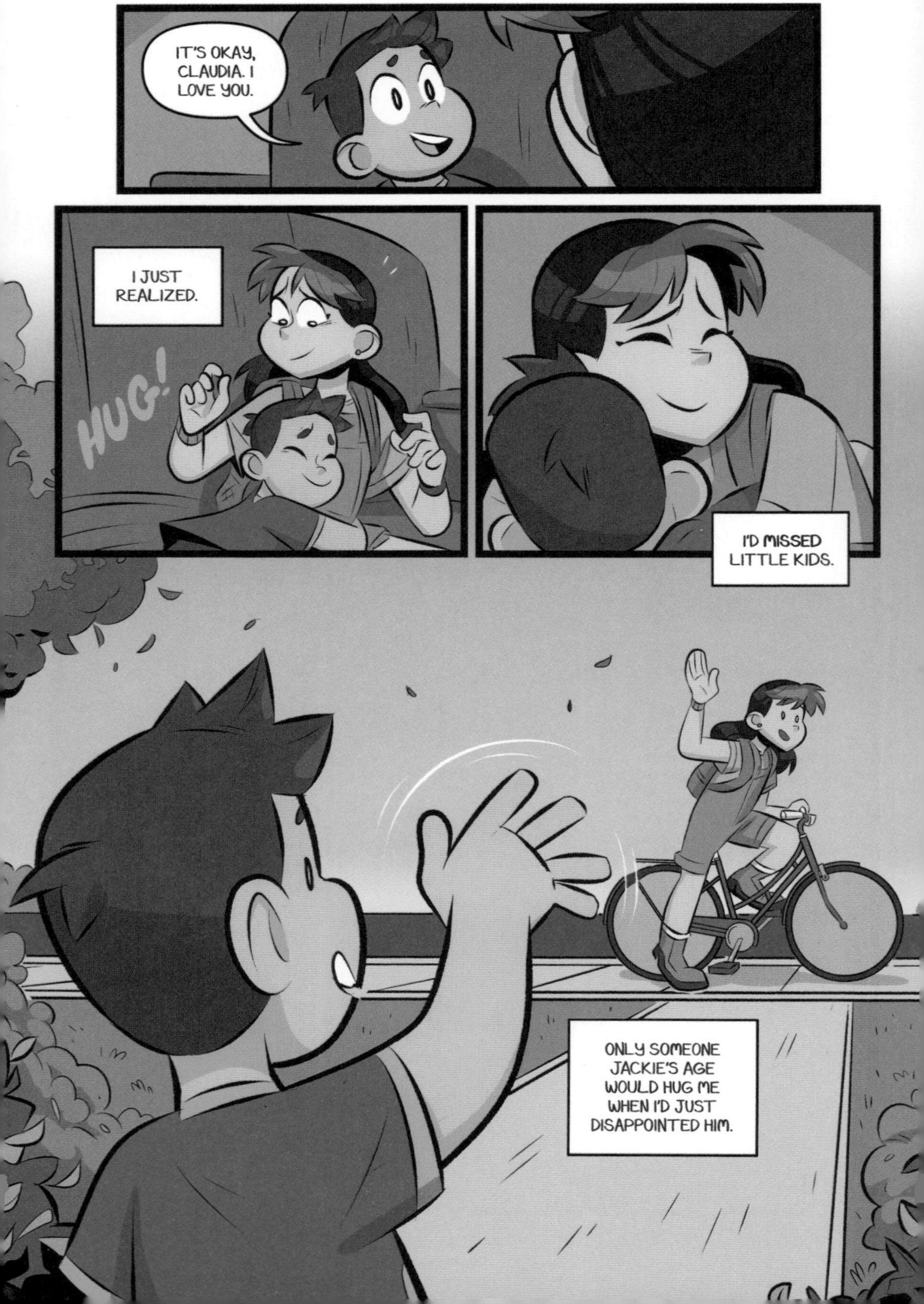
IT'S OKAY, CLAUDIA. I LOVE YOU.
I JUST REALIZED.
HUG!
I'D MISSED LITTLE KIDS.
ONLY SOMEONE JACKIE'S AGE WOULD HUG ME WHEN I'D JUST DISAPPOINTED HIM.

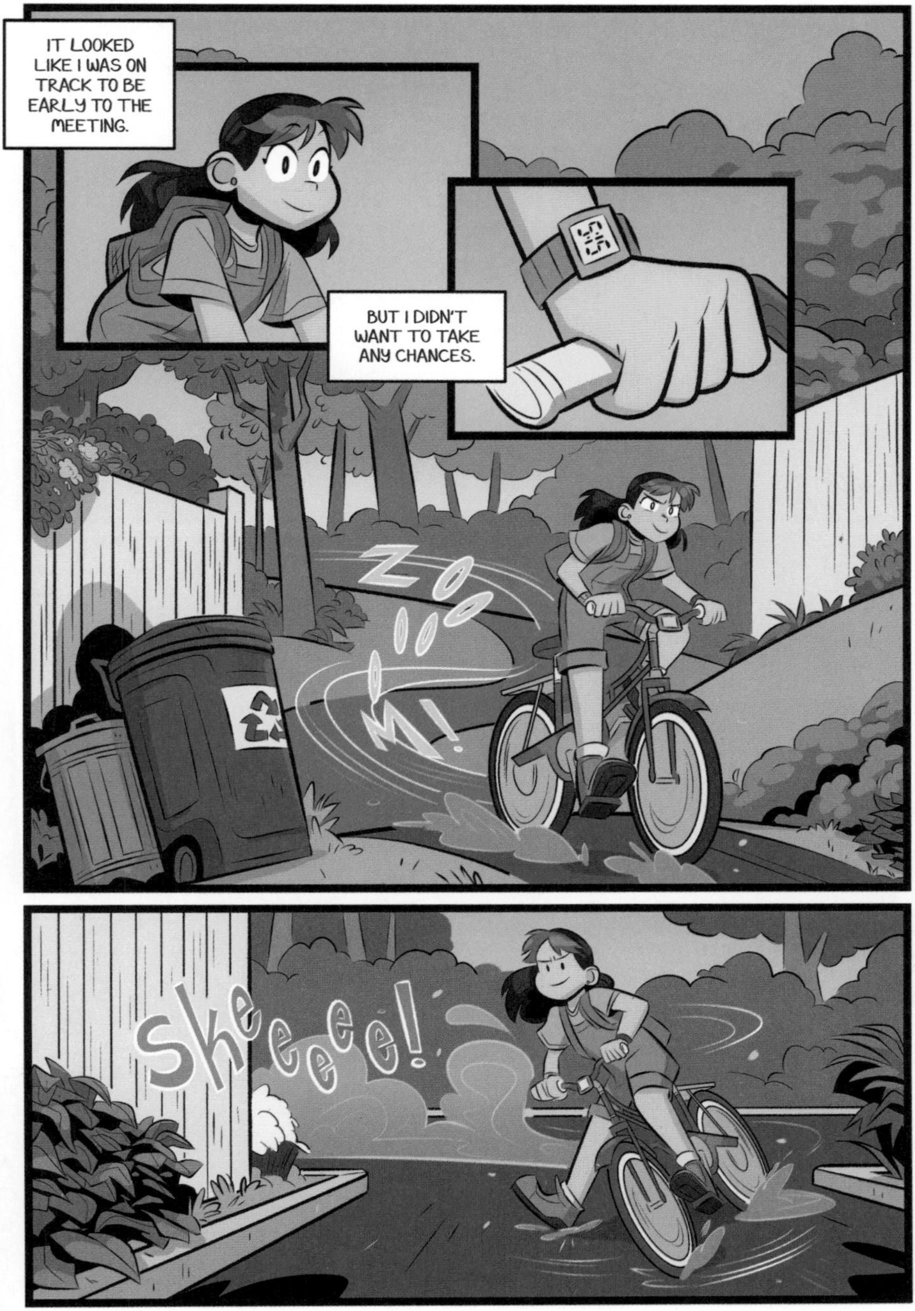
IT LOOKED LIKE I WAS ON TRACK TO BE EARLY TO THE MEETING.
BUT I DIDN'T WANT TO TAKE ANY CHANCES.
ZOOOOOM!
Skeeeee!

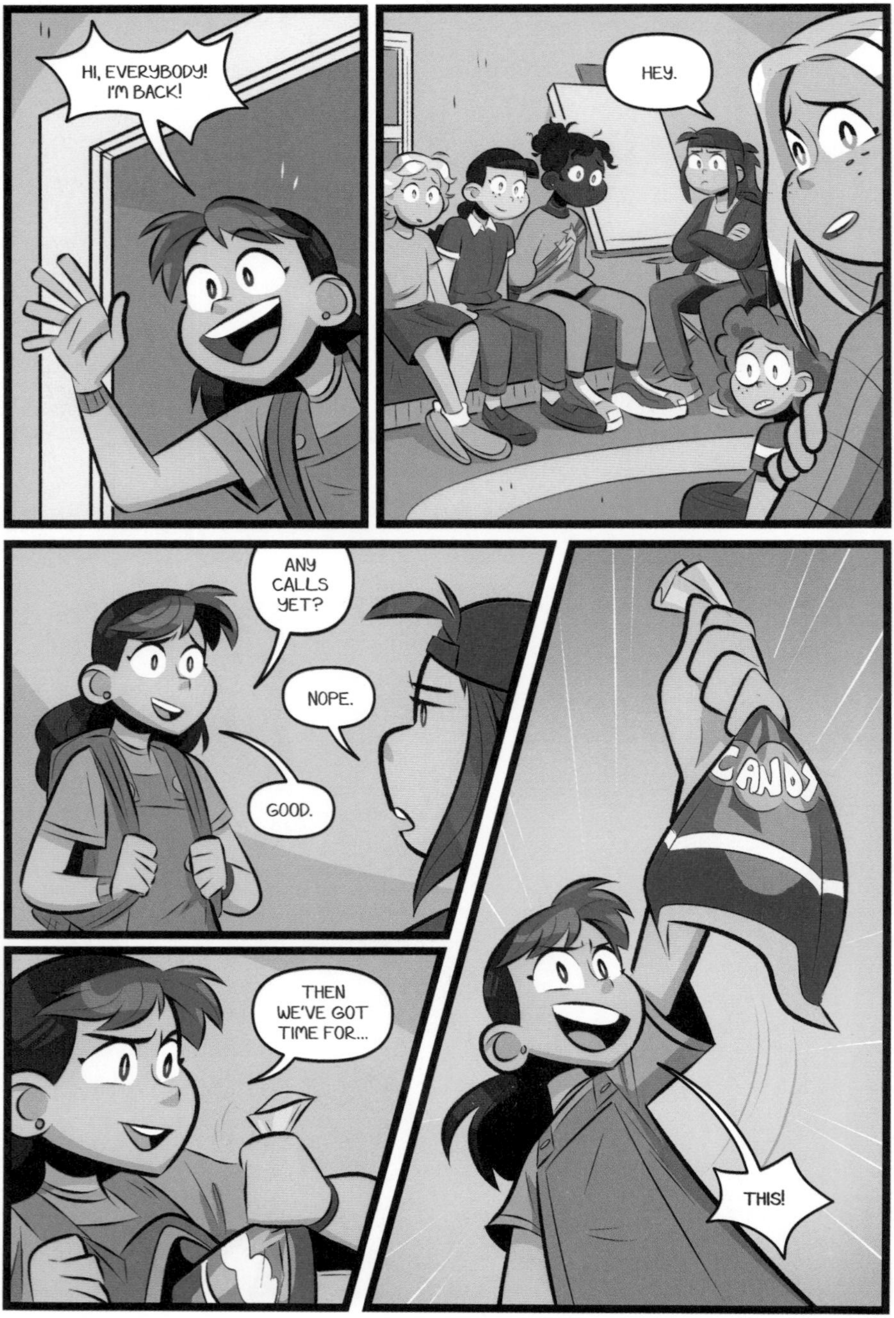
HI, EVERYBODY! I'M BACK!
HEY.
ANY CALLS YET?
NOPE.
GOOD.
THEN WE'VE GOT TIME FOR...
CANDY
THIS!

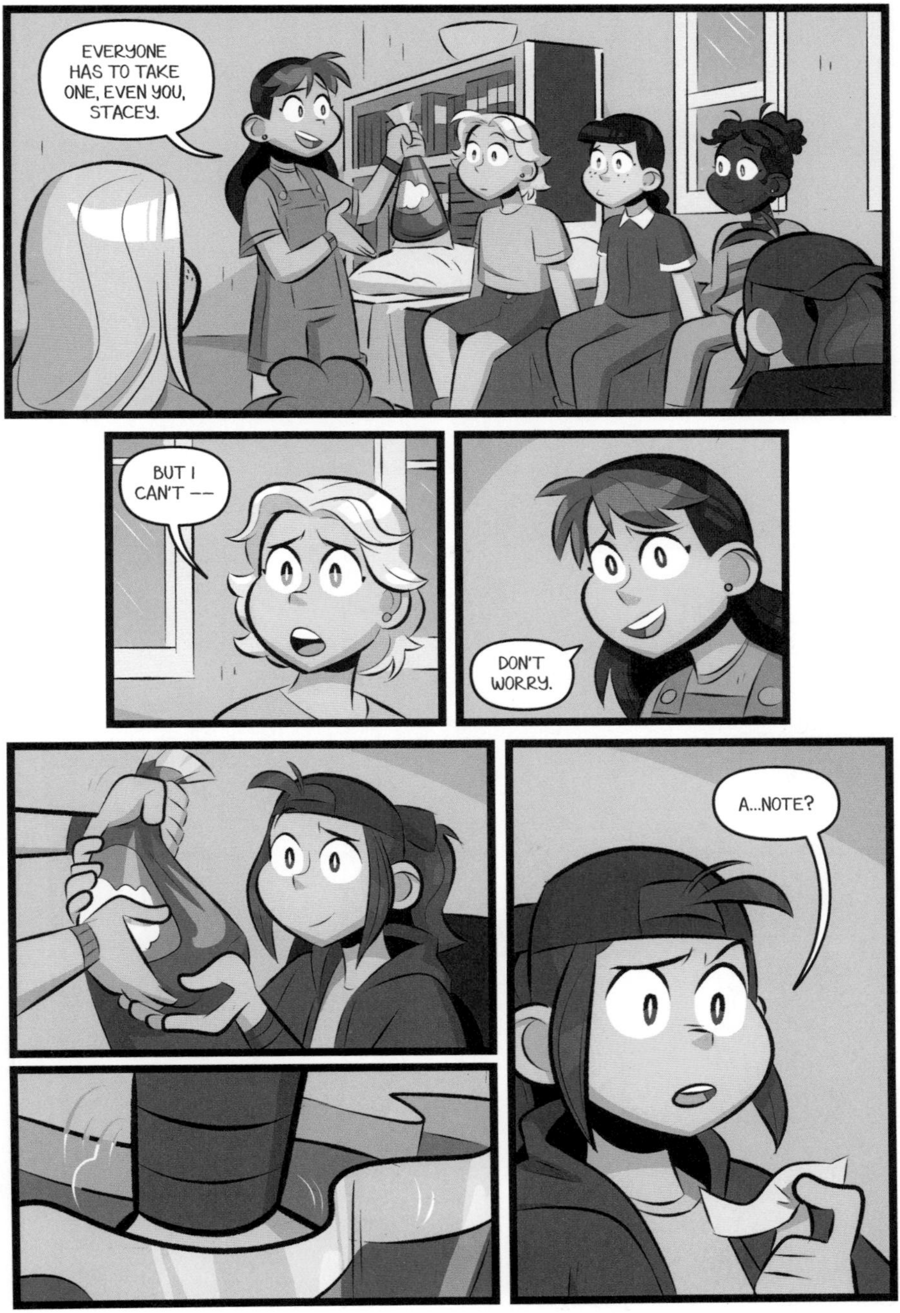
EVERYONE HAS TO TAKE ONE, EVEN YOU, STACEY.
BUT I CAN'T --
DON'T WORRY.
A...NOTE?

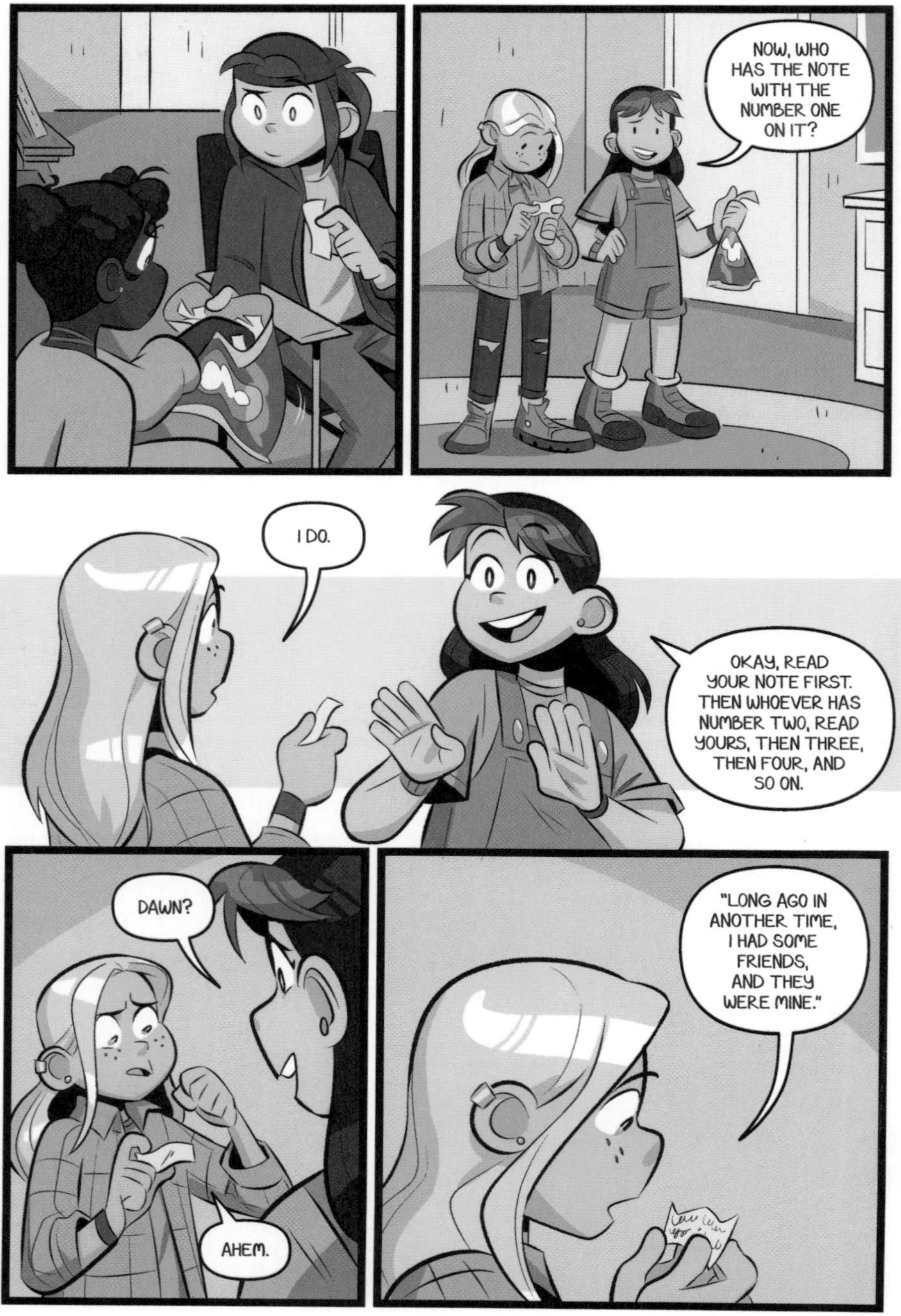
NOW, WHO HAS THE NOTE WITH THE NUMBER ONE ON IT?
I DO.
OKAY, READ YOUR NOTE FIRST. THEN WHOEVER HAS NUMBER TWO, READ YOURS, THEN THREE, THEN FOUR, AND SO ON.
DAWN?
AHEM.
"LONG AGO IN ANOTHER TIME, I HAD SOME FRIENDS, AND THEY WERE MINE."

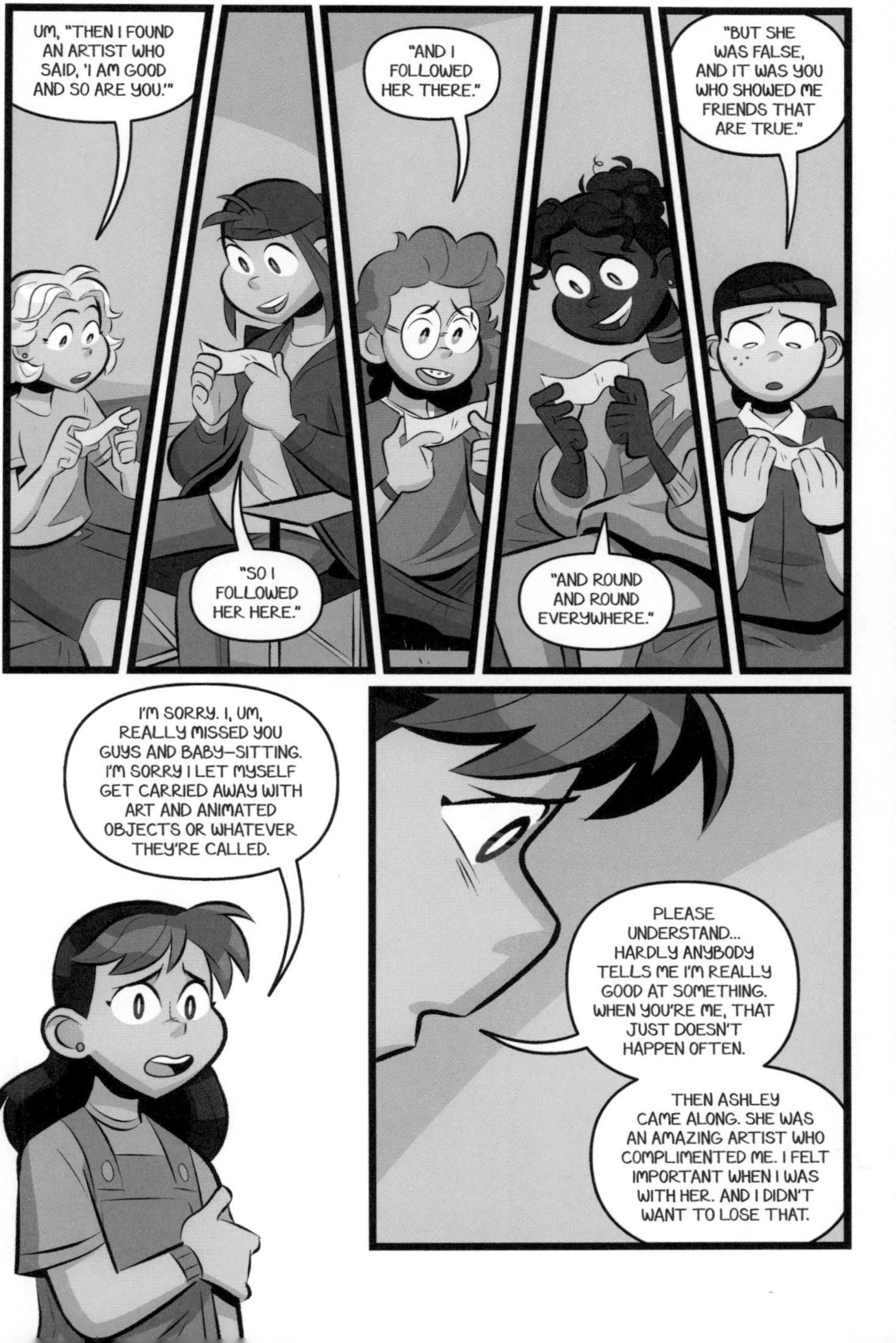
UM, "THEN I FOUND AN ARTIST WHO SAID, 'I AM GOOD AND SO ARE YOU.'"
"SO I FOLLOWED HER HERE."
"AND I FOLLOWED HER THERE."
"AND ROUND AND ROUND EVERYWHERE."
"BUT SHE WAS FALSE, AND IT WAS YOU WHO SHOWED ME FRIENDS THAT ARE TRUE."
I'M SORRY. I, UM, REALLY MISSED YOU GUYS AND BABY-SITTING. I'M SORRY I LET MYSELF GET CARRIED AWAY WITH ART AND ANIMATED OBJECTS OR WHATEVER THEY'RE CALLED.
PLEASE UNDERSTAND... HARDLY ANYBODY TELLS ME I'M REALLY GOOD AT SOMETHING. WHEN YOU'RE ME, THAT JUST DOESN'T HAPPEN OFTEN.
THEN ASHLEY CAME ALONG. SHE WAS AN AMAZING ARTIST WHO COMPLIMENTED ME. I FELT IMPORTANT WHEN I WAS WITH HER. AND I DIDN'T WANT TO LOSE THAT.

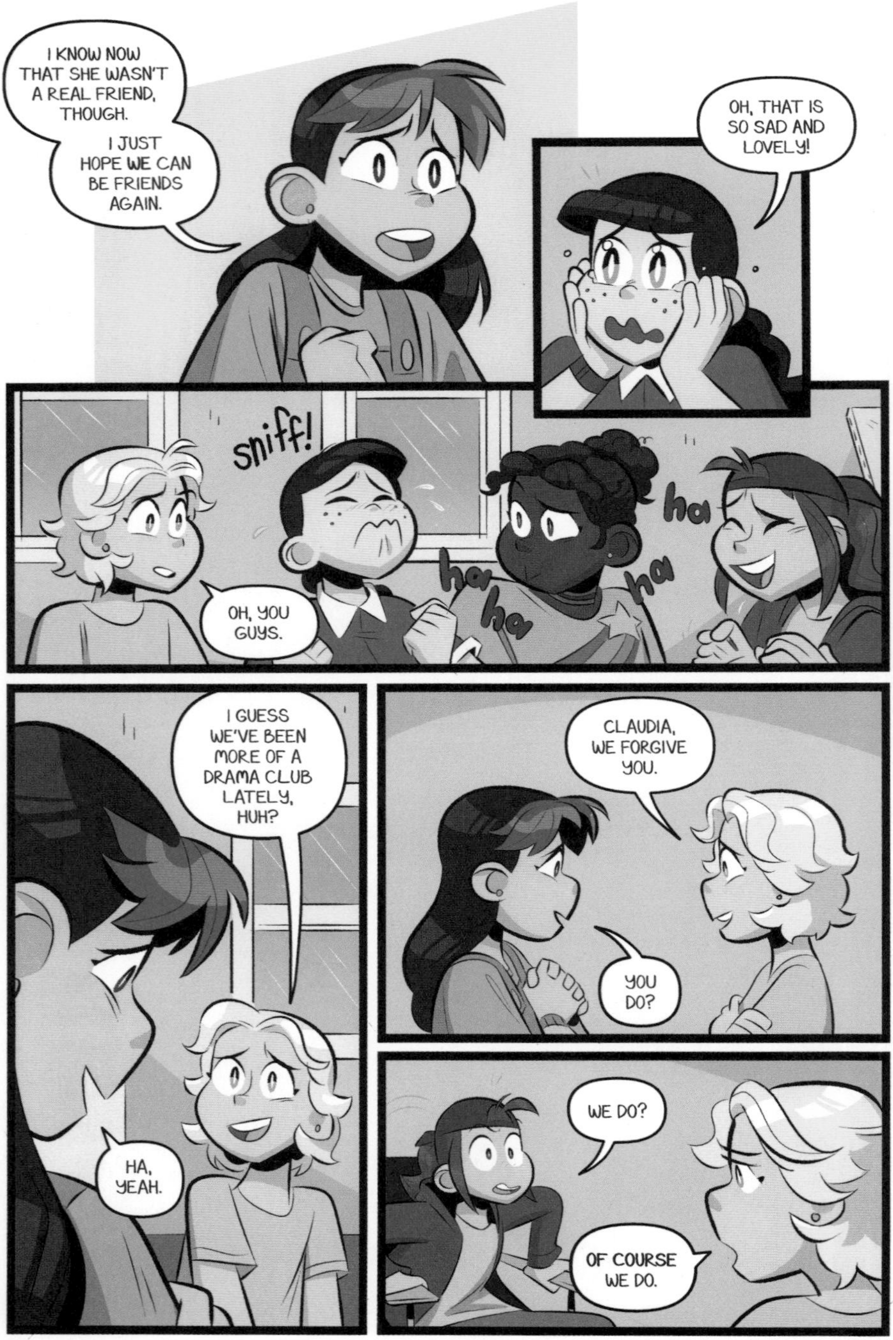
I KNOW NOW THAT SHE WASN'T A REAL FRIEND, THOUGH.
I JUST HOPE WE CAN BE FRIENDS AGAIN.
OH, THAT IS SO SAD AND LOVELY!
sniff!
ha
ha
ha
ha
OH, YOU GUYS.
I GUESS WE'VE BEEN MORE OF A DRAMA CLUB LATELY, HUH?
HA, YEAH.
CLAUDIA, WE FORGIVE YOU.
YOU DO?
WE DO?
OF COURSE WE DO.

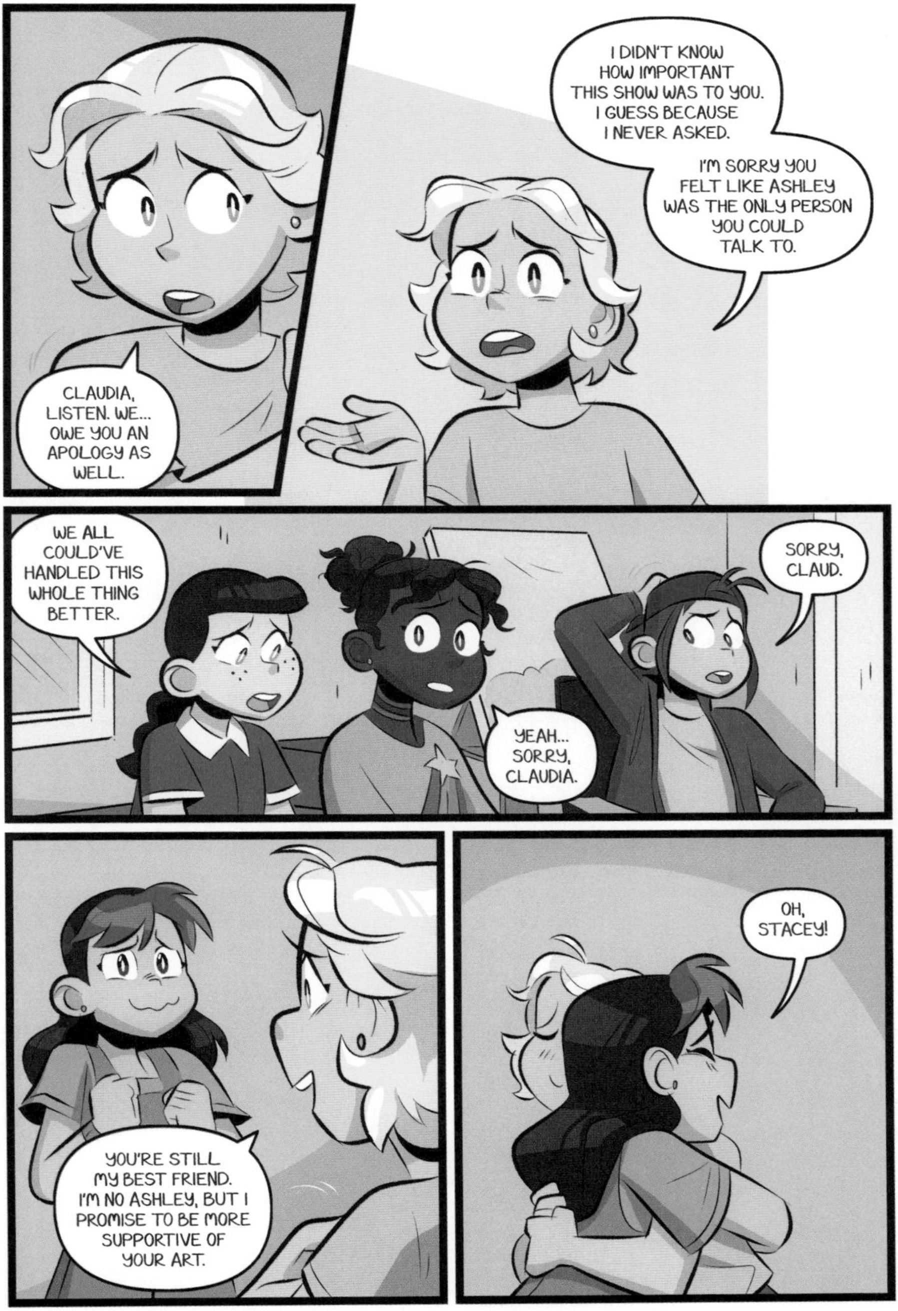
I DIDN'T KNOW HOW IMPORTANT THIS SHOW WAS TO YOU. I GUESS BECAUSE I NEVER ASKED.
I'M SORRY YOU FELT LIKE ASHLEY WAS THE ONLY PERSON YOU COULD TALK TO.
CLAUDIA, LISTEN. WE... OWE YOU AN APOLOGY AS WELL.
WE ALL COULD'VE HANDLED THIS WHOLE THING BETTER.
SORRY, CLAUD.
YEAH... SORRY, CLAUDIA.
YOU'RE STILL MY BEST FRIEND. I'M NO ASHLEY, BUT I PROMISE TO BE MORE SUPPORTIVE OF YOUR ART.
OH, STACEY!

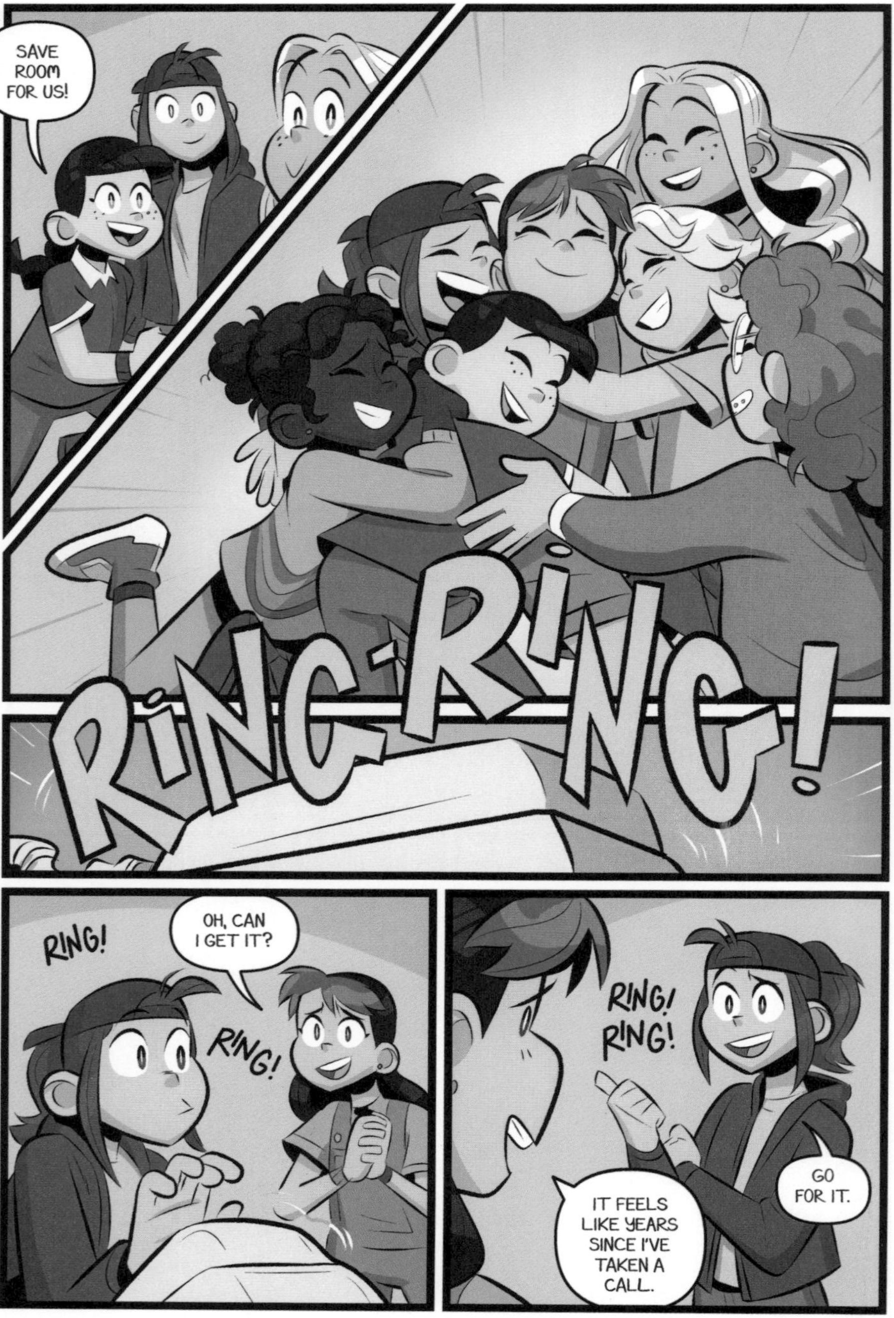
SAVE ROOM FOR US!
RING-RING-RING!
RING!
OH, CAN I GET IT?
RING!
RING! RING!
IT FEELS LIKE YEARS SINCE I'VE TAKEN A CALL.
GO FOR IT.

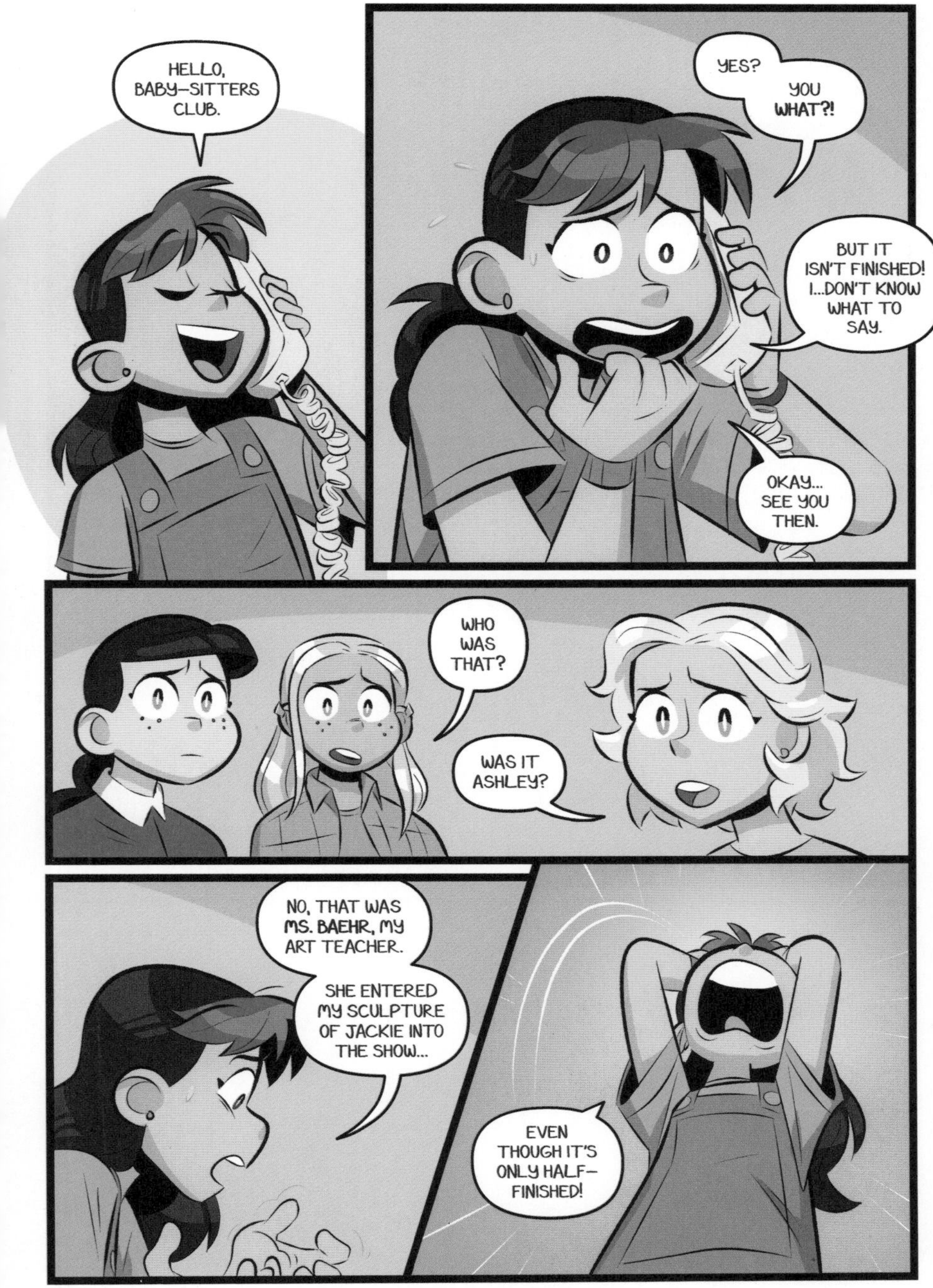
HELLO, BABY-SITTERS CLUB.
YES?
YOU WHAT?!
BUT IT ISN'T FINISHED! I...DON'T KNOW WHAT TO SAY.
OKAY... SEE YOU THEN.
WHO WAS THAT?
WAS IT ASHLEY?
NO, THAT WAS MS. BAEHR, MY ART TEACHER.
SHE ENTERED MY SCULPTURE OF JACKIE INTO THE SHOW...
EVEN THOUGH IT'S ONLY HALF-FINISHED!

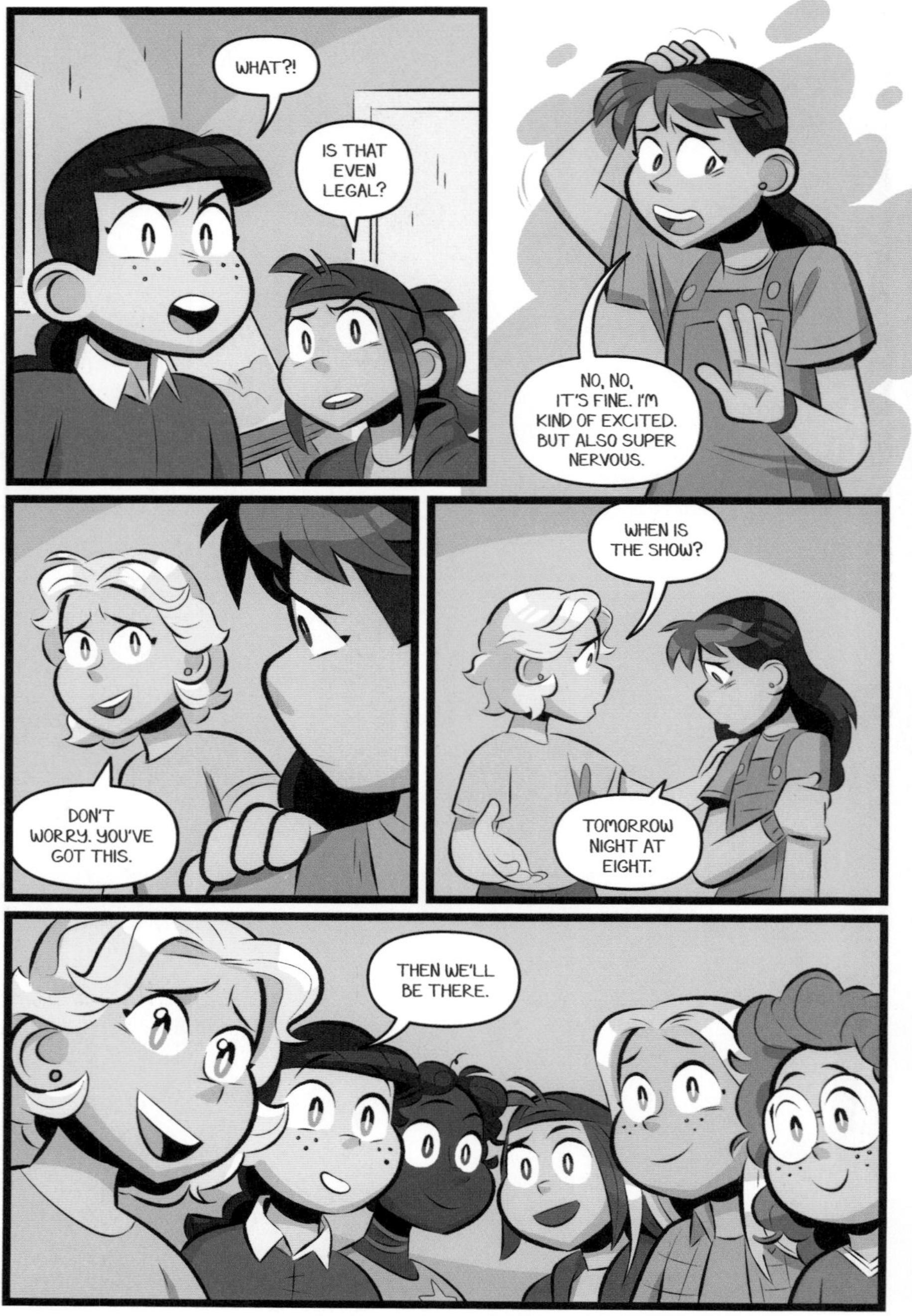
WHAT?!
IS THAT EVEN LEGAL?
NO, NO, IT'S FINE. I'M KIND OF EXCITED. BUT ALSO SUPER NERVOUS.
DON'T WORRY. YOU'VE GOT THIS.
WHEN IS THE SHOW?
TOMORROW NIGHT AT EIGHT.
THEN WE'LL BE THERE.

CHAPTER 13

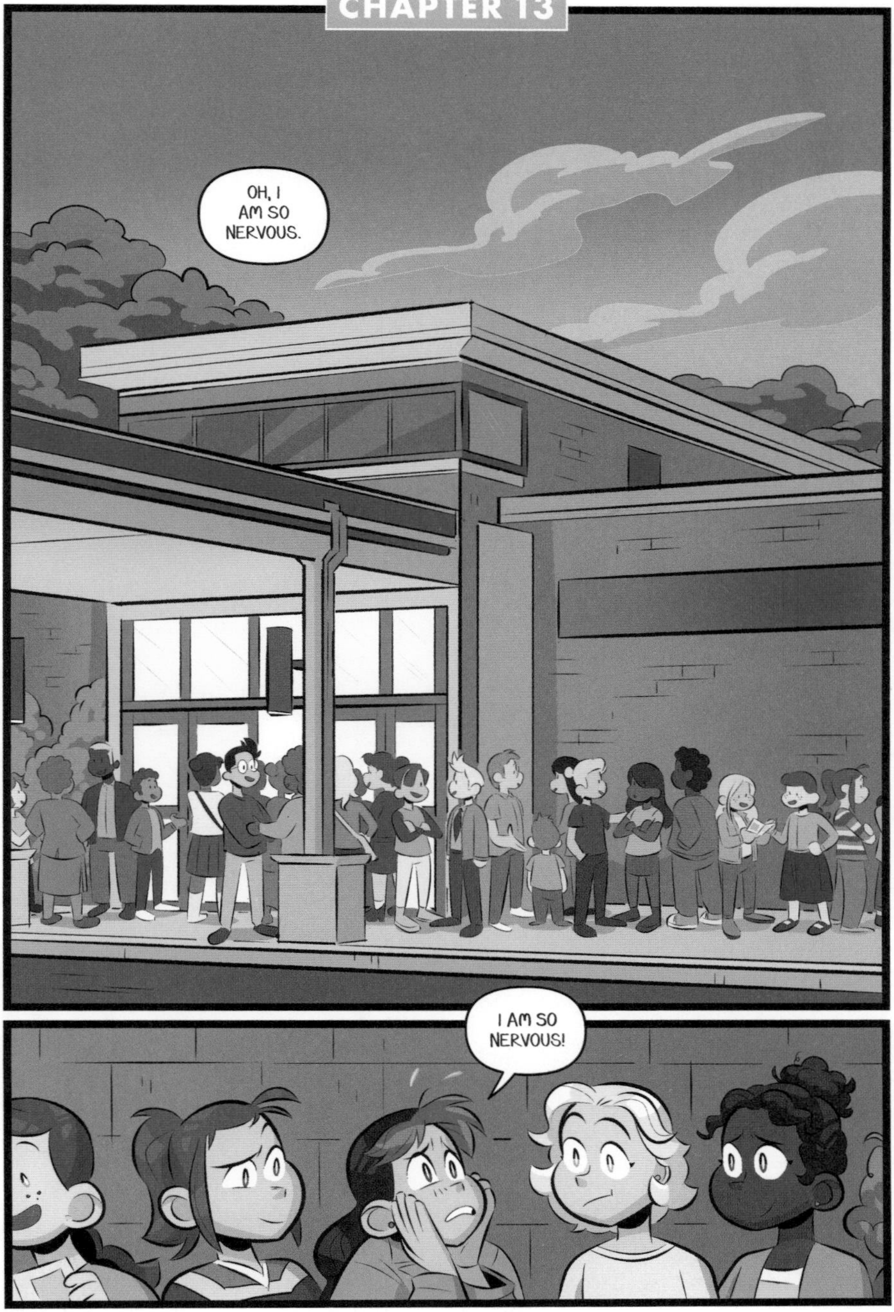
OH, I AM SO NERVOUS.
I AM SO NERVOUS!

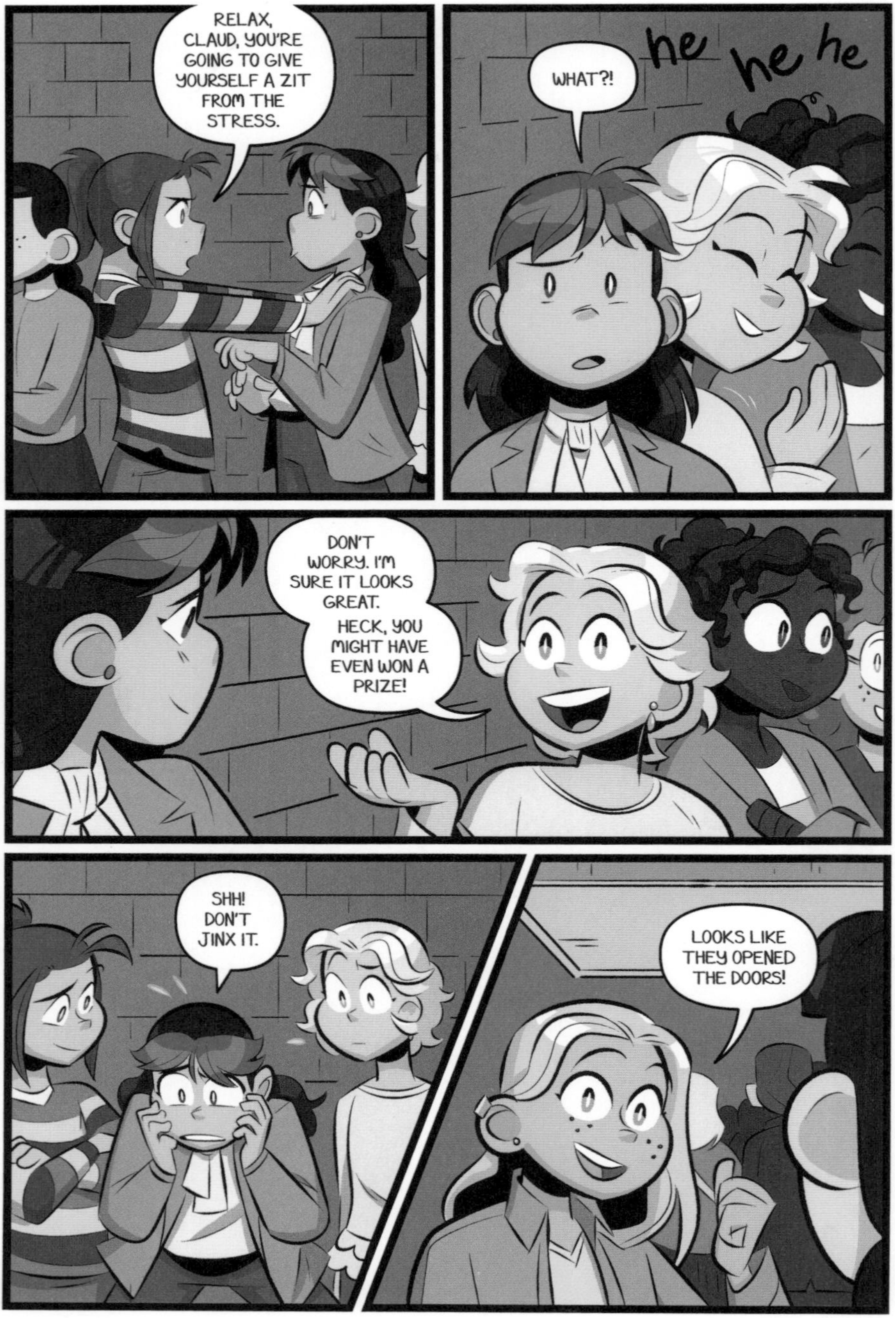
RELAX, CLAUD, YOU'RE GOING TO GIVE YOURSELF A ZIT FROM THE STRESS.
WHAT?!
he he he
DON'T WORRY. I'M SURE IT LOOKS GREAT.
HECK, YOU MIGHT HAVE EVEN WON A PRIZE!
SHH! DON'T JINX IT.
LOOKS LIKE THEY OPENED THE DOORS!

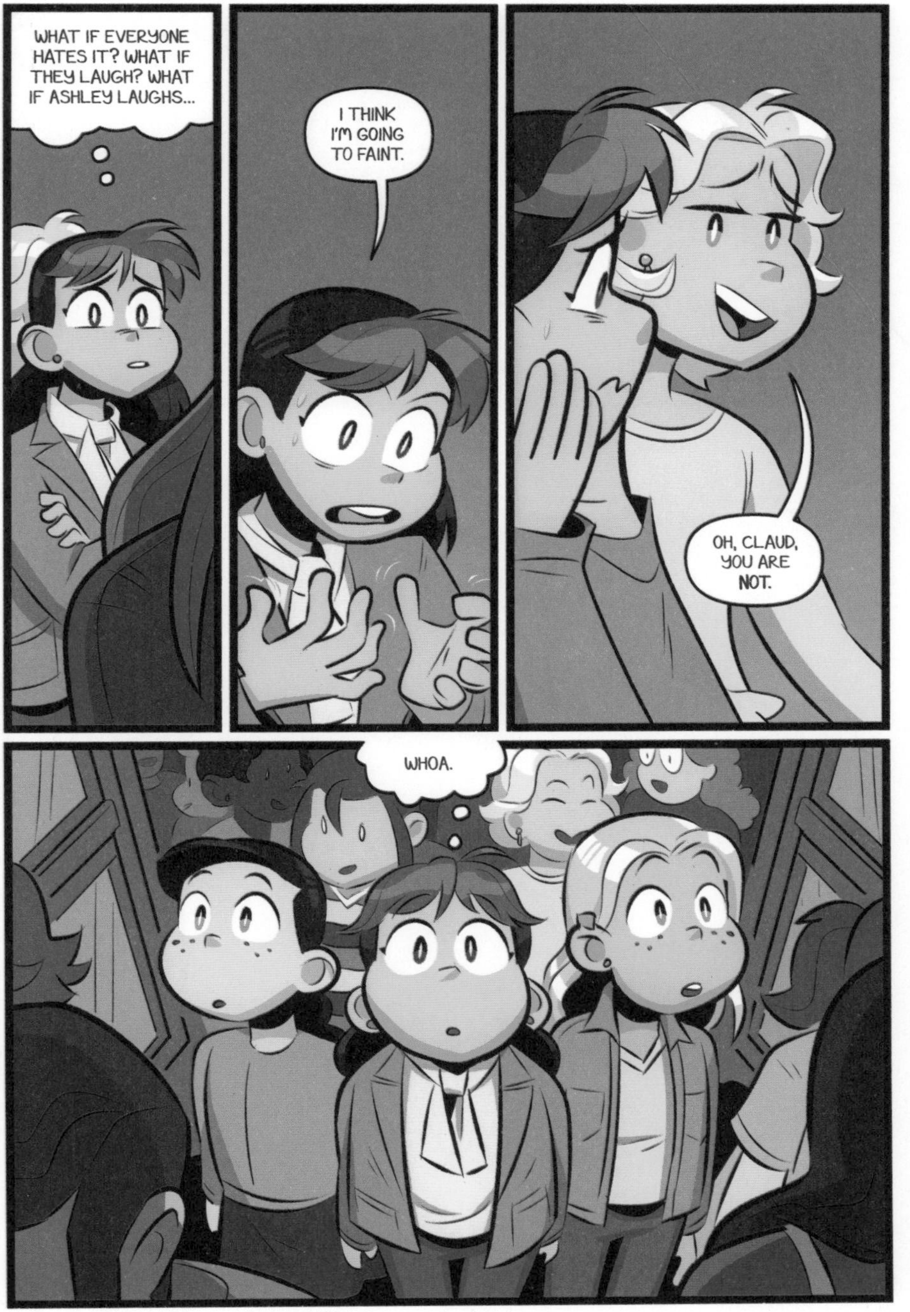
WHAT IF EVERYONE HATES IT? WHAT IF THEY LAUGH? WHAT IF ASHLEY LAUGHS...
I THINK I'M GOING TO FAINT.
OH, CLAUD, YOU ARE NOT.
WHOA.

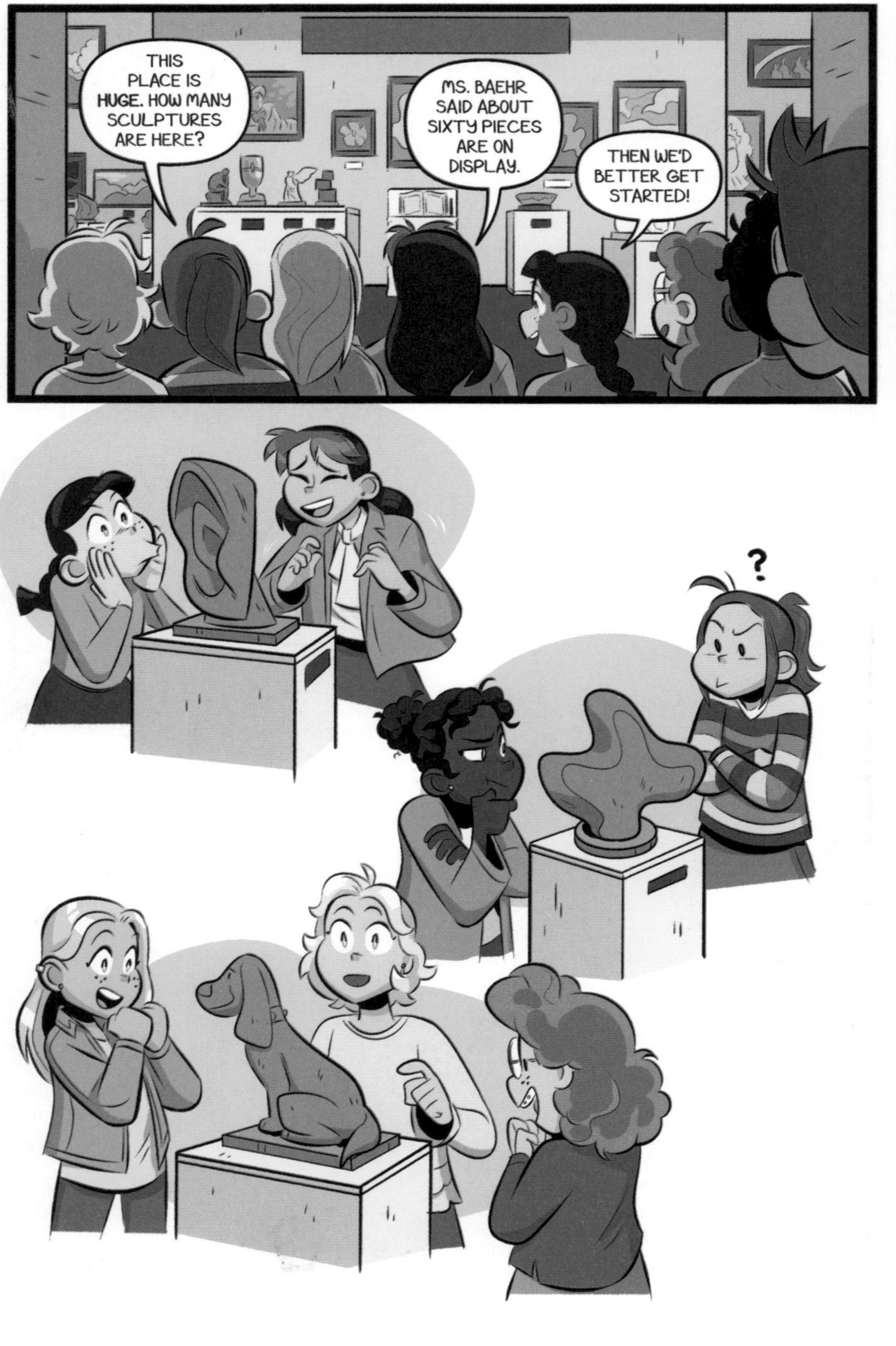
THIS PLACE IS HUGE. HOW MANY SCULPTURES ARE HERE?
MS. BAEHR SAID ABOUT SIXTY PIECES ARE ON DISPLAY.
THEN WE'D BETTER GET STARTED!
?

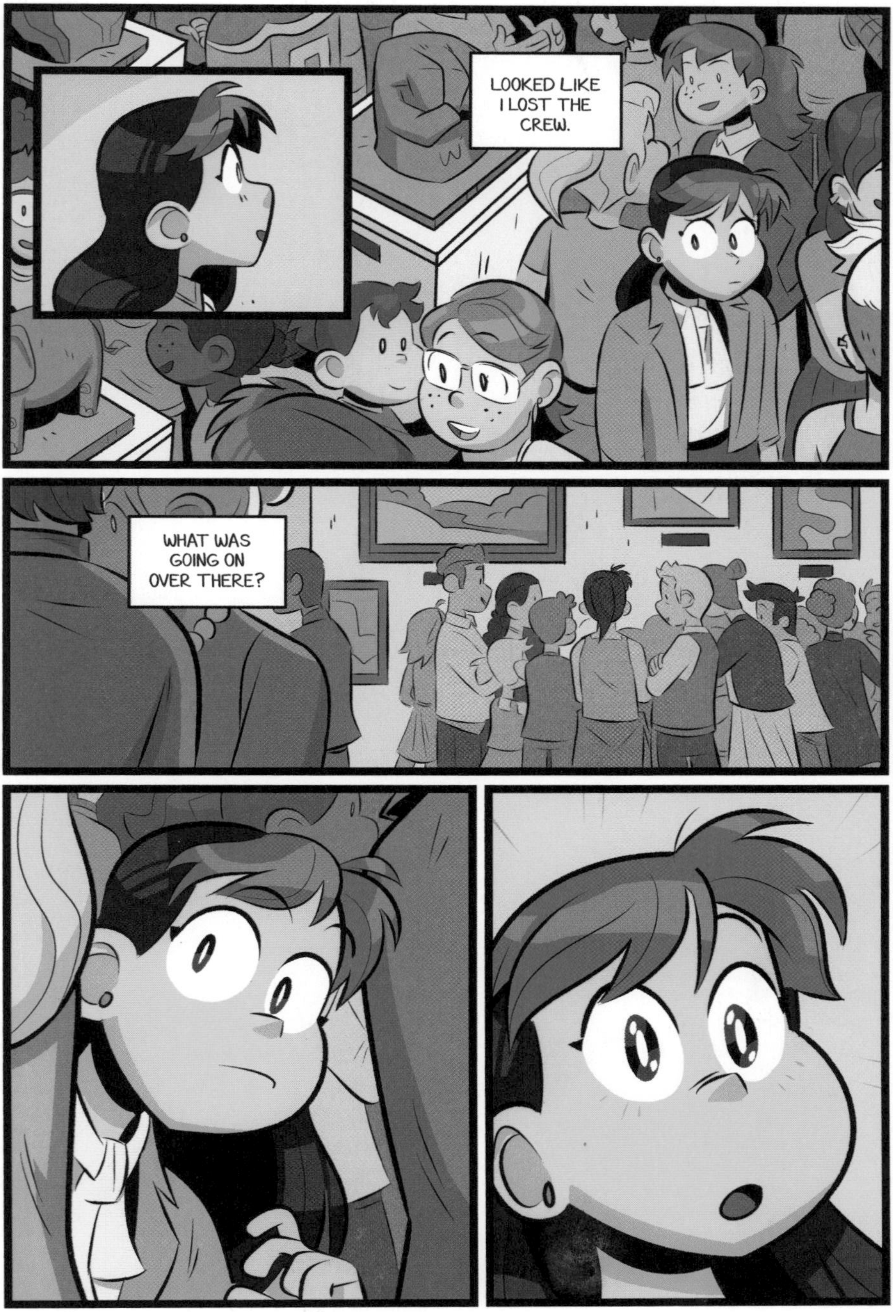
LOOKED LIKE I LOST THE CREW.
WHAT WAS GOING ON OVER THERE?

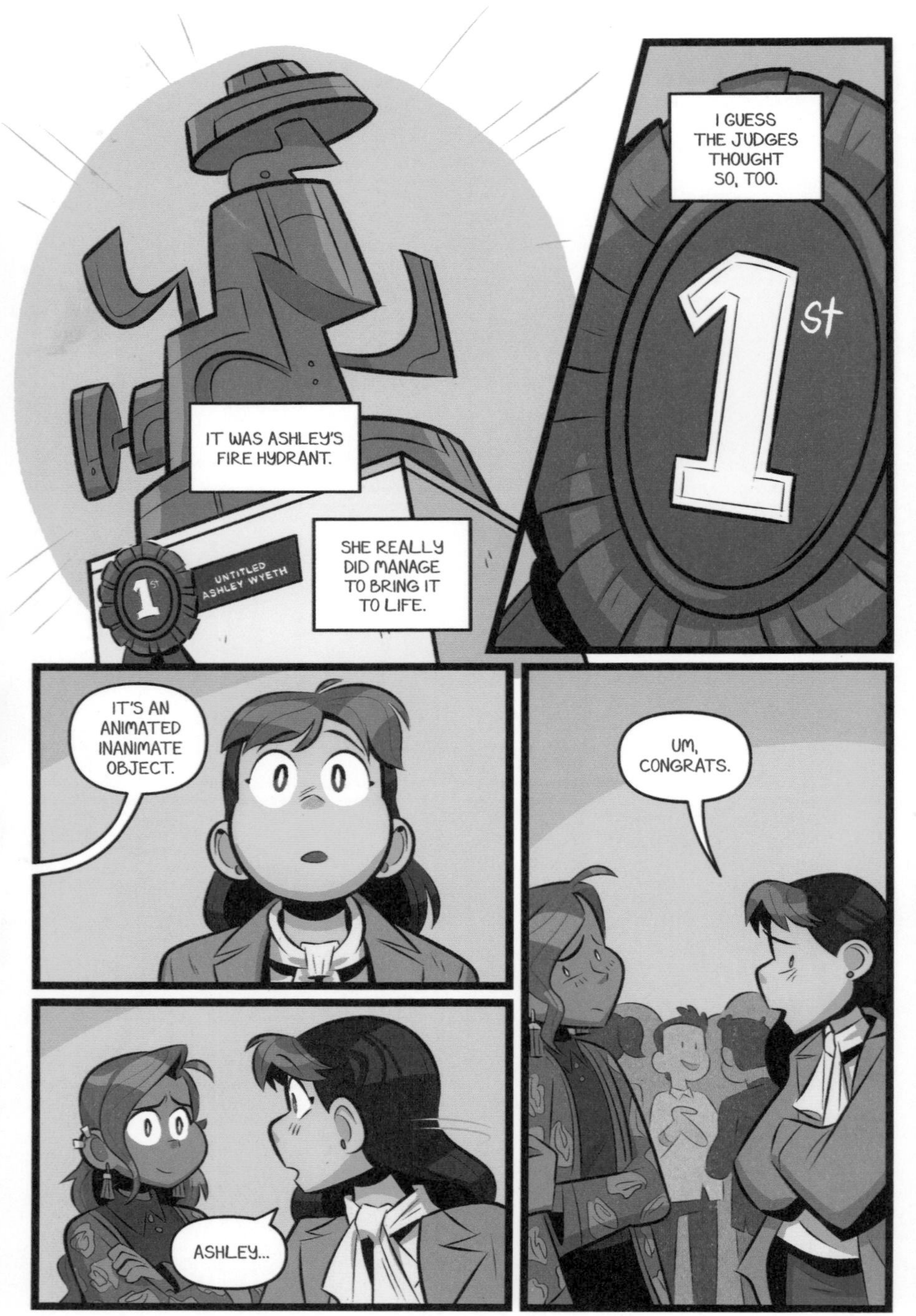
IT WAS ASHLEY'S FIRE HYDRANT.
UNTITLED ASHLEY WYETH
SHE REALLY DID MANAGE TO BRING IT TO LIFE.
I GUESS THE JUDGES THOUGHT SO, TOO.
IT'S AN ANIMATED INANIMATE OBJECT.
ASHLEY...
UM, CONGRATS.

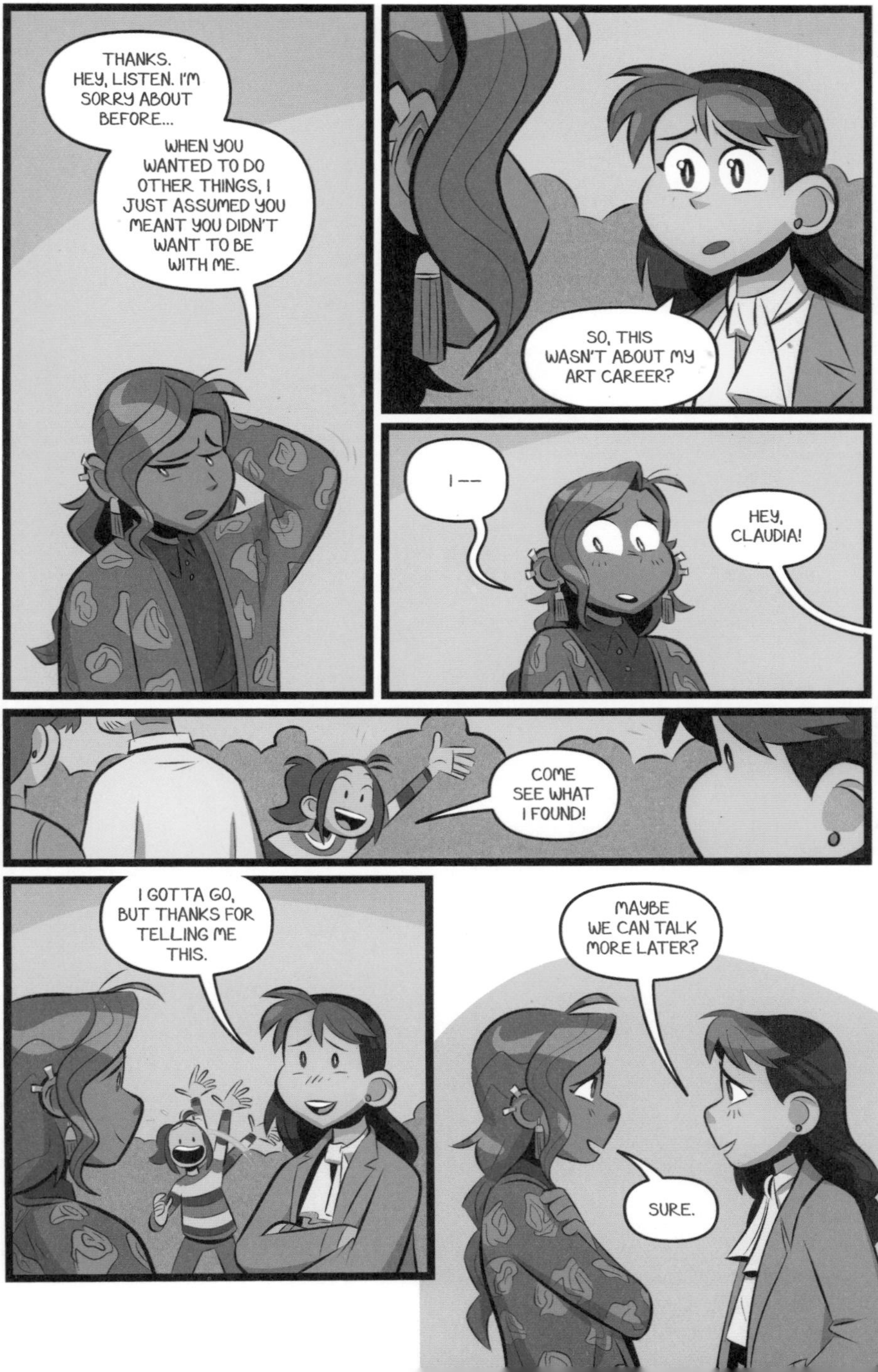
THANKS. HEY, LISTEN. I'M SORRY ABOUT BEFORE...
WHEN YOU WANTED TO DO OTHER THINGS, I JUST ASSUMED YOU MEANT YOU DIDN'T WANT TO BE WITH ME.
SO, THIS WASN'T ABOUT MY ART CAREER?
I--
HEY, CLAUDIA!
COME SEE WHAT I FOUND!
I GOTTA GO, BUT THANKS FOR TELLING ME THIS.
MAYBE WE CAN TALK MORE LATER?
SURE.

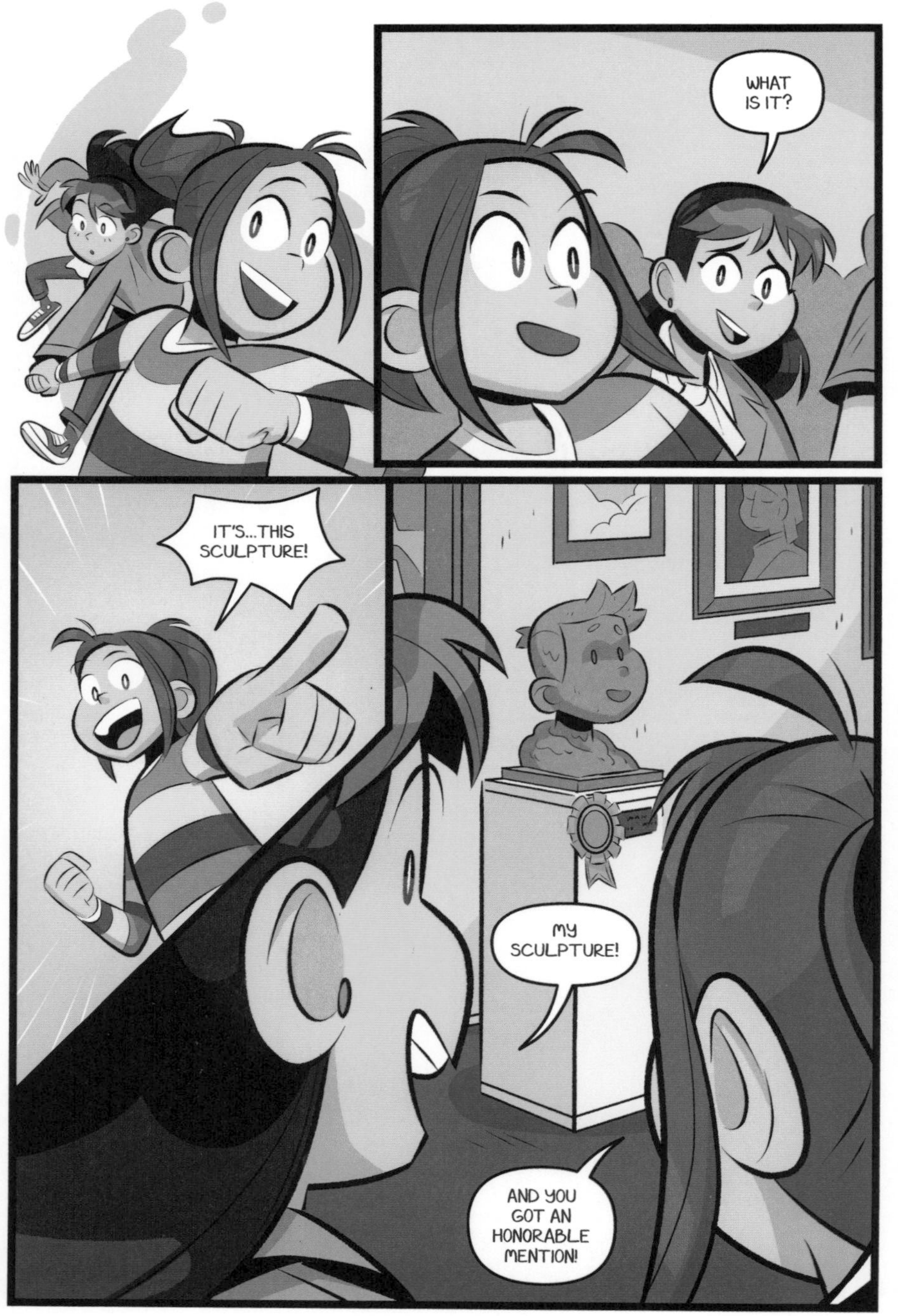
WHAT IS IT?
IT'S...THIS SCULPTURE!
MY SCULPTURE!
AND YOU GOT AN HONORABLE MENTION!

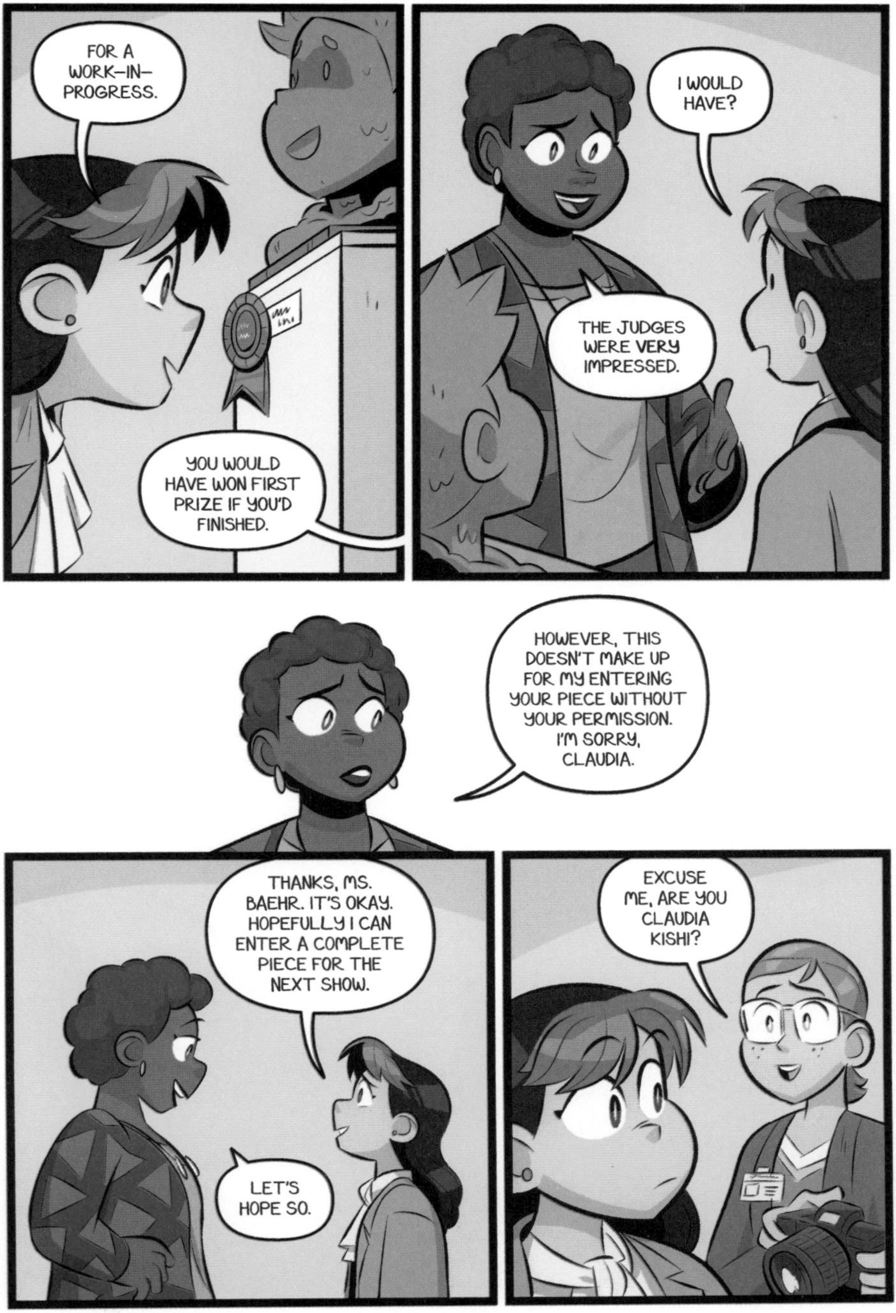
FOR A WORK-IN-PROGRESS.
YOU WOULD HAVE WON FIRST PRIZE IF YOU'D FINISHED.
I WOULD HAVE?
THE JUDGES WERE VERY IMPRESSED.
HOWEVER, THIS DOESN'T MAKE UP FOR MY ENTERING YOUR PIECE WITHOUT YOUR PERMISSION. I'M SORRY, CLAUDIA.
THANKS, MS. BAEHR. IT'S OKAY. HOPEFULLY I CAN ENTER A COMPLETE PIECE FOR THE NEXT SHOW.
LET'S HOPE SO.
EXCUSE ME, ARE YOU CLAUDIA KISHI?

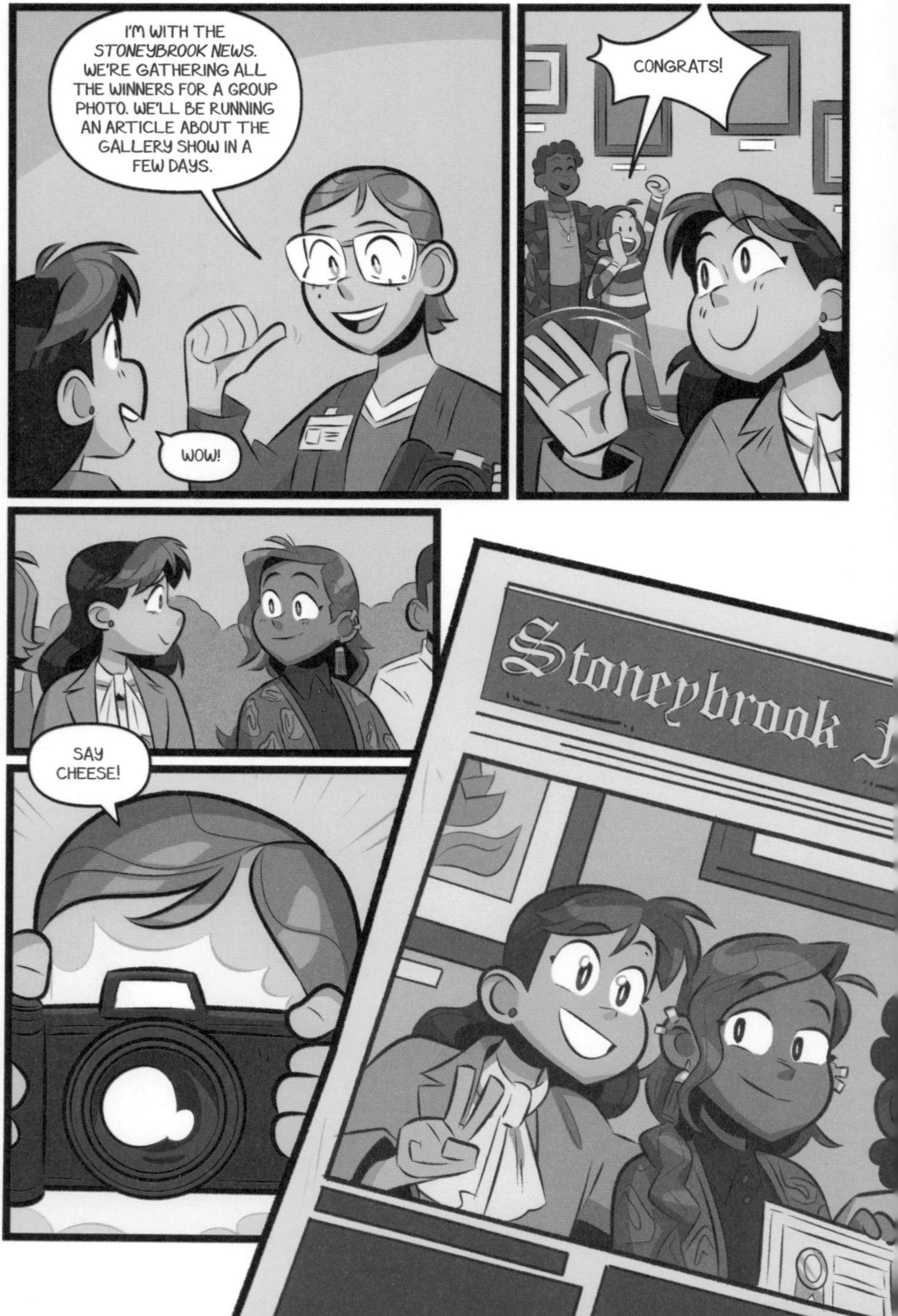
I'M WITH THE *STONEYBROOK NEWS*. WE'RE GATHERING ALL THE WINNERS FOR A GROUP PHOTO. WE'LL BE RUNNING AN ARTICLE ABOUT THE GALLERY SHOW IN A FEW DAYS.
WOW!
CONGRATS!
SAY CHEESE!
Stoneybrook

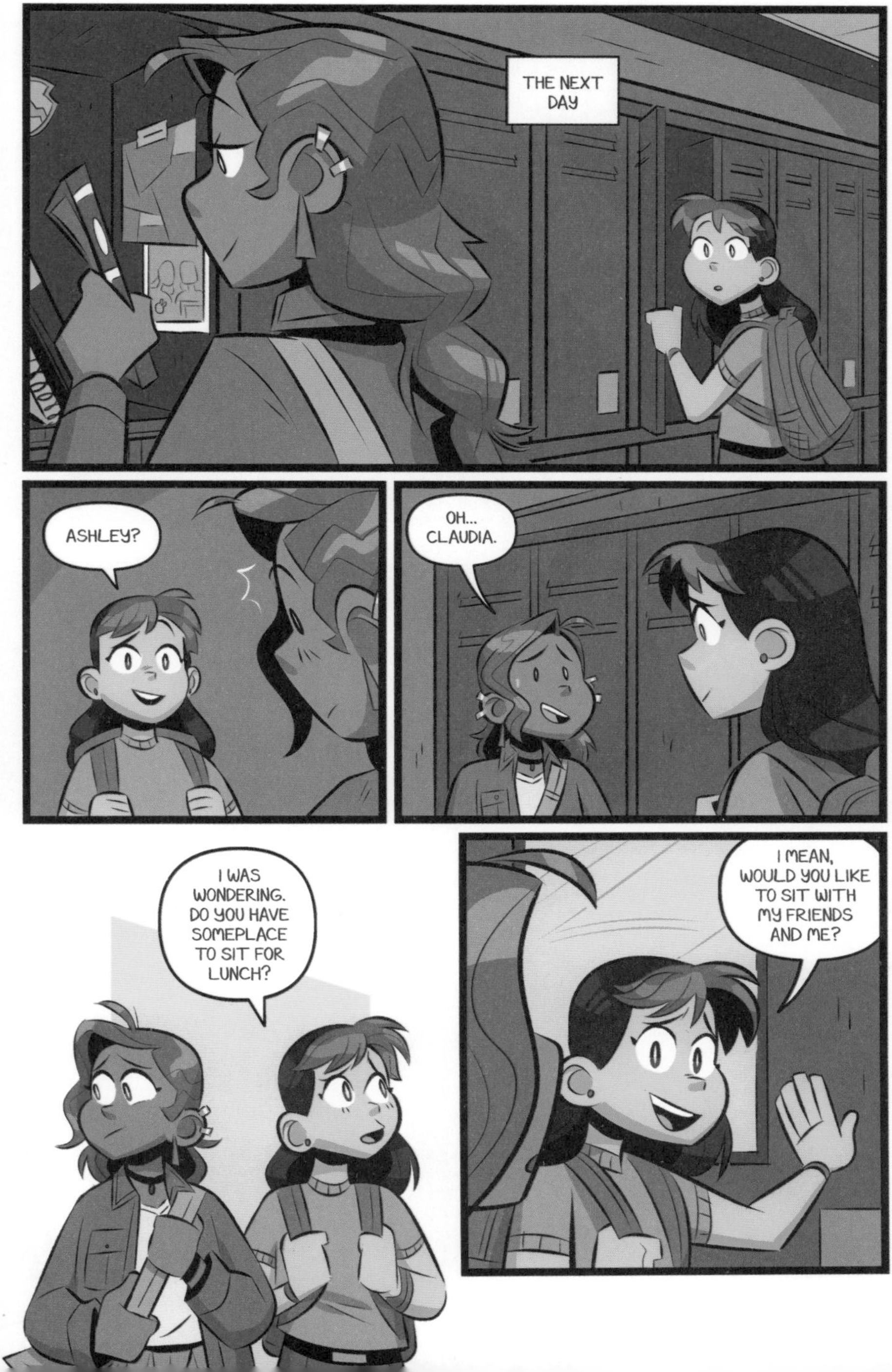
THE NEXT DAY
ASHLEY?
OH... CLAUDIA.
I WAS WONDERING. DO YOU HAVE SOMEPLACE TO SIT FOR LUNCH?
I MEAN, WOULD YOU LIKE TO SIT WITH MY FRIENDS AND ME?

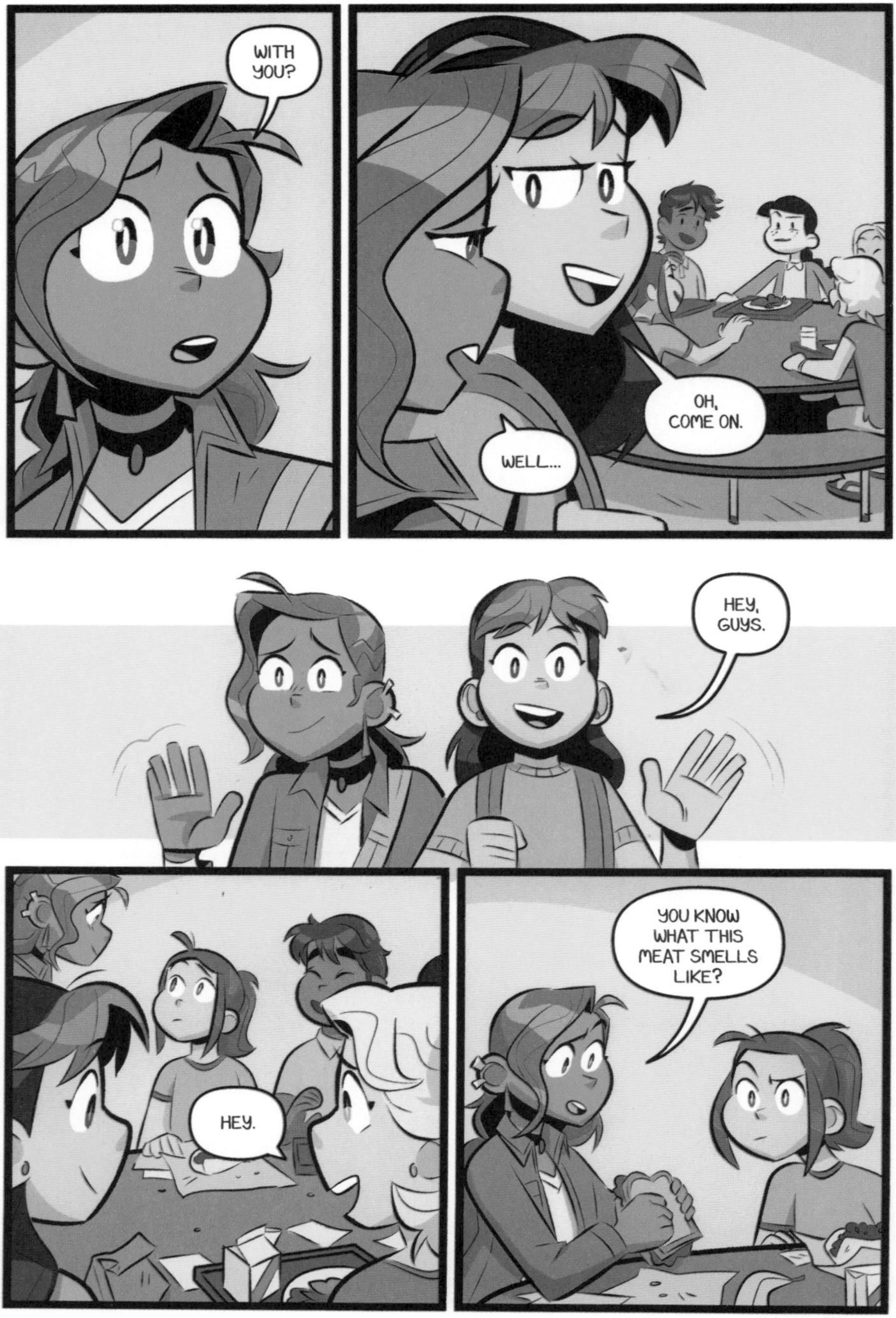
WITH YOU?
WELL...
OH, COME ON.
HEY, GUYS.
HEY.
YOU KNOW WHAT THIS MEAT SMELLS LIKE?

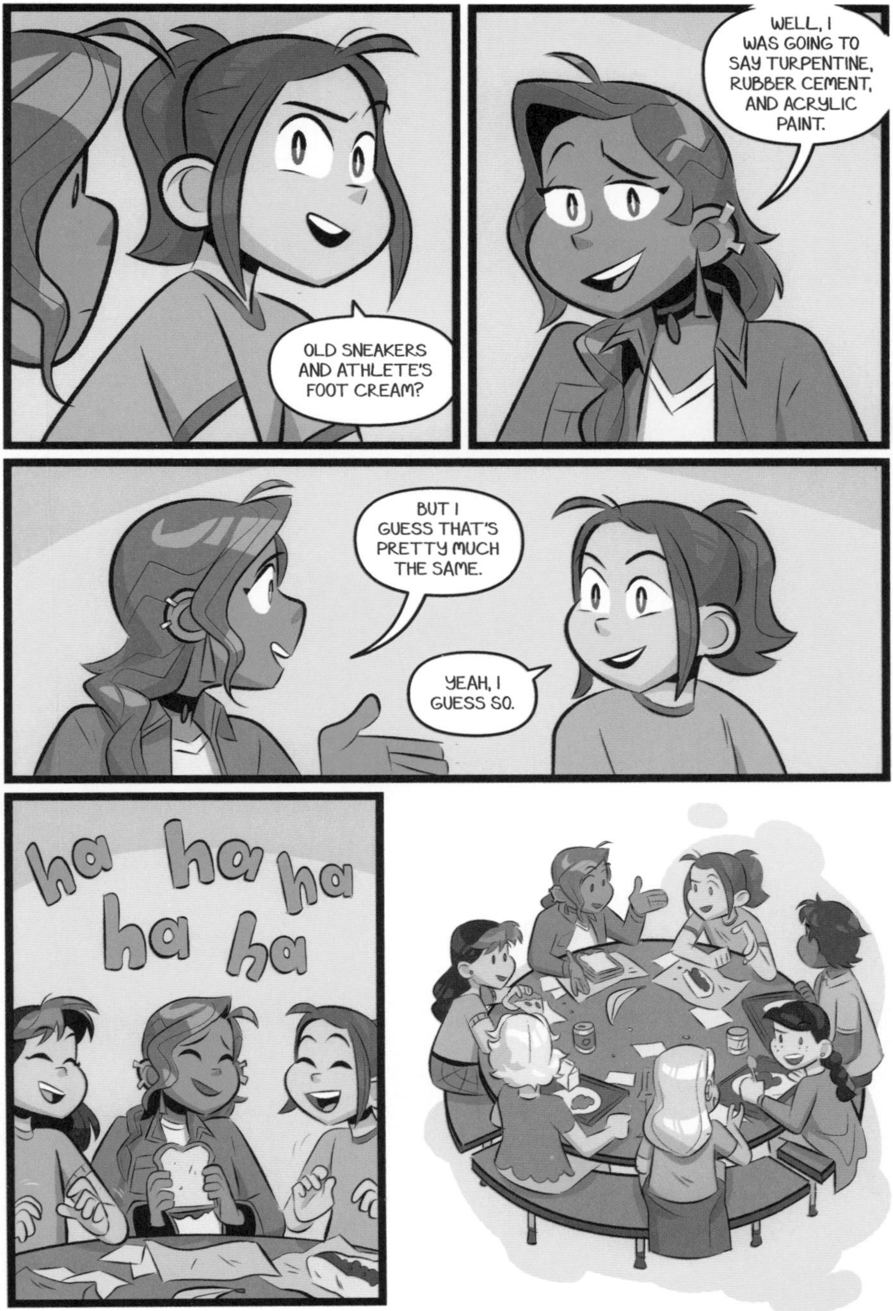
OLD SNEAKERS AND ATHLETE'S FOOT CREAM?
WELL, I WAS GOING TO SAY TURPENTINE, RUBBER CEMENT, AND ACRYLIC PAINT.
BUT I GUESS THAT'S PRETTY MUCH THE SAME.
YEAH, I GUESS SO.
ha ha ha ha ha ha